Deadly Odds

Kim Carter

Published by Raven South Publishing
Atlanta, Georgia 30324, USA
Copyright © Kim Carter 2016

Cover Design by www.mariondesigns.com

Library of Congress Control Number: 2018933818

ISBN 978-1-947140-09-7 (paperback)
ISBN 978-1-947140-08-0 (ebook)

Other Works by Kim Carter

Sweet Dreams, Baby Belle
Murder Among The Tombstones
When Dawn Never Comes
No Second Chances
And The Forecast Called For Rain

Dedication

To my best friend and sister, Pam, the only one who believed in me even before the first word hit the page and continued to believe in me when my book was no more than a few pages held together by an old rubber band. I love you, Sissy!

Acknowledgments

I've certainly learned that no man is an island in this world, and my writing is a prime example. I'm eternally grateful for those who share their knowledge, their friendships, and their kindnesses. To the ones that make this process not only an enjoyable task but a learning experience as well. Many thanks to the following:

- To the Raven South Publishing Team that keeps this ship afloat even on rough seas. Kelly Keylon, President, Publisher, and dear friend. Can't imagine my life without your friendship, love, encouragement, and devotion. Melissa Manes, editor, friend, and the brave woman that lights the fire under my ass when I need it the most. I'm convinced we were separated at birth! Catherine Townsend-Lyons, publicist, friend, and fellow author, you're a light in a dark world and an inspiration to all of us. And last, but not least, Keith Saunders who creates these fantastic covers that never cease to amaze me! This journey wouldn't have been the same without all of you being a part of it.
- To my road dogs, Lisa Mobley Putnam and Greg Headrick, much, much love.
- To John Cross in the Fulton County Medical Examiner's Office, Atlanta, GA. You've been helping me since my first book and still, much to my surprise, take my calls. I couldn't have done any of this without your help.
- To Kevin North, yep, I mentioned you! To my ex-husband and baby daddy, many thanks for answering all of my questions about guns and bullets, bows and arrows, and countless other things—far too many to list. I started writing in a corner of our dark laundry room piled high with dirty laundry. I'll never forget that. Oh yeah, and thanks for the kids.

- To Randy New, our attorney, and friend. You are fierce and funny and you laugh at my jokes. Definitely a keeper.
- To Martha and Cecil Gaddy who've been on this journey since my first book was only a dream, that I never thought would come true, love you both.
- And to my Julius, my heart, my better half... I love you more every day.

Chapter 1

The night air bit at Nathaniel Collier's ears, and he blew on his balled fists, hoping to warm his frozen fingers. He'd spent enough nights on stakeouts to know the drill. Sometimes his work was like that, but he'd learned to adapt to his environment.

Forcing his mind to switch gears, he thought about his current bounty, Mad Dog Consuelos, a small-time pimp accused of murdering one of his prostitutes. Through some whopping screwup, the DA had let the slime out on bond. To make matters worse, an even bigger idiot, a local bondsman, had released him through his office. Collier snickered to himself. Their inept shortcomings meant job security for him.

It was well after midnight, and the housing projects right outside Atlanta were alive with commotion. Children played in the frigid night air in thin T-shirts and worn, faded jeans, their bare knees visible through countless holes and frayed denim. The cracked pavement of the parking lot was smeared with old grease that'd long since drained from abandoned cars while radios blared loud, screaming lyrics that couldn't be deciphered. Nathaniel watched as a group of young men passed a joint back and forth and slugged swallows from a forty-ounce beer.

Nathaniel was acting on a tip that his guy was visiting a young woman in one of the apartments. Because of the children and being outnumbered by Mr. Consuelos's buddies, he'd decided to lay low. He knew from experience that sooner or later, the man's reputation alone would drive him to come out and kick it with the other guys. At that point, he'd call the Atlanta PD and claim his bounty. Years ago, he would've been much too proud to handle it that way, but pride was nothing a few brushes with death hadn't been able to cure.

Reaching for the paper cup filled with coffee, he watched his target exit the apartment. Mad Dog was a small man to have been capable of the intimidation he'd bequeathed upon others for so long. Of course, size meant very little in Nathaniel's line of work. He knew all to well that dangerous things could come in small packages. Guns were rented hearts, and threats were promises that thugs were all too anxious to carry out. He felt his pulse and breathing quicken. It was the rush that kept Nathaniel doing this job.

He watched in bemusement as the crowd slowly turned their heads, following the piece of trash as if he were some kind of a hero. Mad Dog slowly made his way down the crippled stairwell like he was exiting a Hollywood premiere. Nathaniel could see, even from a distance, where he'd earned his nickname. Although he couldn't be any taller than five-four, his body was firm, his walk confident. He walked with a swagger, suggesting he'd have no problem administering violence should the necessity arise. Everyone sensed it, Nathaniel included.

Scooting down in the cold leather seat, Nathanial struggled to keep his eye on his target. He was a little curious as to where the guy would go. He couldn't imagine him sharing a toke with the smokers.

His intuition about that was right. Consuelos made his way past the guys smoking weed, acknowledging their greetings with nothing more than a slight nod. He paused next to a young boy, no more than ten years old, and handed him a small bag of crack rocks. The exchange was so blatant that Nathaniel lost his breath for a moment. A move so brazen could only mean one thing. Mad Dog knew he was being watched.

In that instant, Nathaniel knew he was about to get screwed quicker than one of the ten dollar hookers on the corner. "Damn," he whispered. He'd been in similar precarious situations before, and knew the projects weren't a good place to find himself in such a bad spot. Reaching for the keys in the ignition, he kept his eyes locked on Consuelos. The kid's hand took the crack with the ease of an experienced dealer, but in lieu of cash, he slid a 9 mm from his thin waistband and handed it over to the man who was not much taller than himself.

"Son-of-a-bitch," Nathaniel said. Exhaling deeply, he rested his cold hands on the keys in the ignition. His fingers were numb, refusing to grip the keys and turn them. Captive in his own body, he watched the scene unfold in front of him.

Consuelos turned and walked, calmly and confidently, toward the apartment he'd come out of. The crowd, his audience, had quickly dispersed. Holding the gun steadily in his right hand, he headed to the upper unit. The young boy had already vanished into the night, and the rest of the projects now seemed blanketed with an eerie quiet.

Nathaniel listened to his heart beating loudly in his chest as he watched his breath exhaling in the cold night air. The world was taking on that freeze-frame sensation it did just before something tragic occurred. Following Consuelos's every move with his eyes, he slid his hand across the leather seat of his Pontiac Grand Prix in search of his cell phone. He'd allowed his mind to become too transfixed on his prey and hadn't made the call when he should have. The cops should've been on the way as soon as Consuelos had involved the kid, but he'd failed to alert them. He hit the numbers in the dark and watched as Mad Dog reached the top of the stairs and turned the knob on the apartment door, raising his gun to his side.

"You've reached 911. What is your emergency?"

"This is Nathaniel Collier," he screamed into the cell as he jumped from the car. "Get to Bowen Homes immediately, Apartment C-10. Consuelos…Mad Dog…he's entering the apartment with a 9 mm."

That was all the information he could spare, too much time had already lapsed, and he didn't know who was in danger in the apartment. His mind whirled back to the bounty file as he raced across the parking lot. There had been two witnesses, a prostitute who'd been the roommate and her seven-year-old daughter. The defense would bash their credibility to hell and back.

Jesus, Nathaniel thought. *Don't let the son-of-a-bitch be this crazy. With the system the way it is, he'll probably walk with his current charge. Why would he risk anything else?*

Nathanial was halfway across the parking lot before realizing he had left his bulletproof vest in the car, but it was too late to turn back. Running toward the apartment at full speed, he pulled his weapon, gripping it tightly in his hand. The neighborhood was eerily silent. The sounds of Nathaniel's tennis shoes slapping against the pavement was all he could hear.

Finally reaching the bottom of the stairs, he slowed quickly, making his way to the top as quietly as possible. He strained to hear the distant sound of backup coming, but nothing pierced the barrier of silence. *At least there haven't been gunshots—not yet anyway.*

The apartment door was halfway open, leading into a small living room. Nathaniel passed the door and leaned against the brick exterior of the building, keeping his gun drawn and held securely in both hands. Keenly aware that things were entirely unpredictable and could go either way, he always prepared for the worst.

Closing his eyes tightly for a brief second, he concentrated on his breathing. *I am breathing, right?* There were times when his body had failed to remind him. *Yeah, I'm breathing. Good.*

Nathanial saw movement from the far corner of the room and shifted his weight, turning to get a better shot of those inside. He could see a black woman lying on a couch in a skimpy nightgown. He couldn't see above her waist, but she didn't appear to be in any distress. She was speaking in low whispers, raising and lowering a glass of dark whiskey. Her feet were bare with airbrushed designs on her toenails.

Nathaniel jumped back quickly when a man walked into the room and sat beside her. He appeared to be Hispanic, but much larger than Consuelos. Nathanial leaned forward to get a clearer view, the split-second instinct to switch the safety on his weapon off was beaten by the swiftness of a man that had known nothing but crime and deceit. Nathaniel felt the cold metal of Mad Dog Consuelos's 9 mm as it came to rest squarely on his forehead. He didn't have to be told. The demand would have been rhetorical. Obeying the unspoken command, he just lowered his right forearm and felt the weight of his own weapon descending as it circled around his index finger, then bounced twice on the ground before coming to rest at Consuelos's feet.

"Get that for me, Zandi," Mad Dog demanded of the woman in the nightie. "So...my friends tell me you're following me. Apparently, you don't know who I am, Mr., uh…?"

"Mr. Kiss My Ass to you, buddy. As a matter of fact, I do know who you are. It seems, you skipped out on a little thing called bond, my brother."

"Nobody comes into my neighborhood and disrespects me. Do you hear anybody coming to help you? Respect can buy me at least thirty minutes, you piece of shit."

Nathaniel felt the hair stand up on the back of his neck. Perspiration was beginning to form on his upper lip and forehead. He knew there was some truth to Mad Dog's words, or there would've been a shitload of cops there by now. "Listen, Man, we've all got a job to do, and—"

"That we do," Mad Dog said as he and the other man dragged Nathaniel into the small, unkempt apartment. "That we do."

Zandi was tall, rather attractive, but clearly a working woman. Nathaniel figured her much younger than she appeared. The years on the street had weathered her. Her big, dark eyes mirrored a combination of kindness and pity, but mostly, they exhibited her total, undeniable loyalty to Mad Dog.

"Get him to the couch and tie up his hands."

She led Nathaniel by the elbow and lowered him down.

As Zandi started to tie his hands with an old pair of nylons, a young girl with braids and shiny silk ribbons came out from the back bedroom, rubbing her eyes. "Mommy, can I get some water?"

Zandi looked up in horror. "No, Baby," she stammered. "Please go back to bed. I'll bring you a drink later."

The girl's eyes began to focus as she woke up a little more. "Who's he, Mommy?"

"Go to bed, Gracie," Zandi half-whispered, half-pleaded.

"What the hell is the kid doing out of bed?" Consuelos demanded.

"Sh-she-just-wants-some-water. She's still half-asleep, and she's goin' right back to bed."

"Shit. Get on the couch beside that man right now!" he screamed at the child.

Her eyes now wide, she looked at him and opened her mouth to speak, then thought better of it. "But, Daddy…"

"Shut up, Kid," Consuelos answered. "Just sit your little nosey ass on the couch."

Zandi swallowed hard, picked up the beautiful young girl, and placed her gently on the dirty couch beside Nathaniel. "It's okay, Baby," she whispered. "Just don't say anything else."

The child did as she was told and laid her small head on Nathaniel's shoulder.

Dear God. What's gonna happen here? Nathaniel wondered, looking down at the girl. He'd never been too fond of children, but he couldn't imagine anything happening to her. *Where the hell are the police?* he wondered. Consuelos pushed Zandi down on the sofa, looked hard at all three of them, then concentrated his stare on Nathaniel.

"I hate a punk," he said, seething. "I hate somebody who comes up into somebody else's place and thinks they're gonna disrespect a man's reputation, his family, his hood."

"Look, Man, it's nothing personal. Like I told you, it's a job. Somebody's gotta do it."

"I saw the way you were lookin' at my kid and my woman. They don't mean shit to me, but people like you got a heart for everybody, even a lowdown prostitute who'll sell her body for a buck."

Nathaniel felt sick, especially when Zandi lowered her head as Consuelos spoke.

"Well, I'm tired of pieces of shit like you. You fucked

with the wrong guy this time." With that, he raised the gun and shot Zandi right through the forehead.

She didn't make a sound. Her thin, lithe body slid over on the couch as if she were lying down.

Gracie screamed out, almost like a yelping puppy. "Mommy! You hurt my mommy!" She sobbed, grabbing Nathaniel's arms. "Please help her, Mister."

"He can't help her, Kid." Mad Dog said. "Nobody can. Besides, it's all his fault. He came in here and made me do it."

"You low-down son-of-a-bitch," Nathaniel seethed, his hatred boiling over.

"Just lettin' ya know, Man, that you don't go messin' with Mad Dog. See what your little games have caused? And don't think we won't get rid of all your bodies *and* get away with this bullshit. Your kind is as expendable as the rest of us."

"Jesus," Nathaniel said, realizing the crazy, heartless bastard was actually willing to kill his own daughter. "Don't hurt the girl. She's an innocent bystander in all of this. You said yourself this is my fault. Just let her go, send her into the night. A young kid can be threatened into keeping her mouth shut."

"Fuck you." Then, without another word, Mad Dog Consuelos raised his gun and fired four shots: two into Nathaniel Collier and two into little Gracie Elizabeth Jones.

Chapter 2

Sheriff Reid Langley sat down heavily in the old, tattered recliner and downed a large swallow of warm beer. He was trying to decide which TV dinner to slide into the microwave when the telephone interrupted his thoughts. He sighed and rose slowly from his chair, debating on whether or not to answer it.

It'd been a typical day at the small police department in Hayden, Wyoming. A few townspeople complaining about traffic citations, an accident on Old Mill Parkway, and Elizabeth Shaffer swearing that someone, *one of them out-of-towners,* had stolen her purse, only to find it later in her car. The weather was turning colder as a small flurry of white promised more snowfall for the evening.

The sheriff realized he didn't feel like running any errands or pulling anyone's Jeep out of a ditch. He just wanted to finish his beer, eat a frozen dinner, and watch the game.

The phone stopped ringing only to start up again.

"Damn it all," he murmured to himself as he lifted the receiver. "Yeah? This is Langley. It'd better be good."

"Sheriff, this is Maloney. We've got a problem. Yeah, we've got a big problem."

Reid rolled his eyes as he pictured Deputy Matthew Maloney on the other end of the line. Maloney was only twenty-three and everything was a *big problem* to him.

"Take it easy, Maloney," Reid answered calmly. "What's going on?"

"We just got a call from Madison Aldridge, Joanna Sibley's best friend. They've been best friends for as long as I can remember, even back in grade school, and in junior high, they—"

"Maloney, I don't need that much background. Just get to the point."

"She's dead, Sheriff! Dead! And it seems she's been that way for a few days, at least four. Nobody's seen her in all that time, and then Madison just up and finds her and..." He trailed off, out of breath, sounding like he'd just finished a marathon.

Reid's mind immediately began reeling. He thought he had an idea of who Joanna Sibley was, but wasn't quite sure. The best he could remember was a tall blonde in her early twenties. "Has anyone been sent over yet?" Reid questioned.

"Not yet, Sheriff. I called you first. Poor Madison is hysterical though, I think I need to get over there right away."

Reid cringed at the thought of his youngest deputy trying to calm the chaotic situation. "What's the address, Matthew? I'll meet you there."

"They're at 645 Winding Creek Trail, Apartment B-4, right next to—"

"I know where it is," Reid said, cutting him off. "See you in five." With that, he laid the receiver back on its cradle, then realized he hadn't even asked what'd happened to the girl. His first thought was a drug overdose, even though there had never been a drug problem in Hayden. It just seemed rational explanation for a supposedly healthy young girl's death.

He fumbled for his wad of keys, pulling on a hooded sweatshirt. It was still early in the evening, but the weatherman had promised numbing temperatures by 8:00 p.m. He thought about grabbing a heavier jacket but thought better of it. He knew if he left immediately, he and Maloney would arrive at about the same time. He pulled the door behind him without locking it. That was how things were done in small towns like Hayden, and he followed along with the rest of the trusting, unsuspecting yokels. He still wasn't sure why. Maybe it was because the place seemed so far from the crazy world he'd known three years before.

The sputter of the Jeep's engine reminded him of the situation he was heading toward, and his mind flashed back to Atlanta. He'd spent five years on the elite Red Dog drug unit for the Atlanta PD before going into homicide. He'd been an exemplary cop and had valued his job, but somewhere along the line, the senseless acts of violence had taken their toll. The drug-related murders, carjackings, the random attacks on innocent people seemed to be never-ending, running end to end and wrapping themselves around one another. Reid feared he was becoming ineffective and detached, so when his father's old Army buddy told him about the job opening in Hayden, the small-town cop life seemed like a perfect fit. The little village had a history of being virtually crime free, the cost of living was low, not to mention that Wyoming was considered God's country, with beautiful scenery and fresh, unpolluted air. It sounded like the perfect opportunity for him, and so far, it had been. He didn't seem to have any difficulty letting go of his memories of Atlanta, and hoped this newest problem in Hayden wouldn't turn out to be something that made him regret his move. The people of Atlanta were sadly accustomed to death, violence, and unsuspecting heartache, almost desensitized to it. But his time in Hayden had taught him the locals wouldn't handle it as well.

Reid turned his attention back to the winding road leading to the young girl's apartment. The weather was taking a turn for the worse, just as predicted, and he cursed the old Jeep and its inability to project any heat to speak of. The building soon came into view. Reid sighed heavily when he saw Deputy Maloney's squad car parked in front of B-4. He put the Jeep in park, grabbed his Braves baseball cap, took the keys from the ignition, and made his way quickly to the front door.

Reid was greeted by a chorus of sounds that'd been a familiar part of his past. His chest rose as he took in a big gulp of air. A knot forming in his stomach slowly crawled up his chest and into his windpipe.

Joanna's parents were in the small living room, clinging to one another as they wailed loudly over the loss of their only daughter. The sounds of their grief carried the undeniable tone of people whose lives would never be the same again

"I just got here, Sheriff," Maloney said quietly. "She's back here, in the bedroom. An ambulance is on the way for Madison. She locked herself in the bathroom and is refusing to come out for anyone." The rookie motioned for Reid to follow him down the short hallway, pausing to point out the closed bathroom door.

The bedroom was cluttered with all the personal effects of a young girl, and while the housecleaning was a bit neglected, nothing looked out of the ordinary.

Good sign, Reid thought. *No forced entry to the apartment and nothing's been ransacked.* He wanted to feel some aspect of relief, but the sobs from the living room continued to ring in his ears.

"Right over here," Maloney said, his voice such a light whisper that it was barely audible. His thin index finger pointed to the floor on the opposite side of the bed. "It musta been a heart attack or somethin', Sheriff. She doesn't look hurt at all."

Sheriff Langley looked down at the small-framed, young girl, and his heart sank. He'd seen her in town a few times, a vibrant, athletic type that he recalled jogging at the city park. Her shiny, blonde hair looked like a Palomino's mane, spread out in contrast against the plush, hunter-green carpet. Her lips and face harbored a tinge of blue, but other than that, she could've been simply sleeping. Reid fought the sudden urge to gather her into his arms and lift her onto the bed, but knew better than to disturb what was clearly a crime scene. He also knew young, healthy girls didn't just fall over dead. *There has to be more to this.* "Cover her up, Matthew," he said mournfully to his young charge. "No one else should see her like this. I'm going to talk to her folks. I need you to call Nell and ask her to come down with the ID kit. We'll need some shots of her where she is before they take her to the hospital."

"Sure, Sheriff," Maloney answered nervously, looking much younger than his already tender years. "But why an ambulance? I don't understand. Mr. Sibley called Stephens Funeral Home right after I got here. They're sending someone over to—"

"What? The funeral home? Shit!" Reid shook his head vehemently. "Uh-uh. She needs to go to Mountainside Memorial first. We don't know what she died of Maloney. This child needs an autopsy."

Maloney's fresh face mirrored the shock of someone who'd just been hit unexpectedly in the gut. "An autopsy? On Joanna? You can't mean that, Sheriff. I just knew her as a friend, but I can't think of anybody cutting into her and–" He shook his head as if the words were too bitter to say.

"With all due respect, Sheriff, her family's not gonna allow us to do that."

Reid rubbed his fingers across his forehead and closed his eyes. He was forgetting where he was and needed to regroup for a moment.

"Henry's on vacation, or he'd be here to get her. The only other thing to do is to have the funeral home pick her up."

"We don't know what she died of, Matthew," Reid answered firmly, trying not to sound too condescending. "It's very important we find the cause of death." He considered elaborating, but quickly changed his mind, realizing it was far more important to discuss it with the Sibleys than wasting time with his deputy. "Just cover her up and keep everyone out of here for now. I'm gonna talk to her parents."

Maloney nodded his head like a frightened child and reached over to pull the floral comforter from the unmade bed.

Reid patted him on the shoulder, then allowed his strong hand to rest on the young man's forearm. "Listen, buddy, I know this is hard, and I can't tell you it's ever going to get any easier, but you're a deputy of the law, and people need you to be strong during times like this. I know I can count on you."

"Yes, Sir," Maloney said, looking up for the first time since Reid had arrived. "You can count on me."

"Good. That's what I thought. Now just let me talk to her folks, and we'll see what we can do about getting her out of here."

As he made his way down the hall to speak with the dead girl's parents, Reid's mind drifted to Henry Hartwell, the county coroner. It absolutely appalled Reid that coroners still existed. As far as he was concerned, they were nothing more than a pickup service that received kickbacks from the local funeral homes. They made uneducated guesses and signed off on death certificates with no medical or police training, simply to please their constituents. It boiled down to people-pleasing, ass-kissing, and popularity.

The sobbing hadn't subsided, but it wasn't as loud as it'd been. The initial shock was wearing off, and denial would follow. The Sheriff had seen it enough to know the order of things. Mr. Sibley was sitting beside his wife on the couch, with his arms wrapped around her shoulders. She was rocking back and forth.

Reid felt a sudden pang in his chest as he watched them. He knew they'd need plenty of family and friends to help them through their loss. Making his way over, he sat across from them on a worn rattan chair with a lumpy cushion. "Mr. and Mrs. Sibley," he began, damn near choking on his words. *Shit. Doesn't this ever get any easier?* "I'm sorry about your daughter."

Mr. Sibley looked up, nodding his head in acknowledgment while Mrs. Sibley continued to rock back and forth in unison with her racked sobs. Neither of them spoke a word.

"I'm sorry to bother you right now, but I need to ask you a few questions."

Neither of them responded.

Reid continued, "Did Joanna have any health problems?"

"No, nothin'," her father finally said. "That child was healthy as a horse, always exercisin' and whatnot, trying to stay in shape. That's what killed her, I tell ya. She worked out too hard, and her heart couldn't handle it."

"Did she have a history of heart problems?"

"Nope. Like I said, there was nothing wrong with her. She just ran her body too hard, jogging five days a week and eatin' like a damn sparrow."

A sparrow, huh? Hmm. Maybe we're getting somewhere, Reid thought. He knew eating disorders were common among girls her age and combined with a very regimented, strenuous workout could've amounted to trouble for the girl. "Did she diet regularly?"

"She wouldn't eat any of her mama's fried chicken or desserts no more. All she'd eat was healthy foods, baked this and baked that. She even carried apples around in her purse. What are you gettin' at, Sheriff? You tryin' to make it look like she did this on purpose or somethin'?"

Anger was rising in his voice, but Reid was prepared for it. It was all part of the pattern. Now everyone would turn on him, he would be the bad guy for having the gall to ask questions. "No, Sir, Mr. Sibley," he answered. "I'm not suggesting anything. I'm just trying to figure out the cause of death. It sounds as though Joanna may have been running her body a little hard, but lots of people do that these days. She isn't the only young lady consumed with leading a healthy lifestyle, and—"

"She wasn't *too* damned healthy, Sheriff," he lashed out, his voice failing him. "Now why can't you leave me and my wife be? As you can see, the missus ain't taking it very well."

Reid leaned forward, his voice soft and sympathetic. "I understand that, Mr. Sibley. Honestly, I do, but I have a job to do. My main concern is how your daughter died. I'm not a doctor, and I can't be sure her death was caused simply by overexerting herself." He sat back and waited for his comments to sink in before he continued. The anger wasn't present yet, and it was painfully clear the suggestion of an autopsy was going to hit them from out of left field. He heaved in a deep breath of courage and said, "Mr. and Mrs. Sibley, this is an extremely difficult time, and I will not sit here and even pretend to understand how you're feeling."

"That's mighty big of you, Sheriff. Now, if you'll just leave us alone to tend to our business—"

"I'm sorry, but I can't do that. It's imperative we find Joanna's cause of death. At this point, it appears that—"

16

"Wait a damn minute," Mr. Sibley said, reality finally slapping him in the face. "I don't know where you're a-goin' with this, but I know you ain't about to suggest an autopsy! Hell no! Ain't nobody gonna take a scalpel and cut my baby up..." His face had suddenly turned a dark crimson, and he jumped up on unsteady feet.

Reid stood as well, certain the anxiousness forming in his stomach was going to rise up in his throat and strangle him to death. "Mr. Sibley, please calm down for a moment. We need to talk about this rationally." Reid looked down at Mrs. Sibley, who appeared confused and shocked, her mouth open in a strange, distorted shape. He felt overpowered by the grieving parents and found himself in the rare position of being at a loss for words.

"There ain't nothing rational about cutting on my baby. I won't have it, I tell you. I simply won't have it. Where the hell is Henry Hartwell? Henry'll see that this is handled respectably."

"He's on vacation, Sir. Besides, he's just a coroner, not a medical examiner. He can't give us any answers as to why this happened to your daughter, so—"

"I wouldn't be so sure 'bout that, Sheriff. Henry was here long before you were, and I dare say he'll be here long after they haul your big-city, ass outta our town!"

Reid let the comment go unanswered and sighed as he contemplated his next strategy.

His thoughts were interrupted by a knock at the apartment door. The ambulance drivers were there to extract Madison from the bathroom.

"Evenin', Sheriff," Joe Hill said, his tight uniform snug around his belly.

"Joe, I'm glad you're here," Sheriff Langley answered, grateful for the momentary distraction.

The EMT held up a thin piece of metal used to open locked doors. "I heard she won't come out. Lemme just see what we can do about that. Have you talked to her?"

"Not yet. She seems pretty hysterical though."

The two men, accompanied by Jane Goode, another medical technician, walked down the hall. They'd left one out-of-control situation for another. Madison was still screaming and crying, and the door remained locked.

"Madison, this is Sheriff Langley. I know you're upset about Joanna, but we need to make sure you're all right. Will you please open the door?"

The three waited quietly, but it was clear she wasn't going to respond.

"Okay, Madison," Reid continued calmly. "Joe and Jane are going to open the door and come in to help you. We're all very concerned about you." He stood back as they pried open the door.

The young girl was curled up in a ball in the floor, her small body heaving with sobs.

"Looks like she's going into shock, Sheriff," Jane said as she leaned down over the girl. "Please get me a wet towel. She's severely overheated." Jane brushed Madison's hair away from her face and wiped the damp cloth Joe had given her across the young girl's face and neck. "Madison, honey, do you hear me? It's Jane, Sweetheart, and we're very concerned about you. Do you know where you are, Honey?"

There was only more crying for her response.

"Sheriff, we're gonna have to take her to Mountainside Memorial. She needs a sedative, and she needs it quickly," Jane said, looking back over her shoulder at Reid. With the help of her partner, she was able to get Madison out of the bathroom and into the back of the waiting ambulance. As they slammed the doors to leave for the hospital, it was obvious that Madison was unaware of her surroundings.

"Man, poor Madison's in bad shape," Deputy Maloney said as he walked up to Reid's side. "You think she'll be okay?"

"Yeah, but it might be quite a while. She's takin' it

pretty hard."

Reid turned to go back into the apartment. Just as he did, he saw the headlights of the hearse, a long, morbid-looking car with a "Stephens Funeral Home" decal on the side. "Son-of-a-bitch! Will this day ever end?"

"Listen, Sheriff," Maloney quietly pleaded, "let the funeral home take her. It looks like her heart just gave out. This ain't Atlanta, and none of those awful murders and drugs and things like that happen here."

Reid violently rubbed his temples and thought hard about Matthew's words. *Maybe I'm just being cynical. Maybe my past is clouding my judgment. Maybe this place is freaking Mayberry and nothing bad ever happens here,* he thought, but he had suspicions that wasn't the case.

Reid walked back into the apartment, sitting down beside the Sibleys one more time. "Mr. Sibley, I'm begging with you to let me order an autopsy on your daughter. I don't need anything extensive, maybe draw some blood and do a toxicology report to—"

"A blood test? My girl weren't takin' no drugs if that's what you are gettin' at," he answered. He was much calmer now, almost resigned to the fact that some questions needed answers.

"I'm not insinuating she was," Reid said, trying desperately to avoid the pounding inside his head. "It may be that her heart simply gave out, but we can't ignore other possibilities. She could've been taking some dietary supplement, some fad diet pill that might need to come off of the shelves. I know this is hard for you, but once the shock wears off, Mr. Sibley, you're going to want answers."

"Maybe there's a little truth to that," he answered, consciously ignoring the funeral home personnel as they wheeled in a gurney.

Reid turned slowly, holding up his hand in a gesture for them to stand by before retrieving the body. "Just let me contact Doctor Novus at Mountainside. I'll stay with Joanna myself and make sure the doctor only draws blood and does an external exam. I give you my word."

Mr. Sibley turned to his wife and brushed her thin hair from her face, then leaned to kiss her lightly on the forehead. "God forgive me if I'm makin' a mistake," he whispered, more to himself than to anyone else. Before turning back to Reid, he wiped away a lone tear that'd escaped the rim of his eye. "Sweet Jesus in Heaven," he choked out, "please don't let 'em butcher my only child."

"I'll be right there the whole time, Sir," Reid replied somberly. "I'll have the funeral home drop her off at the hospital, and I'll be in touch as soon as we know anything." He glanced back at the men with the gurney who were heading down the hall, then leaned over to Mr. Sibley. "I don't think your wife should be here when they bring your daughter out. The two of you should go home and get whatever rest you can. If you'd like, Deputy Maloney can drive you."

"Thanks for the offer, Sheriff, but I can drive myself," Mr. Sibley said. He helped his wife to her feet, and on wobbly legs, they walked slowly to their car.

Chapter 3

Nurse Laverne Lewis was standing vigil over Nathaniel Collier's hospital bed for the third week in a row. They'd gone to high school together, so his case was personal to her. Twice he'd coded in ICU, but Laverne was determined to see her former classmate pull through. Apparently, he was determined as well because he was still with them, his body growing stronger every day.

She rubbed her short, stubby fingers over his muscled forearms as she listened to his labored breathing. He was a kind young man, not to mention dangerously handsome. Even after narrowly escaping death, his face still reflected rugged good looks. Laverne brushed his golden-blond locks back from his face as she talked soothingly to him. "C'mon, sleepyhead. It's time for you to come back to us now. You've gotten plenty of rest, Nathaniel."

Much to her shock, his eyelids fluttered, and his deep blue eyes gazed clearly up at her.

"Nathaniel? Can you hear me?"

He managed a confused nod, the best he could do for an answer that fell somewhere between yes and no.

"It's me, Laverne Lewis, from high school. I'm a nurse here at Atlanta Medical Center."

Another nod.

"You were shot. The doctors have you pretty sedated, but you're doing much better now. You're going to be just fine."

"Water," he mumbled. "Thirsty. Need…water."

"Oh! Of course! Let me get you a straw. You can have a little sip—not too much though." She fumbled with a small Styrofoam cup.

Nathaniel drank with a vengeance, wanting much more than she allotted him.

"Sorry, Nathaniel. Let's see how that sits with you first."

He reached for her arm and held on to it much firmer than she expected. "The little girl…please. How…where is she? Did she…did she make it?"

Laverne smiled kindly, thinking of the small, frail child lying in the pediatric ICU downstairs. "She's holding her own right now, Nathaniel, but that's the best news I can give you. She's had a rough go of things, just like you. Why don't you try to get some rest?"

"Please," he whispered, "tell me everything you know." He was tired and weak, but his eyes pleaded with her for information. "Where was she shot?"

"You really need to rest and recup—"

"Please! I just…I need to know. So worried…poor little girl."

"Okay, okay," Laverne answered, pulling up a chair and sitting beside the bed. "All I know is that you were both airlifted in after a shooting at an apartment complex. It had something to do with your job, I think. You were shot twice. The first bullet pierced your left lung, and the second one hit your liver. That was the most extensive of your injuries."

"But her?" he pressed. "Tell me about the little girl."

Nurse Laverne had hoped he'd drift off to sleep before asking about the child again. He didn't need any further worries on his mind. He needed to concentrate on getting stronger, but she could see he wasn't going to stop with the questions until she gave him some answers. "The little girl was shot in the chest and had to have open-heart surgery. She's still on a respirator. It's touch-and-go, but she's quite the fighter. I've been down to see her a couple of times. She's got a big fan club in the unit down there. The nurses are very fond of her, and they're taking great care of her." Laverne watched as tears pooled in his eyes. "Nathaniel, please don't get upset right now. You've got to get better yourself. It's a positive sign the little girl made it this far."

"Is someone watching the...her door...danger," he stuttered, struggling to sit up.

"Is our patient awake, Nurse Lewis?"

Laverne turned and saw Doctor Pennington walking in. "Yes, Doctor," she answered, feeling a little nervous. "He woke up about five minutes ago, and he's very concerned about the Jones girl downstairs, the little one who came in with him."

"Well, I'll see what I can do about that," he answered as he made his way over to Nathaniel's bedside. The older doctor had been on the hospital staff for over forty years, and everyone adored him. He was tall and trim, with thin, graying wisps of hair and half-moon spectacles. His bedside manner had a way of making his patients feel at ease. Rolling a stool up under himself, he sat down and studied Nathaniel's face. "I'm happy to see you're back with us, Mr. Collier," he said. "You traveled quite a long journey to get here. I hate to admit it, but I wondered a few times if you'd still be with us."

"I wanna know about the girl, Doc, the one

downstairs."

"Yes, Nurse Lewis mentioned that. I understand you two came in on the same bird together. It seems you both know some of the same seedy characters."

"Yes, Sir, I-I'm awfully worried, Doctor. She's just...she's so small, and—"

"Mr. Collier, you need not worry about that child. She's a real fighter, much like you. I've made many visits to her bedside, and she's hanging in there. You took a couple of hits to your torso, and one did some pretty severe damage. It's nothing we can't take care of for you, as long as you go easy on yourself."

Nathaniel grabbed Doctor Pennington's smock and pulled him forcefully toward him. "You have to watch that little girl. Her father tried to kill us, and he'll do it again." With that, Nathaniel drifted off in a fitful sleep, before either the doctor or Nurse Lewis could assure him that both he and Gracie Elizabeth were under constant guard by the Atlanta PD.

Chapter 4

Reid used the phone in Joanna Sibley's apartment to reach Doctor Anne Novus. As he expected, she was still in her office, even though it was well after 9:00 p.m. "Doctor Novus, Sheriff Langley here," he stated, as his mind wandered to the young girl in transit to the morgue.

"Hello, Sheriff. How are you tonight?"

He fought off a smile as he pictured her there behind her mounds of paperwork. "Not very good, Doc. We had an unexplained death in town tonight, and the young woman is on her way to you. Her family is against a full autopsy but has agreed for us—or rather, *you*—to run some toxicology tests. I don't know if you'll find much there. She appeared to be in excellent health. The whole thing's just…strange."

"What a tragedy. Was anyone there with her when she expired?"

"Expired? You make her sound like a parking meter."

"Technical terms, Sheriff. The jargon helps us to

remain detached from our patients, which is helpful in doing our jobs. I assumed you'd be familiar with those tactics, in your line of work."

"I am, Doc. Just trying to make light of it is all. Don't be so testy."

"I'm not being testy, Reid. It's after 9:00, and I know you're going to expect me to finish this tonight. Some of us start our day at 6:00 a.m."

"No shit?" He laughed. "Is there a 6:00 a.m.?"

"Jeez. Just let me go," she half-teased. "I have two hours of paperwork to deal with, and they'll be here with the body in a few minutes. Am I to assume you'll be stopping by?"

"You got it, Doc."

"Lovely." She groaned before lightly replacing the receiver.

Reid respected Doctor Novus. She was an extremely intelligent woman, and one of Hayden's most competent doctors. As in many small towns, the doctors were required to wear a variety of hats, and even though she had a specialty, she wasn't necessarily limited to it. Doctor Novus was the most experienced in pathology, so she was naturally the best to take over Joanna's case.

Reid pulled into the circular drive of Mountainside Memorial Hospital and parked his aging Jeep out front. At times like these, he missed the anonymity of large crowds. Being the sheriff of Hayden, Wyoming was the closest thing to being a celebrity, and although he did enjoy it at times, this wasn't going to be one of them. He nodded acknowledgments to a few familiar faces and made his way down the west hall.

The elevator door opened to the hospital basement where it was dead quiet. The basement only housed the morgue, the laundry, and housekeeping supplies. Reid glanced at his watch and discovered it was after 10:00. All of the janitorial staff was gone for the day, so the morgue was the only occupied space. The echoes of his footsteps against the linoleum broke the eerie silence, but didn't do much for his nerves. Reid was relieved to find Doctor Novus in her office, she had a way of putting him at ease, and he was in dire need of her expertise. "Good evening, Doc," Reid said softly as he tapped on the door.

"Same to you, Sheriff," she answered, looking up from a desk piled high with paperwork. "Can I get you a cup of coffee? But be aware, I haven't gotten any better at brewing it since you were here last."

"Yeah? Well, thanks. I'm always a sucker for a bad cup of coffee."

She motioned for him to have a seat and quickly returned with a steaming cup in each hand. She handed him one and took the other for herself as she settled behind the desk.

"Well? You got any gut feelings about this one?" he asked, getting straight to the point.

"Gut feelings are for cops, Reid. Doctors work with facts and scientific evidence."

He studied her face before he answered. *She really is quite attractive, isn't she?* The thought had rambled through his mind more than once or twice. He figured her to be about his age, early thirties, and he knew from the town gossip that she was single. Her long, black hair was pulled into a ponytail, and beautiful green eyes looked at him through stylish reading glasses. She was almost his height, close to six feet tall.

"I wasn't implying you should make an educated guess, Doctor Novus. I respect your profession and the tremendous job you do, so—"

"Pssh. Don't patronize me, Reid," she retorted, pulling her glasses off and laying them on an open medical file. "I know exactly what you meant," she said, struggling against a smile. "I wish I could give you an answer right away, but these things take time. I can tell you that I don't see anything, looking at the outward appearance of the body, that would lead me to believe it was a homicide. It appears to be natural causes, but for a girl her age, so health conscious at that, it's just...*strange*, like you said. How's the family, Mr. and Mrs. Sibley?"

"They're taking it pretty hard, still fighting the damn autopsy." Reid stood up and paced around the small, cramped office, feeling frustrated. "Why in the hell do people do that? Don't they want to know what happened to their daughter? It's as if they expect us to do our jobs with our hands tied."

Anne took a large sip of her coffee, closed her eyes, then let out a long, deep sigh. "You know the answer to that, Sheriff. This isn't your first dealing with autopsy requests. Families never want to visualize their loved ones going through the degrading process. The thought of them being dissected is just too painful for them to bear. The bottom line is, they'd rather live with the thought of her dying in her sleep from a heart played out much too early in life than to think of her being murdered. Sure, it's denial, but it's a hell of a lot easier to live with."

"So what do we do now? She's got to have an autopsy, and God knows it'd be better to do it now than to exhume the body later."

"We both know that, but she's not our daughter. The funeral home is breathing down my neck already, and I'll have to release the body soon."

"That's a crock of shit, Doc, and you know it. I'm going to have to force the issue, and I hate doing that. Hell, in Atlanta it's a law that anyone her age who dies under such questionable circumstances has to have an autopsy."

"This isn't Atlanta, Reid. It's a small town, and these people can't handle their child being cut into after death. Truth be told, a lot of young people have heart problems, inherited and congenital conditions they might not even be aware of. Mix that with excessive exercise and extreme dieting and…well, the heart simply quits. Did you see any signs of foul play at the scene?"

"Not really, but that doesn't mean anything. She's just so damned young and healthy looking." Reid rubbed his fingertips across his forehead and firmly closed his eyes in an attempt to block out the memory of the beautiful, young girl. He remembered her shiny, blonde hair lying across the dark carpet. She looked so much younger than her twenty years. He'd even said a silent prayer of thanks for the condition in which she was found. Rigor mortis had come and gone, and the air in her apartment had been cool enough to preserve her body from the beginning of decomposition. With one last brutal rub across his forehead, he cleared his throat and looked up at Anne Novus. "Could we take a look at her? I know it's late, but what we don't accomplish tonight won't get accomplished tomorrow. Her father is going to demand the body be released in the morning, so we don't have a lot of time with her."

"I expected that," she answered, pulling on her lab coat. "I assume you have a release from the family with you?"

"No, Doc. I don't normally walk around with the forms in my pocket. How many autopsies have I had to order and oversee since I've been here? Hmm. Uh…none."

"You know it's hospital policy, Reid. I can't break protocol just because you're afraid the family might have a change of heart."

"I have a verbal agreement. That should stand up in court if there's a problem. You know we need this autopsy."

"It might or might not hold up. I don't like it," she answered, her voice wavering a bit, making it clear she was about to give in to the Sheriff's pleading. "You know the only way to force an autopsy in this town is if there's reason to believe there was a homicide."

Reid chose to ignore the comment and attempted to change the subject. "Could it be possible that young people are trying out some new drug? Have any been admitted to the hospital lately with symptoms related to drug abuse?"

"You know we don't have a big drug problem here. From what you've told me, her parents were quite involved, cared about her, and were a big part of her life. I think they would've noticed a change in behavior, especially if it were related to drug abuse."

"I don't know about that. I saw a lot of it in Atlanta. Parents are always the last to believe or expect it in their own child. What all does the tox screen test for?"

"The usual—alcohol, marijuana, cocaine, heroin…"

"So if it doesn't show up in those forms, we won't know what it is, right?"

"Sadly, we need to know what we're looking for to test for it. The tests are expensive, and the hospital doesn't want me wasting time on any wild goose chases."

"Wild goose chases? What the hell…?"

"You know what I mean, Reid. Without a few signs, we won't know where to begin testing."

Anne started down the hall, motioning for Reid to follow. "She's right down here. She's the only one we've got tonight."

Reid meandered into the cool autopsy room at a slow gait. It was never pleasant for him to look at a body, much less a kid. He'd seen more than his share of death back in Atlanta—senseless, random, and violent. It'd always turned his stomach, leaving the bitter taste of bile in his throat.

Since Joanna was the only customer of the night, it was impossible to overlook her. The white sheet covering her body let off an almost fluorescent glow.

Reid stood over the body, waiting for Anne to turn the sheet down. He couldn't find the courage to do it. His usually steady hands tended to fail him at moments like this.

Doctor Novus carefully folded the crisp sheet down. "Here you go," she said, handing him a pair of disposable gloves as she snapped a pair on herself. "Maybe you'll see something I missed."

Reid pulled the gloves on and reached down for Joanna's right hand. Her nails were short and looked as if they'd been well chewed. There were no typical defensive wounds or scratches. "Did you swab under these nails?"

"Yep. That's always the first step. Nothing unusual, but she was quite the nail-biter, as you can see."

"Yeah, but everything looks clean. She didn't appear to be fighting anybody off."

"I didn't find any wounds at all."

Reid ran his gloved fingers up her forearm, turning it to inspect the inside as well. "Where are her clothes?"

"Over there in a bag, but if you want to see them, you better look now. The family has already requested them back."

"Shit. What's up with that? I need to send them to the lab. I'll be getting a court order for that, so don't turn them over to the funeral home when they come."

Anne nodded in agreement, turning her attention back to the body.

The light blue shade Joanna had taken on was unsettling but normal for a heart attack. She unfolded the sheet a little more, revealing Joanna's small, firm breasts.

"Any sign of sexual intercourse?"

"I couldn't tell you that, Sheriff," Anne answered, sounding frustrated and tired. "Only an autopsy would make that clear. Again, there aren't any signs of assault. I'm not sure if she had a boyfriend or not."

Reid gently pulled the sheet up and covered Joanna's face, then stared blankly at the white linen.

"There isn't any reason to keep gawking at the poor kid. It's not going to change anything." Anne reached over and placed her hand on his arm. "I'm sorry things are like this, Reid. I really am. If I had the authority to go through with the autopsy, you know I'd do it. But on the bright side, we did get something from this."

"Right. We know she wasn't attacked. I guess that's helpful."

"Actually, we know a little more than that. I don't see any of the normal signs of poisoning. She wasn't covered with vomit, and there's no obvious hair loss. Her blood isn't cherry red, as it would be in a carbon monoxide or cyanide victim, and she doesn't have any injuries or bruising from strychnine-type convulsions. A poisoning victim will typically take on the appearance of someone who has been very ill. As you can attest, she looks fine…um, except for being dead."

"Could she've been injected with something?"

"Anything is possible, but I didn't see any needle marks. You're welcome to look for yourself. I was hoping to find one because that would give me cause to insist on an autopsy."

"I think I should call the State police."

"In my opinion, Reid, you should hold off on that. This town will tar and feather you if you start a crusade like that. There just isn't enough evidence to warrant it, at least not in their eyes. The odds of this being anything other than heart failure are simply slim to none. I know it sounds callous, but you need to let it go. You shouldn't open up a can of worms. Frankly, it probably isn't necessary. You're in Hayden, Wyoming, remember? This is one of the safest places on Earth."

"Yeah, yeah. Famous last words. I hope they don't come back to haunt you."

Anne looked over at the troubled sheriff and felt the sudden urge to hold him. He'd taken the young girl's death to heart, and she could tell he desperately wanted answers. She liked Reid. He was gallant and strong, not to mention handsome. His thick hair was black like her own, but his eyes—a deep, dark chocolate, closer to black than brown—contrasted swiftly with her bright green ones. He also had thick, long lashes that would be the envy of any woman. His six-foot frame was almost majestic. Large shoulders and biceps led to a thin, tight waist and strapping thighs. She wondered if she were more tired than usual because her mind was on things it shouldn't be, especially with a dead girl in the room. She rolled her head around in small circles to ease the growing tension in her neck and shoulders.

Reid looked down at his watch and realized it was well after midnight. Despite all of the grim events of the night, he felt the sudden pangs of hunger, a reminder that he hadn't eaten dinner. "What do you say we go grab a bite at Kaleb's?" he asked nonchalantly. The small diner sounded like a real winner to him at that moment.

His invitation jolted Anne out of her current thoughts long enough to realize her stomach was also growling. "Actually," she said, removing her lab coat, "that doesn't sound like a bad idea. I'll meet you there in, say…fifteen minutes? I need to lock these files up."

Reid smiled and turned to walk her back to her office when he realized they were leaving Joanna there alone. It felt awkward and cold. He stopped and turned slowly to take one last look at the covered girl as if to apologize.

"She'll be fine, Reid," Anne spoke softly. "The funeral home will be here first thing in the morning. We've done all we can for her."

"I know. It just seems so damn wrong."

Chapter 5

Nathaniel struggled with the IV pole as he walked, slowly and deliberately, down the hallway. The nurses' station was coming into view, along with the chair they'd set out for him to rest in when he finally made it there. It looked like a mirage as his face and armpits beaded with perspiration. He thrust his battered body forward and plopped painfully into the plastic chair. Breathing heavily, he fought back tears from the pain of his healing wounds.

"Good morning, Nathaniel," Nurse Laverne said happily as she rounded the corner. "It's so good to see you out and about."

"You sound like you just bumped into me at the mall." Nathaniel laughed, as an agonizing pain shot through his abdomen. He leaned forward until the sharp feeling passed but still managed a smile for the nurse who was helping to make the situation bearable.

"Today the nurses' station, tomorrow the mall. Let

your cup be half-full, Nathaniel."

"Yeah, yeah," he stammered. He reached for the cloth handkerchief in his pajama pocket, but Laverne beat him to the punch and swabbed a damp washcloth across his drenched forehead. "Thanks. That feels a lot better," he said, a bit sheepishly. "Maybe I can make it back to the room now."

"Well, Mr. Collier, you can saunter back down the hall and take a nap if you want to, but I have a proposal for you."

"Can't say I've heard a proposal in a while. Shoot."

"It just so happens," she smiled before continuing, "that I can get my hands on a wheelchair."

"Are you asking me out on a date, Laverne?" Nathaniel laughed. "Because if you are, I accept. I wouldn't turn down a change of scenery for anything."

"Well, not a date with me exactly, but I think you'll be happy just the same. There's another lady downstairs who'd love to see you. She's a lot younger, and she's awake for the moment, but she tires quickly."

"What? She's awake? Then let's stop burning daylight. Go grab that wheelchair."

For the first time since he'd awakened, Nathaniel didn't notice the pain running through his body. His mind was on seeing Gracie, just as it had been the entire time he'd lain in the hospital. A nervousness began growing in his stomach as the memories of that fateful night swirled through his head. She'd been so trusting, only to be betrayed by her own father. He swallowed hard and forced the tears back.

"And here she is." Laverne smiled as she rounded the corner with his transportation.

"A fine set of wheels." Nathaniel grinned, pushing any negative thoughts from his mind.

"Best one in the house." Laverne said as she gently guided him into the seat.

Nathaniel rode in silence until they reached the elevator. "How is she? I mean…well, just give it to me straight, Laverne. I need to know what to expect."

"I wouldn't think of giving it to you any other way. Let's just say we're pretty confident. Lately, she's been staying out of the woods, so to speak. There were many days when her doctors wondered if they'd be able to say that."

"Thank goodness, she made it. I still can't believe anyone could do anything so damned cold, shooting a little girl. Do you think she remembers me?"

"Doctor Pennington said she's been asking about you. He thinks it might help her healing process to see you, that maybe a little reunion might be good for both of you. Just remember, Nathaniel, she's just a little girl. I don't know how much she can handle, so take it slow."

He nodded his head in agreement as the elevator doors opened to the children's wing. He'd wanted to see the girl again for so long, but now he was overwhelmed with nervousness. The brightly decorated hallway seemed to ease some of the tension. Nathaniel had been cooped up in his room for so long that it was nice to finally see color again. He took in the faces of the children in the halls. Some were taking slow walks with nurses, and others were seated in wheelchairs, watching the traffic go by. It saddened him to see them. He'd never really thought about children being hospitalized for anything more than having their tonsils out. By the looks on the faces of some of the parents, he could tell many of the children were there for far more serious concerns than that.

"Here we go," Laverne said quietly. "Room 302. I'll push you in and let you two visit. You won't have long though. You're both in the recuperating stage. You'll be exhausted by the time I get you back to your room."

Nathaniel nodded his head in silent agreement.

Laverne wheeled him over to the side of the bed, then

walked out quietly after patting him on the hand.

Gracie was asleep, but began to stir when she heard them enter the room.

She was more beautiful than Nathaniel remembered, and he sat there frozen, unable to say anything.

"Hello, Mister," she said, a smile curling around the corners of her small mouth. "Do you remember me?"

Nathaniel fought to keep the tears that were forming from escaping the rims of his eyes. "Of course I do," he answered as he reached for her tiny hand, "but the last time I saw you, there were blue ribbons in your hair. Today you have pink ones. I think I like pink best."

She seemed pleased with his recollection and smiled bashfully. "The nurses have been braiding my hair for me. My Mommy used to do it, but…well, she died, you know."

"Yes, I know. I heard about that," Nathaniel answered, unable to look at her. "I'm very, very sorry, Gracie."

She looked at him with large brown eyes, reflecting a sadness and understanding far beyond her years. "I'm sorry too. I'm sorry you got shot, Mister," she whispered. "My Daddy's a very mean man."

"Gracie," he choked out, "you can call me Nathaniel. I know you got shot, too, and I'm sorry about that. I hope we can be friends."

"I'd like that. I'd like it a lot." She smiled.

Nathaniel's eyes began to droop in exhaustion. "I'm going to let you sleep now," he said, leaning over to kiss her lightly on her cheek, "but I promise I'll be back to see you again."

"In the morning?" she asked quickly. "Can you come back then and watch TV with me?"

"I'd like that, Gracie. It's a date. Get some rest now. We both need to get better so we can get out of here."

A frown of concern crossed her face but was soon replaced with the labored breaths of sleep.

Nathaniel sat watching her, wondering what her life

would be like after all the tragedy she'd endured. Her mother was gone, and her father was a heartless murderer.

"Shall I take you back to your suite, Mr. Collier?" Laverne asked, bringing him back to the harsh reality of his own injuries.

"A suite? Gee, if that's what you call my room, I'd hate to see how the other half lives around here."

They both chuckled for a moment, helping to ease the pain of leaving the little creature alone in her hospital bed.

Nathaniel nodded a hello to the Atlanta police officer as they passed. He hoped the guard was taking his post seriously. He was looking after precious cargo, not to mention an eyewitness to one brutal murder and two attempted ones.

It felt good to lie back down in his bed, but the pain was sharp and fearless. "Laverne," he said with a grimace, "I…God, I'm hurting like hell."

"I bet you are. Maybe that little tour was too much for you."

"No," he answered quickly. "I promised her I'd come back in the morning. Don't let me—or her—down."

The nurse's smile reflected a sadness Nathaniel didn't quite understand. "I couldn't possibly do that. In the meantime, I'll get Doctor Pennington to prescribe some pain medication for you. I'll be right back."

She returned within five minutes, and Nathaniel was grateful for the relief his body would soon begin to feel. *Too bad it can't relieve my emotions,* he thought.

"You look like you need to talk," Laverne said, helping herself to a chair.

"I'm just so sad for that little girl. What a short straw she's drawn in life. I wish I'd done something differently. Maybe I shoulda—"

"Nathaniel, you did all you could. This isn't your fault, and you can't carry that burden. She'll be fine."

"Fine? Sure, maybe you guys will pull her through

medically, but what will become of her? What kind of life will she have? Surely, she won't go back to her father."

"Uh-uh. No court in their right mind would give him custody of that girl after what he did to her and mother. Besides, he's on the run, but they'll find him. He won't get away with this."

"Does she have any other family?"

"Not that anyone has been able to find. The Department of Children and Family Services has been assigned the case and they'll find a good home for her."

"Find her a good home? God, Laverne, she isn't a damn puppy," Nathaniel answered angrily, immediately regretting his tone. "I'm sorry," he said wearily.

Laverne leaned over and kissed his forehead lightly. "Get some rest. We'll talk about it later."

"Just one more thing," he said as he tossed his body back and forth to find a more comfortable position.

"What?"

"Is she safe?"

"There have been around-the-clock police guards posted at both of your doors since you were brought in. When she's well enough to leave here, her location will be kept confidential. Her father won't be able to find her."

"Thank you," Nathaniel whispered before letting the painkillers and fatigue carry him off to sleep.

* * * *

The next morning, a ridiculously perky, Laverne awakened him from his sound night's sleep. He was shocked to discover he hadn't stirred once, not even when the nurses had checked his vitals at midnight. "Morning. It's after 9:00. You trying to sleep all day?"

"Had our coffee already, I see," Nathaniel answered groggily. "Would you believe I didn't wake up once last night? You must've given me more than aspirin."

"Your body just needed the rest. You're going to have to start pushing yourself a little more. Doctor Pennington thinks you should be able to go home at the end of the week, as long as you put forth enough effort. You've got to meet us halfway, Nathaniel. We can't do it all."

"No shit," he muttered.

"There'll be none of that," she chirped. "I'm here to wash your hair and help you get changed. You do remember you have a date this morning, don't you?"

"You bet I do." Nathaniel answered. "Let's get on with it."

"Take it easy. One step at a time," Laverne teased as she helped him to his feet.

Gracie Elizabeth was sitting in bed, propped up comfortably with an abundance of pillows. The bed swallowed her whole, making her look even smaller than her forty-eight pounds. Her hair had just been washed and braided, and she'd asked the nurses to put the pink ribbons in again, hoping Nathaniel would notice. She liked him a lot. His face was kind, and she felt safe when she was around him, which was an unusual feeling for her to have around grown-ups, especially a man. Her mother had made her feel that way at times, but those good times had been few and far between.

"Look at that. What a pretty young lady." Nathaniel smiled as he was wheeled into the room. "How are you feeling this morning?"

"Great," she answered, returning the smile in full. "Did you get pancakes for breakfast, too?"

"Not hardly." Nathaniel laughed. "Only you kids get the good stuff. I got a boiled egg."

"Yuck," Gracie said, scrunching up her face. "Wanna watch SpongeBob? You know who he is, right?"

"Of course I know who Mr. SquarePants is! I do live on this planet, don't I?"

She covered her mouth with her hands and stifled a

giggle. Reaching for the remote, she quickly flipped through several channels until settling on one. "It'll start in just a few minutes."

"Good, because I just happen to have a few minutes. I see you're wearing those beautiful ribbons again today."

There wasn't any doubt that she was pleased with his compliment. Her fingers touched her braids, then felt the ribbons, as if to make sure they were all still there. "Do you have any scars? I have a big one and a medium one."

"Yes, as a matter of fact, I do. I have a big one and…well, a big one."

The comment made her laugh, then her eyes settled on his with a seriousness Nathaniel wasn't prepared for. "Mr. Nathaniel, why didn't Daddy like you?"

He glanced slowly around the room, hoping Laverne would return and save him from answering her, but no such luck. He had zero experience with children, and didn't know how forthcoming he should be with a child. "Gracie," he answered warmly, placing his big hands around her much smaller ones, "I don't really know what to say. It's kind of a complicated, grown-up thing."

She curled her fingers around his and kept her gaze on him. "I'm seven years old, not a little kid anymore, Nathaniel," she said in such a matter-of-fact way that it would've made him laugh if the conversation hadn't been so serious. "Did you work with my Daddy?"

"No, Honey," Nathaniel answered, trying hard to conceal the smile that threatened his lips. "I didn't know your daddy at all. See, I'm sort of like a police officer. I catch bad guys and take them to jail."

"And Daddy was so bad that he shot us before you could take him, right?"

Nathaniel squirmed in his chair before answering. "Yes, Gracie. That's exactly what happened. I wish there had been something I could've done to keep him from hurting us and your mother. I guess I just didn't realize how bad things would get that night."

"That's okay." She smiled, squeezing his fingers tightly. "Nobody could stop him. Did you know he shot Mommy's friend, too? She didn't give him enough of her money."

Nathaniel tried to hide his hurt for the child who'd seen far too much violence in her short lifetime.

"Look," she said, pointing up to the television. "It's SpongeBob! He'll make us feel better, I promise."

"I'm sure he will," Nathaniel answered, trying to sound as confident as she did. His attempts were shattered by the ringing of the phone. "I'll get that. I bet it's Nurse Laverne telling me it's time to go back to my room." He picked up the receiver. "Yes, Ma'am?" he said, winking at Gracie.

"That's *Sir* to you," a sickeningly familiar voice said.

Nathaniel felt his blood grow cold, and his face went pale.

"Stay out of my daughter's room, or you'll both die slowly and painfully."

"Wh-wh-where—"

"Don't worry about where I am. I'm closer than you think. Just know you won't get away alive this time, you or the kid."

Chapter 6

Reid held the door of Kaleb's Diner open for Anne, and the two rushed in to get out of the cold.

"Brrrr!" Anne shivered as she took off her wool coat. "The snow is sure picking up out there."

"I know. I'm still not used to this winter wonderland of yours." Reid said. "We had snow once a winter in Atlanta, but it was always gone in a couple of days. It tended to shut the whole city down while it was there though. It'd be comical to you folks around here."

"Yeah, well as you can see, life goes on here no matter how deep it gets."

"Evenin'," Frank Sewell said, greeting them as if it were noon instead of midnight.

"Evenin' to you, Frank," they both answered.

Everyone in town knew the Sewells, the good, honest, hardworking folks who'd owned one of the two diners in town for well over forty years. Between Frank, his wife

Helen, and their two sons, Adam and Aaron, they managed to stay open twenty-fours a day, except on Sundays, since they insisted on closing to 'enjoy the Lord's day' as Frank always put it.

"What can I get for you?" he asked.

"I think we'll start with a cup of coffee," Anne answered, reaching for one of the greasy plastic menus stacked under the salt and pepper shakers.

"Comin' right up." He walked off and was back in an instant. "Two steaming cups right here," he said. He stood over them uncomfortably before pulling a chair up to the end of their booth. "Hey, you folks mind if I yak yer ear off for a minute?" Frank asked awkwardly.

"Not at all," Reid answered, already aware of where the conversation was headed. "What's on your mind?"

"We just hated to hear about that Sibley girl. Real sad. Any news on what mighta happened to her?"

"Not yet. There aren't any signs of foul play if that makes you feel any better," Reid answered, unsure whose mind he was trying to put at ease.

"What do you think, Doc?" Frank asked, turning his attention to Anne.

She hesitated before answering, "We can't ever explain death when it comes to a young person. It's just a tragedy. Lots of things can be going on inside our bodies that we're never even aware of. Young people can suffer heart failure just like older people can."

"So it was a heart attack, then?"

"Not necessarily," Anne answered, feeling more than a little uncomfortable. "That's just the logical explanation at this point."

"Just terrible," he mumbled as he slid his chair back to its proper table. "Decided on what you want to eat?"

"I think I'll take a loaded omelet," Reid answered.

"Same here," Anne retorted, heaving a heavy sigh of relief when Mr. Sewell left their table. "I know better than to discuss cases," she said, looking down at her black coffee. "I just fueled a fire that didn't need to be fed."

"Don't worry. You didn't really give anything away," Reid assured her. "People are going to talk. This is big news for Hayden. Besides, I've been thinking. Maybe you're right and it was just a heart condition. Maybe I'm just being cynical and paranoid. It's just that...well, I've seen too many bad things happen, and it's hard to believe that a twenty-year-old could die of natural causes."

"It happens, Reid. Think of all the athletes, and young, physically fit people, who've literally dropped dead in their tracks."

Reid lifted his cup of coffee, motioning for a toast. "To my future in a safe place. To Hayden, Wyoming."

"Here, here!" Anne toasted, clinking her coffee cup against his. "To Hayden!"

Chapter 7

Nathaniel was still holding the receiver in his hand long after the dial tone started buzzing.

Suddenly, the automated operator jolted him back to his senses, "If you wish to make a call please hang up and try again."

Gracie turned her attention from the cartoon and looked over at him. "Are you all right?" she asked innocently, her eyes full of childlike wonder.

"Yeah, yeah, Gracie, I am," he said, trying to hide the fear running through his veins. "But I need to go back to my room for a few minutes. I-I'm not feeling very well. I'll come back later, maybe for lunch."

Her smile switched to a look of confusion, but she nodded. "Just don't forget, okay?"

He forced a smile. "How could I forget a date with the most beautiful girl in the hospital?"

Her grin showed him she was totally unaware of the

evil lurking nearby. He pushed the nurses' button to summon Laverne to pick him up.

"Hey, you two. That was a short visit. Did Nathaniel behave himself, Gracie?"

A quiet giggle was her only answer as Laverne unlocked the brakes of the wheelchair and headed out of the room.

Nathaniel recognized the officer stationed at the door, recalling him as a quiet, but good cop. He motioned for him to lean down to the wheelchair. "Watch that little girl like your life depends upon it," he whispered. "In fact, it just might."

A dark look of unease briefly flashed across the policeman's face, but he nodded and replied. "I always work that way. Don't worry about her."

"I wish that were possible," Nathaniel answered as Laverne wheeled him toward the elevator.

Neither of them spoke until she was helping him up onto his bed.

"Okay, Nathaniel, what the hell's going on?" The expression on his face frightened her, and instead of pulling up a chair, she pushed his legs over and sat on the bed. *To hell with patient ethics,* she thought.

Nathaniel's hand trembled as he wiped his perspiring forehead. He closed his eyes tight, drawing in a deep breath before answering. "Laverne," he said, his voice quivering as he reached for her warm hand, "Gracie's father just called me in her room. The bastard threatened both of us." He felt that familiar knot crawling up his windpipe. "I'm not ashamed to say I'm scared as hell. Once the two of us are out of the way, there'll be no other witnesses to Zandi's murder or the attempted murder of Gracie and me."

Laverne found herself speechless, her body growing limp. "Jesus. Sweet Jesus. What should we do, Nathaniel?" Her panic subsided somewhat as she thought of the police officers standing alertly outside each of their doors. "The officers!" she said quickly. "They're right outside. He can't get past them. Surely, he wouldn't be so bold as to—"

Nathaniel looked at her, almost envying her naiveté, shaking his head and cutting her off. "What planet do you live on, Laverne? Seriously! Don't you watch television, the news, or America's Most Wanted?"

His comment went ignored as she wrung her hands in exasperation. "There's got to be something we can do. I can help you both escape, and you can take her somewhere where he'll never find you!"

"Laverne, you don't understand," he said curtly, his voice breaking into a husky cough. "Can you please get me a glass of water? My damn gut hurts so bad."

"I'll get you a pain pill. Don't move. I'll be right back."

He laid his head back on the pillow quickly saturating it with sticky perspiration. His mind was reeling. *How can I get her away from him? How the hell can we get out of this place without that monster seeing us and...*

His thoughts were interrupted by Laverne's fingers shoving a pill toward his mouth, followed by a Styrofoam cup of cool water. "What can we do, Nathaniel? I mean, if you think he'll come here, we have to get you both out, doctor's orders or not."

He massaged his belly firmly before trying to explain the situation to her. His face mirrored a grimace as he pushed the button to lift the adjustable bed into a sitting position. When Laverne handed him another cup of water, he sipped from it briefly before continuing. "Laverne, I know you might feel like we need to involve someone else, but you can't tell a soul about this," he said, his voice a low whisper. "Nobody can even know about the call. We have no idea who we can trust at this point."

"Then let's just get you both out of here. I can drive you to another state, or maybe I can—"

"Stop, Laverne," Nathaniel answered, holding up his

hand firmly to quiet her. "If we take that child, everyone and their brother will be looking for us, including the police and federal government. Good intentions don't mean a damn thing when it comes to kidnapping."

"Oh Jesus," she said, standing up and pacing from one end of his hospital bed to the next, her cheeks reddening and her eyes flooding with tears.

"Listen, I need your help, and we've got to hold it together now. Can I have more water?"

The worried nurse moved methodically to the sink and wet a washcloth for his face.

The cool towel brought more relief than Nathaniel had expected, and his thoughts began to form more clearly. "I have a friend in Wyoming," Nathaniel started. "He's a small-town sheriff, in a place that'd be perfect."

"Then what are you waiting for? Let's call him! I can get you there. My brother has a small Cessna he flies out of DeKalb County Airport. No one there will suspect a thing."

"There are still a few problems. This has to be legal, so we don't have the cops on our tail. The first thing I need to do is get a hold of my buddy."

"What's his name?"

"Sheriff Reid Langley in Hayden, Wyoming."

"I'll go get my cell phone out of my purse. I don't carry it with me on the floor."

"That's just it. If we call him from your cell or through anyone Consuelos can connect with me, he'll find us. I'm not going to underestimate the son-of-a-bitch this time."

"So what do we do? Can't we just call from the hospital?"

"That'd make me too nervous, Laverne. He called me on a hospital phone, so he knows the phone numbers to our rooms. I need one of those disposable cell phones, the kind you can buy at a convenience store. We can destroy it after we make the calls."

"I'll get one right away. I'll tell the others I feel sick so

I can leave early. They owe me a few favors, somebody'll cover my shift."

"Wait…" Nathaniel interrupted. Fighting off the pain and fatigue, he struggled to remain lucid. "If he knew I was in Gracie's room, he surely knows we're friends. We have to be very careful. I don't want to frighten you, but Laverne, your life could be in as much danger as mine. If you leave early, and the asshole does happen to be watching, he'll know something's up."

Her face flushed a bit, but other than that, his words didn't deter her. "Then there may not be much time, Nathaniel. We have to come up with a plan."

Nathaniel took several deep breaths. "You said you have a brother. Are you two close?"

"Yes, very. He's three years older than me, but I consider him my closest friend. I'm sure he'll help in any way he can."

"Good. That's what I needed to hear," Nathaniel answered, realizing sleep was close to winning over his mind. "I'm concerned about your safety now. At least Gracie and I are in the hospital, what little security that may be at this point. I think Consuelos was banking on us dying from the gunshots. The quicker we recover, the more uneasy he becomes. I don't think he'll try anything too soon, at least not for a couple of days."

"So…what's the plan?"

"Have your brother pick you up tonight when you get off. Make sure no one follows you. Pick up a cell phone and spend the night with your brother. What's his name?"

"Jeremy. That sounds like it might work."

"Actually, you should take off fifteen or twenty minutes early. Exit through a door you don't normally use and make sure he's there to pick you up immediately. I'm sure Consuelos is aware of our schedules and behaviors."

"You're exactly right. I'll bring the phone in with me tomorrow."

"No, that won't work. You should have someone else bring it in. I don't know what to tell you, but even a Pink Lady with it tucked in a plant would do. We need to leave you out of this as much as possible."

His eyelids began to blink abnormally fast. Laverne knew her patient needed his rest. She wet the cloth one more time and wiped it slowly and gently across his forehead, then the rest of his face, ending with his forearms and hands. By the time she had finished with the impromptu sponge bath, he was fast asleep. She realized there were other patients that she'd long since neglected. Time was of the essence now, and she had to carry on as if nothing were out of the ordinary.

Chapter 8

Reid took his time getting dressed. Joanna Sibley's funeral was still an hour away, and even though he'd offered to pick up Doctor Novus, he saw no need to be in a stuffy suit any longer than absolutely necessary. He'd finally come to terms with the fact the girl's death was nothing more than an undetected heart ailment, and was ashamed at how he'd overreacted. He was aware it was time to leave the brutality of Atlanta behind and enjoy the relative peace and quiet of a crime-free town. *Well, except for a few speeders and Saturday-night drunks.* He couldn't help but allow himself a chuckle.

The ring of the phone turned his attention back to the present, and he debated whether or not to answer it. The number on the caller ID didn't ring a bell. He looked down at the tie in his hand and decided to take the call. "Saved by the bell," he joked as he tossed the necktie back on the bed and picked up the receiver. "Langley," he said.

"Hey, Man. I'm so glad I caught you. I don't have a cell number for you, and—"

"Nathaniel? Nathaniel Collier, is that you?"

"The one and only," Nathaniel answered, still groggy from his second pain pill of the day.

"What's going on, Man? It's good to hear from you. A blast from my past."

"It's good to hear your voice, too, but I need a favor, Reid—a big one. I need…help."

Something in Nathaniel's voice was highly disturbing, a side of his friend Reid had never heard. Not only did it startle him, but it frightened him. "I'll do anything I can, you know that, Nathaniel. Tell me what's up."

By the time, Nathaniel had finished his sordid tale, Reid was awash with worry and concern.

"You may not have much time. It sounds like you're both getting better, and that's scaring the nasty son-of-a-bitch."

"We're better, or at least out of the woods, but we both still need medical care. I don't know where I'd be without the occasional pain pill and some of these nurses."

Reid immediately thought of Anne and how anxious she'd be to help. "I've got the medical end covered here. We just need to get you two to safety. I'm a little concerned about that nurse too. If she stays behind, he may try to get answers out of her. It could be dangerous."

Nathaniel had been worried about Laverne, but he hadn't thought of her needing to leave. *Damn. This gets more complicated by the minute.*

"Do you remember Nick Solomon from Zone 5? Good cop," Reid asked.

"Yeah. Maybe he can watch Gracie here at the hospital. I'd trust him."

"He's with the FEDS now, a US Marshal. Moved up pretty quickly too. I think I need to give him a call. He could legitimately get you guys out of there and into witness protection. I've got a small cabin where you can hole up temporarily, then we can find a rental for you guys until all of this plays out."

Nathaniel was feeling better. His pain lessening as the reality of Gracie's safety was becoming attainable. "Listen, I'm on a disposable cell phone and don't want to make too many calls, so—"

"Smart move…and say no more. I'll call Nick right now and see if he can give us a hand. Keep that phone with you as long as you can. I'll reach you back at this number. After that, destroy it."

Nathaniel held the cheap plastic cell phone with such might that it cracked. "Shit," he muttered frantically, sure he'd destroyed the one line that'd give him some hope. He tried a random number and was relieved to find the phone still worked. His mind immediately went to Laverne, and he hated that he'd involved her, but he didn't know any other way. He tucked the cracked phone under the sheet beside him and wiped his sweaty hand on the blanket. He knew if anyone were to come check on him now, they'd surely call for a doctor. He'd never perspired so much in his life.

The minutes seemed like hours before the phone rang.

"Man, please give me some good news," Nathaniel spoke quietly into the phone.

"I've got good and bad, my friend. What do you want first?"

"Just spill it, Reid."

"Well, the good news is that Nick can help us. The bad news is, it's going to take some time."

"Shit. That's the one thing we don't have."

"I know, and that concerns us too. But listen…I trust Nick. He's a good guy, so when he says he's on it, I know he'll take care of business. He's dropping everything to do what he can, but I don't expect to hear back from him until late this afternoon or even as late as in the morning."

"So what's the bottom line?"

"You'll be going into Federal protective custody. This wouldn't normally happen in a situation like this, but he's bypassing a few of the standard operating procedures. He's taking a lot of risks, Nathaniel, and he might end up with his ass in a sling for it."

"Where are they taking us?"

"He's going to try to get you to me. Like I said earlier, you can stay in my cabin until we can find you a better place. You'll need to stay in Wyoming until the trial, and God knows how long that could be. You know how the system works."

"Unfortunately, I know all too well. I'll hang tight until I hear back from you. Thanks, Reid. I mean it, Man."

"Yeah, I know you do. Listen, I've got a funeral to go to. I'll get back to you as soon as Nick calls."

Chapter 9

Even though it was the nicest one in town, Stephens Funeral Home gave Reid the creeps. Maybe it was just funeral homes in general, but there was something about the place, a gruesome, Alfred Hitchcock, *Twilight Zone* vibe he just couldn't shake. He'd never understand what drove anyone into a business like theirs. He had to tell himself that money was the simplest answer, after all dying guaranteed a constant flow of customers. At any rate, he was there, and he had to deal with it.

Anne was dressed in a simple black dress with an expensive scarf tied loosely around her neck. Even in her funeral attire, she looked beautiful. Reid watched as she carried herself like a runway model through the growing crowd. It was getting harder to deny his feelings for her.

She turned around to find him and grabbed his elbow to pull him up to her among the huge crowd.

The whole damn town is here, Reid thought to himself.

"Let's go into the chapel," he half-whispered into Anne's ear. "There's no need for me to view the body. We've already done that in the morgue."

"Reid Langley!" Anne hissed. "You should be ashamed of yourself. Everyone's watching you, and if you don't pay your respects to that girl and her family, they won't let you forget it."

"Damn it all," he muttered, allowing her to tug his arm as he noticed the spectators eyeing him. "They've heard about the autopsy attempt," he grunted to Anne. "That's what they'll never let me forget."

She ignored his last comment and made her way into the large room that housed Joanna's casket.

Reid diverted his eyes from the ivory coffin, instead, concentrated on the ostentatious room. Perhaps that was what gave him such an uneasy feeling about the place, it didn't fit in with the rest of Hayden. It was too flamboyant, boasting its shiny velvet wallpaper and dangling crystal chandeliers. *Death,* Reid thought, *just isn't the time to be garish.* He took notice of Joanna's profile as he got closer to the casket, and it saddened him to see her lying there.

Mrs. Sibley was sitting in a chair beside the coffin, her eyes glazed over from one too many sedatives. Mr. Sibley was clasping the hands of all the guests. Reid doubted their faces registered any familiarity with him.

Anne tugged firmly at his elbow again, and together they made their way to Joanna's father.

Reid shifted his gaze away from Joanna, but the sight of her youthful face paralyzed him. He could hear Anne speaking condolences, but his eyes failed to leave the fair-skinned young woman. The combination of such an early, untimely death along with the unsettling environment was haunting. He felt a strong pinch on his forearm and had to bite the inside of his mouth to keep from yelping.

"Sheriff Langley is here to express his sorrow, too, Mr. Sibley…for both you and your wife." Anne glared at Reid.

"Uh…yes, Sir. I'm so sorry about this, about your loss. If there's anything the department and I can do for you, please feel free to let us know."

The anger the father's face had mirrored a couple of days earlier now reflected grief. "Thank you, Sheriff. I'll keep it in mind." With that, he turned to thank the following person in line.

Reid quickly jumped on the opportunity to walk outside and smoke a cigarette. It was a habit he rarely caved in to, but today the nicotine was a welcomed comfort.

"My God, Reid," Anne hissed in his ear, "you're acting as though you've never been to a funeral before. What's your deal?"

"Who, in their right mind, would be comfortable at a funeral? It's just…hell, I don't know. It's unsettling."

"Well, get over it," she whispered angrily. "You have a position in this community, and people are counting on you. Quit acting like a child and let's find a seat. There won't be any empty ones if we wait much longer."

Chapter 10

Laverne walked into Nathaniel's room, concern apparent on her face. "I couldn't stand it any longer. What's going on?"

"My friend in Wyoming is working with a US Marshal, a mutual friend of ours. They're going to get us out of here, but I'm not sure how soon. For now, we have to act as normal as possible. I need to visit Gracie. When will you have time to wheel me down there?"

"Are you going to tell her about any of this?"

"No. She's too young to worry about it. Can you take me after lunch?"

"How about fifteen minutes? The floor is pretty quiet today."

"Sounds good. Do they have any stuffed animals in the gift shop?"

"I'll check."

"Grab some money out of my wallet. Better yet, use

my debit card and get as much cash as you can, I may need it."

"This is starting to feel like a James Bond movie," Laverne said, forcing a smile.

Nathaniel regretted he'd inadvertently dragged his former classmate and nurse into all the chaos and danger. She was such a good, happy person, and he didn't want to take that from her.

When she was gone, Nathaniel lay in bed, worrying about how the next few days would play out. He was so accustomed to running his own show, but now his life was entirely in the hands of others. As if that wasn't bad enough, he'd also have to take care of a child, the most foreign thing he could possibly imagine. *Poor Gracie. She doesn't even know me that well. How frightened is she going to be when she has to run away with a stranger? And to Hayden, Wyoming? Jesus. May as well be another planet. Maybe it'll be just what the doctor ordered after all,* Nathaniel thought, trying to think positively.

As promised, fifteen minutes later, Laverne showed up with a wheelchair and a stuffed bear the size of Texas.

"Good Lord, Laverne," Nathaniel said. "Where'd you find that thing?"

"In the gift shop." She laughed. "It's one of a kind. It's been in the window for months, but it was kinda pricey."

"How pricey is *kinda pricey*?"

"It's for a good cause."

"What if she gets attached to that thing? How are we going to make a break for it if the bear won't even fit in a Cessna?"

"You're overreacting." Laverne laughed. "It isn't *that* big. I was only able to get a hundred dollars cash back, but I'll put it in your wallet. Better carry it with you when you leave the room. You can't trust anybody these days."

"I'm in my pajamas. Would you mind holding it for me?"

"No problem," she said.

Nathaniel struggled but managed to get in the wheelchair. It was getting easier every day. He thought back to what Reid had said earlier, *"You're both getting better, and that's scaring the son-of-a-bitch."* He looked seriously at Laverne. "We don't have much time."

"Put on your happy, carefree face, Mr. Collier," the nurse said with a smile. "You're going to see a child. She'll be able to detect if something is wrong."

"I know," Nathaniel answered as he reached for the massive teddy bear and sat back for the ride.

He could hear Gracie's squeals of delight before he even saw her as he pushed the bear out of the way for a full view.

She was looking so much better every day. The color was gradually coming back to her cheeks, and she was able to sit up on her own. "Who's that for?" Gracie asked bashfully.

"Well, I sure didn't get him for Nurse Laverne," Nathaniel teased. "She told me he's been waiting for a home for a long time. What do you think? Would you like to take care of him?"

"Yes!" she exclaimed, her face brightening.

"Well, here ya go, kiddo," Nathaniel said, groaning and exaggerating the weight of the bear.

Gracie seemed pleased as she inspected everything about the stuffed animal. "He's so soft...and look at his big, red bow! I know pink's your favorite though."

"Yes, pink is my favorite on *you,* but I don't think it'd look too good on a boy bear."

That brought laughter from Gracie and Laverne.

"I have to leave you two silly people and your bear and get back to my job. I'll see you in thirty minutes."

"Yes, Ma'am," they both answered.

"Are you feeling better, Gracie?"

"Yes, much better!" She said, hugging the oversized

critter. "He needs a name."

"Hmm. What about Peewee?" Nathaniel said.

Gracie laughed. "He's too big for that. How about Nathaniel?"

"I like it," he said with a smile, "but it might get a little confusing. We won't ever be sure who you're talking to."

"I guess you're right," she answered.

"What about Teddy?" Nathaniel suggested.

"No way! I want him to have a special name. How about...Doctor Pennington?"

"Doctor Pennington it is," he answered. "I bet he'll be pleased to meet his namesake."

"I hope so. That way I can always remember him."

It amazed Nathaniel that Gracie was so full of kindness and love after everything she'd been through.

"How about some cartoons?"

"Okay. You're just in time for *Dora the Explorer*."

"I haven't met her yet, but I'm game. Let me help you move Doctor Pennington over so you can operate that remote." He gently moved the bear beside her in bed, careful to cover him lightly with the sheet. *Damn, Laverne,* he thought. *Now we'll have to cross the country with this monstrosity.*

"Mr. Nathaniel," Gracie asked quietly, "when do I have to go home?"

The question took Nathaniel by surprise, and he had to regroup before answering. "We have to get better first, Gracie, and then we'll talk about going home."

"But I *am* getting better, and I'm just...well, I'm scared to stay in my apartment by myself."

He reached over and wrapped his large hand around her tiny one. "Sweetheart, I promise you'll never have to go back there again. You don't have to worry about anything, okay?"

"Who's gonna take care of me? If I don't live in my apartment, I won't know the bus number to ride to school."

Again, she'd caught him off guard. He was flying by the seat of his pants, and he knew it. "I'll take care of you, Gracie. Would you like that?"

She sat up straighter in bed as tears filled her dark chocolate eyes. "Do you mean it, Mr. Nathaniel? Do you really mean it?"

"Gracie, I've never been a father before, and I can't promise I'll be a very good one, but I'd like to take care of you."

Her thin, tiny arms reached out for him, and she squeezed tightly around his neck. "I love you, Mr. Nathaniel. I love you a lot, and I'm sure you'll be a much better daddy than my real one."

"I love you, too, Gracie."

The hug was interrupted by the phone ringing.

Nathaniel's heart skipped a beat as he answered it. "Yeah?"

"How cruel of you to bring her that bear. She won't have much time to play with it. And as for you raising my kid, that'll happen over my dead body. She's only got one daddy, and that's me, motherfucker."

"Really? Well, we'll see about that. Have a nice day," Nathaniel answered kindly, with just an edge of disgust in his voice. The last thing he wanted was to frighten Gracie.

"Who was that?" she asked anxiously.

"Just somebody admiring your bear. They saw me going down the hallway with it."

"Really? Well, he's a great bear—a really special one."

"Yes, Gracie. Doctor Pennington is one great bear...and I'm glad he makes you happy."

Chapter 11

Consuelos's crew must've bugged the room, Nathaniel thought, his heart beating hard and fast inside of his chest. *How in the hell did they manage that?*

If Gracie sensed anything wrong, she didn't show it. Her eyes were on the latest cartoon, and it took everything in Nathaniel for him to pretend to concentrate on the little Hispanic girl with the talking backpack. He needed to get to his cell phone, but it terrified him to think of leaving Gracie in the room. *Where in the hell is Laverne?*

As if she'd telepathically read his thoughts, the nurse came to wheel him out, right on cue. As soon as their eyes met, she knew something was horribly wrong, and in spite of her excellent bedside manner, she wasn't nearly as good as Nathaniel about hiding her concern. "How was the visit?" she asked, feigning a happy voice.

"Just great." Gracie smiled. "My new bear's name is Doctor Pennington."

"My, my. The doctor will be extremely pleased to hear that. I'll have to tell him to come down and meet your new furry friend."

Gracie's answer was nothing more than a giggle.

"You ready to go back upstairs, Mr. Collier?"

"I guess I have to. Maybe I'll see you later today, Gracie—you and Doctor Pennington." He waved good-bye and put his finger over his lips to motion for Laverne not to ask any questions.

"Can we stop by the snack bar?" he said as she made her way to the elevator. "I haven't been out in awhile, and I feel like a soda. How about you? My treat."

She followed his directions, catching on that something was amiss. "I've never turned down a drink from a man, and I guess I shouldn't start now."

The remainder of the ride was made in silence, which was just what Nathaniel needed. He didn't want to be paranoid, but he wasn't sure how safe he was in the hospital. The officer assigned to guard him walked several paces behind them. He was grateful for that because he was unsure of who could be trusted. For all he knew, they'd bugged his room while he was out.

Laverne pushed him outside on a veranda while she went in to get the sodas. She was back quickly, sat across from him, and eyed him curiously. "Tell me. What is it now?"

Nathaniel turned to make sure the officer was a safe distance away. "They've bugged Gracie's room. They heard everything I said to her. My room must be safe because he didn't mention anything from my phone conversations, but for all I know, they bugged it while I was downstairs. This is getting crazy. Do you have the cell phone?"

She pulled it out of the pocket of her scrubs and handed it to him. "This is scary. You have to get out of here. If no one can help us right away, we'll have to get y'all out on our own."

He knew she was right, but he wanted to give Nick and Reid one more chance to pull it off.

Reid answered on the second ring and listened intently to Nathaniel's latest issue. "I hate to tell you this, Man, but that nurse has to come with you," he said. "Nick will have y'all out of there within twenty-four hours. I'll see to it myself. Destroy the cell phone immediately after you hang up with me. The next call will come directly to your hospital room, from a secure line. Don't talk to anybody, but tell the nurse to be ready. Nick said he'll need everyone's sizes—shoes, pants, shirts, coats, everything. You won't leave the hospital with anything but what you have on."

And a damn bear, Nathaniel thought. "Okay, Man, I'll let you go. We'll be ready."

"Destroy that phone right away, Nathaniel."

"Will do."

Laverne's face grew pale as she waited to be filled in.

"I don't know how to tell you this, Laverne," Nathaniel began, wondering how she'd handle the news. "But you're going to have to go with us."

"What? I can't just—"

"It's the only way. You've had too much to do with both of us. They'll demand answers from you…and believe me when I tell you, they won't hesitate to kill for them."

"But, Nathaniel, what about my apartment, my job, my brother, for Christ's sake?"

"The FEDS will take care of your apartment and your job. You can tell your brother you're leaving, but you shouldn't have any contact with him until the trial is over."

"Jeremy and I only have each other, Nathaniel. Our parents are gone now. It's just the two of us."

"Then he'd want you to be safe, Laverne. I'm sorry—truly sorry—that you're involved in this, but now it's up to me to protect you. It'll only be until the trial's over. Once he's locked up, which I know he will be, you can come back to your old life, apartment, job, brother, and all."

"I don't feel like my life will ever be the same again."

He could sense the tears she was fighting and feared they were on the verge of giving everything away. "Laverne, please. You have to pull yourself together. I'm not trying to make things worse, but our very lives could depend on it."

She looked away, wiping her eyes and fluffing her hair before she turned back to face him. She sighed deeply. "What do I need to do?"

"That's my girl," he said kindly. "The first thing is to destroy that phone…and when I say destroy, I mean *destroy*."

"No problem. Go on."

"I need your clothing and shoe sizes. We can't take anything with us."

"Oh dear Lord." She sighed again. "I'll get 'em to you after I take care of the phone."

"Go ahead and wheel me back now. I'll need my rest."

They made the trip back to his room in silence, both wondering what the future would hold.

Chapter 12

"What was that phone call about?" Anne asked. "You look concerned."

Reid sat back down in the booth and took another bite of his burger, chewing slowly. It was Saturday afternoon, and he'd asked Anne out for lunch. He needed to be around her—around anyone, actually, who could take his mind off the past few days. "It was nothing really, just an old friend from Georgia." He swallowed and took a sip of soda.

"Reid Langley, I haven't known you that long, but I've known you long enough to sense when something isn't right. You know you can talk to me about anything."

He studied her face for a moment. She was so beautiful. *And those eyes! Damn those eyes. They took him to another place, a place he didn't have time for at the moment.* "He's coming out for a visit in the next couple of days."

"That sounds like just what you need."

Yeah, if you only knew, Reid thought sarcastically.

"After all of this with Joanna's death, maybe a visit from a friend will get you back on track."

"What's that supposed to mean?" Reid asked defensively.

"I don't mean to offend you. It's just that…well, this whole situation has been trying on everyone. Now that she's been laid to rest, maybe we can move forward."

Reid looked down at the cheeseburger and fries remaining on his plate and suddenly wasn't hungry anymore. "It's a long story, Anne. I'm not sure how long his visit will be."

She reached over and patted his hand, lightly resting hers around his. "It sounds like you could use a friend. What do you say we pick up a nice bottle of wine and a couple of steaks for dinner? We can take them back to your place or mine and talk over a few glasses of wine while you build your appetite up again."

Reid knew he needed to busy himself with the preparation for his guests, but couldn't deny himself time with her. He had to trust someone, and couldn't think of anyone better than Doctor Anne Novus. "Better take everything back to my place," he answered. "I've got a lot to do. Maybe you can help."

Chapter 13

Nathaniel Collier was trying desperately to fall into some semblance of sleep, but slumber wouldn't come. Laverne had given him a prescription-strength sleeping pill, but it wasn't having any effect. His worst fear continued to surface. He couldn't push the image of Gracie lying in her hospital bed out of his mind. She just seemed so vulnerable and alone. *She's probably watching cartoons, twirling her braided hair through her tiny fingers, with no idea of what lies ahead.* Neither did he, and he hated being in that predicament. He hated it for himself, but most of all, he hated it for Gracie and Laverne. It'd abruptly gotten out of control, and there was nothing for him to do but wait and trust the system would work for them. *That's a fucking joke. How many times has the damn system worked for anybody?*

He sat up on the side of his bed and opened the dusty metal blinds. The view of the parking lot did little to lighten his mood. It was an overcast day, and he watched the parade of hospital staff and visitors as they entered with their umbrellas. The forecast had virtually guaranteed thunderstorms for most of the day. "Lovely," he said aloud.

"Are you referring to the view, Mr. Collier?" Doctor Pennington asked with a smile.

"Yeah. It's a good one, isn't it?" Nathaniel answered sarcastically, reaching out his hand to greet the doctor he'd become so fond of. "How are you, Doc?"

"Doing well, and it looks like you're getting better yourself. Still a little sore and tired?"

"Yes, but I'm doing okay." Recalling the possibility of a bug in his room, Nathaniel decided to be more cognizant of his answers. "Just not quite myself though. I get out a little to walk down the hall, and it damn near kills me. I feel like a ninety-year-old man."

"Your body went through a serious trauma, Nathaniel. It will take time for you to regain your strength. Healing will come. You must be patient."

"Yeah, they tell me that's a virtue," Nathaniel said with a laugh, "but I'm not a very virtuous man."

Doctor Pennington wore a look of concern. "We're going to do a few final tests this afternoon. I've been concerned about you. You should be bouncing back quicker than you are, but not to worry. You know how doctors are. The more tests we call for, the more money the hospital makes, right?" the doctor said. He laughed at his own comment, but Nathaniel detected a note of uncertainty.

"Is there something you aren't telling me, Doc?"

"No. I just think...well, the truth is, I don't want to send you packing until I've covered all the bases. Do you know what I pay annually for malpractice insurance? It'd curl your toenails. Laverne tells me you haven't been sleeping well, even with meds. Try to rest this morning, and we'll get those tests out of the way this afternoon." He reached his hand out to meet Nathaniel's again. "See you later today. Get some rest now."

Nathaniel closed the blinds and lay back on his bed. He struggled to remember just how long he'd been there. A knock at the door drew his attention.

"Hootie-hoo!" Laverne chirped in an artificial tone. "It's me, and I come bearing gifts."

"Gifts? Do tell."

She was holding something behind her back and made her way slowly to the bed. "Give you two guesses."

"Um, let's see…a beautiful blonde in a bikini?"

"Hell no." She laughed, genuinely this time. "Men are all the same. One more guess."

"A new robe? Maybe one that covers my whole ass?"

"Funny. Besides, the nursing staff kind of likes you in that hospital gown." She pulled her present from behind her back, and Nathaniel gasped with delight.

"Oh, my God! The Varsity. Please tell me you brought onion rings and hotdogs and French fries and—"

"Easy." She laughed. "You're still a patient in the hospital. The grease in this food alone could set you back a month."

"I'm willing to take my chances." Nathaniel stared down at the food, taking in the aroma of one of Atlanta's most famous restaurants. Known mostly for its homemade onion rings and other greasy treats, he'd miss it more than anything when he left for Wyoming.

"Somehow, I knew this would make you feel better. Works every time for those patients who overstay their welcome."

Nathaniel thought of a rebuttal but decided to sink his teeth into the chili and slaw dog instead. "Mmm…"

"Make sure you take this medicine," she answered as she made her way toward the door.

"Wait. Can't you stick around a little longer?"

"For some reason, you think you're the only patient I have. It's quite the contrary, Mr. Collier," she teased.

"Your receipt is in the bag, should you decide to reimburse me for your little treat."

He wasn't sure, but thought he detected a slight wink. "Okay, Nurse. I should've known. Everything comes with strings attached."

She left quickly, and he dug into the greasy bag and pulled out the small slip of paper containing all of her sizes. Suddenly, the onion rings didn't taste nearly as good as they had in the past.

Chapter 14

Doctor Pennington and his latest intern ran swiftly down the hospital corridor, slowing only to dodge wheelchairs and curious onlookers. Checking his pager repeatedly, he told his young charge the room number once more. They arrived at young Gracie Elizabeth's room just as the crash cart did, but the doctor pushed himself inside first. He had to look for her twice. Her body was so tiny compared to the vastness of the hospital bed. She looked like an angel lying there, her eyes closed as if she was in a restful sleep. One glance at the monitor and Pennington knew all too well what was going on. The damage to her young body had been too much, and she couldn't carry the burden anymore. "Get her to OR 9 STAT! I've got to open her up if we're going to have any chance at all of saving her."

"Doctor, don't you want to—" the intern began.

"No! CPR will disturb the scar tissue, and we can't afford internal bleeding."

The nurses did as they were told, subconsciously putting the reality of the child's fate out of their minds. They'd seen tragedy before, and knew there was no time for sorrow or reflection in the heat of the girl's battle for survival. Gracie's life depended on every precious second and their training.

Doctor Pennington and his intern slid Gracie swiftly from her bed onto the gurney without a moment's hesitation. It would've normally been up to the nursing staff, but the two men refused to waste a second. Once outside the room, they allowed the nurses to take over so they could dress in their sanitary scrubs and prepare for emergency surgery.

The stunned police officer, still in a state of confusion from the initial alarm, ran briskly after them.

The service elevator was packed with the two doctors, several nurses, the Atlanta PD officer, and the gurney carrying a motionless Gracie. The nurses lightly ran their fingers over her braided hair as she lay there unresponsive up to the ninth floor.

Doctor Pennington breathed rhythmically and kept his eyes virtually closed. Then, as if a revelation had hit him, he opened the doors in a panic. "The bear! For God's sake, one of you nurses go back and get that bear!"

"Wh-what? But why?" one asked, looking blankly at the others.

"For heaven's sake, Doctor Pennington," Nurse Andrews said, "what good will a stuffed bear do her now? The child's unconscious."

"Don't question me! Go get the damned bear right now!"

For a brief moment, the police officer looked as though he might reach for his weapon, then thought better of it, recalling that he was in a hospital, not out on the streets. He held the elevator doors open as Nurse Andrews stepped out, confusion still apparent on her face.

"Meet us in the OR and don't waste any time," Doctor Pennington blurted out frantically. "Hurry!"

The doors closed as she pushed the down arrow for the next set of elevators. *Maybe he's finally burning out,* she thought. The little girl had won all of their hearts, and she knew it could get to even the best of them.

Chapter 15

"Hey," Laverne said as she entered the room with a wheelchair. "Ready to take a ride?"

"Are we going to visit Gracie?" he asked, looking at his watch to see what time of day it was.

"No, Sir, not right now. Your chart calls for an MRI, among other tests. I'm taking you upstairs."

"Should I be concerned? Doctor Pennington seems to think I'm not progressing as well as I should be."

"He's just covering his ass." She smiled, fatigue straining her rounded face.

Nathaniel allowed his eyes to meet hers and held them there. Pointing silently to the phone, he raised both his shoulders, as if to question the fact they could miss a crucially important call.

Laverne's face mirrored the same question, but she pushed him outside anyway. "Doctor's orders come before anything. Without your health, you've got nothing."

"Words of wisdom spoken by a wise woman." Nathaniel managed to laugh.

He thought of his apartment for the first time since being admitted. Unlike Laverne, he wouldn't be leaving anything of meaning behind, least of all his bachelor pad. Nothing about his so-called home had ever been inviting, which was why he treated it more like a motel room and only used it for sleep. His mother had helped him furnish it with yard-sale finds and had gotten him off to a decent start, but he hadn't done anything with the place since her death. The old recliner and couch were now worn to an embarrassing frazzle. His only suit, used if he had to make court appearances, hung in the closet among faded Levi's, sweatshirts, T-shirts, and an occasional polo, all Christmas gifts from his mother. He knew it wouldn't take them long to clear out his belongings, and a fresh coat of paint would welcome the next tenant. He wiped a tear from the corner of his left eye. The only thing he desperately wanted to keep were the three photo albums he'd had since his youth along with the framed eight-by-ten of his mother, taken shortly before she became ill. They'd been ice skating in Centennial Olympic Park, and she'd looked so carefree and happy, her cheeks flushed a hot pink from the cold. Besides his job, she'd been all he'd ever had. Now, he felt like he was losing both of them.

The elevator door shut as he wiped the last of the tears away and sniffled.

"Nathaniel, are you all right?"

"Yeah," he answered. "Just got a little sentimental for a moment, that's all."

"There's no time for that now, Mr. Collier," a deep voice interrupted them.

Nathaniel spun around in his wheelchair to face a tall black man in a pair of tactical cargo pants and a plain gray sweatshirt. The Atlanta police bodyguard instinctively reached for his weapon.

"There's no time for that either, Man," the stranger said. "I'm US Marshal TJ Davis. Ease your hand from your weapon, and I'll show you my credentials."

Nathaniel nodded to the officer, and the Marshal pulled his badge from his waistband.

"There's no time for questions either, so please listen carefully," TJ blurted. "We're gonna get off on the top floor. Mr. Collier, once we're up there, you'll have to get out of the wheelchair and walk. Do so as quickly as possible. Officer, uh…King," he said after looking at the gold bar reflecting the officer's identity, "you'll be met by a Federal agent as soon as these doors open. You'll remain with him while we get these two to the roof. Understand?"

"Yes," was all the cop could muster.

When the *ding* sounded and the doors opened, everything happened quickly. A faint yelp escaped Laverne's mouth as she was thrust into the arms of two large men, who immediately pulled her to the exit door. Nathaniel stood up as quickly as he could, but he felt weak, almost faint. Two sets of arms grabbed his, encircling them around thick, solid necks. It was a whirlwind, a blur.

The metal door swung open, and they were met with the irrefutable sounds of a helicopter in waiting. The wind and earsplitting noise from the chopper blades shook them to the present. They held their heads down as they were rushed to open doors. It was several minutes after they'd taken off before the reality of what'd happened set in.

Chapter 16

The doors opened in a flurry to the ninth floor operating room.

As everyone reached to pull the small body over to the waiting table, the young intern spoke up. "Nobody move or say a word. Time is of the essence." Simultaneously, he pulled out a shiny pistol and equally polished badge, leaving little time for the Atlanta officer to react. "I'm US Marshal Nick Solomon. We're here to rescue this child from a dangerous situation that seems to be mounting."

"But...Doctor Pennington, little Gracie's going to die if you don't operate," one of the older nurses cried.

The doctor's face had taken on a pallid look as he held both of his hands tightly together in an attempt to ease their shaking. "The child has been heavily sedated. She'll be fine. We have to get her out of here. It's the only way to save her life." He looked down at the ground as he spoke, the weight of his years becoming more evident in his posture.

"But we…I don't understand how—" one of the nurses began to argue.

"There'll be time for understanding later," Solomon barked as two more agents stormed the room. "This little girl is a key witness, and her position here has been compromised. She's in grave danger as long as she stays at this hospital." He turned to the doctor. "Doctor Pennington, stay with your nurses and explain everything the best you can. These agents and I will take it from here."

"Where will you take her?" the older nurse asked.

"To the helipad. They're waiting for us now. She'll be okay as soon as she wakes up. Her life will be much better. Trust me."

They were gone in an instant, leaving everyone standing around with their mouths gaping open. The police officer included.

Doctor Pennington removed his glasses to wipe the tears that were flowing steadily from his saddened eyes. He opened his mouth to speak, to answer the many questions, when Nurse Andrews swung open the doors, the big bear covering most of her small frame.

"Thank you, Jesus," he whispered, grabbing the stuffed animal from her arms.

Everyone watched as the old doctor ran toward the exit leading to the roof. He waved off the agents as he pushed his way through the door and into the cold air.

Nick Solomon was inside the helicopter and pulling the door shut when he noticed Doctor Pennington. "Hold up, Man!" he yelled to the pilot.

Out of breath and sobbing openly, Doctor Pennington carefully placed the bear in the crowded chopper. "Please…" he begged, his breath short and wavering, "just let me kiss her good-bye."

Solomon nodded and moved his knees as far over as the cramped quarters would allow. He swallowed hard against the lump forming in his own throat as he watched the tearful doctor lightly kiss the sleeping child. *This kid must really be something,* the Marshal thought, and that gave his mission much more meaning.

Chapter 17

Laverne wrapped her hand around Nathaniel's and laid her head on his shoulder. The tears had started and wouldn't stop. He knew that talking to her would be fruitless. Not only was the helicopter too noisy, but nothing he could say would be enough to ease her fears. They were on their way to a safer place, to a new life, and there was no turning back. He leaned over and hugged her to him, hard and honest. It was only when Marshal TJ Davis shook his shoulder that he realized the blades and engine of the craft had silenced.

"How are you, Mr. Collier?" the Marshal asked sternly.

"Fine. I'm fine. Where have we landed?"

"As I'm sure you understand, we're on a need-to-know basis, and you don't need to know. A car will take you to a safe house until we can work out the details. Red tape. I'm sure you can relate."

"Damn right I can. What about Gracie? Where is she?"

"On another bird. They'll land at a different location, but we'll all end up at the same place, hopefully, around the same time."

Nathaniel looked at the black man's face for the first time. His chiseled features could've easily made him a model, but his eyes were hard and determined. Nathaniel understood firsthand what might've made him look that way, and was sure it hadn't happened overnight. He was certain it was the effect of witnessing the justice system failing people who needed it most. Nathaniel trusted him. "Listen, Marshal...we appreciate what you've done for us. It means a lot, Man."

"I'm just doin' my job, Mr. Collier, nothing more."

"Somehow, I find that hard to believe," Nathaniel answered, reaching his hand over to shake TJ's.

The door of the chopper flew open, and they were back in the hustle, similar to what they'd gone through in their emergency exit from Atlanta Medical Center.

"Where'd all these people come from?" Laverne whispered in Nathaniel's ear. "It's unbelievable. I feel like we're being stalked by the paparazzi."

"No, this isn't the press, Laverne. This is the result of proper planning," he retorted. "They know what the hell they're doing and exactly what they're dealing with."

That was the only opportunity they had to converse before they were swept into a large black Suburban with tinted windows. The agents spoke back and forth in coded conversation for the next twenty-five minutes as the SUV rolled along.

Suddenly, the paved road turned abruptly to dirt, a street that'd obviously been ignored by the city transportation department. They all bumped shoulders as they hit rut after rut.

Laverne's tears had thankfully stopped, but her body was limp as she leaned heavily on Nathaniel.

He smiled down at her, but his attempt to look reassuring failed and resembled pity more than anything else. "We'll be all right," he whispered softly in her ear. "You'll see. I promise."

She nodded slightly.

"Okay, you two," Marshal Davis interrupted in his deep, commanding voice. "You'll stay in this same house for the next couple of days. There'll be more paperwork than you've ever imagined, but in the end, you'll be safe. That's our number-one priority." He motioned his large hand toward a rustic cabin nestled back in a burst of maples and dogwoods. "Can you make it inside, Mr. Collier, or do you need assistance?"

Nathaniel had forgotten about his injuries, and chuckled as he recalled the scars winding like ribbons around his gut. "I'll be fine," he answered. "All this excitement made me forget about being a patient."

"Hmm," was the only answer he received from Davis.

Laverne got out of the Suburban and stretched, deeply inhaling the fresh scent of the outdoors. Nathaniel hobbled out of the vehicle behind her, thrilled with the prospect of a view more splendid than a parking lot.

"Let's step inside please," Davis said, placing his hand on the small of Nathaniel's back.

The rustic look of the cabin was a façade and quite contradictory to what met them inside. It was small but furnished with all the modern amenities of an expensive condo. There was a well-equipped kitchen, and a large conference table, complete with four laptops. A couch and two chairs faced a stone fireplace where a fire was already blazing. Two other agents, one male and one female, and a stuffy-looking, overweight gentleman in a suit waited for them at the table.

"So this is where you hang out, huh? And to think, I always figured you'd be lounging around the local Krispy Kreme!" Nathaniel laughed, proud of himself for finding humor in the whole situation. His attempt at a joke was met with blank stares, making him feel deflated and tired.

"Please," the suit said in a tight-assed, no-nonsense voice, "take a seat. We have a great deal to discuss."

Nathaniel and Laverne did as they were told.

"Can we get you anything? Some coffee or soda perhaps?"

"I'll have a cola," Nathaniel said.

Laverne shook her head nervously.

It was only a second before the female marshal placed a cold soda in front of him.

"Thanks," Nathaniel offered.

"Let's get to the meat of this. I'm State Attorney General Lancaster, Pete Lancaster. Right from the get-go, I want to be honest with you. I go strictly by the book, following standard operating procedures, and this case is as far from protocol as I've seen. I don't like it. However, when politics are involved, it isn't up to my discretion." He remained silent for a moment, looking at both of them as if to ensure his words had sank in. "It's my understanding there's some type of problem that requires the Marshal's protection. This is normally done at the Federal level, but because this is a State issue and not one for the FEDS, it's landed in my lap." He paused again, obviously for affect, before continuing, "In spite of my personal opinion of how things are being handled and resources allotted, I'm all for the protection of a child. From the briefs I've read, this kid hasn't had much of a life up to this point." He pulled a cloth handkerchief from his suit pocket and rubbed it forcefully across his perspiring forehead. "Hey, would one of you be kind enough to bring me a diet soda? Damn, they keep it hot as hell in this place. Anyway, moving right along. The information that crossed my desk made me feel confident we can leave the Atlanta PD out of this. I have a great deal of respect for them, of course, but as in any organization, there are a few bad apples. As I see it, they should be kept on a need-to-know basis. We'll provide them with a contact within our agency and ensure that you'll be at the trial, which is all they really give a damn about." He took several large gulps from the diet soda he'd been handed, then went on to ask, "Am I to understand, Mr. Collier, that you have a friend in Wyoming who's willing to house you temporarily?"

"Yes, Sir. He was with Atlanta PD but now serves as Sheriff in the small town of Hayden."

"Hmm. There's nothing but small towns out there as far as I know, tell me more."

"He's aware of what's going on, and it seems like the ideal situation. He can put us up in a little off-the-wall place, where no one will expect us to be."

Attorney General Lancaster rubbed his temples and requested four aspirin and another diet soda. "Mr. Collier and Ms. Lewis, sometimes people tend to think this witness protection process is much easier than it is. It's nothing like the damn movies. To be honest, it can be complicated and a bit frightening, but when handled properly, it proves successful. As a matter-of-fact, no one who has followed our rules has ever been harmed while in the Witness Protection Program. That's a damn fine record."

"Yes it is, Sir," Nathaniel answered respectfully.

"Lemme tell you how this whole thing works," he continued, "taking for granted now that your case is somewhat isolated. One of the first things we consider is former criminal records, which are nonexistent for both of you. That's good, real good, and it makes my job easier. We also take into account how valuable your testimony will be. In this case, it's crucial. Mr. Collier, what you and that kid witnessed will take that scumbag off the street for the remainder of his natural life. Laverne, you just got shoved into the mix, but for your own protection, you had to leave as well. Tough break, I know, but not as bad as being found, interrogated, and murdered. That may sound harsh, but I've seen it happen, and I don't ever wanna see it happen again. I'm not a fan of innocent people being killed in the damn cross fire, but it happens far too often. Get my drift?"

She nodded and attempted a smile.

Lancaster was out of breath again and stopped to take a break. "Hell, take over for me a minute, Davis. You know the drill as well as I do."

Marshal Davis sat up straighter in his chair, leaning forward as he spoke. "You'll have to sign this Memorandum of Understanding, which basically verifies that you understand the rules of the program and agree to abide by them." He slid a form across the table to the each of them. "You'll have time tonight to read all the small print, but the basic premise of this program is to protect witnesses whose lives are in danger, as in your case. The other criteria is that the witnesses' testimony is crucial to a successful prosecution of the defendant. Mr. Collier, we believe your testimony and Gracie's is definitely critical for a conviction. The tough part is you'll be uprooted from life as you knew it." He turned to Laverne, wearing a look of unfeigned sympathy on his face. "I know this will be hardest on you, Ms. Lewis. I understand, you're leaving behind a brother and a job you love." He reached for her hand but thought better of it. "I never—let me reiterate, *never*—tell people in this program that they'll have the opportunity to return to their old lives. However, in this case, in time, it may be a true possibility. This Consuelos creep is small-time, and once he's put away, I don't think anyone will give a damn about retribution for his life. Anyway, I digress." His face returned to its professional demeanor, and he continued, "As you'll read later in the information I provided, you'll be giving up life as you knew it. You must agree to sever all contact with family members and friends and not return to Atlanta. As Attorney General Lancaster told you, no one has ever been harmed, as long as they've followed these guidelines. We normally provide housing, medical care, job training and initial employment, and a small sum to cover living expenses. I understand that you'll be staying temporarily with a friend of Mr. Collier's, but I'm sure you'll want to find something of your own. You'll receive some funding to help, but don't expect any luxurious accommodations. For some reason, probably those movies Attorney General Lancaster referred to, people tend to think the program will set you up for life, but that's not its intent. We're simply here to assist in making the transition feasible. Ms. Lewis, I don't see why you can't continue to seek employment in your chosen field. Although your names will be changed, you can still keep your nursing certificates. We'll work that out for you."

"I think I'm ready to take over again. Thanks, Davis." Lancaster leaned back in his chair and stretched. His tie was loosened, the top button of his shirt unbuttoned. "You'll need new names and identities. Normally, we allow people to keep their first name and use a surname of our choice. This is a strange situation with the kid especially with her being, uh…of another race. That makes it a little more difficult, especially in Wyoming of all places! Jesus. At any rate, this is what we've come up with. Since you're so fond of the girl, Mr. Collier, for all intents and purposes, you'll be her father. As the story goes, her mother is deceased, and you decided to leave the bad memories behind and move to Wyoming. Obviously, she was a black woman, not Hispanic. Get my drift?"

Nathaniel nodded and smirked. "Yeah."

"Damn. Why do you gotta be a blond anyway? Laverne here, is your sister. She's never married, so she offered to move out here to help you and start a new life herself. Sound okay so far? Believable? Something you can pull off?"

They both nodded in agreement.

"Jesus Christ. Can you believe we're moving a biracial kid from the projects out East to Bumblefuck, Wyoming? I just don't like it, Davis. It makes me feel…hell, just uncomfortable."

"She'll be fine, Sir," Davis answered. "They'll both be housebound anyway until they're completely healed."

"About the girl's mother—" Nathaniel began, only to be cut off.

"Oh yeah, your dark and lovely wife bought it in a car wreck. I forgot about that. The two of you were injured as well. That covers my ass on that part," Lancaster intervened. He wiped his face again with the sodden handkerchief and stood up. "Y'all can take it from here. Just have the paperwork on my desk ASAP. How can anyone think in this sauna? My God. It's hot as hell in here." With that, he grabbed his bulging briefcase and left.

Relief was apparent on the faces of everyone in the room when he was gone.

"Let's take a break," Davis suggested. "How about some food? I'm starving."

"Sounds good to me," Nathaniel answered. "Mind if I move over to the couch? I think I'll be more comfortable."

"Please do. I should've thought of that before. How does pizza sound?"

"Pizza? Hmm…" Nathaniel pondered it for a moment. He hadn't had pizza since before he'd been admitted to the hospital. "It sounds like heaven."

"Good. Agent Harper will pick up a few pies for us." He motioned over to the young man they had noticed when they'd come in.

"Thanks, Man," Nathaniel said. "You don't know what it's like to live on hospital food as long as I have."

The agent grinned as he headed toward the door. "Any special requests or just a variety?"

"Surprise us, Harper." Davis laughed. "Somehow, I don't think anyone will be disappointed."

"Laverne, my name's Agent Julie Harmon. Why don't you come back to your bedroom with me so we can discuss some of the important stuff—like shopping?"

"Oh geez." TJ laughed. "We'll see you two ladies in a few hours."

"That almost sounded chauvinistic, Marshal Davis," Agent Harmon said with a chuckle.

"No offense intended," he teased.

"Laverne, please call me by my first name, Julie. I have your sizes. I just need an idea of what type of clothes you like. You're heading to a much colder climate, so you'll have to do a great deal of shopping when you get there. We just don't want you to show up with the clothes on your back."

"Sounds good to me," Laverne answered.

"And Mr. Collier—Nathaniel, if you don't mind—I'll speak with you next," Agent Harmon said over her shoulder.

"Nathaniel is fine…and I look forward to it."

For the first time in quite a while, Nathaniel began to relax. Of course, he wouldn't be fully relaxed until he had Gracie, his new daughter, in his arms.

Chapter 18

Gracie lifted her small head, squinted, and tried to figure out where she was. She knew it wasn't her hospital room, and for an instant, she was frightened. Trying to get out of bed, she pulled the white sheets back and hopped down. Gracie shivered when her bare feet touched the cold linoleum.

"I see you're up and out of bed, young lady," a kind voice said.

Gracie was afraid to look up.

"I'm Nurse Stanfield, but you can call me Polly."

Gracie lifted her eyes and looked at the small, older woman. *She looks nice enough, but why am I here?* Gracie wondered. *Where's Miss Laverne? Where are Nathaniel and Doctor Pennington?*

"Don't be afraid, Sweetheart," Polly said as she sat on the small bed.

Gracie gave her a skeptical look, forcing Nurse

Stanfield to smile. "Where am I, Miss Polly?" she asked quietly.

"You're at a clinic in the Atlanta FBI Building. Do you know what the FBI is?"

"Yes, Ma'am. They're like the big-time police. My Daddy doesn't like 'em. Why am I not at the hospital? Mr. Nathaniel and Doctor Pennington are gonna be worried about me."

"Don't worry, dear. They know where you are. In fact, as soon as we have a good look at you and make sure you're doing okay, we'll take you to Nathaniel and Nurse Laverne. How does that sound?"

"Back to the hospital?"

"No, not the hospital. We're taking you to a place where you'll be safe."

"So I'm gonna get to live with Nathaniel?" she asked excitedly.

"It looks that way, at least for awhile. You'll be taking a trip, too. No one will be able to find you or hurt you again."

Gracie's whole face lit up.

"I have to check your blood pressure and draw some blood. Did they do that at the hospital?"

"Yes."

"Good, then I know you'll be a big girl and won't cry."

Gracie nodded her head. "Nope. I stopped crying about it a long time ago. Nurse Laverne says I'm her bravest patient in the whole children's ward."

"That's great. Then I'll just draw your blood, and you'll be on your way. You're going to fly in a helicopter. That's really cool."

"Today? Am I going today?"

"In just a few minutes actually. Let me take care of what I need to while you brush your teeth and wash your face. See that bag over there?"

"Yes. It has *Dora the Explorer* on it. She's my

favorite, next to SpongeBob."

"So I heard. Anyway, if you look inside, you'll find some new pajamas, a toothbrush and toothpaste, and probably some new slippers."

"Really? Can you do my hair before we go? Pink ribbons are Nathaniel's favorite. He'll like my new bag too. We like to watch cartoons together."

"That sounds nice. I'll be back in a few minutes with some lunch. I bet you're hungry."

"Yes, Ma'am, but I wanna hurry and get on the helicopter. I know Mr. Nathaniel will be real happy to see me."

"Yes, Gracie, and I'm sure you'll be happy to see him too," Polly said with a smile.

Chapter 19

Anne and Reid got into the Jeep and rubbed their hands together briskly as they waited for the heat to kick on.

"Let's go by Stanley's and pick up some steaks. It's hard to think of supper when we just had lunch, but I probably need a few more things for my fridge anyway. A bachelor's existence is pretty pitiful."

"Oh please." Anne laughed. "You wouldn't have it any other way."

"Maybe you're right. Maybe you're not."

They sat in silence as they made the two-mile drive to Stanley Phillips's family-owned grocery, the place that'd most fascinated Reid when he'd first arrived in Hayden. Atlanta was full of chain grocery stores and mega-marts, but he liked the feeling of the mom-and-pop place. Besides, Stanley's carried the best meat in town, along with a fine selection of wine and beer. He'd learned a long time ago to leave the liquor alone. The produce at Stanley's was always fresh, and everyone who worked there seemed authentically glad to see him. He smiled as he opened Anne's door and followed her into the store.

"Afternoon, Sheriff," Stanley said. "Good to see ya. And you're the doctor from the hospital, right?" he asked, reaching his meaty hand out to both of them.

"Yes, Sir," Anne answered. "I'm Anne Novus. It's very nice to finally meet you. I do a lot of my shopping here, and I've never been sorry."

"Glad to hear it. Yes, Ma'am, real glad to hear it. Anything I can help you find today?"

"Thanks, Stanley, but I believe we can handle it. I just need a few odds and ends, a good bottle of wine, and two of your thickest steaks," Reid answered.

"Well, let me get those steaks for you while you do the rest of your shoppin'. I've got some good Angus in the back. You want T-bones or rib eyes?"

"There's just something about a T-bone. Give us two of them."

"Gotcha. I'll have 'em up front for you when you're ready."

"Thanks a lot, Stanley," Reid answered as he grabbed a cart. They made their way slowly through the store before Reid said, "I better pick up a few snacks for my friends comin' in and—"

"Wait…friends? As in more than one? How many are coming, Reid?"

"Well, at last count, there were three. Let's talk about it when we get to my house," he said, rubbing his temples as a headache instantly assaulted him.

"Let's start with some fruit," Anne suggested, "and I'll grab a few things for a salad and a couple of big potatoes for baking."

"I'll grab some beer. Pick out a nice bottle of wine for yourself and a couple more for me to have on hand. Let's see…chips, dip, pretzels—"

"Oh Lord," Anne whispered under her breath.

The cart was almost full by the time they made it to the front of the store. Reid found himself suddenly feeling enthusiastic about Nathaniel's arrival as he looked down at all the junk food. There were more groceries than he'd ever bought at once in his adult life. *It sure will be nice to have an old friend around,* he thought.

On the way out, he waved good-bye to Stanley and his wife. "They're a good fit, the two of them," Reid said. He envied their happy, comfortable life, and deep down, that was what had lured him to Wyoming. He would never have found such a life in Atlanta.

Anne hadn't been to his small cabin, and Reid wasn't sure whether or not he should be embarrassed. He let his mind wander back to that morning, and hoped he'd picked his dirty clothes and wet towel off the floor. His place was tiny, but suited him well. He'd fallen in love with it the second the realtor had shown it to him. He had signed a contract on the spot and hadn't once regretted it. It had a large front and back porch, both of which he utilized frequently to take advantage of the splendid view. The trees were lavish and not so far in the distance. He could even see the Grand Tetons. *Damn*, he often thought, *no one could ever get used to this kind of beauty.*

The front door opened to a roomy den with thick, pine-paneled walls and a stone fireplace. He was furnishing the place little by little, so for the time being, there was only a recliner, a sofa, and a coffee table. The kitchen was open, off to the left. He rarely used it for more than his microwave meals, but it was sufficient for cooking for a fairly good-sized group. His antique oak table, his latest furniture purchase, reminded him of his mother's, and he was proud of it.

There were two full baths, both of equally ample size, and two bedrooms. It wasn't a large home by any stretch of the imagination, but its charm had won Reid over, and he hoped it would do the same for Anne.

As they wound their way up the drive, the small cabin came into view.

"Well...here she is, home sweet home," he announced.

"I love it, Reid. It looks so...comfortable."

"Thanks. I appreciate that."

They both grabbed armfuls of bags, then Reid unlocked the front door. "Just put everything on the kitchen table, and I'll get the rest," he said.

Wow. This place has such a warm, cozy feel, Anne thought as she pulled the groceries from the bags and started putting items in the refrigerator. *Who would've thought he'd live in a place like this?*

"I think that's it," Reid said when he returned with the remainder of the groceries. "I'll put the snacks in the pantry and grab a beer. Can I get you anything?"

"I think I'd like some Merlot. Thanks."

Once everything was put away, they wandered into the den. Anne sat on the sofa, pleasantly surprised by its comfort.

"Let me get you a quilt. It's getting cold out there, and they're predicting more snow. I might as well throw a few logs on the fire."

Anne watched, sipping her wine as he prepared the fire. "Okay, Reid, curiosity is killing the cat here. Tell me what's going on."

"Well, it's quite a tale," he answered, his forehead wrinkling as he pondered it all. He unscrewed the top of his beer and took a deep swallow before continuing. "One of my friends from Atlanta, Nathaniel Collier, has gotten himself into a pickle, to put it mildly. He's a bounty hunter, and one of his bounties went awry." He took another swig of his beer and stood up to get another one before he'd depleted the one he was already holding.

"This is really getting to you, isn't it?"

"Yeah," he answered as he sat back down in the recliner.

Two beers and a half a bottle of Merlot later, the whole story had been laid out to Anne. "How sad," she whispered. "That poor child."

"Well, seems Nathaniel's fallen head over heels for her, which is very unusual for him. People in his line of work tend to stay to themselves and keep relationships at arm's length. He's one of the best at what he does, but it's a tough existence, to say the least. It isn't like a bounty hunter to take a liking to kids."

"Tell me about Laverne. How's she going to handle this?"

"It'll probably be the hardest for her. She was a nurse at one of Atlanta's largest hospitals, very dedicated and well-liked, from what I understand. Both of her parents are deceased, and her only living relative is a brother. Apparently, they're really close. She just got caught in the cross fire, so to speak, and now she's on her way to Wyoming."

"Poor thing. Maybe I can help her get a job at the hospital."

"I was hoping you'd say that. Nathaniel says she's a damn good nurse, but on top of leaving her whole life behind, Wyoming and Atlanta are like night and day. The cold climate's just the beginning. Some people can adapt all right, but others can't. Also, Hayden isn't exactly the entertainment capital of the world."

"Do I detect a hint of regret on your part?"

"Hell no! I love it here. I got my fill of the fast life and big city. Not to sound like some kind of Bible-toting fanatic, but I truly believe God led me here. He knew I wasn't going to last much longer the way I was living. Hayden is a blessing to me."

"Well, folks either love it or hate it. Let's hope for the best with your friend. What's the plan? Are they going to live with you?"

"Temporarily. We need to find them a reasonable cabin to rent though. I don't know how long they'll need it. The trial could be in a couple of months or a year from now. But, however long they have to stay, I want them to feel at home, to feel wanted."

Anne turned to him with a look of excitement on her face. "In that case, we have some shopping to do. We could spruce the place up a bit and maybe buy some board games and children's books. Do you need more blankets? What about towels and sheets? Pots and pans?"

"Whoa! Like I said, they'll soon be renting their own place. Our first order of business should be helping them find one."

"Oh phooey, Reid. This will be fun, like an instant family. I love the idea."

Reid smiled broadly and thought about it for a minute. "You know, you're right. It will be fun. There's just one thing to figure out."

"What?"

"What should be our first stop on this little shopping spree?"

Chapter 20

Nathaniel sank his teeth into the steaming-hot pizza and sighed heavily as if he was taking a bite out of heaven itself. "Mmm. I don't remember pizza ever tasting this good." He smiled as he chewed slowly, savoring every bite.

"Was the hospital food *that* bad?" Marshal Davis asked.

"You're damn right it was. You don't happen to have any beer in that fridge, do you?"

Davis allowed a wide smile to form on his face and shook his head. "I don't go anywhere where I can't find a cold one." He made his way to the refrigerator and grabbed a Heineken, then took his time opening it. He held it up, offering one to Laverne.

"Why not? Maybe it'll ease my mind."

Nathaniel enjoyed the beer with the same fervor with which he'd devoured the pizza. "Have one with us, Davis," he said.

"Can't say I wouldn't love to join you, but I'm on duty. Looks like I'm your other half until you are safely delivered out West."

"Pisser, huh?"

"Duty calls. The sacrifices we Marshals make."

"You got that one right," Agent Harmon interrupted as she entered the room.

Julie was a perky young woman whom Nathaniel figured to be in her early twenties. She must've landed the job right out of college. Her sandy-blonde hair was pulled back loosely in a ponytail that swished back and forth when she walked. She was wearing only a light dusting of makeup that she really didn't need. Her features were naturally well pronounced, a sharp chin, pouty lips, and tiny, rounded nose. Had she not been so young, Nathaniel would've found her attractive.

"I ordered all your clothes, Laverne. They should arrive tomorrow, and you should be ready to leave these unpleasant memories behind you."

Laverne sipped slowly from her beer, obviously lost in memories of the past few years.

Nathaniel leaned over and kissed her softly on the cheek. "We'll be okay, *Sis*. I promise. At least you'll have me."

"Is that supposed to be comforting?" she asked.

It was the first genuine smile he'd seen from her in several days. "Hell yeah. Now let's drink a few more beers and get a good night's sleep. You'll like Reid, and I think we'll all like Wyoming. If not…well, it's not exactly a life sentence, like the one that bastard Consuelos is gonna get for putting us all through this."

"Before you hit the sack or drink yourselves silly, please review that paperwork," Davis reminded them. "We'll need signatures first thing in the morning. Lancaster's already pissed off about the inconvenience of this whole operation, to say nothing of it being so unorthodox."

"Pull me another beer," Nathaniel answered, "and pass over that mountain of red tape. No time like the present."

* * * *

The sun shone brightly through the stark-white mini-blinds, and Nathaniel squinted as he looked over at his watch. Eight o'clock. He could still taste the beer in his mouth from the night before, but it no longer brought him pleasure. He slid into a pair of jeans, careful to leave the top button open because his belly was still sore. He brushed his teeth and had just finished washing his face when he heard the front door opening. The faint sound of small footsteps skipping across the floor only meant one thing to him. *Gracie!*

"Where's Nathaniel?" she asked excitedly. "I really wanna see him bad. I bet he's worried about me, but I'm okay. Nurse Polly told me so. She even made me spend an extra night with her just to make sure."

"My, aren't you a little chatterbox?" TJ answered. "You must be that young lady Nathaniel wants to see so badly."

"You're damn right she is," Nathaniel answered as he walked across the floor to take her into his arms.

"You get to be my Daddy. Did they tell you? I'm so happy! And they said we're moving to a safe place, one where the bad people will never find us. And Laverne's coming too. Do you like my braids? Nurse Polly found some pink ribbons just for you, and—"

"My goodness. You haven't even taken a breath." Nathaniel smiled so broadly that he felt the soreness in his cheeks. *This must be what happy feels like.* "Just come over here and sit down with me. We can talk about all of that later. Are you hungry?"

The broad grin confirmed she was willing to take the

time to eat, and that was a good thing. They'd both need their strength.

TJ offered to make his famous blueberry pancakes.

It was hard for him not to allow his eyes to wander over at Nathaniel and Gracie. In his line of work, happiness, joy, and trust were far too rare, and he enjoyed the opportunity to witness those emotions.

Chapter 21

With everything packed into the dark Suburban, including the stuffed Doctor Pennington, the group was ready for the trek to the airport. They would be flying a small charter off a short strip of runway north of Atlanta.

Even Laverne had to admit there was more excitement in the air than apprehension. *What the hell?* she thought. *Life's meant to be one big adventure after the next, right?*

Marshal Davis was behind the wheel, with Nathaniel in the passenger seat. Marshal Julie Harmon was in the back seat with Laverne and Gracie. The Suburban was flanked by two unofficial-looking vehicles, which helped to ease the lump of uneasiness in Nathaniel's throat. He was sure Consuelos knew by now that he'd been duped. And *pissed* wouldn't have begun to cover how the vengeful, crazed man felt. *At least the punk isn't as slick as the US Marshals,* Nathaniel tried to assure himself.

The bumpy dirt road soon gave way to smooth

highway, and they all listened as Gracie chatted away. She'd never been on an airplane she told them, and she hoped that she'd get a soda. TJ assured her that she would, and Nathaniel saw him smiling out of the corner of his eye.

"Got any kids, Davis?" Nathaniel asked.

"Nope. Don't have time. I think that calls for a woman first anyway, and it's hard to find one willing to put up with my kind of work."

"I know what you mean. If this hadn't happened, I wouldn't have this ready-made family."

"Well, I believe the Man upstairs always has a plan." Davis's smile was accompanied with a flash of regret and sadness.

"Yeah, I'd agree with that. If you don't devote your whole life to the ungrateful FEDS, maybe He'll have a plan for you."

Davis flashed a grin of straight, sparkling white teeth.

Nathaniel could see a lot of good in the man, and took unspoken pity on him. *It's a shame he's headed down the same path I was,* he thought.

"Okay, Miss Gracie," Julie started, "we have a few things to talk about. As you know, your life will be a little different now, sort of imaginary, like a big game of pretend. It's important you play along at all times. That way, we can make sure nothing happens to you, okay?"

"I understand," she answered, sitting up a little straighter in her seat, an obvious attempt to appear more mature.

"From now on, Nathaniel will be your father. Do you think you can remember to call him Dad or Daddy instead of Nathaniel?"

"Sure!" she squealed. "That'll be real easy, 'cause I've wanted him for a Daddy for a while now."

"Ms. Laverne is going to be your aunt, Nathaniel's sister. Do you understand? You'll need to call her Laverne or Aunt Laverne or Auntie, but not Miss Laverne or Nurse

Laverne. Does that make sense?"

"Yes, Ma'am," she answered, excitement growing in her voice.

"The story is that you and your daddy and mommy had a car accident. Your mom didn't survive, so you and your Daddy, Nathaniel, are moving out here to get away."

"You mean so we won't be as sad about her dying?"

Julie nodded. She'd been handling the situation well so far, but she could feel herself beginning to falter.

"My real daddy shot her, you know? He shot Nathaniel...er, Dad and me too. We almost died."

Julie nodded again, relying on the two years of counseling and psychology classes she'd taken at the university while completing her criminal justice degree. "The good thing is all of that is over, and you don't need to talk about it in your new home. I have a feeling you're going to like Wyoming. You'll see mountains, buffalo, moose, and, most of all, lots and lots of snow."

"Really? Is that true, Dad?"

Nathaniel laughed thinking of the vast difference in climates from the south. "Yes, Miss Gracie, we'll see lots of snow."

"Will we stay warm? Will they cut the heat off very often?"

Nathaniel and TJ looked at each other, saddened by the harsh life the child had lived.

"That's for the grown-ups to worry about," Nathaniel said, "but ya know what? I bet we even get a fireplace. I'll keep logs in it all the time so you'll never get cold."

"A fireplace?" she half-whispered, her eyes widening. It almost sounded mystical to her.

"Yep. And you'll have plenty of mittens and scarves and galoshes—"

"Okay," Julie interrupted, "let's get back to our story. It's important for everyone to understand their part. Laverne, you are a nurse who moved with your brother to assist him with his daughter and help them through their loss. You worked in a little hospital in Griffin, Georgia. Nathaniel, you were an investigator for a small insurance company there. You had a little nest egg and thought about visiting an old friend for a while."

"The big question," Nathaniel said as he laughed, "is what our new last name will be."

TJ and Julie looked at each other and laughed.

"What's so funny?" Nathaniel asked skeptically. "I hope it isn't hard to spell because Gracie has to learn it quickly."

"Oh, it's not." Julie said lightheartedly.

TJ reached his hand over to clasp Nathaniel's. "Nice to meet you, Mr. *Smith*," he said with a chuckle.

"Oh my God," Nathaniel complained. "You couldn't be any more original than that? Why not Doe? Don't any of you people have an imagination?"

"Hey, we're just the yes-men of the operation," TJ answered. "We don't get the big, important jobs like assigning folks names."

The whole car shared a laugh, including Gracie, who wasn't quite sure what she was laughing about.

"Okay, we're almost there, so let's finish up with the business at hand," Julie said. She reached into her briefcase and pulled out a manila folder. "This contains everything you'll need—birth certificates, driver's licenses, Social Security cards, Laverne's college transcripts and nursing license, and a cashier's check from each of your old accounts to deposit into the bank of your choice. You'll receive a small check each month from untraceable sources that won't cause suspicion. You each have an American Express card. Laverne, yours has an eight thousand dollar limit, and Nathaniel, because you're Gracie's guardian, yours has a twelve thousand dollar limit. Once that runs out, the well is dry. Do you understand?"

They both nodded.

"Good. Use your cards wisely. The checks will help, but you will need to supply your new home with many things, along with purchasing more outerwear for the climate." She handed the envelope over to Laverne just as the Suburban pulled up to the small landing strip.

There, a white Cessna was waiting for them, along with a man dressed in a pilot's uniform and a tall, attractive blonde in a matching navy-blue skirt and blazer, with a silk, paisley scarf tied loosely around her long, thin neck. They waved happily to the group as if they were flying off to Honolulu for an extended vacation. The blonde introduced herself as Cecily Libby and immediately took over the duties of showing Gracie around the plane and clipping a set of plastic wings on her jacket. TJ and Nathaniel unloaded the luggage and packed it in the cargo bin.

"We're all set, Cap'n," TJ said. "Packed and ready."

"The gods have been good to us today," the Captain responded. "The skies are clear, and the headwinds are in our favor."

"Can't ask for more than that," Nathaniel said, reaching his right hand out for a shake. "Nathaniel Colli...er, Smith. Nathaniel Smith. Nice to meet you."

"Same here. Captain Russ Robertson, at your service."

Chapter 22

Atlanta police officer Jay Sykes was beginning to show the wear of the past few days. He was still unsure of everything that'd transpired at the hospital, but was well aware Mad Dog would want retaliation. He knew revenge was coming, but didn't know when or where. That was the real pisser.

He couldn't remember the exact moment when he'd decided he could so easily be bought. For all he knew, it was one of those things that simply evolved over time. Like every other rookie, he'd joined the force with naïve optimism, confident he could change the world. After a while, he'd learned to settle for just making a small difference on his beat. Before long, he realized the thugs he was risking his life to arrest were being tossed back out on the streets before the ink on his paperwork was dry. It was infuriating, and Sykes was tired of kicking against the never-ending current that was drowning him.

To make matters worse, his bills were piling up, even

with his overtime and second jobs. Then his wife had to quit her job after the second baby. So, Sykes had decided, what the hell? The bad guys have it easier, and they always get away, so why not cash in on it and help 'em out? The extra money hit the spot. All he had to do was tip off a few dealers every now and then, take a little longer to get to his calls, or overlook a bag or two of crack in a teenager's car—no big deal at all. At least it wasn't a big deal until he got involved with Mad Dog Consuelos.

Things had gone sour for Sykes faster than he would've ever imagined. Mad Dog wasn't smarter than the average thug, but he was ruthless and unmerciful. The man had even put two bullets in his own child. It didn't get any colder than that.

Jay reached for his chest, massaging it firmly with his right hand. Although the pain mimicked cardiac arrest, he knew it was just another panic attack. He was well accustomed to his anxiety getting the best of him, and knew that soon there'd be sweating and a tingling in his arm. He pulled the patrol car over into a McDonald's parking lot, turned on the air conditioning, and prepared to ride out the twenty-minute ordeal. As he laid his head back and closed his eyes, the faint knock on his window went unnoticed.

A young woman had noticed him and was concerned about his pale, sweating face and unresponsiveness. Ten minutes later, thanks to a cell phone call, an ambulance skidded to a stop beside his car.

Jay opened his eyes, suddenly realizing he'd allowed his environment to fade into the background, the biggest mistake one could make in his line of work.

A familiar face rapped on the window and told him to unlock the door. "What's up, Man?" the paramedic asked. "Some lady called and said you weren't responding. Are you okay?"

"Yeah," Jay stammered. "Just a little indigestion. A Big Mac attack," he said, faking a laugh. "I'll be fine. I was just taking a break."

Another young and eager EMT came up with a plastic case full of first-response medical paraphernalia. "Let me take your blood pressure and check your pulse. You're sweating like a pig, buddy."

"No, really," Jay insisted, "I'm cool. I just needed some A/C."

"Gotta cover our asses. Roll up your sleeve and let me get that pressure."

Just like that, things had gone too far. Jay knew if he didn't cooperate, they'd call his Sergeant, and he didn't need that headache. He decided it best to comply with the EMTs' protocol. "Son-of-a-bitch. Can't a guy just pull over for a break around here? Take my damn blood pressure so we can all get on with our day."

"It's nothing personal. We all have jobs to do. Just let us do ours, then you can carry on with yours."

The blood pressure cuff tightened as Jay waited impatiently for the results.

"It's pretty high, Officer Sykes. With that and the heavy perspiration, I'm going to have to insist we transport you immediately."

"Screw that! I'll just go home for the day."

"You know we can't force you to transport, but we're obligated to report this to your superiors."

Jay heaved a sigh of resignation before turning the patrol car off. When another unit pulled up, he could tell from the look on the officer's face he'd be forced to make the trip to the hospital. He let his neck relax and laid his head back on the headrest. There was no point in fighting the inevitable. He'd only get his ass chewed later, maybe even put on some sort of administrative leave he couldn't afford.

"I'll call for someone to pick up your squad car," Officer Talley said in a solemn voice, the tone people use when they think someone isn't going to make it.

The pain was getting worse, so Sykes didn't offer a response. For a brief moment, he feared he was actually having a heart attack.

The ambulance ride was swift as they always were when it came to a cop. The doctors and nurses were waiting on him. As soon as he arrived, they wheeled him into the trauma room where machines were ready to be hooked up to him. Everyone worked quickly and efficiently to pinpoint the extent of his problem. Two hours and several unnecessary tests later, Sykes received the diagnosis he'd already given himself. Panic attack, albeit a severe one, according to the doctor.

The nurse held a damp cloth to his forehead while speaking to him soothingly.

Jay tuned her out as he strained to hear the doctor talking to his sergeant. He dreaded what would come next.

"What's up, Sykes?" Sergeant Hill asked brusquely as he entered through the white curtain. He didn't wait for an answer before continuing, "I don't understand these panic attack things. Must be somethin' new doctors spout off when they're at a loss for a real diagnosis, like that ADD nonsense they use for kids now. You do look like hell, though, so something must be wrong with ya."

"I'm okay, Sarge. I'm just comin' down with the flu or something. I'll just go home and rest for a few days. You know…hot chicken noodle soup, Gatorade, that kind of shit."

"I'm afraid the brass won't allow it. The hospital's gonna admit you for a couple of days, just for observation. Maybe you need a shrink. Ain't nothing to be ashamed of if ya do. We're in a crazy business, and this Consuelos case has been a bitch."

"I don't need a shrink," Sykes answered wearily. "I just feel like I'm under the weather…and, to be honest, Sarge, you aren't helping much."

"Point taken. I'm outta here, but if you need me, I'm

only a phone call away. The LT will be by soon. Nothin' I can do to stop him. Just try to get some rest. They'll be putting you in a room soon, and maybe they'll get you some grub. Have you called the Missus?"

"Not yet. I figured I'd be leaving here after a quick checkup. Guess I better let her know I'll be in lockup for the next couple of days, huh? She might wonder why I'm not showing up."

"Your Meredith's a good girl, Sykes. I recommend you call her as soon as possible. Here. Take my cell phone."

"Thanks, but I can't use it around all this equipment. It might blow up the hospital or something. I'll call her when I get to my room."

The Sergeant patted him on his shoulder, then squeezed it firmly. "I'll be by tomorrow with a burger and fries."

"Thanks," Jay answered. Within minutes, he'd drifted off to sleep.

* * * *

Officer Sykes was awakened a few minutes later by a light tap on his chest. He felt groggy, and it took a few seconds for his vision to come into focus. He saw an officer he didn't recognize. It didn't alarm him because it wasn't uncommon in a department the size of the Atlanta PD to come across cops he hadn't met. This one was dressed in black SWAT clothes, but the fact that his name wasn't embroidered across his chest caused Sykes immediate concern. "Who are you, Man?"

"I'm here to bring a message." He spoke with a faint Hispanic accent, and as he leaned down to whisper the words, thin streams of spittle landed on Jay's cheek, but he was too frozen with fear to wipe it off. "Seems you let our bounty hunter get away," the man said. "Big mistake, my friend."

Jay felt the warmth of the man's breath on his face and smelled a hint of marijuana. "It...happened so fast. The FEDS were in on it. It was well planned. I did the best I could. Really! I just couldn't—"

"That's bullshit, and Consuelos doesn't buy it. You have five days to find them, or that pretty little wife of yours will die painfully...and not at all quickly."

"Meredith? No! Wait! I'll—"

"I don't wanna hear your bullshit. My job was to deliver the message, so I'm done here." With that, the man in black pulled the curtain back, spoke politely to the nurse who was on her way in to draw blood, then continued down the hall.

Chapter 23

Mad Dog was on the run, something he'd never been forced to do in the past. He was on the run and desperate for blood. It didn't matter to him how it happened. He wanted retaliation, and he needed revenge. He felt the manic behavior taking over, but unlike those who scrounged for medication to eliminate the symptoms, he welcomed them. The rage fed his hunger for control.

Consuelos was hiding out in the depths of poverty, in the company of his few trusted men. The poor living conditions didn't faze him. He'd lived a meager lifestyle during his childhood, and in some way, it brought him comfort. Mad Dog knew the cops wouldn't dare step into the bowels of hell to find a fugitive, not even one of his caliber. The old, abandoned apartment smelled of weed, urine, and unwashed armpits. The guys in his circle were there for the drugs and for the simple fact they wouldn't survive five minutes if they betrayed him. It amused him, and Consuelos considered every one of them worthless. Although he was sorely outnumbered, they didn't have enough intelligence between them to outwit him.

As Mad Dog concentrated on the paint peeling in sheets from the graying walls, he let his mind go back to the last time he'd seen Nathaniel Collier and his daughter, Gracie. He'd been sure the shots were fatal. He rarely made mistakes so immense, it wasn't his style.

He was sure everyone, other than his mindless followers, were underestimating him, and he decided he'd replace his feelings of regret with the stimulation of excitement. *Yes, that's my answer for them!*

He cracked the foil that encircled a large bottle of Hennessy, pulled out the cork, and inhaled the enticing aroma. Taking his time to savor the large swallows, he allowed them to rest in his mouth a few seconds before swallowing. *Revenge will be as sweet as this cognac, only this time, it will not be as swift,* he told himself.

Chapter 24

The bitter cold had taken hold of Hayden. It was a little overdue, but that was appreciated. Magnificently large snowflakes floated down peacefully, blanketing the cold ground.

"Yes, this snow is going to last a little while," Lauren Lowe said to herself.

She'd always loved the first few snowfalls of the winter season, but knew she'd soon grow weary of them. She quickly tired of bundling up and making her way to work every morning in the bitter, unrelenting cold.

Pulling the goose-down comforter up around her neck, she wished it was Saturday morning. If it was, she would've been able to sleep a couple more hours. Then she'd get up, pull on her flannel robe, and make pancakes for breakfast. But none of that was going to happen today. It was only Wednesday, and she was on the verge of running late for work. Mr. Phillips didn't accept any excuses when it came to tardiness, and she was in no mood to hear him ranting.

"Our customers make up this business," he often said. "Their time is valuable." Whenever he said such things, Lauren would simply smile sweetly and hurry to her register. He was a kind man who cared about satisfying his customers, and she appreciated that. In fact, it was her motivation to continue working in his store—that and the fact that there weren't a lot of jobs in Hayden, especially for recent high school grads who'd yet to decide on their path in life.

Lauren's parents couldn't understand why she wasn't anxious to go away to college. Most of her friends had opted to do just that, although Lauren couldn't pinpoint a reason, she just didn't feel ready. The small apartment in her parents' basement was sufficient for the time being, and allowed her some semblance of independence. She busied herself with transforming canvases into beautiful paintings of landscapes and places she had yet to see. She was considering attending art school the following year when she felt a little more comfortable about leaving home. Teachers had praised her talents, so art might be the path meant for her. As for today, she still had to shower and get to Stanley's grocery store.

Counting to three in her usual routine, Lauren threw back the covers, grabbed her chenille robe, and let her bare feet hit the piercing chill of the hardwood floor. She scampered quickly across the room until she felt the soft, furry throw rug she'd purchased with her last paycheck. Lingering there for a few seconds, she looked down at her toes as they danced in the faux material, stopping to admire her new nail color, Magenta Ice. It was a dollar more than her usual polish, but it'd been worth it.

Waiting until the water was warm enough for her taste, she hopped in and took a quick but sufficient shower. As she dried off, her thoughts drifted to her meager wardrobe.

She always dressed casually, but she'd been hoping to catch the attention of the new stock boy. He was two years older, as handsome as a movie star, and had a smile to die for. Her new Calvin Klein jeans and the L.L. Bean sweater she'd gotten last Christmas would be perfect. Lauren felt guilty admitting it, but she knew the winter white sweater was becoming on her. It brought out the blonde highlights in her hair, and if she could spare a few extra seconds on her makeup, the bright blue of her eyes would be much more noticeable. She was far from arrogant, but her beauty had been pointed out to her most of her life, by both her parents and strangers on the street. Her Homecoming Queen crown still sat prominently on her dresser, flanked on either side by the dried roses she'd received from her parents that night.

Her small bathroom was still steamy, keeping it warm long enough to put on her deodorant and lotion and brush her teeth. She ran a brush through her hair and picked up the new lotion, a recent gift. It was sort of strange that he'd given it to her, but she'd accepted it with appreciation. Like other young girls, she enjoyed all of the latest soaps and sprays, lotions, and body washes. Shaking it up, she quickly opened the top, inhaling in the aroma of jasmine. "Mmm…" Lauren poured more than an adequate amount in her hand and began rubbing it into her legs. *My skin's always so dry in this weather. Maybe I should go to school somewhere warm, somewhere without snow, maybe Texas or Florida or—*

Before Lauren continued that thought, she felt a tingling sensation in both her hands and her legs. It was faint at first, then almost painful. She reached up to touch her face, which had gone instantly numb. Looking into the steamy mirror, she realized she had no control over her expressions. Her face was unnaturally contorted like someone having a stroke. Easing down onto the floor and leaning over the toilet, she watched the large drops of

120

perspiration drip into the water. Panicking, she lay down on her back, her mind swirling as she tried to grasp the gravity of the situation. Pain radiated from her chest, and her heart was pounding so hard, she half-expected it to explode. She tried to scream out for her mother and father, but her mouth wouldn't open. Her eyes, dry and burning, refused to blink.

Oh God, Lauren pleaded silently, *help me! I-I can't stand the pain.* She lay there as ice ran through her young, healthy veins. All she could think of was the pain—that unexpected, unrelenting pain. Feeling the waves of unconsciousness, Lauren prayed again she'd remain awake and alert, even in the pain. As if her prayers had fallen on deaf ears, blackness settled in swiftly. Her eyelids closed as she vomited profusely, her languid body sucking the regurgitation deep into her lungs. Her final thoughts were of the young stock boy she'd never get to know, the paintings she'd never finish, and the sound of the front door closing upstairs as her mother left for work.

Chapter 25

The Cessna landed uneventfully in a small, secluded airstrip in the midst of the Wyoming wilderness.

Nathaniel had gently nudged Gracie to wake her for the landing. She'd been excited about the flight but had quickly fallen into a deep, satisfying sleep. He watched her lovingly as she rubbed her eyes and brought them into focus. *Oh to see the world through the eyes of a child,* Nathaniel thought. *I finally see what everyone's been talking about.*

"I see mountains," she exclaimed as they came to a complete stop. "They're so big. Do you think anyone has ever been to the top?"

"Sure," Nathaniel answered. "We'll visit the top of some of them too and look down on everything below."

Her chocolate eyes widened and gleamed with anticipation.

"Okay, everyone," Cecily chirped from the door of the

cockpit, "I believe this is your stop. We're officially kicking you out."

"No complaints from me," TJ answered. "I hate flying, and flights over two hours always put me in a bad mood."

Cecily smiled and stood back as Captain Robinson opened the airplane door.

"Welcome to Wyoming," he said, shivering as the cold weather quickly filled the small plane. "Better you all than me. I'm like the birds and prefer to fly south for the winter."

"We'll make the best of it," Laverne said, her tone upbeat.

"To Wyoming!" Nathaniel grinned, taking Gracie by the hand.

"To Wyoming!" she said, grinning back. "Yay!"

Another Suburban was waiting for them on the tarmac as TJ and Julie gathered their luggage, rushing them inside quickly.

"I don't think there's anyone around," Nathaniel laughed. "Do we really need to break into a run?"

"This plane has to get out of here. We're on an abandoned landing strip, and don't want to draw any attention to it. We're only about an hour from Hayden, so your journey with us is almost complete."

"It'll be kind of sad to see you go," Nathaniel teased. "Will we hear from you again?"

"Only if we have news on the trial or we feel there's cause for concern. Everything has gone picture-perfect so far, so I don't expect any problems. Just stay within the realms of the program, as we've already discussed, and you'll be fine. You may decide you like the West better than the East. Most people we put into this program find they like starting over, that it's almost like being reborn. The slate is clean, so you can virtually become a new person."

"I'll have to get back with you on that one," Laverne

answered, shivering a bit. "I have a feeling I'm in for quite a change."

"We'll be thinking of you and wishing the best for all of you," Julie said. "TJ and I didn't just take this job for the paycheck. We hope we're making a difference, especially with people like you guys."

The drive went quickly as they took in all the natural beauty surrounding them. It left everyone speechless, except for Gracie. It was almost too much for her mind to comprehend.

"Look over there! Wow, another mountain! And look over there. That must be snow on the ground. Is it cold? Does it feel soft or hard? Is it wet?"

"My goodness, little girl." Nathaniel laughed. "How can I answer all those questions? You'll just have to wait and see for yourself."

She smiled, but only briefly. She had many more questions to ask.

"Here's the driveway," TJ said abruptly. "This is your friend's place. We'd like you to get out of the vehicle and into the house as quickly as possible. No one here has reason to suspect a thing, but a dark Suburban with a large black man getting your bags out can look a little suspicious, if you know what I mean."

"How will you guys get back?" Laverne asked.

"Commercial airlines, thank God." Julie smiled. "Then I'll take a day off, and it's back to the Witness Protection Program. Another face, a different name. Right, TJ?"

"Something like that. Anyway, it's a pretty nice-looking place. Nathaniel, grab Gracie and carry her in. Laverne, you follow quickly behind. We'll leave the luggage on the front porch by the door. Get it only after we've left."

"We want to thank you," Nathaniel said. "You've done such a good job."

"I'm a sap when it comes to good-byes," TJ answered

as the Suburban came to a stop. "Now get out and get in that house!"

And just like that, it was over, almost like a dream. Nathaniel was glad he wasn't going to have to rush anymore. He was tired and wanted to take things slow.

He knocked on the front door, and it opened before he could reach for the knob. Reid pulled them in quickly, shutting the door as if he'd already been warned. Only when they heard the Suburban pull away did they embrace each other.

"Damn good to see you, Man," Nathaniel said, his voice cracking with emotion.

"You too. You look like somethin' the cat drug in, but we'll work on that. You're going to be breathing clean air from now on, and you'll love it here." Reid then turned his attention to the females in the room. "And you must be Laverne." He smiled as he kissed her lightly on the cheek. "Welcome to my humble abode. I hope you'll feel right at home here."

"I already do," Laverne answered, pulling off her heavy coat.

"And this," Reid exclaimed with great enthusiasm, "must be the young lady I've heard so much about. You're even prettier than Nathaniel said."

Gracie looked pleased and smiled over at Nathaniel. "He's my daddy now," she whispered.

"I know! That's pretty cool, isn't it?"

"It's very cool." She smiled broadly. "My other daddy tried to hurt us, but now we're starting over. My name is Gracie Smith, and that's my dad, and that's my Aunt Laverne."

"Sounds pretty good to me. Maybe I can be an unofficial uncle. How does that sound?"

Gracie giggled and nodded her head in agreement.

"Great! Now, how about something to eat and a drink?"

"I won't fight you on that one, ol' buddy," Nathanial answered.

"How does a beer sound?"

"I'd love nothing more."

"Easy," Laverne piped up. "If you have something to drink, you can't take a pain pill later. You've had a long, tough day, and your body will surely be begging for one soon."

"I'll take my chances, Sis," Nathaniel teased. "A beer sounds like the best medicine."

"A beer it is," Reid said with a laugh. "Michelob or Heineken?"

"Hell, I might as well live it up. Give me the imported stuff."

Laverne shook her head.

"You really are like a sister to me," Nathaniel told her sincerely. "Thank you for everything, Laverne."

"Quit trying to justify that beer. I'm on to you, Nathaniel Smith."

The drinks were followed by grilled hamburgers and hotdogs, chips, and baked beans.

"Just what the doctor ordered," Nathaniel said as they settled down on the couch.

Gracie's eyes were fluttering as she fought off her need for sleep.

"How about a short nap?" Nathaniel suggested. "I bet you'll feel a lot better. When you wake up, we can go out and play in the snow."

She smiled weakly and allowed Laverne to lead her back to bed.

Nathaniel and Reid opened another beer and settled in to talk.

"It's been a long time," Reid began. "I'm sorry about all of this."

"Me too, but strangely, it's been worth it. I mean, I got an instant family out of it, and I don't even have to put up with an old ball and chain."

Reid smiled back at him, but was aware of the pain in his friend's eyes, a pain that ran deeper than Nathaniel would admit.

"Thanks for having us. You've really helped us out of a serious situation. I'm not sure how much longer we could've survived back there. Consuelos is a real piece of work. Can you imagine shooting your child's mother and then your own child? Clearly, he's capable of anything."

"Well, you're all safe here—just clean air, good people, and beautiful scenery. The cold and snow can take a little adjusting, but if I can get accustomed to it, anybody can."

"The main thing is that we're still alive."

"There's definitely something to be said for that."

"Am I interrupting you guys?"

"No, not at all, Laverne," Reid answered kindly. "Come on in and have a seat. Can I get you a glass of wine?"

"Oh, that'd be wonderful."

"Red or white?"

"Surprise me," she answered as she laid her head back on the couch. "Gracie was out as soon as her little head hit the pillow."

Reid returned with a large glass of chilled Chardonnay.

"Mmm," Laverne hummed. "Wonderful."

"I have a friend I'd like you to meet. She's a doctor at the local hospital. It's much smaller than Atlanta Medical Center, but it's a good one just the same. She'd like to offer you a job if you're up to it. Mountainside's always in need of good nurses."

"Sounds great to me," Laverne said with a smile. "I love nursing and would miss it tremendously if I had to give it up. My career is a part of me."

"Can't argue with you there. At any rate, she'll be over tonight for dinner. We thought we'd grill out. You'll like

Anne. She's real down-to-earth." When Reid's phone rang, he excused himself to answer it. "You're shitting me!" he said, his voice high pitched and loud.

Laverne and Nathaniel looked at each other in confusion.

"I wonder what that's all about," Nathaniel said.

Chapter 26

Reid walked back into the room, his face pale, his expression pained. The phone hung limply from the tips of his fingers.

"What's up?" Nathaniel asked, recognizing the ominous expression. He knew someone was dead or in serious trouble.

Reid stood in the middle of the room for a few seconds before answering, his body swaying slightly from left to right. "It's so strange. Another young girl has died of what appears to be natural causes."

"Another one? What do you mean?"

"The second one in two weeks. I tried to get an autopsy on the first one, but the family damn near killed me for suggesting it. They don't believe in that around here."

"What?" Nathaniel asked, unable to believe it. "You've got to be kidding me."

"It's a long story. I…I'm sorry, but I've got to go. My

deputies aren't used to this sort of thing, and I have to take their hands and guide them through it."

"Do you want me to come along?"

"I appreciate it, Nathaniel. I know you'd be a big help, but you need your rest. Besides, I don't have time to explain everything to you right now. Just make yourself at home. If I'm not home by supper, I'm sure you two can figure out the grill."

With that, he was gone, barely taking the time to grab his jacket. Nathaniel felt bad for him. He'd seen enough of that crap for a lifetime, and he didn't envy his friend. "I think I'll take a nap," he said turning to Laverne.

"Same here," she answered and made her way back to Gracie's bed.

* * * *

The snow was falling with a vengeance, making the ride to the Lowe home much longer than usual. As he made his way through the winding, snow-covered roads, Reid dialed Anne's cell phone. She answered on the first ring. Foregoing any pleasantries, he got straight to the point. "Lauren Lowe is dead. Eighteen years old and dead on the cold tile of her bathroom floor!"

"Reid? What are you talking about?"

"I'm talking about another dead girl. Dead, Anne, just like Joanna Sibley! I'm on my way there now."

"Are you okay? Do you want me to meet you?"

"It might not be a bad idea. She's at 446 Elm Circle. It's a big brick house. You can't miss it."

"I'm on my way."

With that, he hung up and called the office. Reid was surprised to find Nell had already left with her crime scene kit, and his two other deputies were en route. They surprised him at times, and it was a relief to know they were on top of it. But how they'd react to the scene was anybody's guess. Even his years of experience hadn't prepared him for what was ahead.

The Lowe home was a big one, perhaps one of the largest in Hayden. Reid had always admired it but had never been inside. It saddened him that his first visit to the place was for such a grim reason. He heard the screams and cries, but his mind thankfully obliterated them.

Maloney was standing across the den, motioning for him to follow. They made their way down a winding staircase that opened to Lauren's apartment. Glancing around quickly, Reid realized it was larger than his entire home.

He looked at Matthew for further directions, then realized he was handling the situation much differently than the last. His face was wearing the same pained look as before, but there was something dissimilar this time. Reid realized it was a growing maturity, and he was proud of him. The deputy was trying desperately to be the young cop Reid expected him to be.

"She's over here, Sheriff, in the bathroom."

They made their way around propped-up canvases of impressive paintings as Nell's camera flashed.

Taking a gulp of air, Reid leaned inside. "Hey, Nell," he said quietly. "What's it look like to you?"

"Hey, Sheriff," she answered solemnly. "I couldn't tell you. I was waiting for you before disturbing the body. I did notice some vomit around her mouth, but other than that, nothing unusual."

Reid motioned for Nell to give him some room. Once she was out of the way, he knelt beside the body. She couldn't have been dead any longer than eight hours because her mother had heard her shower running before she'd left for work and was back home in less than eight and a half hours. Reid was by no means a medical examiner, but he'd talked to enough of them at the scene to be more than a little knowledgeable on the subject.

"Why is she so red?" he heard Nell asking him.

He could tell Lauren was a fair-skinned girl because her hair was such a light color. "It's called livor mortis," he said quietly. "Come here." He motioned for Nell and gently rolled Lauren's body over on her side. "See these white marks over her scapula and buttocks?"

"Yeah. What is it?"

"We can pretty much tell she died here and wasn't moved. The body discolors after death because of the settling of blood with gravity. The white areas are where the bones compressed the skin against the floor and prevented the blood from settling in those areas."

"So that can tell us how long she's been dead?"

"Not really. In this case, her mother's recollection of the shower running when she left and the fact she's still in the bathroom with a wet towel on the floor gives us a more precise time of death than any medical explanation can."

"She's getting stiff, Sheriff. Can we get her out of here?"

"She isn't in complete rigor, but it shouldn't be much longer. Let me talk to the Lowes. I'll get Matthew and James to keep everyone out, even Joe Hill. I see him and Jane out there. They were on duty when Joanna died too. What a pisser for them."

He walked over to James Farmer, one of his older deputies. James was in his early thirties and the father of twin five-year-old girls. The Officer didn't appear to be taking the situation very well.

"Listen, James," Reid began, "I need you and Matthew to keep everyone out of that bathroom. That goes for Joe and Jane as well. I'll be upstairs with the family."

"Sure, Sheriff," he answered weakly. "We'll take care of it."

Reid took his time climbing the stairway, giving himself a couple extra minutes to gather his thoughts. As he reached the top, he was unprepared for the growing crowd.

Word had spread quickly throughout the community, and neighbors and friends were entering with baskets of food and words of sympathy. He found the Lowes seated on the couch in the living room, surrounded by people wearing solemn expressions. He walked up slowly and asked, as tactfully as possible, that the escalating crowd give them a few moments alone. Much to his surprise, everyone dispersed, leaving him alone with the parents.

Mrs. Lowe's eyes, although pooling with tears, were surprisingly clear and alert. "What happened to our daughter, Sheriff?"

Reid stood over them awkwardly until she motioned for him to sit across from her. "I'm not a doctor, Mrs. Lowe," he began cautiously. "I don't know what has happened to your daughter, but she doesn't appear to have been attacked in any way."

Mr. Lowe cleared his throat a couple of times before he spoke, "I just…we don't understand, Sheriff," he said as his hands began to tremble. "Please tell us she didn't hurt herself."

"I can't," Reid answered, "but I can almost guarantee it wasn't the case. We saw no signs to indicate a suicide."

"I feel guilty saying anything is a relief at this point, but I must say *that* is," he said softly.

"Did Lauren have any health problems? A history of asthma, heart arrhythmia, anything of that sort?"

"Not that we're aware of," Mrs. Lowe answered. "She was rarely sick, hardly a day in her life."

"It's difficult to ask you this, but please understand that I need to. Did she, um…ever experiment with drugs or alcohol?"

"Never," Mr. Lowe answered, surprisingly not offended. "We're not naïve, Sheriff. I know parents can't know everything their children are doing, but we never had a minute's trouble out of Lauren." Large teardrops spilled from his eyes, but he refused the Kleenex his wife offered.

Reid was relieved to see Anne entering the room. He stood and shook her hand before introducing her to the Lowes.

"I'm terribly sorry we have to meet under these conditions," she started kindly. "I've looked at Lauren, and I can't find anything that would suggest her cause of death. On the surface, she appears healthy. Is there anything in her medical history that might explain this?"

Both parents shook their heads and continued to look at her for answers.

"What do you think it could be, Doctor?" Mr. Lowe asked, tears still dripping from his eyes.

"Mr. Lowe, it could be any number of things. People tend to assume that because someone is young, they can't die of natural causes, but that isn't the case. We could make the assumption it was a heart attack, and it may have been, but I'm led to believe it was something else."

"Wh-what would lead you to that conclusion?"

"It's too much of a coincidence to find two young girls, both healthy prior to their deaths, according to their families, now deceased. In a big city, it might not be so uncommon, but it's quite different in a small population."

"But it's possible that they both died of heart attacks, isn't it?"

"Well, technically, yes...but it's not probable."

"So you're going at this statistically then?" Mrs. Lowe asked with a hint of resentment in her voice.

"I suppose you could say that," Anne answered honestly, looking both sympathetic and tired. "It's the best way to find answers for your daughter and the other girl who passed away. That's why I'd like to plead with you to allow me to do an autopsy. If it was a heart defect, I'll find that right away. If it was something else...well, I'm sure you'd both want to know."

Reid held his breath as he awaited the hysteria that was sure would follow.

Both parents looked at each other briefly before Mr. Lowe, much to everyone's surprise, nodded his head in agreement. "We have to know. Her death is almost more than we can bear, but the not knowing? I'm sure we couldn't live with that," he said.

Anne nodded and reached for Mrs. Lowe's hands. "I cannot pretend to understand how difficult this is, but you've made the right decision. I'll do all I can to find answers for you."

"Tell us…" Mrs. Lowe started, but she was overcome with emotion and had to pause. When she could speak again, she said, "Tell us what you will do. Please don't…please don't slaughter my beautiful baby."

"Honey," her husband said gently, attempting to ease her pain, "don't think like that. I'm sure Doctor Novus will be as kind as possible to Lauren."

"I assure you we will not be unnecessarily invasive, Mrs. Lowe. I will treat your daughter with the same respect I would treat my own family. Our main concern is finding out what happened to her."

"Where will you take her? When?"

Anne moved over to sit beside her on the couch and took the woman's hand in hers. "The paramedics will take her to Mountainside Memorial where I'll conduct the autopsy as soon as possible. We'll do toxicology tests tonight to see if there are any unknown toxins in her blood. The autopsy itself will be done first thing in the morning." She couldn't bear to tell her they needed time for the rigor to dissipate.

Mrs. Lowe lightly patted Anne's hand, then removed hers from their grasp.

"Take her. Hurry, take her before I change my mind."

With that, the grieving mother got up and left the room, leaving her husband alone.

"We'll take her out through the basement exit," Reid said. "There isn't any reason for your company to see her.

We'll be in touch, but if my department can do anything for you, please let me know."

Mr. Lowe opened his mouth to speak, but his voice failed him. He stood and went to find his wife.

Chapter 27

"I'll meet you at the hospital in a few minutes," Reid said to Anne. "I have to make sure everything is finished up here."

"I understand," she said quietly as he followed her to her car.

"What the hell's going on here, Anne?" he asked as if she had the answer. "I told you I had a weird feeling about the Sibley girl. Something never set right with me about that whole situation."

"I have to agree," she answered quietly, "but I refuse to jump to any conclusions. Let's just wait and see what we find in the autopsy." She dug her keys out of her purse and unlocked the door to the new Lexus. "I should get to the hospital. I don't want them to beat me there."

Reid decided to forego further conversation and reentered the Lowe household through the basement door. It wasn't necessary for him to witness any more of the family's grief, and he didn't have answers to anyone's questions.

He found Nell wrapping up the crime scene investigation, which was sorely limited due to her lack of training and test kits. The black powder smudges that detected fingerprints remained on the counters in the bathroom as an ugly reminder of what had taken place. "I think that's it, Sheriff," Nell said, closing up the plastic container that amounted to little more than a tackle box. "I'm not sure we got anything useful. The prints all looked the same, so I'm sure they belonged to Lauren. I'll forward them to the Bureau."

Reid shook his head in a combination of sadness and disbelief as he paused to study Nell's features. He was ashamed to admit he'd never really paid much attention to her. She was probably in her late forties, ten or fifteen pounds underweight, and had the energy of a young child. Her hair was mousy brown, and her rectangular glasses clung to the edge of her nose. Her job was important to her, and she took it more seriously than any deputy on his staff. Reid made a mental note to plead with the City Council for extra funding on her behalf. The department could greatly benefit from any classes they'd allow her to attend. "How long have you lived in Hayden, Nell?" he asked.

"All my life," she answered, grabbing the small of her back and leaning forward. "I can't handle squatting too much anymore, guess my bones are getting old."

Her last comment went unnoticed. "Doesn't it seem odd for two young girls to die without any explanation?"

"Yeah," she answered slowly, placing her index finger on her chin as though deep in thought. "I didn't think much about the death of Joanna Sibley. She was a health fanatic. You hear about these young girls who try to look like supermodels, waifs, I think they call them. I just figured she was pushing her body too hard. I have to say, I'm not so sure now."

"Any ideas?" Reid asked, aware her job was limited to retrieving fingerprints and taking crime scene photos.

"I'm baffled. The last time a young person died here was about fifteen years ago. Perry Bailey, I believe his name was. Got drunk after his high school football game and flipped his car over. It was a tragedy, but there was no denying what killed him. The family moved away not long after that. It was too painful for them to stay here."

"Any other strange deaths? I mean, unexplained ones?"

"I've had this job for twenty-five years, Sheriff, and can't say I remember one. Let's see…old Mr. Carlson died from cancer a few years ago, Ms. Caldwell shot herself in the chest after her husband left her for a younger woman and moved to Texas, Diane Milton died of a terrible bout of pneumonia, and Roy Stephens died in his sleep of natural causes last year."

"Did they do an autopsy on Mr. Stephens?"

"Nope. No need. The man was ninety-seven."

Reid struggled to maintain his patience. The conversation hadn't gotten him anywhere. He glanced at his watch and scanned the room one last time. "I've got to get to the hospital. I don't want to keep Doctor Novus waiting. Have Matthew lock everything up for me, will you?"

"No problem."

"And would you mind telling the family that the ambulance has taken her?"

"I'll let them know. Do you want me to wipe this bathroom down before I go? There's no need to leave it for them to see. The prints have been collected."

"That'd be nice, Nell…and it's real thoughtful of you."

Chapter 28

Anne was sitting in her office with her glasses pushed back on her head and a cup of steaming coffee in her hand.

The ambulance drivers had delivered Lauren Lowe. The girl lay in the morgue beneath a white sheet, waiting for answers. Her parents had been right. She hadn't been sick a day in her life, except for a couple of ear infections, one bout of strep throat, and a broken arm, all of which had occurred before her teens. Lauren's pediatrician had his nurse deliver her medical chart to the hospital, and although Anne was grateful, it offered little in the way of answers. Lauren had received all of her immunizations, necessary baby checkups, and even a physical exam every year in high school so she could participate in sports. She'd sailed through with flying colors each time, presenting nothing to denote any complications.

Filled with exasperation and deep in thought, Anne didn't even hear Reid as he entered her office.

"You okay?" he asked, clearing his throat and startling her.

"Dear Lord! You scared the hell out of me," she said with a gasp. "Why would you sneak up on me like that? We're in a morgue for Christ's sake. It's creepy enough down here without people trying to frighten me."

"Take it easy," Reid soothed. "I walked in like a normal person. You were just a million miles away and didn't hear me."

She wiped her eyes before pulling her glasses from the top of her head to rest on the bridge of her nose. "I'm sorry," she answered solemnly. "I'm just tired, and these deaths are beginning to gnaw at me."

"Can I refill your coffee? Let's relax for a few minutes and regroup. Rushing to get answers won't help."

Anne looked down at the lukewarm coffee and felt her stomach begin to swirl with disgust. "I've been relying on this stuff as my miracle drug. Frankly, I'm sick of it."

He reached across the desk and offered his hand to her. "I say we go upstairs to the dining room and get some of that delightful grub hospitals are known for. When all else fails me, a stiff drink and a warm meal always come through."

She unconsciously ignored the offering of his outstretched hand, instead standing and reaching for her lab coat.

Reid held his hand up motioning for her to stop. "Let's leave the lab coat," he said softly. "You won't need to play doctor while you eat. I think the public can get along without the world's best Doctor and their fearless Sheriff for at least thirty minutes."

"I suppose you have a point," Anne conceded.

Chapter 29

Nathaniel's eyes opened slowly, and it took him a few seconds to realize where he was. He wasn't sure how long he'd slept, but the sun was already beginning its descent. The cabin was still silent, meaning that Reid hadn't returned and Gracie and Laverne were still asleep. He'd need to wake them to eat dinner, and he didn't want Gracie to be awake all night. A fleeting thought came to his mind: his mother laughing about how, as a baby, he'd gotten his days and nights mixed up. Although she'd laughed heartily about it, it didn't seem like something he wanted to experience.

He went into the bathroom and wet a cloth with cool water, then wiped it slowly across his face. It felt good and helped to wake him and bring a little clarity. He wondered about Reid and what had taken him away. Hoping it wasn't serious, he quietly pushed open the girl's bedroom door. They were sleeping soundly, and he hated to wake them, but knew they could use a good meal. If they were still tired after that, they could turn in for the night.

He approached Laverne's side first and looked down at her for a few moments before waking her. Even in her sleep, she wore a kind expression on her round face. He smiled to himself. She was attractive in a sisterly kind of way. If he'd had a sister, she would've been his pick. Her shoulder-length brown hair was styled the same as she'd worn it in high school, but it didn't seem outdated. She didn't wear much makeup, other than a little blush and mascara. She was probably fifty pounds overweight, but it wasn't unattractive. It fit her personality. If she were smaller, she just wouldn't be Laverne.

He reached to lightly shake her shoulder, but her eyes opened before he touched her. The glazed-over, confused look he'd awoken with was not on her face. Unlike him, Laverne knew instantly where she was and reached over to feel for Gracie.

"She's there," Nathaniel assured her. "Do you sleepyheads want to get up and help me cook dinner?"

"Good Lord," she whispered. "What time is it?"

"It's 7:30. I guess we needed the rest."

Gracie slowly turned over and sat up in bed. "Hey, Daddy. Hey, Aunt Laverne," she said groggily.

"Good evening, little one." Nathaniel smiled. "You slept almost all day. Do you feel like helping me fix dinner? I bet you're hungry."

The girl smiled broadly and jumped anxiously off the bed. "You'll really let me help? Cool! I've never cooked before. Is there snow out there?"

"Why don't you pull on that coat and slide on those snow boots, and we'll go check it out?"

She rambled around the room until she found both items.

Laverne rolled her eyes. "In her pajamas, Nathaniel? Really?"

"Who cares? We're in Wyoming. Who's going to see us? The buffalo?"

"I'll start dinner while you two go frolicking," she said.

Gracie stood in the doorway, her little face bright with amazement.

Nathaniel was equally surprised by the snow showers, something he'd not really experienced in Atlanta. Large, oversized flakes floated slowly from the heavens, sticking to the deck and forming a white, wintry blanket. "Go on, Miss Gracie," he said, nudging her toward the door. "Don't you want to know what it feels like?"

She stepped gently toward the deck as though the white mixture might somehow disappear if she made too much noise. She watched her feet and giggled as she heard the crunch of the snow beneath her boots.

"Touch it. Go ahead," he urged. "It's a little cold."

She bent down, touched it lightly, then jerked her hand back as though it might bite like a stray dog. She giggled again, then pushed her index finger into it until it engulfed her hand. "It is cold N-na...er, Dad! Come on. Feel it. Don't be afraid," she assured him. Forgetting her earlier apprehension, she grabbed a handful and squished it in both hands.

Laverne had been watching from the window, a warm feeling encircling her insides. She opened the door with a forced scowl on her face. "Don't you two know you need mittens? My goodness. I have to think of everything!"

Nathaniel winked at her and accepted the mittens, then helped Gracie put hers on.

"But we won't be able to feel it through these," she complained.

"You're right, but they'll keep our fingers from falling off from frostbite."

"Falling off!" she shrieked.

"Your fingers aren't going to fall off Gracie," Laverne

said, casting Nathaniel a how-dare-you glare. "He's just playing, but it isn't good to let them get too cold. You'll have forever to play in the snow. If your father will kindly light the grill, I can bring out the steaks."

Chapter 30

Officer Jay Sykes struggled unsuccessfully to fight off panic attacks for the next three days. Against his better judgment, the attending physician had released him with a prescription of Xanax and an antidepressant. His return to work would be dependent on several factors, including regular visits with a psychiatrist.

Meredith and her husband rode home from the hospital in silence. Along with concern for her husband, she bore the concern of the family finances. His sick leave was limited, and they were already struggling, even with his extra jobs. She would've welcomed the opportunity to panic, but she had to maintain a level head to keep them afloat. Her mother had come up from Florida to stay with them while she tried to find a part-time job. She was only a few miles from home and still hadn't worked up the nerve to tell him. Jay and his mother-in-law were like oil and water, making her visit a bit of a two-edged sword. It wouldn't help his recovery or mood to have to deal with her, but Meredith needed her mother to help with the kids so she could find work.

"Would it help to talk, Jay?" she asked.

"No, I'm fine. Probably just working too much."

"I've needed a job for awhile. I shouldn't have expected you to carry the load."

"Don't start that shit again," he answered angrily. "Your job is to take care of the family. My kids won't be raised in some generic childcare center. We agreed on that long ago, so don't bring it up again."

She was shocked at how quickly his demeanor had turned to anger. It hadn't been her intent to provoke him, and she knew the next topic of discussion would only infuriate him more. "Jay, we have bills and responsibilities. Your health has to be the top priority right now. If we fall behind, you won't get better. I'm going to get something part-time, at least until you improve. Mom has come up to take care of the children."

"What? Son-of-a-bitch, Meredith! I'll be damned if you're gonna work while that woman takes care of our kids. Are you trying to put me in my grave? Is that what you want? You must really need that life insurance money, huh? Got somebody else to share it with once I'm gone?"

His tirade had been expected, but she was unprepared for the rage. She'd never seen that from her husband. Her hands shook as she struggled to hold on to the steering wheel. Tears stung at her eyes, but she continued to speak calmly. "You have to stop being so proud, Jay. That's not going to help us right now."

"I want her out of my house by tomorrow morning."

Meredith opened her mouth to speak but decided against it. He was too angry to reason with. Hopefully, seeing the kids would help to calm him.

Her hands were still perspiring as she turned the aging minivan into the driveway. Jay hadn't spoken the last few blocks to the house, and she'd refused to look at him. In a matter of minutes, her emotions had changed from sympathy to exasperation. His selfishness was entirely uncalled for.

Shifting the van into park, she turned her gaze to him. "Please give it a try, Jay. I'm sure Mother had others things on her schedule, but she immediately agreed to come here and help us. You two need to act like adults and set your differences aside for the benefit of the kids." She waited for a reply, but when she didn't get one, she added, "I'm going inside. If you want to be a prick and sit out here pouting, that's on you." She snatched up her purse and took the keys from the ignition.

"I'm sorry, Meredith," he said. "I've been under a lot of stress. Please just bear with me. I love you."

"Then let's go kiss those kids. They're ready to see their dad." Masking her surprise from his change of attitude, she turned the knob and shouted, "Daddy's home!"

The silence seemed to echo throughout the small house as Jay's face went ashen.

"I'm sure they're fine. Mother probably took them for a walk to give you time to settle in. You want something to eat?"

He pushed past her and ran through the house. When he reached the master bedroom, a guttural scream escaped his lips, and his legs folded beneath him.

The horrible sight caused Jay Sykes to vomit profusely. The only reason he found the strength to stand was that he had to get Meredith out of the house. When he met her in the hallway, vomit still clinging to the edges of his beard, he grabbed her and ordered her to get out of the house.

"What the hell's going on?" she screamed, pushing past him toward the bedroom.

Lunging after her, Jay caught her right ankle, pulling her to the floor. Her hands clawed at the old shag carpet in an attempt to make progress down the hall. His strength finally overcame her, and he pulled her to him. "You can't go in there. Just trust me on this, Meredith," he pleaded.

Something in his eyes—or maybe the sheer terror in his voice—caused her to stop fighting him. "The kids! Where are the kids, Jay? Are they hurt? Are they…back there?"

"I-I don't know where they are," he said in a pained whisper. "I need you to get the hell outta here. Go to your friend Kelley's house. I'll find the kids, and I'll be there soon." He closed his eyes tightly as if trying to fight back tears. "Meredith, no matter what happens, don't leave there."

A look of brief understanding flashed across her face. She slumped against the wall, the fight all but gone from her. "It's Mother, isn't it? She's dead. She hasn't been feeling well. Oh my God! I shouldn't have asked her to travel, especially with her asthma, and—"

"I need you to get the hell out of here, Meredith! We don't have time for this."

"But the kids, Jay? Where are our children? Why aren't they here?"

"I'm sure they ran to one of the neighbors for help. Just get out of here!"

"Why? Why do I have to leave? Call an ambulance, and I'll go next door to look for the kids."

They were running out of time, and Jay didn't know what had happened to his children, he could only imagine the worst. He grabbed Meredith's arms with more pressure than necessary. With his face only inches from hers, he hissed at her, the warmth of his breath covering her nose and mouth. "It wasn't asthma, Meredith. Your mother's been murdered, brutally murdered, and we might be next if we don't leave. Now get the fuck out of here and go straight to Kelley's! I'll find the kids and meet you there!"

"She was mur-murdered? The kids! Oh, sweet Jesus!"

She made one last exhaustive attempt to reach the bedroom, but Jay pulled her to the front door, catching her as she stumbled.

"If they were going to kill the kids, they'd be lying in there too. Now go, Meredith! You have to get out of here."

"But you and my moth…Mom. I can't just leave you here."

"Get out!" he screamed, his voice raspy and demanding.

This time, with the keys shaking in her hands, she did what he asked, and the smoking, piece-of-shit van skidded out of the driveway.

For a brief moment, Jay forgot about the kids and his mother-in-law and prayed the van wouldn't break down on the road, leaving his wife a sitting duck. The thought was short-lived as he made his way back into the cramped brick house. His feet seemed to be on autopilot, and he found himself in the back bedroom before his mind seemed to catch up with his actions. Jay nervously stood over his wife's mother. A wave of nausea washed over him again, but this time he was able to keep it at bay. There was no note, which was to be expected. He didn't need a written explanation of who'd done it or why. The murder was all the message he needed. He knew his kids would be next if he couldn't locate that fucking bounty hunter.

His mother-in-law had been laid ceremoniously on the bed. *The bed I share with my wife, for God's sake.* She'd clearly been tortured. Several of her fingers were distorted from painful breaks, and the cigarette burns on her body were too numerous to count. The most unbearable part, however, was she'd been disemboweled. He wouldn't need an autopsy to tell him it'd happened before she'd died. He wasn't sure how long anyone could survive like that, but he hoped the shock would've made her pass out.

His next call was to Sergeant Hill on his direct line. Jay wanted the Sarge to know first, so he'd at least be able to find a familiar face in what was sure to become a circus.

Figuring he had somewhere between five and seven minutes before the cavalry arrived, he walked out into the brisk, fall air. He was having one of those out-of-body experiences the quacks talked about on daytime talk shows. His modest home now seemed welcoming and wonderfully familiar. The tricycles, bikes, and rusting swing set seemed to make the house a home, whereas before, they were simply one more thing to move out of his way when he was mowing the grass. He suddenly longed for a Saturday afternoon to grill burgers with the kids and trim the long, out-of-control shrubs. That longing was short-lived, as the sounds of the sirens heading his way broke the silence. Life as he knew it would soon be gone forever, but no one could've calculated what Jay Sykes would've given to have his old life back—the life before Mad Dog, the one where the bills were high, but he still had his character, his integrity.

There wasn't any time for those thoughts now. The circus had arrived.

Chapter 31

The soda and stale honey bun did little to smooth over the fact that a young girl lay dead in the basement below. Anne and Reid's conversation, though limited, didn't include her. As Reid picked up the remaining crumbs with his forefinger and thumb, the inevitable came up.

"I guess we'd better get downstairs," Anne said, standing to push the plastic chair back under the table.

They made their way to the elevator in silence, both contemplating what was going on. Reid had his cop theories while Anne had to rely on her medical ones, but neither really had answers.

Lauren was, of course, still lying on the cold metal gurney, even though Reid halfway expected her to be gone.

Anne flipped on the bright fluorescent lights that ironically seemed to bring the place to life. "Here…put this on," she said, handing him a new set of crisp paper coveralls. She put hers on and donned a surgical mask.

"Why all the precautions? You didn't do this last time."

"We didn't do an invasive autopsy before. You never know what you're up against when you're dealing with bodily fluids."

"So you think it could be some type of poisoning?"

"I'm not saying that, but anything is possible. We simply don't know. I was convinced of a heart attack with Joanna, but this time...well, let's just say it leaves me feeling uneasy."

"Where do we begin?"

"I'm going to draw blood and tissue and request all the toxicology results I can."

"All you *can*?"

He watched as Anne filled vial after vial with blood, her glasses perched on her nose just above her surgical mask. He could make out steady breaths as the mask moved slowly back and forth.

"All the State will fund and all I can justify. I can't imagine all the hell we're going to catch when Henry gets back from wherever his vacation took him. He doesn't like to feel as though anyone has gone over his head."

"Gone over his head? You've got to be kidding me! Who the hell cares? You're a doctor—a *real* one, I might add—and this is a real, unexplained death. I'm hardly concerned about feelings."

She looked up over the top of her spectacles and stared at him just long enough for him to take her seriously. "I refuse to give you the this-isn't-Atlanta speech again, Reid. Frankly, it's getting exhausting. But even in big cities, they have things called...um, what's that word? I think it's *protocol*."

"Protocol? What about those other big words, like *ethics* and *liability*?"

She walked over to a stainless steel pushcart, carefully laid down the vials of blood, then pulled the cart back with her to the autopsy table. Reid started to open his mouth, but thought better of it. He'd overstepped his bounds, and the last thing he wanted was to isolate their working relationship.

"I think I know you well enough to realize you didn't mean to sound so condescending. I prefer to think you're simply passionate about your job. However, no man—not even a Sheriff—is an island. Henry Hartwell may not be a well-educated doctor or even a certified paramedic, but this town elected him to hold the position of coroner. There are laws and chains of command that must be followed, we've just been fortunate that he was unavailable."

"Forgive me," Reid said sincerely. "This is a different struggle for me, a whole new ball game. I just want to do my job."

"Somehow, Reid, I don't think this struggle is much different from your others. You strike me as the kind of man who's been fighting for truth and justice in an unjust world for quite some time."

"Just your average, but exceptionally good-looking superhero," he said with a laugh. "Now, enough about Henry. Let's find out what took this girl from her parents. What tests can we justifiably run?"

"I'd start with testing for illegal drugs, but that's limited to your basic, commonly abused substances, like marijuana, barbiturates, and cocaine. I'll also test her potassium levels."

"What will that tell us?"

"I still can't let go of the possibility this could be the result of excessive dieting. They were young, thin, overactive girls. If their potassium is low, it could be from dehydration, which could point toward water pills or laxatives, both common in eating disorders. Our bodies automatically carry water weight, but for someone who desperately wants to be thin, losing it can make a visible difference."

154

"Won't you be able to find those pills in her stomach?"

"That's extremely iffy, especially with liquid laxatives. They go right into the GI tract, and death would have to occur anywhere from within ten to twenty minutes for us to find it. Chances are, if there's potassium depletion, it's been an ongoing process and wouldn't necessarily have killed her right after ingestion."

"What about other food contents?"

"It takes about an hour for the digestive process to begin. Food should be out of one's system within twelve to twenty-four hours, but some undigested particles can still be found three to four days after death. In that case, the putrefaction is great."

"Sounds appetizing."

"Her death only took place eight hours ago. We may get lucky, but if she took tablets as opposed to caplets, they would've dissolved in the system more quickly."

"Can you do the blood tests yourself?"

Her cynical look gave the answer away, but she responded anyway. "They have to be sent off, but if we're lucky, some of them will be back within three to four days."

"Hmm."

"Have you ever seen an autopsy? I'm tired and not particularly in the mood to take care of a nauseous man."

"Yes," he answered resentfully. "I've seen more than I can count, and I don't appreciate being patronized. Let's get on with it, shall we, Doctor?"

Chapter 32

The circus had arrived indeed, and cops were swarming around like fans at a red carpet event. As sick as it was, many of them lived to see a brutal murder, but few rarely had the opportunity.

Jay was slumped on the front porch steps, his elbows resting on his thighs, wearing a look of shock impossible to feign. He was grateful to see Sergeant Hill approaching, turning occasionally to keep the others a few paces behind.

"Where's Meredith?" the Sergeant asked.

"I sent her to a friend's. I haven't found the children yet."

"I'm sure they're safe, or else you woulda found 'em. How bad is it?"

"Real bad. She was…tortured. Those bastards gutted my mother-in-law like a fish right here in the house I share with my family, Sarge."

"Son-of-a-bitch. I'm sorry, Sykes."

Jay turned and looked around at the growing crowd. With the excess of police units, the neighbors were coming out on their lawns to get the scoop. It wouldn't be long before the media would arrive like the blood-seeking sharks they were. Police scanners were big entertainment, and a murder would be top news, particularly since it was a cop's mother-in-law. The press would be practically salivating to get the story. It'd hit the early news, and before it was over, they'd go so far as to say he was *under an umbrella of suspicion*. That was why he rarely read the paper or watched the news. It all had to be taken with a grain of salt.

The homicide and investigative units pushed their way under the yellow crime scene tape the patrolmen were stringing around the yard. Homicide detectives were known by their fedoras, crime scene investigators by their hard plastic suitcases filled with state-of-the-art evidence-gathering techniques and tools. For some reason, Jay resented thcm both. Maybe because they held positions he'd never reach or maybe just because they were at his home. Either way, he wasn't anxious to speak with any of them.

Sergeant Hill lit a cigarette and tilted the pack, silently offering one to Jay, a comforting distraction the officer welcomed. "Wanna go inside with me, or have you seen enough?"

"I'll go, Sarge. There's something about a bunch of cops snooping around my place that doesn't sit right with me. It's kind of…violating. Know what I mean?"

"I haven't had the experience myself, but I imagine I'd feel the same way."

When they reached the bedroom, it was already filled to capacity. The clicking of Nikons reverberated in his ears.

"Looks like we're in the way here," Sarge said tactfully. "Let's sit at the kitchen table and talk." He'd eaten a couple of meals with the Sykes family and was familiar with the tiny kitchen, so he led the way. He took his jacket off, sat down, and lit another cigarette, a nervous habit adopted by almost every cop on the force.

"I've got to find my kids," Jay said, thinking of them for the first time in thirty minutes.

"I've got patrol going from house to house. We'll put out an APB on them in the next couple of minutes. Do you know what your kids were wearing?"

Jay's thoughts were consumed with survival.

"Sykes? You with me?"

"Yeah," he stammered, taking one last drag on his cigarette before snuffing it out in the ashtray. "I don't know what they were wearing. We just got home. Hell, I can't even tell you what Meredith had on, and I saw her thirty minutes ago."

"Here...have another," the sergeant said, tilting the pack in his direction. "Do you want something to drink?"

"No thanks." Jay took the cigarette mindlessly. "It's all just...so hard to believe."

"I haven't looked around much, but from what I can tell, it wasn't a robbery. Why would someone want to kill your mother-in-law? She hasn't even visited more than a couple of times, from what you've told me. Would anyone even know her or know she was here?"

"I've gotta talk to you about that, Sarge."

"Sounds serious."

"Yeah, about as serious as it gets."

"Let's go out back. There's no need for anyone else to hear this."

As Jay slid open the glass door, he heard the screen door slamming in the front of the house and the happy squeals of his children.

"Mom? Dad? Grandma?"

"In here!" Jay screamed. "I'm in the kitchen!" As soon as they ran in, he grabbed them both and squeezed them with such gratefulness that they tried to get away.

"Ouch, Dad. What's the matter? Why are the

policemen here?"

"That doesn't matter," he answered. "What matters is that you kids are safe. We couldn't find you two. Where have you been?"

"This nice man took us out for ice cream sundaes. He told Grandma he works with you, and you gave him money to treat us to whatever we wanted. Thanks, Dad."

Sergeant Hill caught Jay just as he passed out on the kitchen floor.

Chapter 33

It had been almost a week since the disappearance of his daughter and that piece-of-work bounty hunter. The gruesome murder of Sykes's mother-in-law had brought instant gratification, but even that didn't satiate his growing appetite for revenge. He was like a caged animal, pacing back and forth, exuding hatred.

Consuelos had four of his most trusted cops working on it, along with two FEDS. He knew he could trust them, but they weren't that good, mostly low-level grunts who had shallow hopes of moving up, something that'd never happen. He did get some information from them though. The FBI was almost positive that his daughter and the bounty hunter had been taken into witness protection. Even Consuelos knew that wasn't good news because the witness protection agents' reputation alone kept any of them from being bought. Not even the FEDS or the CIA could break into their operation. It was sealed as tight as a drum, and no one with any authority would attempt to touch it.

He went back to the filthy tenement and ordered one of his thugs to get takeout and another large bottle of Hennessey. He wouldn't be able to think clearly without filling his belly with junk food and his bloodstream with the strong cognac. He wasn't John Gotti, but he knew everyone had a price and that *no one* disappeared into thin air. The pieces just had to be placed carefully together, then he could set everything straight and move on to other business. Every day he tied up his mind with the bounty hunter's bullshit, he was losing money. He would have to find a different city soon because he never knew who'd turn on him and hand him over to the cops. *Just a few more days, and we'll close in on that bastard.* Of that, he was certain. He wasn't sure who'd suffer his wrath next, but eventually, word would get around. Mad Dog wanted the business taken care of, and as long as there were loose ends…well, anyone was fair game, even their precious families.

Chapter 34

Although deep in sleep, Nathaniel could sense a presence over him. He stirred slightly when he felt a soft fingertip tracing along the edge of his face. "Gracie? Is that you?"

"How'd you guess?" she asked, giggling. "You haven't even opened your eyes yet!"

"I'm magic," he whispered, realizing that day was just beginning to dawn. "Is Laverne still asleep?"

"Yes," she whispered back. "Can I climb in? My feet are cold."

Nathaniel slid over and folded the covers back just far enough for her to slide in. "I don't know if I can let little girls with cold feet in."

"They won't be cold long," she promised. "Do you like my new pajamas?"

"I love them, but when I was a little boy, my mom always bought me pajamas with feet in them. They kept my piggies warm in the bed and even when I got up in the morning."

"You had shoes on your pajamas?"

"Not shoes," he said, laughing. "They were just like your pjs, only they covered my feet too. Maybe we can find some of those here. We'll ask Laverne to take us shopping."

"I'd like that," she said, her eyes beginning to glaze over with sleep.

Nathaniel fluffed the pillow around her little head and kissed her lightly. "Let's see if we can catch a few more minutes of shut-eye."

A confused look briefly crossed her face, but before Gracie could question his meaning, she was fast asleep.

Reid was weary and desperate for sleep as he quietly opened the front door. The wind had picked up outside, but he hardly seemed to notice. After closing the door behind him, he slid out of his coat and tossed it across a chair, then looked over at Nathaniel and Gracie, asleep on the fold-out sofa. He'd almost forgotten about them being there and instantly regretted not being courteous enough to give them a phone call sometime the night before. He unlaced his boots and stepped out of them, feeling the cold that instantly enveloped his toes. The chill seemed to run up the length of his body, so in lieu of collapsing directly into bed, he started a pot of coffee and took a long, hot shower.

After pulling on an old pair of Levi's and a sweatshirt, he walked to the kitchen to get his warm cup of coffee.

Nathaniel was at the table with his fingers laced around a steaming mug, and an empty one sitting next to the pot for Reid. "Looks like you had a late one," Nathaniel said.

"You know what's so weird, Nathaniel? I haven't had any of those since I left Atlanta. I hope you didn't bring 'em with you."

"If I did, it was an accident. Want to talk about it?"

Reid ran his fingers through his damp hair and poured coffee into the mug. He held up the carafe to see if

Nathaniel needed a refill.

"No, I'm cool. Haven't had but a couple of sips."

"I don't even know where to begin. I just know I'm glad you're here. Sort of takes the edge off."

"If you're not too tired, why don't you start from the beginning? I've got nothing but time."

Reid did just that, starting with the death of Joanna Sibley, the debates about the autopsy, the vacationing Henry Hartwell, and the recent death of Lauren Lowe. When he was finished recounting it all, he said, "I just don't get it. After we buried Joanna, I'd completely convinced myself that I was just a paranoid, burned-out cop. Now another young girl is dead, presumably from the same thing."

"I take it Doctor Novus completed the autopsy last night?"

"As much as she could. It's just crazy here, Nathanial. No one even wants to consider an autopsy. It's as if they think it's some sadistic ritual. They don't see any need for it, and they think I'm an uncaring, ruthless, son-of-a-bitch for even suggesting it."

"Go a little easier on yourself, Reid. I haven't been here a full twenty-four hours, but it seems like a good place to live. Not only did you and I live in the city, but we hung out at all the crime scenes. Hell, even people living on the outskirts of Atlanta have no idea of the crime that goes on there. Do you think the people living in those lofts in Buckhead know that drug dealers are selling to kids a few miles away? Hell no! They'd be the same way if you insisted on an autopsy for their kids."

"Yeah, but I wouldn't have to. The medical examiner's office would have to deal with that shit."

"Oh, I see. Not so fun being the bad guy, huh? You feel helpless, and that's understandable, but you shouldn't take it personally. I'm sure you're a terrific sheriff, and they're damn lucky to have you."

"Yeah, yeah, but the bottom line is, we've still got two dead girls and no answers."

"Anything unusual in the autopsy?"

"Nope. Organs looked healthy, average weight and size, no injection marks or burning in the esophagus to indicate poisoning, and no defensive wounds. All we can do is wait for the toxicology reports, and you know how that goes. Unless it's the typical illegal substance, we're back to square one. Anne thinks it may have something to do with dieting, but it'd be a long shot to prove. The girls were healthy and physically active, but they didn't show any signs of malnutrition."

"Well, herbal remedies are on the rise. I can't believe so many people are still falling for it. It's dangerous as hell and not regulated by the FDA. They sell them for any ailment, from constipation to hunger control. I don't know why it can't be shutdown, but people can buy that so-called natural shit in drug stores and over the internet."

"We haven't found any capsules or tablets in the digestive tract or stomach contents."

"First of all, that may not be the problem, and secondly, you know how quickly those things dissolve. You said the second girl was dead eight hours before she was found and the first girl maybe even days. You wouldn't find any pills, tablets, or herbs in an autopsy. Have you searched their rooms and belongings? That'd be your best bet. Maybe you should get one of your detectives on it."

Reid stifled a laugh before explaining the totality of his budget and his undertrained staff.

"You've got to be kidding me," Nathaniel said, shaking his head.

"As with anything, Nathaniel, I've got to take the bad with the good. We're in the least populated state in the nation, to say nothing of it being the third largest. Technically, it has the same per capita crime rate of big cities, which leaves me with very few problems and, hence, a major lack of funding."

"Hmm," was all Nathaniel could muster.

"But it's not a bad place. In fact, I'm the happiest I've been in my life. I thought I'd miss all the big-city excitement, but I don't. I think that's why I'm taking this so hard. I hate to see this place contaminated. The people are so sheltered from the rest of the world. Hell, they rate Atlanta and Detroit right up there with Beirut, like they're some crazed, faraway places where people are just shot down in the streets."

"They may not be too far off," Nathaniel said with a chuckle.

As they finished up the rest of their coffee, the shuffle of tiny feet could be heard approaching. Gracie was rubbing her sleepy eyes and smiling at the same time.

"Good morning, sleepyhead," Reid said. "I saw you all snuggled under the covers when I came in."

"Mornin'," She said smiling bashfully.

Nathaniel reached down and pulled her into his lap.

"This is where I want to raise my little girl, a place with plenty of fresh air, nice people, and a good, honorable Sheriff. What do you say, Gracie? You want to stay here for a while?"

She thought about it seriously for a minute. "Yes, Daddy, I would."

Chapter 35

He sat down deep in the dog-eared leather armchair, sipping slowly on a bottled root beer, savoring each sip as though it might be his last. He had a lot on his mind, and needed to think. There were some critical decisions to make. Groaning as he climbed out of the comfortable spot, he walked to the doorway to turn off the lights. The darkness was welcoming, and it blocked anything from disrupting his thoughts. He didn't need any disruptions as he sorted through the deaths in his mind. It was exciting to know that he alone had caused all the hoopla in town, all the sadness and grief, all the doubt and curiosity. It was stimulating to know he'd caused all of it without anyone in town ever thinking he could possibly be party to it.

Joanna Sibley had been the most amusing. Maybe it was because she was the first or because the mortality of her death had slapped the little piss-ant town right across the face. As he took another thoughtful sip from the brown bottle, his mind drifted to Lauren Lowe. Her cold body was still lying in that makeshift morgue in the basement of the hospital, and word of the autopsy would be getting around soon. The Sheriff would take a hell of a lot of heat, and people would be shaking their heads at the Lowe family, wondering how they allowed their baby to be butchered. He had to give kudos to the Sheriff who'd turned out to be a little wiser than he'd expected. Either Langley was really convinced that something wasn't right about Joanna's death, or he was one of those arrogant cops who didn't want anything happening on his watch. Either way, the small-town sheriff would be fun to play with for a while.

After the final sip from the bottle, he stood to fetch another and maybe a candle or two. *Yes, candlelight will be a nice touch,* he thought as he settled in to plan the next big event in Hayden. He slipped in and out of the kitchen like a cat burglar for no other reason than to humor himself. The candles were in the hall closet. He grabbed four and carried them back to his den.

The room was small and sparsely decorated, just the way he liked it. It provided a quiet place to think, to ponder the day's events without the interference of a television or any tempting reading material. The dark, mahogany paneling and dark leather furniture gave it the appearance of a cave, especially when the fireplace was roaring. It was where his first plans had come together about the murders, small thoughts at first that later became a foolproof strategy, figured down to the last intricate detail. *They'll accept the lotion like I'm giving candy to a baby.* If the girls had given it even a moment's thought, they would've realized how odd it was that he'd give them a gift. *Ah, the naiveté of youth. It works every time.* It also didn't hurt that they'd been raised to respect people and not to hurt their feelings. *Ha! Thank you, Mom and Dad, for teaching your little girls manners!* It had taken over a month to come up with the lotion idea, but it'd turned out to be effective. He could just envision the young doctor and her beau, the Sheriff, trying to find a puncture wound or injection site. His only concern had been that it might leave a rash, but as of yet, word of that happening hadn't gotten out.

He'd successfully completed his first plan of action. The community wouldn't believe the two girls had died naturally, so it was time to step up his game and really get them going. The first two girls had the luxury of a quick death, but the others would not.

He'd carefully pick two more victims from his list, always young, pretty girls. The sad truth was that people didn't really concern themselves with ugly, unpopular kids. *Even teachers favor the cute kids and treat the fat, sweaty ones who wear hand-me-down clothes, nasty* he thought.

"Yep," he said aloud as he slugged the last of his root beer, "they really don't give a shit about the ugly ones."

Chapter 36

"Well, guys, I hate to do it, but I've got to get some sleep. I guess I'll leave it to you two."

"Good night, Uncle Reid," Gracie said, "or is it good morning?"

"I'll take either one." Reid laughed, standing to rinse out his coffee cup.

"I thought maybe we'd do a little shopping today," Nathaniel said. "Where do you suggest?"

"There's a small mall and a Wal-Mart about an hour and a half away, but I find the family-owned stores around here are best. Sometimes their winter clothes can be pricey, but they're high quality and worth it. Take a left out of the driveway, and you'll run right into town. You should find just about anything you need, from small cafés to clothing shops, from ice cream stores to liquor joints. The people are really friendly, but be prepared to answer a few questions. They know every name and face around here, so you two will stick out like sore thumbs. Your Southern accent won't help either, but don't take it personally. The locals just like to know who's in town. It actually makes my job a lot easier."

"I can understand that," Nathaniel said. "Mind if we borrow your Jeep for a few hours? I'll try to get my own car as soon as possible."

"No problem. In fact, just plan on using it for as long as you need to. I've got a patrol car and don't mind using it. I'll get one of the deputies to pick me up later and take me to the station, so take your time. This little girl looks like she needs to get out for a while."

"Yes, I think it'd do all of us some good. To repay the favor, we'll pick up dinner for tonight."

"Sounds like a winner to me," he said as he tossed over his keys.

As Reid strolled off for his much-needed sleep, Nathaniel nuzzled his cheek up against the top of Gracie's head. "What do you say we wake Aunt Laverne and take her to town for breakfast? Do you think she'd like that?"

"Yeah! C'mon."

Against Laverne's urging for them to stay home and rest, they headed to town. The weather and scenery were quite a contrast to Atlanta, and they didn't waste a moment taking it all in. Big, beautiful trees, still white from the previous night's snow, formed a warm, comfortable canopy, and the two-lane road wound like a well-curled ribbon as they took in the beauty around them.

"Seems almost too perfect, doesn't it?" Nathaniel asked of no one in particular. "Almost makes me leery. There's no such thing as perfect."

Gracie had her nose pressed firmly against the window, and small puffs of white were filling the air around her as she exhaled.

"Nathaniel, honestly," Laverne answered. "You're a father now, and pessimism can no longer rule your life.

Take the world as you see it, and you just may find yourself much happier."

A comfortable silence followed as they made their way into the small town.

"Not quite the big city, huh?" he asked.

As the town came into full view, so did the sense of what was to come in all of their lives. It wasn't a large place, but it offered all the necessities for just about any occasion.

"It reminds me of Little House on the Prairie," Laverne commented.

"Where's the little house?" Gracie asked.

Nathaniel and Laverne looked at each other, then back at Gracie.

"We're dating ourselves," Nathaniel said. "When was that? Back in the seventies, early eighties?"

Laverne ignored his comment and turned her attention back to Gracie. "It was a great television show. They make the whole series on DVD now. If we find it, we'll buy it and watch it together. That was back when they had wholesome TV."

The town square was literally that, shops that formed a square block, and in the middle were sidewalks leading to a large statue who must've been an important figure in the town's history. Green park benches dotted the snow-covered park, inviting anyone to sit for a spell, as one might have said down South. On another day, Nathaniel would have been tempted, but he had shopping to do. He slowly circled the block, taking in each store and the displays in their front window. "Kind of impressive," he said, turning to Laverne. "Seems they have the basics covered."

"Nathaniel, today's our first day out. Let's not make it too long. Neither of you are even up for breakfast out. Let's find a diner and maybe one shop, then head back to the house."

Gracie looked disappointed but didn't say a word. She was used to being out of sight and out of mind. She'd been taught her place early in life and didn't want to frustrate Nathaniel or Laverne.

"A-ha!" Nathaniel said as he read aloud the sign above the building nestled between a clothing store and the town grocery. "Dina's Diner. Why it even rhymes. Hope the food is good."

"Food in little greasy spoons is always the best," Laverne answered.

"What do you say we try it?" Nathaniel said, looking back at Gracie.

"Yum! I'm starving."

He pulled into a parking place conveniently located right in front.

A sign telling customers to seat themselves was taped to the cashier's station, so they chose a table near the back. Their appearance had already spawned a few raised eyebrows, so the less visible they were, the better.

It was only a few seconds before a young girl appeared, bearing menus. "Hello," she greeted them cheerfully. "My name's Cassie. You folks just passing through or new in town?"

So much for subtlety, Nathaniel thought, grateful Reid had warned them. He returned a heartfelt smile, knowing the girl meant no harm by her question. "Actually, we're staying for a while. It's quite a beautiful place you have here."

"Yes, it is," she almost murmured. "There's just not a whole lot to do for the young folks. It can get kinda boring. So where are you from? The South, I take it."

"Is it that obvious?" Nathaniel laughed. "I only answered one question. Guess my accent is more pronounced than I thought."

Cassie tried to hold back a giggle but failed miserably. "No offense," she added. "I like it."

"Cassie!" a man toward the front grunted. "I need a refill on this coffee, gal."

"Guess I'd better go," she answered over her shoulder. "Anything to drink?"

"Two orange juices and a milk," Laverne answered to her back.

Balancing a tray carrying their drinks, she reappeared within minutes and pulled out a tablet from her frayed smock. "So...what'll you folks have for breakfast today?"

"Any recommendations?" Nathaniel asked.

"It's all good, especially lunch."

They ordered more than they thought they'd be able to eat but ended up devouring the majority of it.

As Nathaniel attempted another bite of his butter-soaked biscuit, a middle-aged woman appeared. "Name's Dina," she said, reaching her hand out to each of them. "Hear you're new in town. We're so accustomed to the regulars that new faces are a pleasant surprise."

"Why, thank you," Laverne answered. "We're looking forward to a new life here." *What the hell?* she figured, knowing that if anyone could put the word out so they wouldn't have to keep repeating themselves, it'd be the owner of the town diner. "Unfortunately, a sad situation brought us here, but we intend to make the best of it."

"Oh dear! Nothing too serious, I hope," Dina said, leaning forward in anticipation of a juicy bite of information.

Laverne looked down at her plate and sighed a little too long for Nathaniel's taste.

"My wife was recently killed in a car accident," he lied, just as he'd rehearsed. "It was extremely hard on all of us, especially our daughter, Gracie," he said grimly, turning his head sideways to nod at the girl. "I'm fortunate to have a sister with no marital ties, so she agreed to come with us."

"Well, my sympathy for your loss. Hayden certainly is a soothing place, a nice place to relax and heal, but how in

174

the world did you ever find us?"

This is it, where the rubber meets the road, Nathaniel thought. *Don't let me screw it up this early in the game.* He cleared his throat and held up one finger as he took a quick sip of his juice. "It just so happens that I'm an old friend of your Sheriff's. He recommended the place for some respite, somewhere we can escape the horrible memories. So far, it's been great."

She patted him lightly on the shoulder and smiled broadly at all of them. "I'm glad to hear you'll be staying for a while, and I'm sure Sheriff Langley will take good care of you. If you have any questions about our town, just let me know. I've been here all my life. I'd tell you my age, but you being a single man and all…well, it just wouldn't be proper," she said, grinning playfully. "My conscience won't allow me to let y'all leave without also recommending Kaleb's Diner around the bend. They've got excellent food and are family owned, just like this place. We try to share the business. That's the only way to keep the peace in a one zip code town!"

"Thank you, Dina. That's awfully kind of you," Nathaniel said, smiling up at her.

"I hope you enjoyed your breakfast, because it's on the house today, a welcome-wagon gift from us."

"Thank you very much, but we couldn't possibly do that," Laverne said.

"You can and you will," Dina retorted sternly as she leaned over to admire Gracie. "My goodness! What a beautiful little mulatto." She smiled warmly. "You're just darling, little one!"

"What's a mulatto, Daddy? Am I part of an Indian tribe?" Gracie asked.

Nathaniel could feel the blood rush to his face, but words failed him when he opened his mouth to speak.

"Why thank you very much," Laverne quickly answered. "I guess we'd better get going. I'm sure we'll be seeing you again."

"I'd be delighted," Dina answered, not once considering that she'd said anything offensive.

Nathaniel held his tongue until they were out of the diner and on the sidewalk before he blurted out, "Why in the hell would she call Gracie that? How backward can you get?"

"Nathaniel, really," Laverne huffed. "She certainly didn't mean to offend anyone. That term is often used in places where biracial children are not plentiful. In Atlanta, they call them mixed. How offensive is that?"

"Well, it sounds demeaning, and I don't like it!"

"Just let it go. It's listed in *Webster's*, you know."

"So is 'ain't,' but it *ain't* proper."

Gracie grabbed Nathaniel's hand tugging him toward some of the town shops.

"Let's not worry about it, Daddy," she said quietly. "I'm different, but that only makes me special. I thought Ms. Dina was a very nice lady."

A stern look from Laverne forced him to agree.

"So…where to first, Gracie?"

"First? I said one store is our limit, remember?" Laverne scolded them firmly in her nurse voice. "You two should be in bed! I'm not about to spend the next week nursing you back to health because you refuse to take it easy."

"Okay, Aunt Laverne. Let's go in here," Gracie answered.

It looked like an old-fashioned five-and-dime, but it was large and adequately supplied. Nathaniel and Gracie went straight to the DVD section and picked out several princess movies. Laverne walked quickly to the other side of the store and gathered several workbooks for Gracie's grade level. They all met at the checkout counter.

"Looks like somebody's going to have a good time with these," the older cashier said. A genuine smile crossed her kind, wrinkled face. "Can I suggest some microwave popcorn for all these movies?"

"No, I think we'll be fine." Laverne answered. "But thank you so much for asking."

"New in town or just passin' through?"

Nathaniel suddenly felt exhausted. He was still nervous about the whole situation, and his health was obviously frailer than he'd originally thought.

"We're here visiting Reid Langley but hope to make it a permanent arrangement," Laverne answered as she picked up the paper bags containing their purchases. "Thanks again."

They could feel her eyes following them as they made their way out, but it didn't feel threatening.

Maybe, just maybe, things will be all right, Nathaniel thought.

They stopped by the grocery store and sat in the car while Laverne went in to pick up items to make dinner. Gracie was already asleep, and every few minutes, small whimpers came from her tired and recuperating body. Nathaniel felt the same way, realizing they'd overexerted themselves on their little excursion to town.

Laverne did her shopping quickly and was back to the car in less then fifteen minutes. "You don't look so good, big brother," she said. "Hate to say it, but I told you so."

"You must not hate it too much since you said it anyway."

She smiled to herself as they headed back to the cabin.

Chapter 37

As suspected, Nathaniel and Gracie slept for hours and woke up feeling almost as tired as when they'd gone to bed. Laverne was busy in the kitchen, preparing a small turkey breast with homemade cornbread dressing. It was a meal that smelled delicious and was reminiscent of home and the holidays.

"Didn't realize I was hungry," Nathaniel said.

"Well, just grab a piece of fruit to tide you over. It'll be awhile before the food's done. Reid called and said he'll be home within the hour. He sounded pretty bummed out. I hope it isn't because we're staying here."

"No, that's not it. There are problems at work, and cops tend to bring their jobs home with them. It's the nature of the beast."

The ringing of the phone ended their brief conversation.

Nathaniel picked up the receiver and answered, "Reid

Langley's residence."

"Hello, Nathaniel. This is Anne Novus. How are you making out?"

"Feeling a little rough around the edges, but mostly tired. It's Gracie I'm concerned about. I hope she's healing properly."

"I'm sure Laverne is taking good care of you, but I have some meds I'd like to drop off. They're samples, so no one will miss them in the pharmacy."

Nathaniel put his hand over the mouthpiece and quietly asked Laverne if there would be enough dinner for one more.

She nodded affirmatively.

"Listen, if you're coming over anyway, we'd love to have you for dinner. Laverne has made plenty, and we're expecting Reid within the hour."

"I never turn down a home-cooked meal. Let me finish up a little paperwork, and I'll see you soon."

Chapter 38

Even all the experience and knowledge the town sheriff brought with him from his big-city job isn't doing him a damn bit of good. In fact, it's probably driving him crazy that he can't be the damn superhero and make it all right.

He snickered to himself as he sat in his candlelit room with a root beer and imported cigar. "It's well past time for this town to have some more excitement, and it's my pleasure to accommodate them."

The dimly lit room seemed to offer him not only solace but a place for his deep, dark ideas to formulate. Laying his head back on the soft leather chair, he closed his eyes and smiled to himself. *This time I'll really stump 'em.* It was just a matter of how he'd be able to get the latest approved sleeping tablet into her system. Then, when the girl was sleepy and defenseless, he'd flush the poison down her ear canal with a syringe. It was really an ingenious idea, and he was proud of himself for conjuring it up. *They'll never think to look there during an autopsy, and even if they do, they won't find a damn thing.* During his very thorough research, he'd discovered the sleeping aid wouldn't be found in the bloodstream.

A sinister smile crept across his face as he felt the surge of arousal, though not of the sexual kind. He couldn't care less about sexual satisfaction, and he refused to be the average, overly profiled serial killer. He had a job and didn't live with his mother, stutter, or take trophies. He didn't need some shocking MO, some brutal, crude weapon, or sick little fantasy fetish. He was simply satisfied with how the town reacted. He loved watching the townies grieve and scrounge around like savages, trying to find answers. He wasn't a serial killer at all, for that was far too cliché. He simply enjoyed knowing that it was all in his hands.

Now, ...who'll be the next broken beauty?

Chapter 39

Anne and Reid arrived within minutes of one another. Dinner was already prepared and on the table.

"Mmm. I could get used to this." Reid smiled, his face reflecting exhaustion and concern. The aroma of Laverne's excellent cooking seemed to soothe his nerves a bit.

"Well, now that everybody's here, let's dig in," Laverne answered.

The conversation during dinner was generic, nothing to indicate the trouble that was driving the town into a panic.

"I'd really like to find our own place soon," Nathaniel commented. "I'm sure you're already sick of having extra bodies in your beds, and I think it's time that Gracie has her own room."

"You know I don't mind, Nathaniel. It's been kind of nice coming home to something other than empty rooms, especially now. But I understand wanting a place of your own. There are a lot of rentals around here, which I'd recommend first since it'd be difficult to secure a home loan without a job."

"Oh yeah. A job. I haven't even thought about that," Nathaniel said with a laugh.

"Speaking of jobs," Anne interrupted, "I have one at the hospital for you, Laverne—that is, if you're interested. They need some help on the geriatric ward."

"Wow! That was fast," Laverne answered. "I'd be delighted. Just let me know when I can start."

"How does tomorrow at 3:00 p.m. sound? I tried to find something on another shift, but 3:00 to 11:00 was the best I could do."

"No problem at all, but what do you think about leaving these two knuckleheads alone?" she asked, pointing to Nathaniel and Gracie.

"They appear to be healing nicely. I brought another dose of antibiotics for both of them and a small sample of pain meds, but only if needed," she said, looking at Nathaniel with a scrutinizing physician's eye. "It wouldn't be a bad idea for you to take a couple now. You had no business going out today, and if you don't take something now, you'll certainly be paying the piper later."

"Maybe the Doc is right," Nathaniel said. "I am tired, and my gut is aching like hell. How are you, Gracie?"

"Really tired," she answered with a yawn.

"Too tired for an ice cream sundae?" Laverne asked.

"Yes, Ma'am."

"Wow. That *is* tired. Let me put you to bed."

While Laverne busied herself with Gracie, Anne, Reid, and Nathaniel sat down in the den.

"Any luck with the autopsy?" Nathaniel asked.

"Hell no," Reid answered, "and I don't expect to have any. This place is so far back in time that I'm surprised they embalm people."

"Reid, come on," Anne answered. "You're really starting to piss me off, exaggerating like that." Turning to

Nathaniel, she continued, "We're waiting on toxicology reports, but to be honest, I don't expect anything. All I can point to right now is how obsessed both girls were with their health."

"From what Reid has told me, I'm not so sold on that idea," Nathaniel offered. "I hope that doesn't offend you."

"Not at all," she answered. "We need all the ideas we can come up with, and three heads are better than two."

"The whole world is on this weight-loss kick. Don't you ever read the front pages of the tabloids? All they talk about are either overweight celebrities or anorexic ones. There are all these fad diets, exercise routines, advice to drink lots of water and brush your teeth more often to fight off hunger pangs. Men's magazines are filled with ads for protein supplements, shakes to help you add muscle while losing weight. It's exhausting and just plain ridiculous if you ask me. But the diet industry hauls in billions of dollars every year, exploiting people's poor self-images. Still, when you think about it, how many deaths have occurred because of it? We could Google it, but to be honest, how many have we heard of? From what you've said, neither of the deceased girls were bulimic or anorexic, thin, but certainly not malnourished," Nathaniel said.

"So where does that leave us?" Reid asked.

"What unnerves me the most, are all these so-called supplements kids can find in herbal stores, with no prescription or age limit necessary to buy them. In town today, though, I didn't see any places that would sell those. Fortunately, it doesn't appear that craze has hit Hayden yet."

"If herbs are the culprit, then where are they getting them?"

"Easy. Over the internet. Hell, you can buy a baby over the internet these days. Not to sound old-fashioned, but I think it's the worst thing that's ever come into existence. The World Wide Web is just that, and everybody's caught in it like a damn fly."

"But like I told Reid," Anne interjected, "you have to know exactly what you're looking for in an autopsy to test for it."

"Some of them, especially the diet ones, are extremely large, like horse pills. They wouldn't dissolve as quickly as capsules. Did you find any of those?"

"No," she answered, "but even large tablets are absorbed through the GI tract over time. We haven't gotten to either victim quickly enough."

"My first thought would be to go through their belongings, even their underwear or private drawers, places where they'd hide things from their parents. Then I'd scour their computers and other gadgets and see what websites they've been visiting. Have you talked to any of their friends?"

"There hasn't exactly been time to do that," Reid grumbled. "I wish I could get you to head this investigation, Nathaniel, but we don't have the money in the budget."

"I'd be willing to volunteer my services to help an old friend until I can find employment."

"Sounds great, but of course I'll have to run it past the City Council and the Mayor. There's always political, bureaucratic bullshit, only on a smaller scale here. Some things never change, huh?"

Chapter 40

After the medics finally managed to bring Officer Jay Sykes back to consciousness and hydrated him with water and a saline solution, they were dismissed by Sergeant Hill. The two men sat stoically in the wrought-iron chairs on the patio. The Sykes children were being looked after by one of the female officers, who had four children of her own, and their mother was en route from her friend Kelley's house. At the moment, the family was no longer in imminent danger.

"I have a feeling about what you're going to tell me, Sykes," Hill said quietly, with both a hint of disappointment and sadness. "He had you on the take, didn't he?"

Jay cleared his throat. His thoughts were so tangled that they wouldn't form into anything coherent, much less leave his mouth. He looked his superior in the eye and simply nodded his head in agreement.

"Lemme guess. It started small. He knows you're underpaid, like all the guys on the force, and you have a family to support. At first, you really didn't see much harm in it because the perps walk as soon as we book 'em anyway. Little by little, you began to get in deeper. He had you in his sights, and you had no choice but to give him what he asked for. The threats soon followed, and as much as you wanted to stop, you knew you couldn't."

"If you knew all this, why haven't you turned me in?"

"I didn't know until now, Sykes, but I see it every day, and it always ends the same. Most dirty cops start out as clean ones. You didn't intend to endanger anyone or do any damage to the society you're sworn to protect and serve. But what you don't realize is, if you play with snakes, you're eventually going to get bitten. What starts small escalates, and before you know it, they've got you in a corner. Tell me…who is it?"

"Consuelos."

"Holy shit! Mad Dog? Damn, Sykes, you're in deeper than I thought. I don't mean to sound callous, but you're lucky your mother-in-law was the only one to take a hit. He's not finished, you know."

"Yeah, I know," Sykes answered, his face falling into his hands. He wished tears would come, but he was beyond crying. The pain was deep down, so sadistic that it wouldn't even allow him the release of shedding tears. "It's all over, isn't it? The job? Not only is my family in danger, but I'm going to lose everything I've worked for."

"I hate to tell ya, but that's usually the case. You'll have to face Internal Affairs and, quite possibly, a judge and jury."

"Son-of-a-bitch!"

"There may be a way to save you, at least temporarily anyway."

"Tell me, Sarge.

"We'll go to the brass. You can give the big boys

whatever dirt you've got on Consuelos. Maybe we can lure him out of his lair and prosecute him to the fullest. It may not ultimately save you, but it's worth a shot."

"I'm willing to do whatever it takes," he choked. "I'm a desperate man, ready to take desperate measures."

"Careful now. You shoulda learned about the dangers of desperation by now."

"Yeah, you're right," Sykes said.

Chapter 41

Consuelos knew his time was limited. He had to get out of Atlanta. He sent one of his largest, most intimidating men to pull one of his enlisted FEDS into the situation. He got up to pee in the corner of the room. *This is the last time I sink this low,* he thought as he shifted his feet so the golden spray wouldn't get on his shoes. He looked around at the peeling walls, and for the first time allowed his nostrils to really take in the stench of the hellhole he'd almost become accustomed to. Empty food cartons were shredded from rats scrounging around for the sticky remnants of leftovers. For the first time in all his years of living in poverty, he vomited until there was nothing left but yellow bile. *Yep, I'm outta here, and until I find that little brat and the son-of-a-bitch who took her, I'll live like a king. Maybe…Miami. Yeah, sunny Miami sounds like a good place to start.* He had enough money to get his drug and prostitute business back up and running, and with so many other issues going on in that part of the country, he'd simply blend in with the rest of the criminal element.

Two hours later, his goon showed up with Agent Massey, who had a look of sheer aggravation on his face. "What's this all about?" the agent asked brusquely. "I can't leave in the middle of an investigation, especially with one of your thugs."

Consuelos looked at him smugly. "You're here, aren't you? Massey, you're playing with the big boys now. Walking away is no longer an option. Investigation or not, you'll leave when I say you'll leave."

"I've got two hours before I'm due in a meeting I can't miss," Massey hissed. "What the hell is so damn important?"

Glancing at his watch, Consuelos grinned. "Looks like you better get your ass moving then. I need four Armani suits with shirts and ties to match, and it goes without saying, I'll need shoes and socks as well—the whole nine yards. Money is no object."

"They'll need you there to take the measurements. You know how that works by now."

Handing over a folded sheet of paper, Mad Dog sneered. "The measurements are here, and they haven't made a mistake yet. Tick-tick-tick, Agent. Your minutes are eating away."

"Don't you think it'll be a little suspicious for me to show up at the only Armani shop in town, demanding suits and accessories fit to some other man's measurements? Why not Neiman Marcus? Their suits are sharp. Only the trained eye can spot an Armani anyway. I can get in and out quicker, and no one will remember the transaction thirty minutes later. Besides, I assume since money is no object, you'll be paying in cash."

"Money is money as long as it's green."

"I doubt very seriously that Armani does thousands of dollars' worth of business in cash, especially in one transaction. It'll throw up red flags."

Consuelos paused briefly, and furrowed his brow, his mind obviously deep in thought. He didn't want to admit Massey could be right, but on occasion, his overinflated pride had to be put aside for the good of the operation. "Point taken, Agent. Order the suits before you go back to work and deliver them to the Motel 6 in East Point. I'll text the room number to you. Tell them the suits need to be altered by first thing in the morning. If they hesitate even for a moment, offer them a couple of hundred bucks. Trust me, they'll be ready."

"Do you mind my asking where you're going from here? You know things are too hot for you in Atlanta. In fact, I expect to see your mug on *America's Most Wanted* any day now."

"Miami…and I may need your help on that too. Like I told you, Massey, there's no walking away until I say so. You've been faithful though, and I know you want out. Just get the clothes and find a safe route to get me to Miami, then I'll cut you loose."

Relief washed over Agent Massey's face, and for a minute, he thought he might actually pass out. Instead, he nodded his head in agreement.

Consuelos pulled out a wad of cash, making Massey more than a little uneasy. Getting caught with that kind of money would be all the proof his superiors needed to prove he was on the take.

"I'll see you in the morning," the Agent rasped. "Just give me that text." As he walked from the filthy tenement, he couldn't resist the need to pull his lapel up and ensure the stink wasn't embedded in his clothes. He feared the smell wouldn't wash off his skin soon enough, no matter how hard he scrubbed.

Chapter 42

Neiman Marcus did, indeed, have the suits altered the following morning, pressed and ready to go. Massey needed assistance carrying out the packages, so he opted for his own personal vehicle as opposed to an agency-issued one.

Thirty minutes later, he was standing at the door of Room 29, knocking lightly on the door.

Consuelos opened it, looking much different from the day before. He'd sobered up, eaten a decent meal, showered, shaved, and doused himself with expensive cologne. With a thick chenille robe wrapped around his short, stocky body, it was obvious he was waiting on his clothes. He hadn't taken much with him when the manhunt for him had begun.

"Here you go, just as you ordered," Massey said, passing over two suits before turning back to the car to continue to unload.

Consuelos appeared pleased with his decisions and picked a gray pinstripe suit, a gray shirt, and solid black tie. All cleaned up, he looked like money, but anyone could tell not the honest and certainly not the old kind. He looked like a mob boss, making it the perfect camouflage for Miami. It wasn't that far from Atlanta, but he'd be a world away. Massey couldn't thank the Lord enough for that.

"What are the plans for transportation to Florida?" Mad Dog asked, primping as he looked in the mirror.

"A rental car is too risky because they'll require ID. I was able to hack into those who've stopped their newspaper delivery, indicating they're out of town for vacation or some other reason. I've got an address, but one of your men will have to pick up the car. Chances are, the vehicle won't be reported stolen for at least a week. That'll give you more than ample time to get settled and find something else. I don't need to tell you that it needs to be pushed into a river or left somewhere where it'll never be found."

"Don't patronize me, Massey. You can't possibly think I'm that ignorant."

Massey struggled not to tell the little wimp that he was nothing more than a lowlife psycho who'd stooped so low as to shoot his own daughter. He wanted to tell him about the real criminal masterminds he dealt with on a daily basis, but he was too grateful that the man was cutting him loose. Mad Dog wouldn't hesitate to kill him if he said or did anything that upset him. Massey was grateful to be single and not have a family that Consuelos could threaten. He reached into his pocket and handed Mad Dog a piece of paper with an address scribbled on it. It was a pitiful attempt to disguise his own handwriting. "Here's where your guys will find the automobile. I've got to get out of here," Massey said.

"One more thing," Consuelos said.

Massey resisted the urge to sigh. "Yes?"

"Do you have the capability to break into the US Marshals' Witness Protection Program?"

"You've got to be shitting me!" Massey snorted. "Good luck on that one, because it's not going to happen. The only hope you have is for your daughter or the bounty hunter to screwup and contact someone back here. That program is wrapped tight, and they're not going to fuck up their stellar record now. If anyone even suspected I was looking into it, we'd both be sitting in a Federal Penitentiary."

"Again, don't underestimate me." Consuelos sneered, "You, Agent Massey, are free to go."

The agent felt a shiver run up his whole body as the words reverberated over and over in his mind, *"Don't underestimate me."*

Chapter 43

The funeral for Officer Sykes's mother-in-law was very low key. A small obituary was printed neatly among the rows and rows of others, and because she was from out of town, it could be easily overlooked. A small paragraph of diminutive size was squeezed in a corner of the daily paper to verify a weekly, random murder. No one wanted to give Consuelos any credit.

Internal Affairs hadn't been shocked over Officer Sykes's betrayal. They were aware such turncoat behavior ran deep within the ranks of any police department. Over time, many officers were tempted, and as hard as they tried to hold out, it was like a strong drink being offered to an alcoholic, always hard to keep at bay. There were times it brought a mild form of sympathy from the seasoned IA officers. In this case, it was obvious Sykes had his reasons, regardless of how unjust they were. In the end, he'd lose everything: his wife, his kids, his home, and his job.

Internal Affairs Officer Cyndi Lloyd was assigned his case and given the important task of gathering enough Intel from Sykes to reel Consuelos in. In one way, she was betraying Sykes herself, by using him. *If he'd done his job,* she told herself in an effort to ease her conscience, *two people would still be alive and two others left uninjured.* For some reason, even that didn't make her feel a hell of a lot better.

Sykes remained a gentleman, reaching his hand out to shake hers when they met. His eyes were clouded over from days of torment while the black circles puffed heavily under his eyes reached as far down as the middle of his cheekbones. His baggy clothes indicated he'd missed a few meals.

"Where are the wife and kids?" she asked, her voice even and professional.

"With her cousins in Tennessee. They'll be safe there. We've never received even so much as a Christmas card from them at our house, not even a phone call in years. Nobody can link them to us. Sergeant Hill contacted them from his office, and they agreed to take my family in. One of Meredith's friends drove them down, and Sarge received the verification call they'd arrived safely." Tears started to form slowly, spilling over like raindrops onto his cheeks before dripping onto the interview table. Cyndi reached for a tissue and passed it over. Sykes took it, but balled it up in his hand instead of wiping away the tears.

Here comes the anger and self-pity, she thought. *It's all part of the process.*

"My wife is simply beside herself," he said, his voice cracking. "I don't think I'll ever get her back."

"I know it's hard, Officer Sykes, but we have to focus on nailing Consuelos. No one will be truly safe until he's caught. Maybe then you can work out your personal issues."

He cleared his throat and wiped the tissue quickly

across his face. "What can I do? I just took orders. I certainly wasn't one of his thugs, or mixed up in any type of inner circle. I would've stuck out like a sore thumb. The money was passed easily, either by him or another Hispanic man who never even opened his mouth. We both preferred it that way. The less I knew, the better off I was. I never thought it'd get to this point. Shit. I got my mother-in-law killed, and almost..." His voice trailed off in an inaudible attempt at forming words. "To be honest, I thought he was small-time."

"He is, compared to many others, but he's also a ruthless psychopath, which puts him right at the top of the list." Again, Cyndi noticed tears forming. "Listen, Sykes," she said sternly, "get off the pity pot. That's not doing anything to help either us. If you don't have anything to offer, you're just another dirty cop facing jail time. Pull yourself together or get the hell out of my office and quit wasting my time."

Sykes tried to hide his shock but managed to sit up straight and look her in the eye. "To be honest with you, I don't think he's going to come after me. Consuelos made his statement with that murder. It wasn't just meant for me, but for any cop stupid enough to get caught up in his schemes. He doesn't need me, for God's sake. What can I do to him? He's on the run for his life, and he knows I don't know a damn thing about his operation. You're right, I'm nothing more than a dirty cop. I deserve everything I get!"

Cyndi reached over, closing the file containing what little information they had. She took off her drugstore reading glasses, then stood, indicating that the interview had reached its end. "We'll be in touch. I assume we can reach you through Sergeant Hill?"

"Yes," Sykes answered, suddenly emotionless. He held his head down in shame as he walked out of the police station for the last time.

During the interview, Cyndi had lost any pity she might have originally felt for Jay Sykes. There was still a great deal of sympathy for his family, but none left for him. The real shame was that he couldn't even offer any assistance in finding the man who'd broken up his family and ruined his life. For only a moment, Cyndi Lloyd wondered where he'd go, but then shrugged her shoulders and quickly reminded herself she really didn't give a rat's ass.

Meanwhile, the Fugitive Task Force would keep their noses on the trail of all of Consuelos's known associates, in the hopes one of them would break.

"We'll get the bastard," Cyndi vowed under her breath. "No matter what, his ass is ours."

Chapter 44

The autopsy wouldn't reveal anything until the toxicology reports came back, and that would take several weeks. Anne's only choice was to release Lauren's body to Stephens Funeral Home so her family could pay their respects and put her to rest.

Reid sat in his office, looking at the messages piled high on his desk. He wanted to grab them, wad them up into a ball, and toss them into the trash, but he was the Sheriff, and didn't want to be replaced. In spite of his snide remarks about Hayden, he actually liked the place and his job, and didn't want to leave.

A knock at his door was actually welcome.

"Come on in!" Reid shouted.

"Hey. I hope I'm not bothering you," Nell said.

"No, not at all. Just sitting here trying to figure some things out."

"I know what you mean. Kind of reminds me of Jaws,

with all the town panic."

The comparison made Reid laugh. It was really quite accurate, minus the ocean. "We won't know much until the blood work comes back. We just need to be strong for the community. They expect us to remain professional and be detached so they can enjoy the luxury of breaking down."

"Yeah, I know. In a place this tiny, we're the only ones they can look to for guidance."

"You've lived here all your life, Nell. What do you think's going on?"

"Oh, Reid," she answered, instantly feeling awkward. She was unaccustomed to using his first name. "I have no idea, but there's one possibility we've overlooked."

"And what's that?"

"The sheer coincidence that two girls died of heart attacks that close together."

"Haven't exactly overlooked that angle, but for now I have to follow any leads pointing to something else."

"Um…" She hesitated as if she didn't want to bother him with her next words. "There's something else I need to talk to you about."

"Spit it out. You don't have to mince words with me, Nell."

"I'm a little worried about Maloney. He's young, Sheriff, and not experienced in police work. He's been taking this kind of hard, and I was wondering if he might need some counseling."

"Counseling? Shit."

"I'm serious, Reid," she continued. "He knew both of those girls, and he's been struggling hard to hold it together. Maybe you could talk to him."

"I guess it couldn't hurt. I'm just not the hand-holding type."

The ringing of the phone signaled the end of their conversation, and Nell exited quietly.

"Sheriff Langley," Reid answered.

"Hey," Anne said. "Stephens Funeral Home picked up Lauren a couple of hours ago. I'm going to have to hire a secretary to answer all the calls from people wanting to know what killed her. I'm contemplating leaving a message on my machine and never answering the phone again."

"May not be a bad idea," Reid said.

"Funny. I wish that were the answer. On another note, Laverne showed up thirty minutes early for her shift and seems to be fitting in well. I'm sure she'll work out just fine."

"That's good to hear. I like her. She's a tough gal."

"Yes, she is. I'll talk to you later."

"Hang on a sec'. Can you tell me how long Stephens Funeral Home has been in existence?"

"From what I know, about thirty years. Ira Stephens and his son run it. It's the most prominent funeral home in Hayden. Of course, there's not much competition since there are only two others."

"I might take a ride over there. I'm not sure why, but maybe they saw something we didn't. At the very least, they've got some experience with deceased bodies."

"That's kind of strange, Reid, especially since you're no fan of funeral homes. I'm not so sure it's a good idea."

"It can't hurt."

"Suit yourself. I've got a lot of work to do. I have other duties besides dealing with autopsies, you know."

"Really? I didn't know that."

A dial tone let him know she didn't have time for his foolishness.

He smiled and picked up his radio. "Maloney, what's your twenty?"

"Just left the station, Sir."

"Well, turn back around and pick me up. I'll be out front."

"Ten-four."

Reid grabbed a thick jacket and wrapped a wool scarf

around his neck as he walked out of the station. Maloney was already waiting for him, so he jumped in the car, grateful the heat was on full blast.

"What's up, Sheriff? Not another body, I hope."

"No, nothing like that. How are you holding up? I know this is really tough, especially since you knew both of them."

"Yeah, it's hard, but it's sad for the families too."

"What do you know about Stephens Funeral Home?"

"About as much as anybody, I guess. It's been around since before I was born. It's nice, but from what I hear, it's twice as expensive as the others."

"Are the Stephenses nice people?"

"Well, to be honest, they're not exactly the kind of people my family is on a first-name basis with. They live in a mansion right outside of Hayden. They don't socialize much, other than going to church, but everyone knows who they are and choose to use their services."

"So, it's kind of a prestige thing then?"

"You make their funeral home sound like owning a Mercedes."

"No, I'm not implying that. People tend to want their loved ones put away as nicely as possible. For some reason, many believe the more money they spend, the better off the deceased will be."

"That's not very kind," Maloney answered.

"Well, if you haven't realized it by now, I'm not known for my tact. I was thinking we'd take a ride over there."

Maloney looked like he'd seen a ghost. "You can't be serious," he croaked. "Why would we do such a thing?"

"They've been exposed to dead folks for years. Maybe they've detected something we haven't."

Maloney's face was still ghastly white, and he faced straight ahead as he drove.

"What's the matter? You scared of funeral homes?"

"I wouldn't exactly call it scared, Sir, just uncomfortable. It's almost like you can feel spirits in the air or something." Maloney said.

"Doctor Novus said Mr. Stephens and his son run the place. Do you know the son?"

"Yeah, Jonathon. He's a couple of years older than me. Guess there wasn't much left around here for him to do but join the family business."

"Were you friends with him? I mean…did you know him very well?"

"I don't like speaking ill of people, but—"

"Shit, Maloney, grow up. Law enforcement is about honesty and grit and telling things like they are. Was the kid weird or what?"

"That's putting it lightly. I kinda felt sorry for him because he didn't really have a chance with the kids at school."

"And why was that?"

"On top of the fact that his family is in the funeral business, he's also a bit, uh…girlish. That doesn't sit too well with folks around here."

"You mean gay?"

"I don't know for sure. He's just strange. He was a loner, always dressing in black like those Goth teenagers do in big cities. He was always pale, almost like he'd put makeup on or something. Looking back on it, he reminded me of one of those Columbine shooters, those misfits with the trench coats."

"And now he's in the family business, huh? Have you seen him lately?"

"Only at a couple of funerals. He kind of stands in the background and blends in. Every now and then, I'll see him at Phillip's, getting groceries, but that's about it."

"Did the Stephenses have any other kids?"

"Yeah, but that's kind of weird too."

"How so?"

"They have a daughter named Melanie, the hottest thing ever to set foot in Hayden. She has black hair and these dark eyes, almost black too. She was real popular, a cheerleader and in the student government—the whole nine yards."

"What's the age difference between her and the brother?"

"About two years. She's my age, but she never noticed me. I was definitely out of her league."

"Why'd the kids pick on Jonathon and not her?"

"I guess because she was so pretty and had so much going for herself. In fact, she ostracized her brother right along with everyone else."

"Where is this Melanie now?"

"Some big-time New England college—Tufts or something like that."

"Does she ever come home?"

"I'm sure she does on the holidays, but I don't ever see her. Last summer, I saw her in Kaleb's Diner, and she actually spoke to me. Made my week."

Reid rolled his eyes, realizing the youth of his young officer. *Hell, maybe the kid does need counseling.*

The rest of the ride was a silent one, which Reid preferred. He wasn't anticipating stepping into the funeral home any more than Matthew was.

The wind had picked up, and the sky was painted a gray, hazy color that hinted of snow or sleet. They pulled the cruiser into the closest parking spot, and both sighed before getting out.

"Pretty nice place," Reid said.

"Mm-hmm," Maloney replied.

Back in Georgia, most of the funeral homes were big, Victorian houses that'd been converted. Rocking chairs often dotted the large front porches, and healthy green ferns hung from the eaves. Those places had creeped Reid out too, but the Stephens Funeral Home was far more ominous.

It didn't look at all like an old, welcoming home. It was more like a fancy office building with a ridiculous number of parking spaces. Two polished hearses sat under the oversized carport awaiting the next funeral.

A doorbell rang as they opened the front door, alerting the staff that someone was in the building.

Mr. Stephens appeared from out of nowhere, like Lurch from the Addams Family. "Hello, Sheriff," he said, wearing a thin smile that didn't reveal his teeth. "I'm not sure if we've formally met, but I'm Ira Stephens."

Reid reluctantly held out his hand to meet the fishy handshake. *My God,* he thought. *A limp handshake says a lot about a man, and none of it's good.* "Nice to meet you, Mr. Stephens. I should've been by long before now. I need to make it my business to meet everyone in our town."

"And this must be young Matthew Maloney. I remember you as a high schooler. Now, you're all grown up and protecting our community."

"Trying to, Sir. Thank you."

Reid noticed perspiration forming on Matthews's forehead and hoped it wouldn't get any worse.

"What brings you here, Sheriff? Is it business or pleasure?"

Pleasure? Reid thought. *What kind of pleasure would bring me to a funeral home?* "I thought you could be of assistance to us in our investigation into Joanna Sibley's and Lauren Lowe's deaths."

"I'd help, but I'm not sure how I could. Isn't Doctor Novus handling things over at Mountainside?"

"Yes, and she's doing all she can."

"Then, with all due respect, I don't see where I fall into any of this," he answered.

Reid denoted a slight bit of animosity, and knew it was time to stroke the Crypt Keeper's ego. "Mr. Stephens, I'm sure you understand, like I do, the hesitation of the families to do autopsies. It can be quite a demeaning procedure."

"Of course," he agreed sternly.

"I've heard nothing but accolades about you and your business," Reid forced himself to say. "Even the best investigators and doctors can overlook things. So, I just wanted to see if you could assist us."

"How? I have no medical expertise. I simply embalm and prepare the deceased for burial."

Reid didn't like the man and couldn't imagine anyone else liking him either. He felt his jaw tightening as he continued, "I understand. I was thinking that during your careful preparation, you might have found some type of injection mark or something else we might've missed."

"We clean the bodies very well before and after embalming. I'm sure we would've noticed if there were marks on either of the girls. As I recall, we didn't see anything even slightly resembling that on Joanna Sibley. As you know, we received Lauren Lowe's body less than two hours ago, but we've already begun tending to her. It's against the law for anyone to enter the embalming area without a license, but I suppose this is an exception, since you are, after all, the Sheriff."

Reid felt the weight of Matthew's shoulder as it leaned heavily against his. Huge, half-moon circles of sweat were forming under his armpits.

"Would you like me to sit out here, Sheriff?"

Reid thought back to what Nell had discussed with him earlier and decided to cut the kid a break. "Yeah, that's fine. Mr. Stephens is already breaking the rules by allowing me back there. I don't want to take advantage of his good nature."

Looking relieved, Matthew quickly found a stiff-looking sofa and eased his body onto it.

Reid felt his own armpits deceiving him as sweat formed and dampened his uniform. He felt as though he was walking through that *Valley of the Shadow of Death* the Bible referred to. They passed rooms with waiting bodies and caskets for viewing, a few offices, and a large room filled with more caskets and cremation urns. His breathing became labored, like a pregnant woman practicing Lamaze. Mr. Stephens's smirk showed his enjoyment at the Sheriff being ill at ease.

They went through two more doors and down a long, dark staircase before Stephens opened the door to the embalming room. The cool air met them as soon as the door opened. Reid followed behind his ghoulish guide, step for clunky step.

When Reid looked up, he was face-to-face with none other than Jonathon Stephens. Everything Matthew had said about the man was on target. He looked like some odd character straight out of a low-budget horror movie.

Jonathan raised his eyes briefly and continued with his work. Lauren was lying on the large porcelain table that served as a shallow pool to bathe her, her head resting on a plastic covered piece of foam.

"Jonathon, this is Sheriff Langley. Sheriff, my son Jonathon."

"Yes," Jonathan answered as he peered through dyed black hair that obscured his eyes from view. "I've seen you in town." He motioned at his hands and rubber gloves. "Can't exactly shake your hand, so forgive me for being rude." With that, he went back to sponging Lauren off.

A chill ran up Reid's body, almost making him tremble, and the hair on his neck stood up. *Surely, this guy's not molesting dead bodies,* he hoped, staring suspiciously at the younger Stephens.

"The Sheriff wants us to scrutinize the bodies for any injection marks, Jonathan. You know how odd we find it that two young girls, your sister's age, were found deceased."

"I always look for anything out of the ordinary and nothing has been suspicious," he answered, his voice soft and feminine. "I look them over from head to toe and everywhere in between," he said as if it were something to be proud of. He continued to wash Lauren's torso without offering any other conversation.

"Perhaps the genitalia," Ira suggested. "That could be a possibility, could it not?"

The thought of either of these creeps examining the girls in such an intimate way almost made Reid vomit. His mouth began to water, and a bitter, burning stream of bile rose in his throat. He prayed it wouldn't come up and spew across the room. "I don't see how that could be a possibility."

"And why is that?" Ira asked, his face expressionless.

"Because it would've required someone to get close enough to them while they were naked to give them an injection. There weren't any defensive wounds, no unknown skin under the fingernails, no bruises of any sort, or any unknown fingerprints at the crime scenes."

"Sheriff, surely, you're not naïve enough to think that young women today don't have premarital sex. In fact, most of them are quite whorish, going from one young man to the next."

Reid looked at him, grappling for a response. It was a cold statement, and he was shocked anyone would have the gall to make it, especially in the same room with the young girl still lying on the embalming table. He watched briefly as Jonathon began rubbing the sudsy washcloth over her bluish-gray breasts before turning away in disgust. "Thank you for your time, Mr. Stephens. I won't be bothering you again. I think I can let myself out." Neither of the Stephenses offered a good-bye, and Reid was grateful not to have to respond.

Chapter 45

Reid spent the rest of the day answering phone calls and meeting with the Mayor and City Council. They were on the fence between a murderer invading the town and natural deaths. For a few brief moments, Reid sat there with them, swaying one way, then another. They reluctantly agreed to let Nathaniel assist with the investigation, but only in the background. That came as an unexpected relief.

Exhausted and exasperated, Reid headed home. He hadn't picked up anything for dinner, but was sure there were still a few things in the pantry.

The aroma of a roasting hen in the oven met him at the door, and he suddenly felt the deep pangs of hunger.

Nathaniel and Gracie were sitting at the kitchen table, with workbooks spread out around them.

"Looks like classes have begun."

"Yep," Nathaniel answered, "and she's doing quite well. I guess we need to get her into school."

"The schools around here are good ones. I think you'll be pleased."

Nathaniel's furrowed brow betrayed his worry.

"She'll be fine," Reid answered, reading his friend's thoughts. "Contrary to what you might think, this is not a prejudiced place."

A feigned smile crossed his lips as he gathered up the books. "What do you say we call it a day, Gracie?"

"Okay," she said. "Can I watch a new DVD?"

"Yes, Ma'am," he answered and walked over to put it in, knowing it'd keep her busy while they talked.

"So...anything new?"

"City Council and the Mayor have given me the go-ahead to let you assist with the investigation behind-the-scenes. Frankly, I was surprised."

"That's good. Besides that, how did today go?"

"Well, if nothing comes back on the tox, we're screwed, plain and simple. We'll have to let it go."

"So we wait for the screen. Patience is a virtue, they say."

"I might listen to that bullshit if it were coming from anybody but you."

"I still think you need to look into their computers and belongings. That might yield some clues that tox screens won't. If it's somehow related to something they were taking, you'll need to find it soon. It could prevent another death."

Reid told him about visiting the funeral home and his suspicions. "I'm telling you, both of them give off serious molester vibes. You should've seen the son giving that poor girl a sponge bath."

"Reid, everybody gets a quirky feeling when they enter those places. It's like entering a morgue. It's a place of death, and if you felt comfortable, I'd have to think there was something wrong with you."

"I know what you mean, but it's more than that. The

kid has a younger sister the same age as the dead girls. Maloney told me the kids in high school shunned him as a teenager. He looks like he walked right out of some vampire movie. It's weird."

"So what would his motive be?"

"Geez, haven't I given you a few already? His popular sister was in the same class with these young girls who probably snubbed him."

"Kids are cruel, and everybody gets made fun of in high school. They don't all turn into murderers. Hell, I didn't."

"Almost every school shooting has been the result of students being bullied or ostracized."

"You're right there, Reid, but what's that? One in approximately two million? We can consider it, but we shouldn't put all our eggs in one basket. A murderer could just as easily be your run-of-the-mill average Joe. Let's roll with the computer and diet pill theory first."

"I don't think the Sibleys or Lowes would object to us looking into their daughters' computers. They'd probably be more comfortable having Nell go through the girls' personal belongings. I'm sure they haven't cleaned out their things yet. I'll talk to Nell in the morning. In other news…have you heard anything about the trial?"

"Not yet, but I'm sure Nick would've contacted us if there was a possibility of it making the docket in the near future. I've been reading the *Atlanta Journal-Constitution* online, and it appears Consuelos is still on the run. If they'd found him, it would've made the paper."

"That's a pisser."

"Yeah. Right now, I've got to think of Gracie and get her settled in a stable environment."

"I talked to Troy Adamson today. He's a realtor in town and has a couple of rentals that sound viable. His office is smack in the middle of town. He said he could see you at 9:00."

"I'll be there."

After the men talked, the three of them, minus their fearless leader, Laverne, sat down for a good meal.

Nathaniel watched Gracie as she ate. He decided he'd asked Doctor Novus to take a look at her, even though she was much better, she was still awfully tired.

Chapter 46

The car that'd been lifted for Consuelos was an older Buick, about the size of a small yacht. It apparently belonged to an elderly couple because it had very few miles on it for its age. It was in immaculate condition, but reeked of mothballs. It wasn't what Mad Dog had in mind, and not at all the *nice set of wheels* Agent Massey had mentioned. But he hadn't been in a situation to bargain.

He loaded his small arsenal, fifty thousand in cash, and the new suits into the trunk before heading south. If he could make it to Miami without being pulled over on the way, he'd be home free. He had a few contacts there who'd be willing to hide him, offer some form of protection, and help him get his businesses rolling. Once all of the logistics were out of the way, he could concentrate on finding Nathaniel Collier and Gracie Elizabeth. Then he'd finally settle the score that should've been handled the first time. He did wonder, however, who'd buried Zandi. Her family had long since disappeared into the background, and none of her hooker friends could pay for their next hit, much less a burial. Zandi had once been a beauty, but he'd taken care of that. For some reason, Consuelos felt a pang of guilt, but it didn't last long. He didn't have time for emotions. They only got in the way of his work and his money.

His men in Atlanta were keeping their eyes on people his targets might contact. Nathaniel's mother was dead, and she'd been his only family. Gracie certainly didn't have anyone to contact, that left the nurse who'd disappeared with them. She was expendable, and with only a brother left in her family, she was their best bet. Wherever they were, it had to be isolated, and Consuelos was sure she'd eventually weaken and contact her brother if nothing more than to tell him she was safe. His FBI buddies could easily enter the brother's apartment when he was away and put taps on the phones and bugs in the room.

All I've gotta do is wait, Mad Dog thought. Even though he wasn't the most patient of men, he had no other choice.

Chapter 47

"Shit!" Anne said to herself as her office door burst open. She'd been dreading this confrontation for two weeks.

Henry Hartwell stood before her, looking as though he may jump across her desk and strangle her. "What in the world were you thinking?" he seethed, his teeth clenched so tightly together that she feared they may all break off. "I fucking leave for a long-overdue, well-deserved vacation, and when I come back, all hell has broken loose."

"I'd hardly call it that, Henry," she answered calmly, her face turning crimson.

"What? Hardly call it that! Have you lost your mind? The last time I checked, I was Coroner of this town, and have been since your mama was powdering your ass and changin' your diapers! I come back to a town in complete turmoil, young girls being violated by autopsies and families on the verge of suicide."

"Henry, you're overreacting. If you'd just calm down

for a moment and let me—"

"Calm down? I'm not just the coroner here, Anne. I'm a political figure, a representative of the people. It's up to me to keep peace, especially during death."

Doctor Novus found it almost comical that he considered his outdated, unnecessary position so important. "With all due respect, Henry, you were out of town, and I had to take the lead. This was an unusual situation, and it required immediate investigation. The last thing the Sheriff and I intended was to bring any unnecessary grief to the families. But as you're fully aware, certain things need to be done when a death is suspicious."

"Speaking of the Sheriff, his uppity-ass is next on my list for chewing. I intend to meet with the Mayor and City Council to have him immediately relieved of his duties."

"I don't believe they'll back you on that, and you'll only make yourself look foolish. You may not agree with the steps taken thus far, but both Reid and I did what was required of us in your absence. Sheriff Langley is a very competent man, and we need him on this investigation."

"You don't get it, do you, Doctor? This town won't tolerate such inexperience, and neither will I. If I were you, I wouldn't feel too comfortable with your own job security. Furthermore—"

"Furthermore, nothing," she said, cutting him off. "I've had enough of your ranting, Henry. There are other things that need my attention aside from the tragedy of the two girls' deaths. If you choose to impede this investigation by going to the City Council and the Mayor, I can't stop you. In the meantime, I have patients to attend to. Now, if you'll kindly leave my office, I can be on my way." She reached for her lab coat, put it on, took one last sip of coffee, and stormed past him.

Henry turned to watch her leave, his mouth dropping open in disbelief. Never in his life had anyone spoken to him in such a way, especially a woman, and he vowed then and there that he wasn't through with her or the self-righteous Sheriff Langley.

* * * *

Reid sat at this desk enjoying one of Dina's famous tuna melts. Just as he took his third bite, the door slammed open. His first reaction was to jump up and come out swinging, but then realized it was Henry Hartwell. Reid casually reached down, picked up a chip, and chewed on it slowly, a move that only seemed to agitate the coroner more.

"Of all of the nerve!" Henry spat. "You certainly don't know your place around here, do you, Langely?"

"I prefer *Sheriff*," Reid answered condescendingly.

"Well, your *preferences* are soon to come to an end if I have anything to say about it. What makes you think you can come in here and violate this town, tellin' families what to do with their dead?"

"Hmm..." Reid pondered, holding back a smile. "Maybe because I'm the *Sheriff*."

"You stuck-up son-of-a-bitch. You've done more harm to this town than good. Things were never this bad in Hayden till you got here with all your big-city bullshit."

"That's pretty harsh, don't you think, Henry? How old is this town anyway? A century or two?"

"I refuse to have a battle of wits with the witless. Just know that you and that doctor friend of yours haven't heard the last of me!" he retorted as he slammed the door again.

Reid stifled a laugh. If Henry hadn't looked so harmless, it wouldn't have been nearly as funny. He was short and more than a few pounds overweight. His hair hadn't been kind, leaving him only a few wisps around the circumference of his head. He was always perspiring and stressed as if he were carrying the safety of the entire town on his shoulders. Reid expected him to have a massive heart attack any day. *Of course, that'll probably be my fault too*, he thought.

Chapter 48

Jeremy Lewis lay on his couch, watching a rerun of *Cheers,* one of the shows he'd always enjoyed with his sister, Laverne. He missed her terribly, but wasn't worried about her safety. The US Marshals had made him comfortable with the process and had assured him she was in a much safer place than Atlanta. It was still strange to him that she'd gotten caught up in such a situation, but he knew it wouldn't last forever. Jeremy was certain that as soon as the trial was over, she'd be back in Georgia, working at the hospital. Then they'd be able to sit together again, laughing over sitcoms, eating takeout, and reminiscing about their childhood.

When Jeremy heard the doorbell ring, he sat up slowly and took a quick sip of his beer before making his way to the door. He didn't bother to ask who it was. He had several buddies who stopped by unannounced for a drink several times a week on their way home from work. The lock was twisted and the knob half-turned when the door pushed him unexpectedly to the floor. He tried to jump up to challenge his attackers, but they were on him before he could sit up. "What the fu—"

"Where's your sister?" the intruder demanded.

Jeremy's mind was racing, and for a moment, he couldn't even comprehend the question.

A large, tight fist made contact with his cheekbone, making his head swirl with pain. "There will be many more of those if you don't tell us where she is!"

"I-I..." he attempted to answer, but his words trailed off as warm, salty tears streamed down his cheeks from both pain and fear.

Another blow followed, this time causing a long laceration across his face. He could feel blood flowing from the deep gash.

"I-I-really-don't-know. Witness Protection, I think," he gasped. "That's all I know. I can't talk to her. I've got no idea where they took her." He wasn't sure how many people had broken into his house because his vision was blurred, but they were all over him, pounding and kicking him with brutal strength.

"Why is she in Witness Protection?" a deep voice demanded.

"I...man, I-I-can't-breathe," he said, hissing and gasping. Jeremy spat mouthfuls of blood out onto the carpet.

"Pull him up," the same voice demanded. "Give him a minute to catch his damn breath."

As waves of nausea threatened unconsciousness, Jeremy prayed for a few more minutes of clarity before he blacked out. "Somebody tried to kill his daughter, and...the police...they're looking for him, so she—"

"Where did they take her?"

"I told you already, I don't know!" he shouted. "I guess this is why they kept me in the dark."

"I don't think he knows a damn thing," the deep voice insisted. "Let's just finish him off and get the hell outta here."

Then, just like that, everything went black.

* * * *

Jeremy woke up to the glare of bright fluorescent lights in a hospital room. His eyelids felt heavy, and small slits were all he could manage to see through. Pain radiated throughout his body, and he let out a pitiful yelp, loud enough to alert a passing nurse, who rushed to his bedside.

"Hello there, Mr. Lewis," the nurse said kindly, leaning down to talk softly into his ear. "My name is Rose, and I'm a friend of your sister's. They tell me you ran into some pretty dangerous men. Lucky for you, a group of your friends came by and scared them off. If your drinking buddies hadn't shown up to bum a beer, you might not be here with us today."

"Is-sh-she-okay? Laverne?"

"I'm not exactly sure about any of that, but there's a man I'm supposed to contact now that you're awake."

"Please call him now. She may be in danger."

"I think everyone is safe for now. You're still on some pretty heavy meds. Just rest through the night, and you can speak with him in the morning."

"It's not safe for me here. Call him now."

"Don't worry about your safety. There are two police officers outside your door. Just get some rest now, and you'll feel a great deal better in the morning."

Jeremy looked at her as closely as his vision would allow and wondered if she was somehow involved in this whole scheme. He'd never met Rose before, and he had no idea whether or not she was telling the truth about being Laverne's friend. It didn't really matter because he was at her mercy. He didn't feel like he could even lift a finger, much less get out of bed to defend himself. His mind darted back and forth from the attack, to Laverne, over and over again, until he finally fell into a fitful sleep.

* * * *

The morning sun stung Jeremy's eyes, but he was able to open them wider than the day before. He wasn't sure if the pain had lessened, but he did feel more aware, more cognizant of what had happened. He stirred a little, trying to pull the sheet up over his shoulders, but the pain shot through him like a bullet.

"Let me help you with that," a man said, lumbering slowly over to his bedside.

Jeremy wasn't sure, but he thought he'd heard the man's voice somewhere before. His skin prickled with fear, and he knew not to speak a word. The last thing he needed was for the man to think he was going to call for help. He couldn't withstand another violent attack. Out of his peripheral vision, he saw a large body sitting in the chair next to the bed.

"Jeremy, I'm US Marshal Nick Solomon, and I helped your sister out of here." He paused long enough for information to sink in.

Jeremy heaved a painful sigh of relief.

"You're a lucky man. If it wasn't for your pals, you'd be six feet under."

"That doesn't sound quite so bad right now," Jeremy answered.

"That's just the pain talking. You'll be good as new in a few days."

"Laverne?" he asked frantically, trying desperately to sit up.

"She's okay, and everything is under control. Only a few of us know where she is, and we won't talk. Don't try to sit up, you have several broken ribs, and moving around will just make it worse."

When Nick paused again, Jeremy wasn't sure if it was for affect, or if he were contemplating what he'd say next.

"I have to tell ya, I feel pretty bad about all of this. We all knew there was a possibility they'd connect you and Laverne. We should've had someone trailing you, but hindsight's twenty-twenty."

"Who were they, and will they come back to finish me off?"

"We're certain they were some of Consuelos's goons, and we're just as certain they won't bother you again. From now on, you'll be followed everywhere you go."

Jeremy felt rivers of sweat running down his face and the middle of his back. The pain was just about more than he could stand. "What's a guy got to do to get some painkillers around here?"

"I'll get you some in just a minute, along with something to make you sleep."

"Wait..." Jeremy choked out. "Where do I go from here? Why can't you send me to wherever Laverne is? That way, we'd both be safe."

"That's true, but they've already established their identity in that community, and it wouldn't be feasible. That threesome is suspicious enough without you being suddenly thrown into the mix. Unfortunately, our best bet is to leave you where you are and see if we can lure these assholes out."

"So, I'm the bait?"

"It doesn't sound very kind, but I suppose it's true. We have to do everything we can to make sure they don't get to your sister. Get a full day's rest and a good night's sleep, and we'll get some mugshots over for you to look at tomorrow."

Chapter 49

With the attack on Jeremy Lewis thwarted, Consuelos was back to square one. He didn't like it, but he had to concern himself with getting settled in Miami. It hadn't taken him long to hook up with some of his established connections, and he'd be back in business within a couple of weeks. He desperately needed to find his daughter, a child who could easily put him out of commission, but his first priority was to start over.

He was sure it wouldn't be long before the Atlanta PD would catch up with his idiot henchmen who hadn't finished off the nurse's brother. When the police did catch them, they'd sing like canaries with the slightest threat of lockup. Nevertheless, Mad Dog felt safe in his new world, accompanied by old-timers who couldn't be threatened into dropping the dime on anyone.

But he had to get to the two eyewitnesses before they could seal his fate in court. He knew he'd eventually be caught, no one stayed on the lam forever, but without witnesses, the DA would look like a babbling idiot. Even as cocky as he was, Mad Dog Consuelos knew he was on borrowed time, and the uneasiness in his gut never let him forget it.

Chapter 50

Haley Monroe was very concerned about her appearance, sometimes to the extreme. She ran three miles a day and worked out diligently with the weight set her parents had given her for her birthday two years earlier. After all, her looks and well-honed figure earned her more tips waiting tables at the new sports bar and grill outside of town. Sometimes the men got out of hand, but even in their drunkenness, they never forgot to tip her graciously.

Needless to say, Haley's parents weren't happy about her career choice. To them, waiting tables in a bar was the equivalent of working in a strip club. But, Haley stuck it out because she knew it'd eventually pay off, and she'd someday be able to purchase her own greenhouse and open a nursery. She'd always loved working with flowers, and had been studying horticulture books since she first learned to read. Her parents' yard was a proud display of the fruits of her labor.

Since she wasn't due into work until the five o'clock shift, she decided to do a little weeding after her run. Gathering up her tools, she let her Pekinese out in the fenced yard to play, and went back around front to pluck whatever uninvited greenery had decided to rear its ugly head. After more than an hour, she went inside to get a bottled water, then quickly made her way back to the weeds again. The chill in the air didn't seem to affect her as she worked.

"Oh, this is almost too easy." He sneered as he watched from a hundred yards away. "A piece of cake."

Haley put the top on the water, replaced her gloves, and continued to manicure the perfectly landscaped flowerbed. She was pleased her pansies were full of color, ignoring the sometimes ugly winter weather.

An attempt at a brutal bark came from Curly, her dog, as he ran circles around her. The ornery dog loved to race through the front yard and tease her with his attempts to get near the road.

"How'd you get out, fella?" she asked, her voice reflecting exasperation. Haley went after him, calling his name in a discouraged tone. She knew he'd come back as soon as she yelled, loud and stern.

The dog distracted the beautiful girl long enough for her stalker to slip the already diluted poison into what was left of her bottled water. "Perfect," he whispered to himself. He was well aware of her routine, at least to the extent of tending her gardens. He hoped someone would see the grizzly event and be able to share it with Doctor Novus and the Sheriff. Things were about to take an ugly turn, and relished the thought of it.

It took Haley about ten minutes to gather up her irritating dog and put him back in the house. Letting him out had cost the snippy little shit his privileges of running loose in the fenced backyard.

He was about to give up on her retrieving the bottled

water, when she reached over and took an excessive gulp. It actually took longer than he expected for the concoction to take effect, and for a moment, he wondered if he'd held back a little too much of his brewed concoction.

By sheer luck, her mother came out with the phone, obviously a call intended for Haley, just as the symptoms began.

"This is good, real good," he whispered with a smile, but he knew he'd have to ease himself out of there without being seen.

Haley's thoughts swirled, and she fell over onto the cold, neatly-manicured lawn.

Her mother raced to her side. "Haley! Haley, are you okay? What's the matter?"

She tried to speak, but her mouth twisted into the form of a severe stroke, and her face sagged to one side. Her body was itching terribly, but her arms seemed paralyzed when she attempted to relieve herself from the aggravation. "So…cold," she whispered.

It was almost inaudible, but her mother was able to catch it. "A blanket! Let me get a blanket!" she wailed. The dial tone alerted her that she was already holding the phone, and she dialed 911 in a frenzy. "This is Alice Monroe. Please send an ambulance! My baby needs help! Please help us!" she screamed as she turned back to her suffering daughter.

Ice flowed quickly through Haley's veins, and her body began to convulse. Vomit spewed violently from her mouth. And with every breath she took, she aspirated some back into her lungs. The pain, mixed with desperate and futile attempts to breathe, made her plead silently for her own death. She fixed her sights on her pitiful, helpless mother and closed her eyes for the final time.

The ambulance raced down the short driveway and made its way to Haley, just moments short of assisting her. Even if they'd reached her before her final breath, it wouldn't have helped, the death she suffered was way out of their league.

Joe, in his too-tight uniform, leaned down to assess the situation.

Alice Monroe's thoughts seemed to focus on how profusely he was sweating. Joe always seemed to be perspiring, and she found it strange in the climate they lived in. But she found it even stranger to have noticed it while her daughter lay dead on the lawn.

Jane and Joe turned Haley to one side, and with gloved hands scooped the remaining vomit from her mouth. From their experience, they knew the aspirated vomit deep inside her lungs had killed her. There wasn't anything they could do to keep her from drowning in it. CPR would've been fruitless. A pulse could not be detected, and her lips were already turning bright blue from oxygen deprivation as her body temperature decreased.

Already knowing the tragic outcome, they placed her quickly onto the stretcher and loaded her into the ambulance. There was no hope of saving her, but it wasn't their place to make that determination.

"We'll need to transport her to Mountainside immediately, Mrs. Monroe. Please call your husband or a family friend to drive you there. Hopefully, you'll be able to see her soon."

The last thing they wanted to do was let the terrified mother know it was over. She needed to get to the hospital so one of the doctors on staff could take her to the *dreaded quiet room* and give her the news. That was not a job for EMTs, and neither Jane nor Joe wanted to deal with it.

Chapter 51

The charge nurse in the emergency room immediately alerted Doctor Novus about the young lady en route to the hospital. It was reminiscent of the other recent deaths, and because Doctor Novus'd handled the prior two, she found it pertinent and ethical to let her know.

Anne rushed upstairs, leaving important slides unattended under the microscope, to meet the incoming ambulance. As soon as she caught sight of the girl, she knew it was too late. Hanging her head, she whispered a few choice words, and headed toward Jane and Joe. "Put her here," she said, motioning to a small, curtained-off area in the ER. "Are her parents here?"

"Not yet, thank God," Jane answered. "The mother is out of it."

Anne attempted to insert a breathing tube, but Haley's throat was full of vomit, and she'd been without oxygen for far too long.

"What's going on around here, Doctor?" Jane asked quietly. "Do we actually have a serial killer in Hayden? I didn't think that was supposed to happen in places like this."

"Hush," Anne answered, a little harsher than intended. "Don't you dare let anyone hear you saying that. You'll incite an unnecessary panic."

"I'm terribly sorry," Jane answered, her face reddening from the sting of the angry words.

"Forgive me," Anne answered, "but we don't need a pitchfork mob around here. I know this is hard for you two, but we'll take it from here."

They slid Haley over onto the small hospital bed and wheeled their own gurney back to the ambulance.

"Another sad day," Joe said. "Another sad day."

"It's sad when anyone dies, but all these young girls?" Jane answered. "This is crazy. How many dead people have we picked up since we've started working together? Maybe two, and they were elderly. Most of the sick die here at the hospital."

Joe didn't offer a reply. There was nothing left to say.

Doctor Novus interrupted Doctor Jameson as he finished stitching up a small laceration, asking to speak with him in the hallway. "Sorry to bother you, but this is the third mysterious death we've had. It looks like she choked on her own vomit."

"I'm sorry to hear that. Have you talked to the parents?"

"No. They just arrived," Anne answered, her voice quivering violently.

"Do you need some help? All you have to do is ask."

"I feel…well, inadequate having to ask you, but yes, I could use all the help I can get. We need an autopsy, and it goes without saying that such a suggestion won't be welcome. It's going to be tough enough to tell the Monroes that their little girl isn't coming home, but to hit them with the autopsy…I just don't think I can do it by myself."

"No problem. We're all on the same team here. Do you need some water, maybe a cup of tea to settle your nerves?"

Anne shook her head. "No, that'll only prolong the inevitable. I understand Mr. and Mrs. Monroe are in the lobby. Let's go get them."

The scene they witnessed in the lobby was to be expected, a family huddled together in grief.

"Hello," Anne began. "I'm Doctor Novus, and this is Doctor Jameson."

"I'm Terry Monroe, Haley's father. This is her mother, along with my sister and her husband. How is she?"

"Let's step back here out of the way, where we can talk in private," Doctor Jameson said, attempting to sound emotionless.

The chapel would be a dead giveaway, so they opted for an empty room used for this particular purpose. Four chairs awaited them, the fabric so weathered that Anne's first thought was one of embarrassment.

"Please take a seat," Doctor Jameson said kindly. He stood beside Anne and crossed his arms, willing himself the courage to say the necessary words. "I'm very sorry. We weren't able to save your daughter."

The wails that followed were heart-wrenching, causing Anne to struggle back tears herself.

"This can't be true. It…she can't be!" Mrs. Monroe screamed. "Go back and check on her again. You're doctors, for Christ's sake. You can't just give up! What kind of people are you?"

Her husband's attempts to calm her only worsened the situation.

"Don't touch me, Terry!" she hissed, pushing his hand away. "Don't you even care that this hospital is incompetent? I want to see her! I demand to see my daughter right now!"

"She doesn't look like herself," Doctor Jameson said,

knowing his warnings were pointless.

"We'd still like to see her," Mr. Monroe interjected, much more calmly than his distraught wife.

"Give us just a few minutes, and we'll allow you to," Anne answered. "I'll send a nurse in shortly." As Anne left the room, she reached for the wall.

"You okay, Anne?" Doctor Jameson asked.

She fainted before he could break her fall.

Chapter 52

It was amazing how well the Witness Protection Program worked. Gracie's permanent records from school were flawlessly fabricated, and her immunizations had been given to her before leaving Atlanta. For that, Nathaniel was thankful. A school physical would've revealed her injuries weren't from a car accident but the results of gunshot wounds.

He'd gone by the school the afternoon before, enrolled her, and met her teacher. He liked the woman, who appeared very interested in her students. The alphabet was stretched in an extra-long border above the chalkboard just as it'd been when he was a child. Nathaniel asked several questions, then carefully brought up the subject of Gracie's race.

"There shouldn't be a problem," the teacher said sincerely. "I'll see to it, Mr. Smith. I'm sure I can head off any problems at the pass. Second graders don't tend to worry about race. They're very accepting."

"Thank you for your time, Mrs. Hoffman. We'll see you in the morning. Gracie still has some hard days, so please call if I need to pick her up early."

"I most certainly will," she answered as she walked him to the door.

Gracie was up an hour earlier than necessary, but so was Nathaniel. It was a big day, one he wasn't quite prepared for. He wasn't sure if he could handle leaving her at a strange school.

"I wanna wear my pink dress," she said. "It's my favorite."

"You'll have to wear tights," he answered. "It's cold out there."

"I know that, Daddy. You look worried, but you don't need to be. I'm a big girl, and I've been to school lots of times before."

"I know," he answered, attempting an encouraging smile. "What would you like for breakfast? Pancakes, eggs, or Pop Tarts?"

"I'm not really hungry this morning."

"Uh-uh, missy," he said, remembering his own mother's insistence that he eat a healthy breakfast before school. "A good breakfast will help you do better in school. It'll keep you alert."

"But I've never had breakfast before school. My mom never had time to fix it before she…before her car accident."

"Well, your new Daddy has all the time in the world for you. If I'm going to decide, it'll be pancakes and bacon."

"Okay. I'll try to eat."

"Go on and get dressed for school. Laverne will help you with your tights. She's excited about your first day too."

Nathaniel was filled with mixed emotions. While the

pancakes cooked, and the bacon seared, he made a peanut butter and jelly sandwich, filled a snack bag with chips, and placed an apple in her *Dora the Explorer* lunchbox. "Breakfast is served!" he yelled through the house.

Gracie looked like a doll, and Laverne offered a big smile as she entered the kitchen in her chenille bathrobe. Gracie was so excited that they were lucky to get a few bites down her. Each year was a new beginning, even at the same school, with the same friends. He was surprised that Gracie didn't appear to be scared or anxious.

The ride to school was filled with chatter. Gracie informed him that she preferred bananas to apples in her lunch, a problem he'd remedy the following day. She also hoped she'd get to color and listen to a good story at circle time.

Nathaniel, on the other hand, felt the knot growing in his throat the closer they got to the school.

"Wow! Look at the playground. Cool! Look how high that tower goes! They've even got monkey bars!"

"Gracie, you must be careful and remember that you aren't completely well. You have to take it easy. If you overdo it, you'll have to come home to rest."

"I know," she answered. "Don't worry about me, Daddy." With that, she grabbed her lunchbox and her backpack filled with the requested school supplies, which amounted to little more than crayons and a glue stick.

Her excitement was contagious, but Nathaniel still felt uneasy. *What if the kids make fun of her?* he thought. *What if they call her a mulatto...or worse?*

"Come on, Daddy," she said, pulling him by the hand. "I want you to show me my room."

He tried to walk slowly to prolong his departure, but she tugged at him relentlessly. The hallway seemed much shorter than it had the day before, and they reached her room quickly.

"Well, hello! You must be Gracie," Ms. Hoffman said

as she squatted down to look her in the face. "We're so happy to have you. You can put your lunchbox and book bag in this cubby, and I'll show you to your desk."

"Okay! I love school," Gracie proclaimed, taking in the bright colors of the room around her.

"You better hug your Dad before he leaves."

Gracie turned and squeezed Nathaniel's legs tightly. "I love you, Daddy...and don't worry about me. I'll have fun."

"I know, Baby. I'll be right outside at 2:30."

"I'll see you then," she said happily.

Chapter 53

Anne and Doctor Jameson gave the Monroes time to visit with their daughter. The shock of their loss wouldn't truly sink in until long after they'd left the hospital. A shot of Valium had aided Mrs. Monroe with her anxiety for the time being. She sat, huddled in the corner of the small, hospital room. Others looked on as if they wanted to offer solace, but their bodies wouldn't allow the movement.

After Anne's fainting incident, Doctor Jameson refused to leave her side. He tried to encourage her to go home for the day, but even before he spoke the words, he knew she'd never agree to it. He finally got the entire group together to discuss their next steps.

"We obviously want answers," Mr. Monroe stated harshly. "Could it have been a bite of some kind, maybe a poisonous spider? She was so healthy, but her mother found her working in the yard, and—"

"We'd like some answers, too, Mr. Monroe. To get a

concrete conclusion on what happened to Haley, we have to run some tests."

"Tests? What exactly do you mean? My girl is dead. What kind of tests could you possibly want to run?"

"Toxicology reports and maybe have a look at her brain and heart."

Anne felt the distinct wave of dizziness again and sat down in one of the nearby chairs to steady herself.

"That sounds quite...invasive, considering she's already gone."

"Sir, as I'm sure you understand, it'll be done as respectfully as possible. Three deaths in three weeks are quite troublesome for the entire community. Three healthy, young women don't die of heart attacks without a cause."

"I understand that, but isn't there any other way?"

"Unfortunately, we need to do this. I know you want to make sure no one else has to go through anything like this. Allowing these tests might help us put an end to it."

Mrs. Monroe rested her head against the wall. The Valium had thankfully taken effect, and she was close to emotionless.

Her sister stood and joined Terry, who seemed to be in shock. "Terry, I hate the thought of it, too, but you have to let them do this. Haley won't rest in peace if you and Alice have to live with unanswered questions." She patted her brother-in-law's hands kindly. "Let's take Alice home and let her lie down. We all have a hard few days ahead of us."

"A few days?" he whispered. "What about a lifetime?"

"Doctor Jameson, is it?" she asked.

The doctor nodded.

"Do you have any forms that need to be signed? We should get Terry and Alice back home so they can rest."

He reached over to the rectangular coffee table and retrieved his clipboard, thankful he'd already grabbed the necessary forms before coming down. He didn't think they would've waited around if he hadn't had them on hand.

Mr. Monroe scrawled his signature across the bottom and initialed on the designated lines. He reached for his wife, and a few moments later, they were gone, leaving their deceased daughter and any future joy behind them.

Chapter 54

Anne made a quick phone call to Reid to fill him in on the most recent death. "There's no reason for you to come up here," she said. "It appears to be the same thing we've dealt with before. I'm beginning to agree with Nathaniel."

"How so?"

"The answers may not lie with the bodies as much as the places where they died."

Reid felt like releasing his usual explosion of expletives, but knew it wouldn't help anything. "Maybe you're right," he answered as calmly as he could. "I'll go home and talk to Nathaniel, I need him on this. The tough part will be getting him in there without everyone becoming suspicious."

"To hell with them if they do," she answered, fed up with the whole situation.

"You're right. The hell with small-town curiosity."

* * * *

Reid found Nathaniel at the kitchen table with half a sandwich in hand, looking through ads for rental homes.

"What's up?" Nathaniel said, looking up from the paper.

"We've got another one," Reid answered.

"Shit! You're kidding? Where? In town somewhere?"

"Yep, right here in Hayden. Someone's pulling our fucking chain, and it's pissing me off."

"Don't flatter yourself, Reid. This is just some sick son-of-a-bitch who gets off on killing young girls, simple as that. The FEDS kill me with all that behavioral science bullshit, so please don't fall prey to it. You've got yourself a certified whacko here. We have to find him."

"How?"

"For starters, you've got to get me into the girls' rooms. There may be more answers lurking there than you think."

"The Monroes are the latest family to be hit, and I don't want to burden them right now. I guess we should start with Joanna Sibley's apartment."

"Then what are we waiting for?" Nathaniel asked.

"I'll carry you in the patrol car. It'll look more official to prying eyes, and there'll be fewer questions to contend with."

"Gotcha."

The ride to Joanna's apartment was a short one, and before they had much time to talk, they were pulling onto Winding Creek Trail. Reid looked for the apartment manager's office and found it in the small clubhouse facing the miniature pool. An older woman with dyed gray-blue hair was sitting behind a faux maple desk, reading an *AARP* magazine.

"Hi there, Sheriff," she said. "What brings you out here? Bet it's somethin' ta do with that Joanna Sibley, ain't it?"

Reid hadn't ever met the woman, but that wasn't

surprising as there were many people in Hayden he hadn't yet seen. Nevertheless, everyone seemed to know him and more about his business than he would've liked. "Yes, Ma'am. This is an old detective buddy of mine, Nathaniel Smith."

The two exchanged the usual pleasantries before Reid continued. "Is her apartment empty, or has a new tenant moved in?"

"Her mama and daddy already paid for the remainder of the lease, six months' worth, and demanded that everything be left as it was. Six months! At five hundred and fifty dollars a month, that's quite a lot of dough. I know it's a bit morbid and all, but I couldn't turn down thirty-three hundred dollars."

"Well, Ms…"

"Call me Lizzie. It's Lizzie Williams."

"Okay, Lizzie," Reid said, stepping softly into his next question, hoping she hadn't seen enough episodes of *Cops* or *Law and Order* to know she should ask for a warrant, "we were wondering if—"

"What're y'all lookin' for?" she asked excitedly, instantly alleviating any doubts Reid had about the search.

"Not sure. Just anything that might give us a clue about the cause of death."

"It *was* suspicious, wasn't it?" she asked, leaning forward in her seat, keeping her beady eyes glued on the two men, and perching her chin in her hands as her elbows rested on the desk. "See, I told everybody that, but they kept tellin' me I was crazy, claimin' it was just a heart attack. Now you're here, sayin' I was right about a murder or some kinda foul play or—"

"No, no, Lizzie. We aren't saying that at all. We just wondered if you might be so kind as to let us in for a few minutes."

"You're the Sheriff," she answered, pulling open the center drawer to retrieve a ridiculously large ring of keys.

"You got every right. Follow me." It only took her a few seconds to locate the right key. She opened the door wide, extending her arm as she motioned for them to enter. She looked more than a little disappointed when they didn't ask her to follow them.

"We'll let you know when we're finished so you can lock up properly," Reid said, all too aware of the scowl that crossed her face.

The Sibleys had left the place intact, exactly as it'd been on the day of Joanna's death. Reid was sure they visited often, hoping the shrine would somehow help them feel closer to her. Many people did that, often for years, sometimes even their whole lifetimes. *I guess it's better than the cemetery,* Reid assumed, glancing around at where the girl once lived. "You take the bathroom, I'll take the bedroom," he said to Nathaniel. "I've got a feeling we'd better make it quick. Something tells me innocent Lizzie down there is making a whole lotta phone calls."

Nathaniel rummaged through the bathroom with a vengeance. It smelled of recent disinfectant, so he figured Mrs. Sibley had cleaned it well. The drawers were filled with makeup and hairbrushes. The countertops held the latest perfumes and lotions, along with a small stack of washcloths sitting next to a container of Noxzema. A lone toothbrush stood in its holder beside a half-used tube of Crest. *There must not be any regulars sleeping over,* Nathaniel thought. *An extra toothbrush is usually a dead giveaway.* "Nothing much here!" he yelled to Reid. "I could look longer, but I don't think I'll find anything."

"Okay," the Sheriff answered. "Come on in here."

Normally, the two men would've felt uncomfortable searching through a young woman's panty and bra drawers, but their experience meant it was nothing out of the ordinary, one of those means-to-an-end type of things.

"Not a damn thing," Reid answered, "not even contraceptives."

Together they flipped the mattress, but it didn't yield anything either.

"Let's get out of here," Nathaniel said, looking down at his watch. "I can't be late picking Gracie up on her first day."

"I'll go with you. I can't think of anything that'd lighten my mood more."

"I bet she's the only kid who gets picked up at school in a cop car," Reid said with a laugh.

"She'll be thrilled, but I'm sure she's exhausted. I better go to her room to help her carry her lunchbox and backpack."

"You're kidding, right?"

"What?"

"Would you've wanted one of your parents to come to your classroom after your first day?"

"This is different."

"Why? Because it's *your* daughter?"

Nathaniel smiled. It sounded good to hear someone refer to Gracie as his. "Maybe you're right," he said.

"I know I am. That's why there's a line of cars in front of the school. None of the kids want their parents to embarrass them by coming inside."

After sitting in the pickup line for over twenty minutes, Nathaniel finally said, "There she is! Gracie!"

She was smiling from ear to ear as she talked to another little girl.

"Her ribbons are still in her hair. I was sure they'd fall out."

"You're sick, man. I'm telling ya."

Gracie noticed them and flagged them down with both hands.

Maybe she wouldn't be the kind of kid who'd be embarrassed if her dad showed up in her classroom, Reid thought.

They listened to the constant chatter about her new

244

teacher, her new friends, and her desk, which was apparently in just the perfect place for her to see the blackboard. She couldn't wait to tell Aunt Laverne how everyone loved her pink dress. "Tomorrow, I'm going to wear the yellow one with daisies," she said with a grin.

Chapter 55

After their rounds, Doctors Jameson and Novus met in the basement of the hospital. Neither was sure whether they were putting it off or hoping the whole situation would just disappear like a nightmare.

"Thanks so much for assisting me," Anne said, her eyes reflecting sorrow and exhaustion. "I'm no more a formal medical examiner than you are," she said. "I've just got a bit more training in pathology."

"Doctors are trained in a bit of everything. We're all that Hayden's got, so…well, we're all they've got."

"I suppose you're right, but one more of these, and we're going to have to call in the State."

They sipped lukewarm coffee as they stepped into their white surgical suits.

The opening and slamming of the door caused Anne to spill her coffee right down the front of her scrubs. It only took the blink of an eye to see Henry coming at them so quickly that for a moment, she feared for her safety. He was wearing muddy overalls and boots, leaving a mud-caked trail behind him with every step. Apparently, it was quitting time at his trash removal company. "What in God's name do you two heathens think you're doing? Obviously, you've lost your ever-loving minds. Do you know what you've done to that poor family, the Monroes, much less to the other two? I leave for two damn weeks—just two damn weeks—and you let the whole damn town go to shit. I'll be damned if you're gonna cut open that child on my watch! I'll take it to the Supreme Court if I have to. Don't think I won't," he threatened vehemently.

For a moment, Anne couldn't maintain her professionalism. She did something she rarely did, especially on the job. She laughed until her gut hurt and had to lean over to offer her stomach some relief. Tears flowed down her cheeks as she looked at Henry and wondered when he'd become so disillusioned.

"Laugh if you want to, but you're not going to perform an autopsy on that child!"

Doctor Jameson gestured at Anne, motioning for her to go into the office and get control of herself. Once she was on her way, he said in a stern, condescending tone, "Mr. Hartwell, I understand you hold an elected position in this town, but these situations require medical expertise. I have a signed affidavit from the family of the deceased, giving us legal permission to perform the autopsy. I guarantee you it will stand up in court. I also guarantee that if you thwart any of our attempts to do our job, I will personally have you brought up on criminal charges. It would be nothing short of neglect not to offer these young women and their families some answers, some vindication, and some closure. Furthermore, I will not allow you to enter this hospital and talk to anyone in this manner again. If you don't get the hell out of here right now, I intend to call security, and it won't stop there!"

"Why you...you little..." Henry sputtered and spit as saliva shot out with every word. "You're through in this town, Doctor! You might as well pack up your belongings and those fancy framed diplomas over your desk and get the hell out. You're done here!" Surprisingly intelligent enough to realize he was in over his head, both legally and intellectually, Henry marched out the door ceremoniously, with his head held high.

Anne finally had herself together enough to come out of her office in time to applaud her coworker. "I've got to say," she said, "I didn't know you had that in you. Quite impressive. Of course, you know that good ol' Henry will continue to be a thorn in our side, right? He's all talk and will never make good on any of his threats, but he won't make our lives easy."

"We're doctors. Since when have our lives ever been easy?"

For the first time, Anne studied Doctor Jameson's face. He was a kind man, an attribute revealed in his pleasant eyes. She figured him to be in his early sixties. He had two or three kids and several grandchildren whose pictures took up virtually all the extra space on his desk. He offered the type of bedside manner every patient hoped for, and was well-liked by all of his colleagues. He was also an excellent physician. Anne regretted that she hadn't taken the time to get to know him better. She'd never witnessed him showing any signs of anger or impatience before. *But it sure was justified. Oh boy, was it justified.*

"While you change those scrubs, I'm going to slip out of mine and get us something to eat. We've been through an emotional day, and this little outburst didn't help. Go rest in your office and heat the coffee up to an acceptable temperature. I'll be right back. Then we can plot out our strategy and go at it with clear heads."

Anne couldn't argue with that, and was already slipping out of her jumpsuit. She went into the bathroom and looked in the mirror, only to be appalled by the reflection staring back at her. Her makeup had long since faded away, and her hair looked as though she'd just gotten out of bed. She cupped her hands and splashed water across her face, then took her wet hands and smoothed down her hair. *Geez. Many more days like this, and I might as well go back to a large medical facility where I'd be surrounded by others who could share the workload and the heat.*

By the time Doctor Jameson returned, Anne was asleep at her desk, her face resting on folded arms.

"Ahem…" He cleared his throat, trying to gently wake her without startling her. "Still hungry?"

She rubbed her curled fingers across her eyes and looked up at him. "Yes, but what time is it?"

"About 7:45. I went to Kaleb's to grab some burgers and fries, and I got sodas out of the machine upstairs." He reached into the greasy bag and passed her a double-cheeseburger.

Anne opened it immediately and began eating as though she hadn't eaten in days. After a few minutes, her face turned crimson, and she apologized. "My goodness. I must look like a cavewoman. I don't remember if I ate anything else today."

"Me either," he said. "Nothing wrong with enjoying a meal, if you can call this one. I take the grandkids for burgers, but the wife and I try to avoid the luxury of cholesterol. I guess it's kind of a double-standard, eh?"

They finished the rest in silence before changing, once again, into their scrubs.

"What do you expect to find?" Jameson asked. "I know very little about this situation, other than the scuttlebutt winding through the grapevine."

"Then you know as much as I do. Toxicology hasn't come back on either of the other two autopsies, but that's to be expected. We found no attack or defense wounds, no injection marks, and no signs of foul play, other than the vomiting and diarrhea. The GI tract had absorbed any sign of pills. All we can come up with is that it could be either something herbal or a type of diet pill."

"Have you received the others' medical records?"

"Yes, and there's nothing there. All three were healthy, with no indication of heart disease. Reid and I came up with the herbal supplement idea, but we can't find anything to confirm it. He and his friend, a detective from Georgia, are searching the girls' rooms in hopes of finding something of significance."

"That may be the ticket. As much as I hate to say it, we'd better get on with this autopsy."

It took over four hours, but when they pulled their gloves off, they were no better off than they'd been when they'd started.

Chapter 56

With Laverne still working the late shift, Nathaniel was responsible for dinner, so he browned some ground beef, drained it, and added a jar of spaghetti sauce.

The noise of him searching for a pot to cook the pasta in summoned Reid to the kitchen. He was toweling his hair dry from his recent shower, and after pulling out an appropriate pot for Nathaniel, he sat down at the table. "I'm not going to call Anne, I'm sure she's busy. She'll let us know when she's finished."

"Yeah, she's got to be exhausted."

"Grab a beer and let's brainstorm."

"Sounds good. Get a tablet and some pens, and I'll put Gracie in the tub. She's tuckered out. I just hope I can keep her up long enough to eat."

A few minutes later, Gracie padded in with her pajamas and house shoes on. She looked like the picture of innocence, and one would've never suspected all the pain and heartache she'd been through in her short lifetime.

Nathaniel carried a pillow and a blanket and motioned for her to lie on the couch.

She did as she was told as he turned on the television, putting in a DVD. She was instantly engrossed in it.

Reid cracked a beer open for each of them, then sat down in front of the blank sheet of paper. "Where do we start?" he asked.

"You know, methamphetamine is a grave problem everywhere, even in sheltered places like this."

"They didn't show any of the signs of being meth-heads. If they were on the stuff, though, it'll come back in the blood work. Besides, they were health nuts. Why would they risk contaminating their bodies?"

"For years it's been used as speed. It would up their energy level and decrease their appetites."

"I don't know. It seems like a long shot. Also, we've never busted any meth labs here, thank God. I'm not sure where they would've even gotten the shit."

"Are you suggesting the girls never left Hayden? Come on, Reid."

"I'm sure they did. Haley Monroe, the most recent victim, worked out of town at a sports bar. But consider the statistics, Nathaniel. Meth is highly addictive, and the odds of them just doing it a couple of times to decrease their appetite is a stretch. I say we scratch that theory before we get lost on a rabbit trail we don't need to be on."

"Okay, maybe you're right. The tox screen will answer that anyway. The other theory is murder. Who would want to kill them, and how the hell is the killer doing it?"

"That's anybody's guess."

The steam coming from the pot signaled the pasta was ready, and they all sat down to eat.

Gracie almost fell asleep in her food, making Nathaniel wonder if he should keep her home the following day. He put her to bed and kissed her good night, but she was asleep without even feeling it.

A ten o'clock knock at the door proved to be Anne, who walked in and literally plopped down on the sofa. "Nothing, Reid—zero, zilch, nada. There's a smart murderer out there, and you two have to find him. The autopsies aren't going to help, that's for sure."

"I'm going to talk to the Lowes and the Monroes tomorrow and introduce them to Nathaniel. If they'll allow it, he can look for anything unusual in their rooms and will hopefully find something that'll help us."

"Do you think they'll go for it?" Anne asked. "They've been so adamantly opposed to and hesitant about these autopsies. It's almost as though they're afraid we'll dig up something that'll soil their daughters' reputations."

"Nathaniel has an easy manner. He's a charmer and I'm sure he'll be able to convince them."

"But they don't even know him. For all they know, he could have something to do with the deaths."

"Anne, I think you're too tired to think straight. Maybe you should crash here for the night."

"No," she answered as she covered her yawn with her hand. "I should get home. I need to be at the hospital early in the morning."

"Well, keep us abreast of anything new, and we'll investigate as much as we can."

She stood to grab her purse and coat just as hard pounding began on the door.

"What the hell?" Reid asked. Instinctively, he grabbed his weapon and turned on the outside light. "Oh, for heaven's sake," he said, shaking his head in disbelief. "Damn if it isn't Henry." He opened the door less than two inches.

Before even being greeted, Henry was shoving his way in, the stench of liquor strong on his breath. "I need to talk to you, Sheriff...and it ain't gonna wait," the old Coroner slurred.

"Henry, we have a child in the house. You've been drinking, and it's late. Let me take you home, and we can discuss anything you'd like in the morning."

"Hell no! I won't have you tormentin' this town. I can't even answer my phone anymore without somebody calling for my resignation. I take pride in my position, and I've never had problems servin' as the Coroner till now." His body swayed back and forth from the excess alcohol in his system, but he wasn't finished with what he had to say. He pushed his way further into the house, looking for a place to sit.

"Henry, you've been drinking," Anne reminded him. "Now is not the time for this. You might say things you don't mean, and—"

"I mean exactly what I say!" he slurred again. "You might think your some big-time doctor, but being the Coroner is my job. I've held this post as long as I can remember, and nobody's ever doubted my judgment before."

For a brief moment, Reid pitied the man. He needed his position to feel important and respected. Henry's trash removal service didn't exactly have people looking up to him.

It was then that the tears began. At first, there were just a few, which he wiped away with the back of his filthy hand, but before they knew it, Henry's tears were flowing in a torrential downpour.

"Shit," Reid said, more to himself than to anyone else in the room. "Come sit down, Henry. Let me put on some coffee."

Henry followed the Sheriff's orders and sank down in the recliner.

Anne returned with a wad of toilet tissue for him to wipe his face and blow his nose. "Now, Henry," she said, "there's no need for this. We can all talk like adults. It's no more your fault that these girls are dying than it is ours. We can't seem to figure it out, but we could use your help," she said in an attempt to make him feel that he was still respected and his duties necessary.

Dabbing at his eyes, he said, "I only took two weeks off. I haven't taken a vacation in ten years. I just went to see my sister in Idaho and my brother in Pennsylvania. Folks are unforgiving around here, I tell ya. One minute they're on your side, votin' for ya, and the next, they want to lynch ya."

"Well, if you think about it," Anne answered kindly, "that's how you've made us feel."

"I-I never meant to," he said sincerely. "I didn't mean to make nobody feel bad."

Reid handed him a big mug of coffee, and they sat in silence as he sipped slowly.

Chapter 57

Miami was certainly the hot spot Consuelos hoped it'd be. For the first couple of weeks, he lived the good life. The drugs were as plentiful as the women, and most of the scantily clad ladies loved the thought of being with a bad boy. They also loved the money flowing from his pockets

The trouble was, he knew the money wouldn't last much longer. He was beginning to feel the nervousness of his partners, and knew he had to finish his business. They wouldn't turn him in, but they wouldn't keep him around long enough to take the heat for him either. Once again, Mad Dog found himself living on borrowed time.

Back in Atlanta, the Fugitive Task Force was making his thugs' lives hell. They weren't difficult to break. Almost every one of them had active warrants, and with a few small promises, they'd turn him in. They were a little uneasy themselves, and with Consuelos in jail, they'd be safer on the streets. They all knew he was crazy and unpredictable, and didn't have any desire to be on the other side of his wrath. So far, the task force knew he'd made it to Miami, and since the Dade County cops were on the ball, they had no doubt they'd soon have their man.

Even with the fat having been cut from the task force budget, the chief begrudgingly agreed to send two of his top men to Miami. The only reason he dared to do so was because he was one hundred percent certain they'd be successful in The Sunshine State. Photos of Consuelos had been faxed to every TV station, and the cops in Miami were on it before their plane even arrived.

Consuelos was feeling the heat, and panic began to set in. He was desperate, and desperate men did desperate things.

He was sitting in the expensive penthouse of one of his acquaintances, watching his mugshot on the news, when his buddy came in with a beautiful blonde who was high as a kite. She didn't look like someone who'd be strung out, but it was hard to tell who took the stuff anymore.

"I think we've found our weak link," Mad Dog's friend said.

Consuelos felt his heart skip a few beats. "Tell me you ain't shittin' me, Man. I'm at the end of my rope with this shit."

"Mad Dog, meet Cecily Libby. Just so happens, she's a flight attendant, employed as an independent contractor for the US Marshals. Took me a while to get her to take the cocaine, but money and the possibility of a successful man breaks the bitches down every time."

"Aren't you lovely?" Consuelos said, smiling at the girl. "Let me show you a view of the city. This is one of the most expensive penthouses in Miami, but you can see that for yourself. You, my dear, have met one of the most eligible bachelors in town."

The cocaine was still taking its toll, but Cecily was coming down enough to have a conversation. "Yeah…" she smiled. "Nice, really nice."

The two men let her sleep it off on the sofa, and after a couple of hours, they woke her.

"I hear you're a flight attendant," Consuelos said as he eased into the conversation.

"Yes," she answered as she crossed her long, lithe legs.

Consuelos knew the move was intentional to make sure their beauty didn't go unnoticed. Like the rest of her, her legs were gorgeous and inviting. That, however, never swayed him, especially when it came to getting what he wanted. "So," he continued, pretending to admire her toned calves, "do you travel internationally or just domestic?"

"Mostly domestic," she answered, her eyes still reflecting a hint of the cocaine.

"Well, that's certainly safer these days," he said, toying with her.

"Yes, I suppose so."

"What airline are you with? Maybe I'll see you around. My business requires a great deal of travel."

She stammered for a couple of moments, but without the aid of sobriety, she wasn't able to come up with an answer.

"You okay?" Consuelos asked, leaning forward until he was within inches of her face.

Startled, her first impression was to quickly back away.

Now was his opportunity to quit playing the game. He'd enjoyed it for a while, but it was time to get down to business. "We know where you work, Cecily, is it? And if you thought you were running with the big dogs before, you're sadly mistaken." He watched the fear grow in her eyes as a slow grin crossed his face. *Nothing like terror to sober a girl right up.*

"I-I don't understand. How do you know me? Wh- what do you want?"

"We're interested in some of the passengers you

dropped off recently. We wanna know where you took them."

"But-I-I-can't-give-away-that-information. It's my job, and I've made a commitment. Besides, I never really know where anyone goes. They're dropped off at deserted airstrips, and I don't know where they take them from there. Honest, I don't," she whimpered, aware that what was coming next wouldn't be good.

"But you remember where the airstrip was, right?"

"I just...I don't remember everybody. There are so many, and—"

"Oh, but I bet you'll remember this group. White guy, white woman, little mixed girl, seven years old. The guy and girl would've needed some medical attention." When Consuelos saw the recognition flash instantly across her face, he knew they were home free. "Tell me now," he said calmly, reaching for a large hunting knife that he traced lightly down her beautiful face and across her neck. "I hardly think strangers are worth your life, are they?"

Her breathing was fast and furious, and for a minute, Consuelos was certain she'd hyperventilate. He had no patience for that shit. He slapped her across the face with medium force, causing her cheek to turn crimson.

"I think it was Parson, Wyoming. It was in the middle of nowhere, and a black Suburban took them away. It all happened so fast, and—"

"But you had to hear something. Where did they say they were taking them?"

"They didn't even trust the pilot or me. We're just independent contractors," she said, panting, in absolute fear of what they would do to her once they got the information.

"Where'd they take them, Cecily?" Consuelos asked. His patience was gone, and he'd beat her within an inch of her life if that was what it took to get the information he needed.

She could read the evil intent in his eyes and knew she

had to cough up anything else she could recall. "I-I honestly don't know where they took them. I swear," she whimpered, "but I do know it was an hour away. I'm not sure which direction, but the Marshals told them they only had an hour left before they'd get there. It could be a broad circumference. That's all I know. Please don't hurt me. I'll never tell a soul if—"

"I know you won't, Baby," Consuelos said, turning on the charm. "Let's celebrate!" With that, he opened a bottle of fine wine. "Then we'll drop you off wherever you want to go."

The relief rendered Cecily limp, but she took the Merlot, sniffed it, swirled it in her glass, and sipped its goodness. "Mmm," she said, relaxing a little. "Good year."

"Yep," Consuelos answered as he threw her body over the balcony, "a real good year."

Chapter 58

He spent the following evening in the obscurity of his den. After a ham sandwich dinner and a root beer, he followed it with a Bailey's Irish Cream. He laughed to himself at the thought of an after-dinner drink in the wake of such a sparse meal, but he could do anything he wanted. He'd already accomplished three murders, and the stupid town was trying to figure it all out while he was the only one with the answers. It was a rush, and he loved the feeling.

He thought of putting possible victims' names in a hat and drawing them randomly but decided against it. *No, I'd rather think it through and make each decision individually. That's a lot more fun.* The first girl that came to mind was Cassie. She was only an adequate waitress at Dina's, but everyone loved her bubbly personality. She was a possibility, but it would break the pattern of pretty girls, since she was more than a little chubby. She wasn't really ugly, but fortunately for Cassie, her fluffy figure and not-so-great appearance took her out of the running.

Madison Aldridge, Joanna Sibley's friend, was definitely a cutie. She hadn't taken her friend's death too well and was still staying close to home while she mourned. *Yep, she'll be next, but how do I lure her out? Hmm. That might pose a challenge.*

Word had started to get around that herbal remedies for obesity and weight gain had caused the girls to go into premature cardiac arrest. He laughed when he thought of how ludicrous it was. "Close, but no cigar. Maybe I should lead them on a chase for a while. Nobody, not even the *Sheriff*, will ever figure this one out," he said to himself.

He had allowed Haley to suffer a little longer, and he'd enjoyed that, but now, it was a whole new ball game. Madison would suffer long enough to know who was killing her. She'd watch hopelessly as he gave her the final dose of poison that would end her life. "Mmm. Doesn't that sound…delicious? Even better than ham on rye!"

Chapter 59

After dropping Gracie off at school, Nathaniel met Reid at the station. They planned to meet with the three families at the Lowes' home. It was gracious of the grieving parents to open up their home, and it came as a welcome surprise.

They went over their dialogue on the way and with nervous stomachs entered the foyer.

Mrs. Lowe took them into the living room, where the others were already assembled.

"I understand you want to speak to us," Mr. Monroe said, his face drawn from his recent loss.

"Yes," Reid answered slowly. "Thank you all for coming." He took his time, choosing every word carefully as if easing into it might somehow help. "First of all, let me introduce you to my friend and fellow detective, Nathaniel Smith. He's from Georgia and has relocated to Hayden to relax and regroup after...uh, some troubling family issues."

"Troubling family issues, huh?" Mrs. Lowe asked,

somewhat skeptical. "What kind of family issues? Seems to me we've got plenty of those here."

"Unfortunately, my wife, daughter, and I were in a very serious accident. My wife was killed, and my daughter and I spent weeks in a hospital. Gracie is only seven and took it hard, as did I. When my friend Reid, your Sheriff, bragged about how wonderful Wyoming is, I decided a fresh start might do us good. My sister, Laverne, has no family of her own, so she came with us to help me with Gracie. She's now working at Mountainside Memorial as an RN."

"That's quite tragic," Mrs. Lowe answered, feeling cruel for misjudging the man. "Forgive me for intruding, Mr. Smith."

"No, please don't apologize. I understand your skepticism. We're from a small town, too, and I'd be more than a little suspicious if a stranger showed up asking a bunch of questions."

"The City Council and Mayor have agreed to let Nathaniel assist in this investigation, and I'd appreciate your cooperation," Reid interjected.

"Investigation?" Mr. Sibley questioned. "Since when did this turn into an investigation?"

"I can't say I'm using the word lightly," Reid said, carefully considering what he was about to say. "Because, at this point, there is no medical evidence that indicates your daughters died of a heart attack or any other natural cause." He felt the room grow rigid, but continued, "What I'm trying to say is—"

"What the Sheriff is trying to say," Nathaniel chimed in, "is that your daughters may have taken a pill or herbal supplement of some kind they thought would make them healthier or thinner. Or, at this point, we have to speculate...well, murder."

"What?" screamed Mrs. Monroe.

"Have you lost your mind? Where are you from,

Mister?"

"As Reid said, I'm from Georgia, Ma'am. As you know, herbal supplements are sold over the counter and via the internet, and none of them are regulated by the FDA. That scares me. They make many promises for health and weight loss benefits, and your daughters could've fallen prey to that. This does not, by any stretch of the imagination, suggest the girls were drug addicts or responsible for their own deaths. Furthermore, it's just a possibility. We are waiting on toxicology reports that we hope will provide us with a little more insight. The invasive autopsy showed a healthy young girl with no heart disease whatsoever." He leaned forward, his face mirroring the genuine concern in his voice. "On the other hand, your daughters were all very attractive young women, innocent, respectable girls who lived their whole lives here in Hayden and didn't seem to have any enemies. It's likely they would've been suspicious of a stranger, which means they wouldn't have been likely to take anything from one. Therefore, we feel it may have been someone they all knew."

Reid wasn't sure, but thought he heard a quiet gasp from the group. They seemed transfixed on Nathaniel so he let him continue.

"What I'd like to do," Nathaniel continued, "is to eliminate all possibilities that this could've had anything to do with an over-the-counter pill. That would give us some answers or would at least solidify that we're on the right track."

"And what does that entail?" Mr. Lowe asked.

"What I'm asking is for permission to search your girls' belongings and go through the recent communication on their computers."

The mothers were already shaking their heads slowly, and rivers of tears were forming.

"I assure you that we'll handle this with the utmost

respect, as it is something I've done many times before. Also, you're welcome to be there to assist and answer any questions I might think of. I know this is a bit shocking, but we believe it's necessary. I'm sure no one wants to see another family go through this."

They shook their heads in unison, and one of the mothers sniffled loudly.

Reid heaved a sigh of relief, glad that Nathaniel had pulled it off. "I will be checking out other angles," the Sheriff told the group. "Nathaniel will be in touch with you to arrange a time, but if you have any questions or concerns, you know my line is always open."

For the first time in a while, Reid left *almost* feeling like the good guy.

Chapter 60

Jay Sykes was allowed into the precinct to gather what few personal belongings he'd left in his locker. They amounted to little more than a few family photos taped to the inside, an extra deodorant, and a change of uniform. He obviously didn't need the uniform, but thought the deodorant would come in handy. He carried the items in his hands. A bag wasn't even necessary. It was a pretty sad show for all his years on the force. He felt the blood flow to his face and ears as he walked past his coworkers. There weren't any handshakes or good wishes, just stares, some were sad while others looked disgusted. What amazed him most were the looks of disdain from the cops he knew were guilty of the same misgivings. They naïvely thought it'd never happen to them and that they'd never get caught. For their own sakes, he hoped his actions had been a wake-up call.

Sykes had been given a letter by the Chief informing

him of his need to retain a lawyer. If he couldn't afford to hire an attorney to defend him, the State would provide one. However, his case wasn't scheduled on the docket in the near future. Even after all he'd done, they'd try to keep him free for as long as possible.

He'd talked to his wife a couple of times since the death of her mother, but Meredith had made it painfully clear there was nothing left of their marriage to salvage. She blamed Jay for her mother's death, and was too scared of Consuelos being on the loose to let him attempt to see the kids. She requested that he not call for a while. In so many words, something short of never again,.

It didn't come as a surprise. Jay knew he'd lost everything, and there was no one to blame but himself. His insides were riddled with guilt at the thought of the deaths he could've prevented. It was one thing to overlook a couple of bags of crack rock, but homicide was indefensible.

He stopped his old truck in the driveway of his home. He hadn't been here since they'd removed his mother-in-law's bloody remains. Somehow, the place looked different. It was quiet and unnerving, a place he didn't want to be. Jay couldn't believe he lost his family for taking kickbacks that didn't even provide them with more than this broken-down hovel.

He'd thought about stopping at the liquor store on the way to the house for some rotgut whiskey but had decided against it. He knew it'd only numb the pain and wouldn't ultimately take it away.

Turning his truck off, he took the keys out of the ignition. He fumbled around with them for a minute until finding the key to the house, then slowly walked to the front door and opened it. His thoughts drifted to how badly it needed repainting and how long he'd neglected it.

Inside, he couldn't bear to go back to his own bedroom where his mother-in-law had died. Instead, he walked into the kids' room, picked up some of their stuffed animals, and smelled them. *Funny,* he thought, inhaling the scent of youth and happier days, *how smells can make memories so vivid.*

He ambled into the kitchen and pulled a soft drink out of the fridge. After popping the top, he slugged it down in one gulp. Jay hadn't realized just how dry his throat had been. Then he reached up to the cabinet above the refrigerator, taking down his own personal backup weapon, the one thing they hadn't required he return. He'd purchased the beautiful .357 Magnum with his first paycheck from the department. He rubbed his fingers across the barrel, then took his shirttail and wiped away his prints. He'd thought about it for a long time, and knew more than one person would be better off with him gone. His wife couldn't possibly grieve any more than she already was, the kids weren't coming back, and he'd soon be placed in administrative segregation in a prison in South Georgia. The time wouldn't be hard, because as an ex-cop, he'd be protected from the other animals whose fate had been his responsibility. He let his chin rest on his chest and closed his eyes. *How did it come to this?* he thought.

Jay opened his eyes, concentrating on the finger paintings and school calendar on the refrigerator. There could be worst visions before his death. Pondering all the usual positions—the temple, the heart, center-mass—he placed the gun just below his chin. All of them had the potential to take him out with one shot, but they also had the potential of totally fucking his life up for years. He'd seen it go both ways, instant death or vegetative state. He hoped his death would be fast. He felt his pulse quicken and the sweat forming on his fingertips, and he hoped that it wouldn't cause him to slip on the trigger. The last thing he wanted was to be paralyzed, yet more of a burden to everyone.

Suddenly, Jay's mind took on a spinning effect, one

he'd heard often happened before certain death, the whole *life-flashing-before-his-eyes* sort of thing. He didn't notice he was losing his grip on the gun, but heard the weapon clang against the cheap linoleum floor. For a brief moment, he thought he'd actually shot himself. He was unsure of how much time had lapsed as he sat there with his eyes closed and his breathing labored. As resolved as he'd been to put himself out of everyone's misery, Jay Sykes suddenly felt that some type of fate had intervened. *I'm not meant to leave here—not just yet anyway. I've still got business to tend to, and I intend take care of it!*

Chapter 61

Gracie was waiting outside with her belongings in her hand.

Nathaniel pulled up to the school a bit earlier than usual, and as he waited his turn in the pickup line, he enjoyed watching her interact with her classmates. She'd come through everything with flying colors, and he hoped she'd continue to improve. He knew, deep down, that all of that darkness had to be lurking somewhere in that head of hers. But he was happy to see she was full of smiles in spite of it all.

"Hey, Dad!" She grinned, regaining more and more of her color every day.

"Hey, kiddo. How was school?"

"Great. I have to bring my painting home tomorrow though. Mrs. Hoffman said it wasn't quite dry yet."

"I can't wait to see it! How about an ice cream? I thought we could grab one before we go look at the house we might rent."

"You mean a whole house of our own?"

"Yes," he said, laughing, "a house of our own, for you, Aunt Laverne, and me."

"Can we see the house first and get ice cream later? Please?"

"We have to meet the realtor in thirty minutes, which gives us just enough time to grab a cone."

"Okay," she agreed.

They found a parking spot right in front of the drugstore. It still had an old-fashioned soda fountain in the back, something long gone in Nathaniel's part of the world, so it was a treat for him too. They held hands as they made their way to the back, smiling at a few customers along the way.

Nathaniel helped Gracie up onto the stool at the counter. He ordered a caramel sundae, she opted for a strawberry cone. He had to lick around the edges more than once to keep the ice cream from running down the side.

The elderly server made his way over to them as he wiped the counter with a clean, damp rag. "How's that ice cream, young lady?"

"It's good," Gracie answered, licking her lips.

"Glad to hear it. And that sundae, Sir?"

"Just great. My name's Nathaniel Smith, by the way, and this is Gracie. We're new in town." He reached his hand out to meet the gentleman's.

"Nice to meet ya. Name's Harold Hoffman. I've been 'round here since the day I was born. Wouldn't have it any other way. Hayden's a great place to raise a family," he said, motioning his head toward Gracie.

"Reid Langley is an old friend of mine. He gave the place rave reviews, so we couldn't turn him down."

"I know someone whose last name is Hoffman," Gracie said with a smile. "She's my teacher."

"That's my daughter," the old man said, laughing. "Is

she a very good teacher?"

"Yes, Sir!" Gracie answered without missing a beat. "I like her a lot." She looked Mr. Hoffman over as if she was sizing him up. "So you're her Daddy? This is my Daddy," she said, leaning her head over onto Nathaniel's shoulder.

"He seems like a pretty nice Daddy to me especially if he brings you in for strawberry cones from the best ice cream shop in town," Harold said, his face serious and attentive.

"I bet you are too." She said. "And you do make good ice cream cones."

"Why, thank you, Miss Gracie. I'll tell my daughter I've happily made your acquaintance."

"Thank you, Mr. Hoffman."

"We'd better get going, Gracie," Nathaniel said.

"Good luck to you, folks," Mr. Hoffman answered as he continued to wipe down the countertops.

* * * *

It took Nathaniel less than five minutes to find the house, and from the car in front, he could tell the realtor was already there. From the outside, it was just the type of cabin he'd envisioned, and he hoped the inside would be just as welcoming. They stepped up onto the large covered porch and tapped on the door.

A young man, probably in his mid-thirties, introduced himself as Troy Adamson. "Mr. Smith, I take it?"

"Yes, and this is my daughter, Gracie."

They shook hands and walked inside. It was nice and cozy, much like Reid's cabin. The walls were made of logs, and a sizeable fireplace greeted them as they entered. It offered high ceilings, and the kitchen was big enough for him to accomplish any meal. He was certain Laverne would be satisfied with it. There were three decent-sized bedrooms, which met one of his main requirements. The master had its own bath. There was another off the hallway, near the den. However, the biggest plus was the loft. A ladder led up to a small area that could be an extra bedroom, an office, or a den.

Gracie was delighted and instantly flew up the ladder and looked down from the banisters. "Look, Daddy!" she squealed. "It's just like Laura's house on Little House on the Prairie!"

"It sure is," he said, "except we've got electric lights instead of candles."

"Can this be my bedroom?"

"We'll see, Gracie. I'd really prefer your room to be closer to mine, but it looks like it'd make a great place for you to do your homework and watch television."

"Or a painting studio, so my paintings could dry at home!" she shouted.

"Mr. Adamson, I think we'll take it."

"You sure you don't want to look at some others? We have some really beautiful places, and—"

"I think the loft has sealed the deal," Nathaniel said, pulling out a check and filled it in including the security deposit and first and last months' rent before handing it to the shocked realtor. "When can we move in?" he asked.

"Typically, I'd have to wait until the check clears the bank, but I don't see any need for that," Mr. Adamson said. "Here are the keys. You folks can move in whenever you're ready." He handed over his business card and pointed to the address. "You can either stop by or just mail your check in every month. We're right in town, so you may want to save the postage."

"Will do," Nathaniel answered, offering a final handshake. "Now to pry her away from that loft."

"Hope you enjoy the place. The utilities are all on, but you'll need to stop by City Hall to get them put in your name."

Nathaniel decided to take Gracie home for a nap and start dinner. He was almost as excited about the new place as she was. He hadn't realized how much he wanted his own home and could hardly wait to move in.

He decided to put off searching the girls' rooms until after the weekend. It would give the families time to absorb the idea. The Monroes had not yet put their daughter to rest.

He waited up for Laverne, which wasn't an easy task, but he had to share the good news. "We've got a place," he said and went on to tell her all about it.

"If Gracie loves it, it sounds like a winner to me," she said smiling. "Tomorrow's Saturday, so it looks like we'll be shopping for furniture."

"Sounds damn good to me," Nathanial answered as he pulled out the sofa bed.

Chapter 62

The burial for the Monroe girl was scheduled for Saturday morning. Alice Monroe had to be sedated, which wasn't surprising.

Reid and Nathaniel were dressed and ready an hour early. They wanted to make it to the funeral home, not only to pay their respects, but also to scout out the attendees. Profiling taught them the killer would make an appearance for the pure enjoyment of it. But in small towns, people didn't seem to notice who attended as much as who didn't.

There wasn't anyone there yet, which gave the two a slight advantage. The funeral home had done well in preparing Haley's body. There were more flowers in the room than either of them had ever seen. They each started at different ends, reading the cards attached to the arrangements.

The sound of someone clearing their throat caught them both off guard. They hadn't even realized Jonathon

Stephens was in the room. He was like some obscure painting they'd seen out of the corner of their eye but hadn't really noticed. "The room next door," he said, pointing to his left, "is also filled with flowers for the deceased."

"Thank you," Reid stammered, still a little rattled by his undetected presence.

"You are most welcome. Should you need anything, we are at your service."

"I bet you are," Reid muttered, then shivered.

"What a creep," Nathaniel whispered after he was sure the young man was out of earshot.

"Yeah," Reid whispered back. "That's Jonathon Stephens, the owner's son. Apparently, he gives a lot of people the heebie-jeebies around here."

"I can imagine. He might be worth a look."

"I've thought about that more than once. Let's keep an eye on him during the service."

Apparently, the whole town had sent flowers, and Reid and Nathaniel didn't even have time to read all the cards before the family began to arrive.

Mrs. Monroe had the same glazed-over look she'd displayed at the hospital after being given the Valium. She didn't seem to have any idea what was going on until she saw her daughter's lifeless body tucked neatly in the casket amidst the pink satin lining. She opened her mouth to wail but instead collapsed into her husband's arms.

The service was a nice one, and many of Haley's friends spoke about what a great person she was.

Nathaniel and Reid made it their duty to keep an eye on the Stephens' son.

Just as Maloney had told Reid, Jonathon blended into the background so well that one wouldn't know he was there unless they were looking for him.

Chapter 63

Paramedics Jane Goode and Joe Hill thought they had the perfect job. They didn't have to punch a clock or even show up at the fire station unless there was a call. While they both lived right outside of town, they could be at the station within ten minutes if their presence was required. Since they were always on call, to put it mildly, their lives revolved around their jobs.

Joe and Jane made the perfect working pair. Neither had a social life, and they got along impeccably. They respected one another's ability to do the job, and after so many years, the two were a well-equipped team of EMTs. They were often first on the scene whenever anything happened in Hayden, which was rarely a big significance until recently.

Jane left the funeral filled with sorrow. It'd been hard to watch the Monroes go through so much anguish. She started to head home, then thought better of it. She didn't feel like reading or working on her latest stamp collection, and sure didn't want to eat a grilled cheese sandwich alone. It was something she rarely did, but Jane drove the opposite direction of her own small cabin and made a pit stop at Dina's. Joe hadn't been feeling well lately, so Jane picked up two chicken noodle soups to go.

With the bag tucked under her arm, she rang her partner's doorbell. She could count the times on one hand that they'd been to one another's home through the years. It wasn't intentional, they just saw enough of each other at work.

He opened the door and motioned her in. "Well? How was the funeral?"

"Bad...I mean, in the sense that it was mournful. There were some very kind words said about her."

"I'm sure there were," Joe answered, taking the bag from her hands.

"Mmm. Smells like soup," he said, forcing a smile. "Just what the doctor ordered."

"Still got that cold?"

"Yep. Can't seem to shake it no matter what I do." He pulled two spoons from the drawer and two cans of soda from the fridge. After he moved a few days' worth of newspapers out of the way, they sat down at the kitchen table.

"Speaking of the doctor, have you actually been to one?"

"Nope," he answered, motioning toward a wide array of over-the-counter antidotes.

"What you've invested in all that garbage, you could've gone to the doctor several times."

The soup seemed to help his mood. He moved over to the couch after he'd finished.

"I think it just might be you're a little overweight," Jane commented.

"Ya think?"

"Joe, I'm being serious. Your uniforms are too tight, and you sweat so much that I'm afraid you'll pass out on the job or even worse, while driving. It's unhealthy and dangerous."

"Is that why you came over here, to badger the hell out of me?"

"Actually, I came over because I could use some companionship. All these deaths are getting to me."

"Yeah, I know. My apologies. It's just one shock after the next. I feel like my cell phone is gonna go off any minute."

Jane looked on the coffee table and picked up a fat, hardback book entitled *Home Remedies*, then shook her head. "Remedies my ass. It isn't working for you, Joe. It just isn't working."

Chapter 64

After the funeral, Nathaniel went straight home to pick up his two girls and go shopping for furniture. He'd have to be somewhat frugal, considering he had a limited amount of funds. With little savings of his own, he'd been relying on the line of credit allotted by the Witness Protection Program. That twelve thousand was running out, and he knew he'd have to find a paying job soon.

Laverne and Gracie were ready for him, and they decided the shopping trip for their new place would require going outside of Hayden. Not only would they need furniture, but all the other things needed to run a household as well.

They made the hour drive to Wilhelm where the selection of large chain stores was plentiful. The first stop, of course, was for lunch. They opted for McDonald's. It'd been so long since they'd had the good fortune of sinking their teeth into a Big Mac, and Gracie was anxious to order a Happy Meal. Laverne was grateful there wasn't an indoor playground.

The first store they stopped at after lunch was a large one that Nathaniel hoped they'd not only offer all he needed, but would deliver. He was in luck. "If what you order is in stock," the salesman told him, "they'll deliver on Monday."

It took well over three hours, but with Laverne's help, they had furniture for every room. He was so fortunate to have her, and wasn't ashamed to let her know it. Nathaniel's egotistical days were over, and he didn't want Gracie living in a home that looked like a bachelor pad.

The next stop was for linens. Gracie decided on neon pink for her room, which came as no surprise. Besides the bed linens, they picked up bath and dish towels and washcloths.

Laverne paid half of the tab for all the furniture and linens, which left Nathaniel with a decent balance on his card. He was uncomfortable with her doing it, but she insisted. "I have a job now, and we're going to be living in the same place," she said defiantly. "I want to be part of this and pitch in."

When they arrived at the appliance store, Nathaniel turned to the back seat to let Gracie know they'd arrived and found her sound asleep. "Just let me run in," he told Laverne. "You two wait here. The cabin is equipped with a refrigerator and kitchen appliances. All we need is a washer and dryer. I should be able to handle that."

Although delivery would be several days behind the furniture, they could manage. The sheets and towels could be washed at Reid's, and they had enough clothes to wait for the washer.

"What now?" he asked, his voice weary.

"Just a few little things, like kitchen accessories," Laverne answered. "I can handle all of that in Hayden. We need to head back and let you two get some rest. I have a pork roast for dinner, so we're covered there. Y'all can take a long nap while I cook."

"Have I told you lately that I love you?" Nathaniel sang.

"Not often enough, big brother," Laverne answered as they made their way back home.

Chapter 65

The Miami PD was not at all surprised to find the beautiful dead woman, lying on the parking lot, below the expanse of towering luxury condominiums. It wasn't something that happened every day, but it wasn't exactly uncommon either. She had drugs in her system, but they were still unable to determine whether it was a suicide, an accident, or someone simply tossed her over the balcony. At any rate, it'd be difficult to tell, at least for a while. Her fingerprints offered no identity, and after the exhaustive questioning of the tenants, they could only conclude that none of them had seen her before. The doorman had conveniently stepped away for a few minutes the night before, leaving a window of about fifteen minutes for anyone to come or go. The cops doubted his story but were forced to accept it.

The medical examiner's office picked up the body, and the complex sent a crew to clean up any remnants of human remains. It was unsettling how quickly someone's life could be erased.

From what the detectives could tell, she was attractive with fairly expensive clothes, professionally manicured nails, and a beautiful tennis bracelet. Even if she'd been a high-priced call girl, someone would be missing her, and they hoped it'd happen sooner rather than later. In the meantime, she was a Jane Doe on a gurney, rolled into a refrigerated room in the county morgue.

The Atlanta detectives spent several days meeting with the Miami PD and all the scumbags they thought may have some knowledge of Mad Dog and his whereabouts. Thus far, their trip had been a bust, and budget constraints had put them back on the plane to Georgia, forcing them to leave the investigation to the locals and their fugitive squads. That left it up to the Miami PD to put two and two together and figure out that Cecily Libby had been murdered for her information.

Chapter 66

The skies were clear, in fact, the weather would've been perfect if not for the frequent gusts of strong winds. A brisk walk in the sunshine was pleasant, though, and he'd enjoyed it. It helped to clear his mind, and he made an extra loop around the house to get his heart rate up.

His plants were calling as he entered the house, almost as if something were physically tugging at him. The two back bedrooms served as his greenhouses. One was a dark room, the other filled with fluorescent lighting. He loved to dry old flowers from the cemetery and make potpourri. He added extra strong oils filled with scents to make it last longer. It made a great gift for anyone, and he shared large bags with his mother and sister. They never seemed to tire of it, or so he thought.

Today, however, was not a day for pretty flowers. He put on his gloves and opened the door to the now dank and smelly room. The roots and flowers of the monkshood plant were drying nicely, but he needed a new supply to continue his mission. It'd proven to be the perfect killing machine. He felt such a high when he thought of how he'd fooled the girls with the lotion. It went straight from the skin into the bloodstream, and they'd been so trusting they never saw it coming. What excited him the most was, they went to their deaths knowing they were going to die, pleading with the Grim Reaper to come and take them from their misery. They had made fun of him—not outright, but he knew they found him strange. *I wasn't born beautiful and talented. Too bad they were.*

His mind wandered, as it often did, to Doctor Novus. *What a know-it-all bitch. I'd love to see her trapped in the misery of her own body as it betrayed her.* Then again, she could bring his whole house of cards tumbling down. He knew his limits. *I'll stick with the younger ones for now, but who knows? The good doctor's number just might be coming up.*

Chapter 67

Mad Dog Consuelos soon learned what'd been big money in the projects wasn't anything in the underworld of Miami. The real crime bosses soon figured him out, and receiving any help from them to get to Wyoming was now out of the question. He'd have to rely on his own instincts, which would mean stealing a car in every other state and lying as low as possible. He had enough money to get there, but would be cutting it close. The budget didn't really matter though. What was most important was getting to his daughter and the bounty hunter before the cops put two and two together and figured out who the dead flight attendant was.

He had studied the map of Wyoming on the internet on at the public library. He was aware it could take days or even weeks to find them, but he'd do whatever it took. He was closer than he'd been before .

He knew by now that all the lowlifes in Atlanta had

dropped the dime on him, but that wasn't a cause for concern, and certainly came as no surprise. He just had to stay on the run and hope the authorities would busy themselves with scouring every nook and cranny of Miami.

Nothing would come between him and his revenge: his daughter and the bounty hunter.

Chapter 68

Nathaniel dropped Gracie off at school and headed immediately to Joanna's apartment.

Mrs. Sibley met him at the door and showed him in. "If there's anything I can do to help, Mr. Smith, I'm more than willing," she said with a strong look of determination. "The only change is the bed in her room has been made and I removed the food from the refrigerator."

"Thank you," Nathaniel answered as she led him back to her daughter's bedroom.

"I'll try to stay out of the way, but promise me you'll let me know if you find something."

"I certainly will, but feel free to stay back here with me." He turned and looked at her, trying to hide his pity. "I don't want to offer you any false hope, Ma'am, but we'll do all we can."

She ignored the comment and said, "I think it'd be better if I sit in the living room."

"That'll be fine."

He hoped his search would give him more time than he and Reid's last hurried visit. He didn't want Mrs. Sibley knowing that they'd already been here.

When the television news came on, he began his search for clues. He started with the dresser drawers, removing everything carefully. He didn't find anything other than what was to be expected for a girl her age: panties, bras, T-shirts from different places she'd visited, and pajamas. There wasn't any remotely sexy lingerie. Her closet held a selection of purses, none of which netted anything of interest. There was summer and winter clothing, so he was sure he wouldn't find anything boxed away. He went over the bedroom like a prison guard would search a cell, but as much as he wanted to, he couldn't find anything that'd lead to a killer.

The bathroom was like any other female's with bath gels, lotions, and basic toiletries. The kitchen was neat and tidy and filled with hand-me-down dishes.

Mrs. Sibley shared his disappointment. "Would it help to check her old room at our house?" she asked.

"How long did she live here, in this apartment?"

"Close to two years."

"I believe anything of importance would be here, especially since the deaths happened recently." Nathaniel felt terrible as soon as the sentence left his lips, but he couldn't retrieve it.

The heartbroken mother started to cry and sat back down on the sofa. "I just don't understand this. I was so sure she died of natural causes. The thought of her suffering is almost more than I can bear."

"We still can't rule out a natural death, Mrs. Sibley. Sheriff Langley just wants to cover all the bases, which I'm sure you can appreciate."

He reached for her hand and laid his over her small, curled fingers. They sat there in that awkward position for what seemed like hours to Nathaniel until she finally let go and stood up.

"Thank you for your help, Mr. Smith. Maybe you'll find something in the other girls' homes."

"Yes, Ma'am. We're not finished yet. If you can think of anything, please call Reid. He really is a good Sheriff, and he cares about this town."

"I know," she answered softly, "but when one is filled with grief, they need someone to blame."

Chapter 69

Jay Sykes still had one friend on the force, and he wouldn't hesitate to ask for his help. He was determined not to leave this Earth until he'd taken vengeance on the one man who'd cost him everything. Picking up the phone, he dialed Sergeant Hill's personal line.

The Sarge answered on the first ring. "Atlanta PD. Sergeant Hill speaking."

"I need to talk to you," Jay pleaded, instantly feeling vulnerable.

"Sykes, what the hell are you doing?"

"I need to talk to you right away, Sarge," he reiterated. "I almost shot myself a minute ago."

"What? For God's sake, don't do that! Gimme twenty minutes, and I'll be over there. Walk around outside or something while I'm on my way. You need to get out of that house…and stay the hell away from your weapon."

Jay hung up and tried to pull himself together. He went

to the kitchen sink, turned on the water, cupped his hands, and splashed some on his face. Much to his surprise, it seemed to help. Hill was right. He needed to step outside, where the gun couldn't tempt him.

True to his word, Sergeant Hill pulled in the driveway less than twenty minutes later, only to find Jay sitting on the front porch with a wad of tissues in his hands. "Listen, Sykes," Hill started sternly, "I feel bad for ya, Man. Really, I do, but the last thing the department wants is for me to continue any contact with you." His voice sounded defiant, but the empathy in his eyes told another story.

"I know, but I-I need your help."

"It's out of my control now. You know I don't have any say in what happens from here on out."

"I just need some information, nothing that'll hurt anybody. Really, Sarge."

Against his better judgment, Hill sighed heavily and pointed toward the front door. "Let's go inside."

Jay walked in and sat on the loveseat, leaving the wingback chair for his former Sergeant.

"Get on with it, Sykes. I don't need anyone seeing my car in this driveway."

"I need to find the bounty hunter and little girl Consuelos shot."

"What the hell are you talking about?"

"I'm serious, Sarge They both disappeared after they were released from the hospital. You know what that means."

"Not really. Maybe they're just hiding from their shooter. I know I wouldn't want to be shot again."

"It's not a joke," Jay said. "It only points to one thing, Witness Protection."

Hill let out a forced laugh. "You've gotta be shittin' me, Sykes. You expect me to break into their files and tell you where they are? Sure, Man. No problem. I think you've gone crazy. The Marshals are FEDS, as in the *Federal*

Witness Program. Those two wouldn't qualify because this is a *State* case. Besides, what do you want with them? What do you plan to do, send 'em flowers?"

"I want to find them. Wherever they are, that's where Consuelos will be headed."

"So you're lookin' for a showdown?"

"No. I want justice."

"Shit," Hill said with a sneer. "You weren't interested in justice when you were taking that maggot's money."

Jay felt the sting of his jab but refused to let it deter him. "Nathaniel Collier was a legend. He caught all the major cases from the surrounding bond companies."

"And?"

"And that means he had to have friends on the force. Most of the bail-jumpers don't go much further than Atlanta, just like Consuelos. They feel protected in their own neighborhoods."

"Even if I do find his friends and they know where he is, they sure as hell won't give it away, besides the fact that it'd be strange for me to ask."

"Just see if anyone has quit in the last couple of years or transferred to another police department. Even if it's not that far away, they could offer them some cover."

"Yeah, but nobody could just take the kid. That's illegal. The Division of Family and Children Services would take over."

"They wouldn't risk that."

"Look, this is the last thing you need to be involved in, Sykes. Vigilante justice won't change a thing. You're already in enough trouble."

"I don't expect it to change much, but it would ease my conscience."

"I can't promise anything, but I'll check around. In the meantime, get the hell outta this house. Stay in a hotel and leave that gun here. Do you need any cash?"

"No. I've got a credit card."

Chapter 70

The search of Lauren Lowe's small apartment in her parents' basement netted the same findings as Joanna Sibley's. Nothing. The two definitely had beauty in common, but they hadn't exactly been close friends.

Nathaniel decided to wait until the following day to visit Haley Monroe's home, a visit he dreaded more than all the others. Her family'd had less time to heal.

He picked Gracie up at school, and she jumped in the car, proudly displaying a finger painting of her family. "That's great, little one," Nathaniel said with a smile. "Just think, our very first picture for the refrigerator!" He'd heard some of his buddies bragging about their kids' artwork being posted on the fridge. He had to laugh now, at this odd, pivotal moment in his life.

Their mouths gaped when they opened the door to their new home. The furniture had arrived, and Laverne was standing in the middle of the den with her arms outstretched, as if to say, "Look at this, folks!" She smiled at Gracie. "Well, don't just stand there, Honey. Go check out your room…and you too, Mr. Smith."

Nathaniel gave up the master bedroom to Laverne because he knew women appreciated a larger area to primp in. He walked around, struggling with his emotions, aside from living at home when he was young, the rental cabin was the only other place he'd ever felt at home.

"Thank you, Laverne. This is beautiful. How did you do it?"

"Let me tell you, the moving men aren't very fond of me. I asked them to rearrange several times before I was satisfied."

"Oh my," Nathaniel said with a laugh. "I bet they loved that."

"So…does this get me out of cooking dinner tonight?"

"You bet. You pick the place, and I'll pick up the tab."

"You got it, big guy. Listen, I think we should invite Reid and Anne. She was so nice to get that job for me. I'm surprised I'm fitting in so quickly. My coworkers are really friendly."

"Sounds good to me," Nathaniel answered. "I need to give Reid a call anyway. I didn't find anything today to suggest foul play, but I'm sure he'd like to hear what I did find."

The phone call to Reid was short. There wasn't much to talk about, but he accepted the dinner invitation for both himself and Anne. He even suggested Nell as a babysitter so Gracie could get her rest for school the following day.

"I'm just not sure if I'm ready to leave her like that," Nathaniel answered. "She's just so…vulnerable."

"No, Nathaniel, *you* are vulnerable. No one's going to harm her here, especially Nell."

The comment was true. Nathaniel hated to admit it, but he was the one who didn't want to let go. "Do you think she has plans tonight?"

"No, but I can ask. Call you back in a few."

All the arrangements were confirmed and Nell showed up to look after Gracie. She was excited about Nell's visit and already had the Monopoly board set up on the kitchen table. The four left the house, glad to be going somewhere other than funeral homes and morgues.

Laverne delegated her restaurant choice to Reid, and he suggested a nice restaurant about thirty minutes from town. The ambiance was restful, and they offered a variety of steaks and seafood.

After ordering, Nathaniel talked about his day.

"You know," Anne interjected, "I'm not a detective, and I'm certainly not finding anything on my radar, but I've been thinking. I have a friend named Vaughn Edmondson, a forensic psychiatrist who works part-time as a professor at a small college and with the prison system. I'm sure Vaughn would be happy to come talk to us. A good forensic psychiatrist can tell us a great deal about the deaths we're finding here, especially if they're being committed by the same person."

Nathaniel tried to contain himself but rolled his eyes instead. "I just don't get into all that behavioral science BS. I'm sure profilers hit it on the head sometimes, but even a broken clock is right twice a day."

"Oh ye of little faith." Anne laughed. "It looks like we're running out of options. What do we have to lose?"

"What's with forensic psychiatrists anyway? Do they try to treat the dead?"

"Come on, Nathaniel," Anne said with a sneer. "They deal with the living and, I suppose, the dead as well. They are experts on criminal behavior patterns, psychological testing, abnormal psychology, but they are also investigators. They're frequently asked to bring their expertise into the courtroom."

"I guess that makes them legit, then?" Nathaniel laughed. "No harm intended. In any case, weren't not in a position to turn down any help. I'd like to meet your friend. Set it up."

"Will do. Now let's talk about something more pleasant. Laverne, I understand everyone on the third floor loves you. They tell me you're doing a good job and have an excellent bedside manner."

"I can attest to that," Nathaniel said. "I don't know what Gracie and I would've done without her. I'm still here only because of her."

"Oh stop it." Laverne smiled, her cheeks turning a light shade of pink.

Their food arrived, and the conversation slowed as they dug into the delicious meal.

The evening had been enjoyable, except for Nathaniel's concern about leaving Gracie with someone else. He was relieved to get back home to her and find her sleeping peacefully. "Thank you so much, Nell," he said.

"Anytime, Nathaniel. I'd be happy to babysit again."

He kissed her lightly on the cheek, then went back to check on Gracie one more time.

Chapter 71

He had stalked Madison Aldridge for four days and discovered she rarely wandered outside the confines of her home. She didn't follow any patterns or routines, and she never left the comfort of her own property. *This may prove to be a challenge,* he thought, *but the bigger the challenge, the better. I'm getting pretty good at this.*

It could prove to be his most difficult role yet, but he was sure it could be done. He would boil the root to make a deadly liquid. Then he'd suck several milligrams up into the plastic syringe he'd purchased from the drugstore just on the outskirts of town. He wouldn't leave an injection mark, the one crucial clue the Sheriff and Doctor would be hoping to find. *No, I'll just squirt it down her ear canal.*

"Pretty damn brilliant," he said aloud before laughing. "I should've made more of my life. I'm just…wasted talent."

As the night wore on, he dressed in the perfect

ensemble for the job: pants, sweatshirt, socks, and shoes. He would wait until the last minute to put the black cotton ski mask on. By now, he was familiar with the property and knew the shortest and safest route to her bedroom window. He'd have to rely on the family being heavy sleepers.

His car coasted to a stop on a deserted stretch of road not more than a mile from the Aldridge home. He placed the syringe in a plastic box before putting it carefully inside the pocket of his jacket. He had to be cautious. He knew all too well the power of the poisonous plant. He waited outside Madison's window, concealed by overgrown shrubbery. Waiting patiently and silently, he watched the white puffs of steam caused by his warm breath against the cold night air. The penlight shining on his watch revealed it was just after midnight. The house had been dark and silent for over an hour, if he was going to make his move, there was no time like the present.

Madison's bedroom was on the ground floor and took little effort to pry the window open. Then, with more effort than he expected to exert, he eased his hand first followed by his head and body like a serpent into the dimness of her room. The cool air rushed in from outside, but closing the window would cut off his escape route.

Madison had her back to him and didn't even stir as the cold breeze filled her bedroom. The covers were pulled up to her shiny, brown locks. He watched her body rising up and down with the gentle rhythm of her breathing. She looked so peaceful that, for a brief moment, he almost changed his mind, but that moment hadn't lasted long.

He moved slowly toward her, pulling out the syringe. He was anxious for her to be awake, and she would be soon. He pushed the needle end of the syringe into her ear canal, careful not to touch any part of her skin, then let the deadly poison flow. He administered it in short, quick squirts, giving it just enough time to drain into her ear. He didn't want it to overflow onto the sheets or her pillow and leave any suspicious stains.

She turned over onto her back, her eyes glazed over with confusion. He took out the penlight and held it to his face so she'd get a good view of him. Madison's face mirrored shock and fear as she struggled to scream. She tried rolling away, but her hands reached up toward her throat as she fought to breathe

"Don't worry, Honey," he said with a grin. "You'll go fast. The damage is done, and there's nothing anyone can do for you now."

She began clawing at her chest while sweat formed instantly on her face. Then the convulsions began. Her small body writhed, jerking up and down in uncontrollable seizures. Her body starting failing.

He knew it was only a matter of time before the family woke up from the commotion. He wasn't as careful this time but exited as quickly and quietly as possible. By the time he made it back to the car, he was holding his aching side and gasping for air. He knew he had to get out of there. They'd soon be calling for an ambulance.

Chapter 72

Phones were chirping, ringing, and buzzing simultaneously all over Hayden. First Jane's and Joe's, then the Sheriff's home phone, along with Henry Hartwell's. A deputy was dispatched as well.

Reid called Nathaniel, giving him quick, concise directions, hoping he'd be able to follow them. By the time Reid got to the house, the place was overflowing with emergency personnel. Floodlights bathed the lawn in bright light accompanied by police lights, Henry's portable blue bubble light, and the ambulance lights. *Hmm. This can't be good,* Reid thought.

He bypassed the overwhelmingly emotional family and went straight to where the crowd had gathered. Madison was lying in a pool of her own vomit, her eyes opened in a frightened stare. "Nell, snap what you can," Reid said, almost having to yell across the room. "Come on, people. This is a crime scene. Why is everyone in here? Shit! Let

Joe and Jane do what they can. The rest of you get out!"

Henry Hartwell entered the house with a bang, holding up a hand to the distraught family and turning on his heels to see what the ruckus was all about. "What've we got here?" he asked loudly, pushing others to the side and shoving his way into the bedroom.

"Gee, I think it's another dead girl," Reid answered rudely, feeling instantly like an ass.

"Is there a pulse?" Henry demanded.

"Nothing," Joe answered breathlessly, sweat rolling down his nose and onto the victim's face.

"Well, get her to the hospital," Henry demanded, waving his arms like wands, motioning everyone away. "Get the gurney in here. Are you people crazy or just lazy?" he screamed at Jane and Joe. "This young girl may have a chance of being revived if you two would've done more than just stare at her!"

Reid and Nathaniel looked at one another questioningly. For a moment, Reid thought of taking over the situation but then thought better of it. Unfortunately, Henry was right. Getting Madison out of there would give him his crime scene back, and he'd let Henry deal with the family. Henry seemed to revel in being the one who talked to them in hushed tones, assuring them everything would be all right. With Madison on her way to the hospital and Henry driving the family in his official coroner car, they could go over the room with a fine-toothed comb and look for evidence. Once again, Reid was grateful Nathaniel was there.

The comforter was so contaminated with vomit and diarrhea that their best option was to simply fold it up and carry it to the morgue where better lighting could confirm any foreign hairs or debris. The window had been left open and offered several prints, although they'd likely belong to the family. The ones on the windowsill and blinds were just smudges, so the intruder had clearly thought to wear gloves. *Damn it. Looks like we're not dealing with an idiot here.*

Nathaniel and Reid went outside to look for footprints, but were unable to find any that could be cast.

Without any further clues at the scene, they hoped more would be found with Madison herself and her comforter.

Reid knew Anne had already been notified, so he thought it best not to call her. "Come on," he said to Nathaniel. "Let's head straight over to the hospital."

As Reid drove entirely too fast down the narrow, winding roads, Nathaniel braced himself with a hand on the dash. "We can't do any good for anyone if we wind up dead ourselves, you know," he scolded, keeping his eyes on the road.

"I want answers, and I don't want to lose precious minutes. There's no telling who's down there, rambling through what may just solve these deaths."

"You know Anne better than that," Nathaniel answered. "She's the consummate professional, and I hardly believe she'd allow anyone near her workstation."

"You're right," Reid said, sounding a little better as they pulled into the ambulance entrance and jumped out.

Anne was already in her *astronaut suit* as Reid referred to it, with the mask covering her beautiful and deeply concerned face. Henry donned his as well, as if he knew what the hell he was doing. Anne was kind enough to allow him in.

"Any defensive wounds?" Reid asked as soon as he walked into the room. "Patience," Henry whispered. "The doctor has just readied herself for the procedure. This might take some time."

Nathaniel and Reid cringed. There was one too many people in the room, and they didn't like it.

Reid ignored the remark and continued, "Can we use the other autopsy table to lay out the bedspread? The lighting in here is so much better."

"Knock yourself out," Anne answered as she studied Madison's arms and hands closely.

Henry stood back at a safe difference. He'd never liked postmortem investigations. He much preferred to sign off on death certificates as natural deaths. Henry'd always enjoyed the way people appreciated how he treated their deceased.

Nathaniel and Reid picked away at every piece of vomit and loose stool with small tweezers, hoping to find a hair or fiber that might lead them to their killer.

"Got anything, Doc?" Nathaniel asked, trying to sound patient.

"These bruises aren't defensive wounds. They're from the convulsions. I can't understand why a victim wouldn't put up a fight. He must be poisoning them with something quick, something normally undetectable until tested for. I'm going to do an invasive autopsy."

"What? I simply refuse to allow it," Henry said strongly. "You don't have the family's consent, and they'll shit a brick if you even ask for it. I'm shocked by your lack of compassion Doctor Novus."

"It isn't a lack of compassion, Henry," she answered dismissively.

"There are laws to abide by…" he tried to continue.

Reid could almost see his mind reeling, trying to come up with some State code.

"Yes, there are laws, but after four unsolved deaths, I am within State guidelines to order an autopsy, with or without family consent. If you don't believe me, call the State medical examiner's office. The number's on my desk, and I've already checked with them."

"Well, I don't like it. When the parents are unhappy, it makes my job hell."

"You can't be serious," Nathaniel said. "You're worried about what the registered voters might think about you while these girls are obviously being murdered? Unbelievable!"

"Down boy," Henry answered, motioning with his hands for Nathaniel to take it easy. "We all have jobs to do."

"And what is your job exactly?" Nathaniel retorted.

"Okay, boys," Anne interrupted, "we can't work under these circumstances."

As soon as she began her Y incision, Henry dropped to the floor with a *thud*.

"Get some smelling salts and get him out of here," Anne said. "I knew the incision would do it."

Chapter 73

For four long days, Sergeant Hill plowed through personnel files, unsure why he was even doing it. Sykes had been a decent cop who'd gotten too desperate. But, that was no reason for Hill to give confidential information to a civilian. He was taking a huge risk, breaking the law himself. *Shit*, the Sergeant thought. *What the hell's the big deal about passing along five names?* The odds of any of them having a connection with Nathaniel Collier were slim to none anyway, and once he handed them over to Sykes, he'd make it perfectly clear that he was done: no more phone calls, no more favors, no more contact. With that, he picked up his phone, and dialed Sykes.

"Yeah?"

"Wow. Some phone etiquette ya got there, buddy," Hill said, anxious to get to the bottom line.

"I'm nervous, Sarge. What've you got for me?"

"Five names, none of which stand out to me. Officer

Dannon left the force and took up with the city of Zebulon. Apparently, his wife wanted to move out of the city. They still operate under the good ol' boy system, so I wouldn't bank on Collier taking the girl there. Officer Washington got fired two years ago and is working for a dry cleaning place on Tenth. Sanders's mother died, and he moved to Macon to take care of his invalid father. Doesn't sound like a situation with room for three more folks. Remember Officer Kathy Lyons?"

"Yeah."

"It was quite a scandal a couple of years back, but she was fired for stripping on the side. Apparently, she kept the job since it was much more lucrative than public service."

"You said there are five."

"Yeah. The last one on the list is Reid Langley. He left the force a couple of years ago to take a Sheriff's job in East Bumblefuck, Wyoming. I don't think he's got anything to do with it. A Sheriff wouldn't let anybody bring a fugitive's child to his town. It'd be too risky. Besides, it sounds like a pretty safe place, not one they'd wanna lure Consuelos to. The rest were just your basic losers who couldn't possibly hack it—you know, those types who flunked out of the academy or just last a couple of years. Collier wouldn't have turned to any of them. He's an intelligent guy, and I think he'd want to go somewhere sheltered. My advice would be to check out any family he might have. Other than that, I don't have squat."

"Okay."

"Sykes, I gotta tell ya, this is it. Don't call me anymore. I hate you took a fall, but I can't take one with you."

"Where in Wyoming?"

"What? I told you it won't be Langley, and you don't need to go out there and get involved. You're in deep enough without showing up there asking a lot of questions."

"Just tell me where, and you'll never hear from me again. I may not be a cop anymore, but I still have gut instincts."

"Hayden's the name of the town. Hayden, Wyoming." With that, Sergeant Hill hung up the phone and considered himself through with his subordinate, and, it was a great relief.

Chapter 74

Laverne had taken Gracie to school, and it was well after noon before Nathaniel, Reid, and Anne decided to pull off their autopsy gear.

"I've got to pick Gracie up at 2:30," Nathaniel said. "We need some serious help here. Reid, I recommend calling in the Wyoming Bureau of Investigation."

"Yeah, I know," the Sheriff answered. "Clearly, we're in over our heads."

"I'm releasing her to the family this afternoon," Anne said. "We need to figure out what we're missing. Can both of you make it to my house tonight around 7:00? I'll make dinner."

"I'd like to, Anne," Reid answered, "but we've got a lot of investigating to do."

"My friend Vaughn is coming into town."

"The forensic psychiatrist?" Nathaniel asked sarcastically.

"Just give it a shot," Anne retorted. "If it doesn't work, we won't be out anything but a couple of hours."

"A couple of hours we don't necessarily have." Reid interjected. "But we'll be there." His last thought as he left the hospital was whether or not Vaughn Edmondson was going to stay over at Doctor Novus's house for the night.

* * * *

Nell was available for babysitting duty again, and after feeding Gracie a bowl of pasta and a salad, Nathaniel followed the directions to Anne's house. He wasn't as nervous this time about leaving, but he'd have to call at least once to check in. The last thing he wanted to leave her for was to hear some bullshit theory from a shrink.

Anne's house was modest, but new and decorated professionally. Four plates were placed on the table, flanked by tossed salads and tall glasses of iced tea.

"Glad you could make it," she said with a welcoming smiled. "Reid and Vaughn should be pulling up any minute. They're both busy, and I didn't expect either to be on time. Can I get you a drink?" she asked, pointing to a well-stocked wet bar.

"I'll have whatever you're having," he answered, making himself at home and sitting on the stark-white couch.

"A martini it is." She smiled and handed him one with extra olives.

He took it appreciatively, wishing he'd just requested a beer.

A knock at the door proved to be Reid, still in his uniform. "Sorry, I'm late, but it takes effort to hide from the people of this town."

"No problem," Anne answered. "We're still waiting on Vaughn." She didn't even bother to ask him about his drink preference, but just handed him a beer.

"Nice place you got here," Reid said as he accepted the cold drink.

"Yeah, I like it. It's a little small, but it's just me, so I don't need any extra space. It'd just be more to clean."

Their conversation was interrupted by a soft knock at the door. Nathaniel could already feel his defenses going up.

"Why, hello!" Anne said, as she swung open the door, then offered a big hug.

Nathaniel and Reid sat in stunned silence. Apparently, they'd both been expecting a man, but instead, they were greeted by a beautiful woman. They stumbled over each other as they rose to shake her hand.

"Let's have dinner first," Anne said. "We can get to know one another better before moving on to business." She pulled a pan of lasagna from the oven and carried it to the table, along with a basket of garlic bread.

They tried to find enough conversation to fill the thirty minutes as they ate, but found it difficult not to discuss the reason why they were there.

The two women cleared the table then joined Reid and Nathaniel in the den.

Vaughn pulled out a briefcase and removed a legal pad with information scribbled all over it. "From what Anne's told me, it sounds like you have a serial killer on your hands."

Nathaniel fought back his incessant need to be a cynic before he asked, "And how do you figure that? We haven't even determined what these women have died of. Forgive my disrespect, but I'm not a firm believer in the art of profiling. I think it's nothing more than a bunch of logical guesses."

"Nathaniel, you haven't offended me. My job is filled with a constant barrage of skeptics, and I've become accustomed to it. A profiler is much more than a gypsy consulting a crystal ball. We've spent years studying crime scenes and rely a great deal on statistical data."

"Just because someone is a murderer, doesn't make them a certain type of person. Sometimes birds of a feather don't flock together. But humor me. What makes a serial killer? A bed wetter? Someone who stutters? Mutilates animals?"

"Nathaniel," Anne said impatiently, "let's give this a chance. It seems like we're stuck between a rock and a hard place. This information can't hurt."

Vaughn sat back deep into the sofa, removed her shoes, and curled her socked feet under herself. "Okay," she said, changing her tone to a professional one, "let me give you a few facts, and we can go from there." She reached for her legal pad and put on a pair of bifocals. "The statistics I'm going to give you may waiver a few percentages, but for the most part, they are proven data, not simply guesses. The majority of serial killers have a particular method of killing. For example, they don't normally change from, say…strangulation to shooting their victims. Your killer seems to have a method we can't target, but all of the victims died quickly, with vomiting and diarrhea. They all had healthy hearts and bodies. An average of sixty percent target strangers, which is what I find odd here. A town this small would notice a stranger. They may welcome him, but they wouldn't be especially trusting. These girls haven't even put up a fight. Over seventy percent of serial killers are known to operate in a specific location, which, in this situation, hits the nail on the head. I could go on and on, but every law enforcement officer and anyone who watches true crime TV knows the basic verbiage. Over eighty percent are white males, and the majority have been somehow ostracized by society somehow. The average age at which they kill their first victim is twenty-eight, but most are in their twenties or thirties. Of course, this doesn't eliminate the possibility of it being someone older or younger, but it's something to consider."

"That doesn't exactly narrow it down enough for us, Ms. Edmondson," Reid said. "That could be practically anyone in this town."

"In that case, we need to find a motive and cause of death," she answered, peering over her glasses. "First, let's look at motive. The girls were all young, in their early twenties, and from what Anne has told me, quite attractive. It isn't exactly like picking off members of a losing football team, but it narrows it down to a grouping. Could there be someone in town who has something against pretty girls? Say…someone who's been shunned in the past?"

Reid's mind went straight to two misfits: young Matthew Maloney, simply because of his age, and Jonathon Stephens because he was just weird enough to pull off the murders. He also had access to the chemicals and tools.

"I'm sure we can come up with some suspects," Reid said, "but we need to find out how the killer is doing it."

"My initial thought was herbal supplements," Nathaniel interjected, "but I've beaten that dead horse too long. I can't see them dying from taking it once, and we've found no evidence of any such thing in their rooms. None of the girls had ordered or researched them on their computers."

"Hmm," Vaughn said. "The herb theory may not be so far off. There are herbal supplements that can be fatal if taken in excess, but you said there weren't any in their personal belongings. It would be hard to get someone to take an overdose of pills or capsules without them putting up some type of resistance. I'm not an expert on this topic, but the internet can help us tremendously. I do know that each supplement contains several different ingredients, and many have been removed from shelves because at least one them can be found in each one. Natural ingredients have been used as poisons for years, from Indians putting them on the tips of their arrows as they hunted, to poisoning the food or drink of a political figure. Plus, teenagers will try anything for a high. I had a colleague years ago who told me about a young kid who boiled a lily of the valley because he'd heard it would make him high. He drank a glass of the boiled water and died a terribly painful death. If his mother hadn't seen the plant in the pot on the stove, they wouldn't have ever figured out what happened to him."

Reid, Anne, and Nathaniel looked at one another as if something had clicked in their minds all at once.

"It sounds like you just discovered our murder weapon," Anne said excitedly. "But how do we find it in the autopsy?"

"Not so fast," Vaughn said with a laugh. "I came in here to a houseful of people who thought I was full of foolishness, and now you're ready to accept my first proposition."

"It makes sense," Nathaniel said, excitement obvious in his voice. "Maybe the killer gave them a lethal dose of something natural, something that we can't confirm via tox. Maybe he put it in their drinks."

"Again," Reid interrupted, "they would've had to trust that person enough to let them in their rooms to offer them a drink. Even a young girl would find that suspicious from a stranger. The guy broke into Madison Aldridge's bedroom while she and her family were sleeping, so why would she have accepted a drink from him? I don't know, Nathaniel."

"Maybe it's not in a drink," Vaughn said. "That was simply an example."

"What if they find the one ingredient that's taken from the supplement because of its potential for serious side effects? Maybe he put it in their vitamins or something."

"It would be difficult to do that, especially in the US. He could order it, but it'd bring on a great deal of suspicion if it were shipped here, a red flag even for those who are just making money off the stuff. And how would he have put it in their vitamins? It's a long shot at best. He would've had to break into all their houses. The bad thing about herbs is that they're used legally all over the world to treat ailments from arthritis to rheumatism. The key is to know what that person is taking and why. Any ideas?"

"No," Anne answered, "but what about flowers? What if he had some delivered?"

"If he did, they wouldn't have eaten or boiled them. Some can be lethal with prolonged touching, but a local florist wouldn't have anything like that on hand. A larger florist with any knowledge of plants would certainly report it. Besides, if the girls had received bouquets, especially from a stranger or secret admirer, I think they would've shared this information."

"Jonathon Stephens is as weird as they come," Reid said, right out of the blue. "He has access to plants, and he was certainly shunned in high school."

"That might be a possibility," Vaughn said, "but I've learned in this business not to jump to conclusions. The most obvious is usually not your guy."

Reid and Nathaniel exchanged glances.

"Let me get the pie and ice cream," Anne said. "Vaughn has to get home. She's got a long day tomorrow, and we have a lot to deal with here. Enough of this talk for now."

They talked leisurely over their dessert. Nathaniel found Vaughn both fascinating and extremely intelligent, not to mention she was easy on the eyes. "I have to apologize for my lack of faith earlier," he said. "You've given us a lot to think about, and I appreciate it."

"I've enjoyed meeting you, too, Nathaniel," she said. "Please keep me in the loop about the investigation, and if you have any questions, feel free to give me a call. I think you guys are looking on the wrong computers though. The killer would've had to consult the internet. I bet his computer is where you'll find your answers."

"We have to find the killer before we can get a warrant to go through his computer."

"Stranger things have happened," she said.

Chapter 75

Jay Sykes was grateful for the credit card he and Meredith had kept for emergencies. They hadn't even charged a penny on it, no matter how bad things had gotten. His rainy day had come, and he needed the extra funds. No one in the police department or the DA's office had told him he had to stay in Atlanta, so he called the airport and booked a flight to Casper, Wyoming. It was over two hours away from Hayden, but the little town wasn't equipped for commercial flights.

He packed his warmest winter clothes, turned off the heat in the house, and locked the door behind him. If he never saw the place again, it'd be too soon. The truck sputtered and spat, but he got to the airport in record time.

He arrived two hours early because security at the Atlanta airport had become a bitch, and he didn't want to miss his flight. Even after waiting in the long lines, he still had over an hour to kill. He made his way to a bar down the concourse and ordered a scotch on the rocks and an eight dollar burger.

He was going to splurge. The card had a five thousand dollar limit, and he didn't give a damn if he spent it all.

After one too many drinks, Jay headed toward his gate, just in time to board his flight.

An overweight woman squeezed in next to him, her breathing loud and labored.

This should be a great flight, he thought sarcastically.

She gave him a flirtatious smile before pulling out a paperback.

Maybe that'll keep her occupied, he hoped.

The drink cart came by, and *romance-reading passenger* ordered a red wine, which was quickly followed by another. Unfortunately for Jay, that second glass got her talking.

"Where're you headed?" she asked.

"To visit a friend," he answered.

"Does your friend live in Casper?"

"No. Actually, I'm going to a little place called Hayden. I have some extra time off and thought I'd visit an old friend. He's the Sheriff there."

"Get out!" she laughed, playfully nudging his shoulder, invading way too much of his personal space. "Can you believe I'm headed to Hayden myself? Unfortunately, it isn't to visit an old friend. I have to attend the funeral of my young niece."

"I'm sorry to hear that," he answered. "What happened to her?"

"The sad thing is, they aren't really sure. She was only twenty-one and quite a beauty, I might add. My sister is all broken up, and I need to get out there as soon as possible. I was hoping to get a flight that'd take me closer."

"Yeah, me too," he answered, feeling the hair on his neck stand up. He hoped Consuelos wasn't already there, trying to intimidate Collier. He subconsciously leaned forward in an attempt to push the plane faster.

She slapped his leg, a little harder than intended. "Hey, since we're both headed to the same place, why don't we share a rental car? Nothing like saving a few bucks here and there."

Normally, he would've never considered it, but he quickly agreed. "Why not? Maybe the ride will go faster with company."

She smiled, obviously pleased with herself.

They waited in line for over thirty minutes to get their car. They rented a small compact, and while it was quite inexpensive, it made Jay uncomfortable. The last thing he wanted was to be cooped up with an overweight wheezer. Nevertheless, he put the charges on his credit card, and she reimbursed him her half in cash, which he appreciated.

As expected, she talked the whole way, but before he knew it, they were passing the sign that welcomed them to the town of Hayden. She used her cell phone to get directions to her sister's house, and he dropped her off with little difficulty. She thanked him, and they parted ways without even asking one another's names.

Jay found a local motel off of the beaten path and checked in for a week. He wasn't sure if he'd need to stay that long, but at $28.99 a night, he figured it was worth it. He unpacked his bags, washed his face, and lay on the bed to plot his strategy. He wasn't sure if contacting Reid Langley was the smart thing to do, but he didn't have anyone else to turn to. Jay hoped his sudden and unexpected appearance wouldn't be resented.

Chapter 76

Consuelos found the State of Wyoming to be nothing short of a pain in the ass. He'd always hated the chill in Atlanta during the winter months, but the wintry Wyoming weather was fucking ridiculous.

He drove into Wilhelm and checked into a cheap motel. It wasn't much to look at, but it was clean. He pulled out the map he'd picked up at a BP station and laid it out on the small desk in his room. There was a lot of ground to cover within a one-hour circumference, but he could do it. He had to.

The first order of business was to go shopping and buy some inconspicuous clothes. He didn't need to look like a pimp. Being Hispanic in a predominately Caucasian part of the country was enough to draw a few stares in itself. He drove to the nearest Wal-Mart and bought a whole wardrobe, along with a thick coat. "Damn, that place is amazing," he said with a laugh as he walked out of the store with his wares. "I should've come up with that idea myself!"

He changed and headed to dinner at a chain steakhouse. It was the same as the one in Atlanta, and for some reason, that gave him a boost of confidence.

The next day, he'd begin his search. For two people, that search wouldn't have a pleasant ending.

Chapter 77

After going through the hard drives of several computers, Nathaniel and Reid decided to grab a bite at Kaleb's. They weren't used to the constant glow of monitors, and their eyes had soon tired of it.

"Afternoon, Sheriff," Frank Sewell yelled, greeting them from across the restaurant.

The two waved and took the nearest booth.

"Laverne, Gracie, and I have eaten at Dina's but not at Kaleb's yet," Nathaniel said. "Seems like the same kind of down-to-earth place."

"Yeah, it is," Reid answered. "It's been family-owned for years, definitely a mom-and-pop place. They're open twenty-four hours, except Sundays, when they're closed."

"That still shocks me about these diners. How many people go out to eat in the middle of the night in Hayden, Wyoming?"

"Probably not many. I think they use the time to

restock and clean up."

"How are ya, Sheriff?" Frank asked, squeezing Reid's hand with his big, beefy paw.

"Doing about as well as can be expected. This is one of my old friends, Nathaniel Smith," he said, pointing across the table. "And Nathaniel, this is Frank Sewell, the owner of this fine establishment."

"Nice to make your acquaintance," Nathaniel said, pushing his hand forward, hoping Frank would go easy on him.

"Can't say I haven't already heard about ya. You know how small towns are. Everybody needs something to talk about. Haven't heard anything bad if that makes ya feel any better."

"I have to say it does. You never know how people will react to a stranger."

"That's true. It doesn't hurt that you've got such a beautiful little girl. How's she doin' 'round here, being a mulatto and all?"

Nathaniel could feel his blood starting to heat up, but took a few deep breaths and attempted a calm answer. "She's fine. The children and adults in the community are actually treating her like a normal kid."

Frank's cheeks brightened with embarrassment. "Forgive my ignorance," he said sincerely. "I certainly meant no harm. It's just rare around here, but I assure you that everyone finds her quite beautiful."

"No offense taken," Nathaniel answered, trying to lighten up a bit. "She is a beautiful little girl if I do say so myself."

Just as the situation was becoming less uncomfortable, a friendly woman rounded the corner. "Afternoon, you two," she said cheerfully. A fresh yellow apron covered her rotund belly. "I'm the brains of the operation." She said playfully, reaching for Nathaniel's hand. "I'm Helen, the mother of this dysfunctional clan. It's nice to meet you, young man."

"You too." Nathaniel smiled, taking an instant liking to her.

She looked around before pulling up a chair.

Here it comes, Reid thought, *all those questions about the deaths.* But he was pleasantly surprised the conversation wasn't geared that way at all.

"Mr. Smith, is it?"

"Yes, Ma'am. Nathaniel Smith."

"Well, I hear you brought your sister with you."

"Sure did. Laverne works over at the hospital, she's a real sweetheart."

"Funny you should say that," she said, leaning forward and lowering her voice. "My two boys, Aaron and Adam, need a good woman."

"Helen, please!" Frank interrupted. "This is hardly the time or place."

"Whatever you say, Frank," she answered, waving him off like a fly. "There's never a time or place, according to you. Those boys are driving me crazy, Sheriff. They need a life. They live and breathe this diner, and it isn't healthy, I tell ya. They need a social life. After they left high school, they started helping with the business, and haven't stopped since. They're workaholics, and as much as I appreciate their help, I want more for my boys. For starters, a couple of nice young ladies."

Nathaniel and Reid shared a hearty laugh.

"I wouldn't worry about it, Helen. It isn't like there's a large pool of single women around town. Buy them a couple of tickets to take a cruise somewhere, and they just might come back hitched."

Frank let out something resembling a snort, but Helen clapped her hands at the idea. "Maybe I'll do that," she said. "It couldn't hurt. Anyway, if your sister should ever dine with us, I'd love for the boys to meet her. It's so hard for fellas to find a good woman these days, especially one with a job!"

"Let's let these gentlemen eat," Frank scolded as he made his way back to the kitchen. "I recommend the special today," he said over his shoulder. "I'll bring out two."

Reid graciously offered to pay for lunch, and Nathaniel took him up on it.

Before they left the diner, Nathaniel turned to Helen. "Mrs. Sewell, just how old are your boys? I don't want my sister cradle-robbing!"

"They're of age, Mr. Smith, twenty-four and thirty-two. There's no hope, I'm telling ya, just no hope at all."

Chapter 78

"Okay, Reid," Nathaniel started as soon as they got into the patrol car, "you need to get out that big dry-erase board of yours and set it up at home. It seems we may have two more suspects."

"I hate to agree with you, but at this point, we've got to consider all our options. I've been holding off a town meeting, but it's inevitable. I need to meet with the Mayor while you get Gracie. Can you come over about 5:00?"

"Yeah, I think so."

"I'll order a pizza. Don't forget to bring a DVD for Gracie."

Nathaniel was late getting to Reid's. He wanted Gracie to have her bath first, in case they got home late. She didn't like the idea of going to someone's house in her pajamas and robe, but a bribe of pizza finally settled the issue.

Reid had the board set up in front of the fireplace and had already written down the suspects fitting the age range.

"Well? What are your thoughts?"

"Um…" Nathaniel pondered as he assessed the list. "Aaron and Adam Sewell and Jonathon Stephens? I can agree there, but Deputy Maloney? He's just having a hard time dealing with it. I don't see it as being him."

"That's the point, Nathaniel. The killer can't appear suspicious."

"One point I've been pondering," Nathaniel started, "is that if this guy is using poison, he'd most likely need a place of his own. Do any of these guys still live at home?"

"We can check it out. I know Maloney has his own apartment, but I'm not sure about the Sewell boys or Jonathon Stephens. That shouldn't be hard to check."

"I like Vaughn and think she's an intelligent woman, but I'm leery of limiting our prospects to her statistical outline. Let's look at all the oddballs around town."

"I'll think about it, but we'd have a board full if I wrote them all down. Small towns are home to a lot of real characters, Nathaniel."

Chapter 79

After weighing his options and deciding to go out on the proverbial limb, Jay Sykes drove to the sheriff's office. He asked for Reid by name and was quickly greeted by the him. They hadn't met before, at least that he could recall. "Hello, Mr. Langley," he offered, a smile refusing to form on his dry lips.

"Good Morning," Reid said. "How can I help you?"

"If it'd be possible, I'd like to speak with you in private, Sheriff."

"I can give you five minutes," Reid answered. He was more than a little suspicious of a random stranger showing up with all that was going on.

"I'd appreciate it."

After moving a mound of paperwork from a leather chair across from his desk, Reid motioned for his visitor to take a seat. "I'm afraid I didn't catch your name."

"Jay Sykes. I was formerly with the Atlanta PD." He

watched as the color drained from Reid's face. A few uncomfortable moments of silence followed.

"Atlanta, huh? What the hell are you doing here?" Reid asked.

"I'm here to find Consuelos. He ruined my life."

"And how did you find me? Find...*us*?"

The Sheriff's tone was getting aggressive, making Jay wonder if he'd made a dire mistake. "I...uh, it was really just a good guess. It's kind of a long story."

Reid got up and closed his office door. "I know I told you I've only got five minutes, but I like long stories. Why don't you tell me one?"

An hour later, it was all laid out on the table: the dirty cop story, the shame, and the dreadful need for revenge.

Reid got up and paced the floor relentlessly. "Damn it! If you found us this easily that means Consuelos can."

"I don't think so. It was good luck on my part."

"We don't welcome shootouts here, Mr. Sykes. Hayden is a peaceful place, and we don't need or want you here."

"You can't make me leave. The last time I checked, it was still a free country."

"One phone call to the Atlanta PD and I'm sure they'll front the money to get you back there."

"Look, I'm not here to cause trouble. I'm staying in a cheap motel on the outskirts of town. You won't even see me. I'd think you'd welcome an extra set of eyes."

"I don't have time for this, Mr. Sykes. It appears you've made up your mind, but if I lay eyes on you again, I won't hesitate to make that call."

"Thank you, Sheriff, but one more thing. Do you think Consuelos could be responsible for the death of that young girl?"

"What young girl? What are you talking about?"

Jay held up his hands in surrender. "It was all a coincidence. I caught a plane from Atlanta to Casper, and by sheer chance, I was seated next to a woman who was coming here to attend her niece's funeral. It sounded like some of Consuelos's handiwork, perhaps a warning."

"Well, it isn't. Please let yourself out. I've got responsibilities to attend to."

Jay knew when to leave well enough alone, so he stood up, nodded a good-bye, and left the police station without looking back.

Chapter 80

The last thing Reid wanted to deal with was a telephone call, but he took it anyway. To his surprise and relief, it was Anne. "Hey there," he answered. "It's been quite a while."

"Yes, too long."

"To what do I owe this privilege? Business or pleasure?"

"I'd like to say pleasure, but I'm afraid I can't. What are you doing for lunch?"

Reid glanced down at his watch and realized it was well after 2:00. "I guess I'm meeting you. Name the place."

"The hospital dining room?"

"Damn, Anne. Couldn't you think of something a little more romantic?"

"I don't have the time. I'm squeezing lunch in as it is."

"I'll be over in twenty minutes."

"Save a table if I'm not there."

When he finally arrived at the hospital, Reid gave

Anne the once-over. He'd never seen her so tired and frazzled. Her hair was clean but carelessly pulled into a ponytail, and she wore very little makeup. "What can I get you?" he asked.

"Nothing. I don't have much time."

"Listen, Anne, you've got to eat. You don't look so good. It's important that you keep your energy up."

"It's called working too hard and trying to find justice for young, dead girls."

"Ouch. That stung. My apologies, but I'm still going to insist you have a bite. Stay put, and I'll grab a sandwich. You can eat it on the go if you don't finish."

A couple of minutes later, he returned with two turkey sandwiches and two cartons of milk, only to find Anne had paperwork spread all over the table. "What is this?" he asked as he unwrapped the sandwiches and handed her one.

"I started thinking about what Vaughn said in reference to the plants. It seems pretty logical. The other things would have to be given in pill or capsule form or diluted in something they took soon after. There were no injection marks, no positive tox results. Just think about it, Reid. I've been doing some research on poisonous plants found in the US," she said. She thumbed through the papers with one hand and ravenously ate the sandwich she held in the other.

"And what have you come up with?"

"Well, there's poison hemlock. It originated in Europe, but it's found its way to the US. It can be put in a salad and looks and apparently tastes like spinach. The leaves are even similar. The girls were very health conscious, but it would've been odd for them to accept a random salad unless they'd actually ordered or bought it."

Reid's mind went straight to the Sewell brothers, but he continued to listen.

"If they did eat a salad with hemlock in it, the symptoms would've started fairly rapidly, but it would take several hours for death to occur. That might have worked in the situations of Joanna Sibley and Lauren Lowe, but I don't think Haley Monroe was eating a salad while she was gardening, nor was Madison Aldridge as she slept. Besides, the symptoms had a rapid onset in both of the latter deaths."

"So we scratch the hemlock. What's next?"

"There's also jimsonweed, otherwise known as stinkweed. The whole plant is toxic, and there are numerous documented cases of it being boiled in tea. The berries, if eaten, are also highly toxic. One of the symptoms is convulsions, and we know that happened in three of the four cases, due to the bruises and contusions we found. Stinkweed contains belladonna alkaloids, which we could test for."

"Stinkweed, huh? That's some name."

"I know. Next, we have the monkshood plant. There are several species all over the United States. Like stinkweed, the whole plant is poisonous, but it contains aconitine and aconine, both of which can be easily found with tests. It can be ingested or absorbed through the skin, so there wouldn't have to be injection marks or anything in the stomach contents. Depending on the dosage, death can occur within minutes, caused by paralysis of the heart muscles. Monkshood really captures my attention because there's no known antidote, and our killer apparently knows that. It can also be eaten in a salad, but it doesn't tend to be as fatal that way. You're free to look through all this information, but I'd say monkshood is the most likely culprit. I'm surprised, I can say, by the number of highly toxic plants found in our backyards."

Reid looked down at the thick stack of papers and printouts about deadly poisons. "It'd be great if we could get a positive tox on one of these, but it still doesn't get us any closer to our killer."

"Maybe, maybe not. At least if we catch him, we'll

have all our ducks in a row, so to speak. The evidence will be there, and we'll have a cause of death."

"I guess you're right. We could use another visit from your friend Vaughn."

"A-ha! Do I detect a change in attitude, Sheriff?"

"I'm not ruling out the potential of an intelligent woman assisting our investigation."

"Hmm. Should I be jealous?"

"Give me a break, Anne," he answered, winking at her. "I'm glad you devoured that sandwich. I've been worried about you."

"I'm a big girl, Sheriff. You don't have to worry."

"There's a brainstorming session at my house at 7:00, if you can make it."

"I'll try. These days, that's all I can promise."

Chapter 81

Continuous calls from the Bureau and Captain Russ Robertson set off a stream of suspicion. Cecily Libby was officially missing. She'd been estranged from her family for years and hadn't attempted any recent contact, leaving them at a loss as to when she'd actually disappeared.

Her picture was sent out to every agency in the United States and Europe, and within twenty-four hours, they had their answer. She was one of the Jane Does still taking up space in the Dade County morgue. A brief description of how the body was found left no doubt she'd been murdered. They just wondered how much she'd given away before she was tossed to her death.

Cecily had been fairly new on the job and, thankfully, hadn't flown on many flights. That narrowed it down to some extent. What ultimately confirmed their suspicions was that Mad Dog Consuelos had been rumored to be in Miami when it happened. There was little doubt that she'd spilled the beans about something while she was high.

The mission would have to be altered and the small family extradited from Wyoming. The Witness Protection Program was not about to screw with its record, especially when a little girl's life was at stake.

Chapter 82

Once Gracie was fed and in her pajamas, she and Nathaniel rode over to Reid's for yet another night of the guessing game that was getting the best of them. Nathaniel carried in two buckets of chicken and some side items Mrs. Sewell had chosen for him while Gracie carried her backpack with the newest princess release and her teddy bear. She'd started to have nightmares, and Laverne thought the new furry friend might help.

Reid sat at the table with papers spread erratically across it. He stood up as soon as he saw the food. "Thank God, I'm starving! We'll have to eat on the coffee table. After you guys left, I couldn't possibly get this place organized again."

He walked over and scooped Gracie up in his arms.

She wrapped her thin arms around his neck. "Hey, Uncle Reid. Your hair is wet." She giggled as she reached up and touched it.

"Yes, it is, young lady, I just had a shower. Now let me see that new teddy bear. I hear it's more portable than huge Doctor Pennington."

She quickly fished out the new bear from her backpack, briefly showing it to Reid before hugging it close.

"Should we wait for the girls or go ahead and eat?" Reid asked.

"Girls? I thought it was just Anne."

"She's bringing Vaughn. Apparently, they're big on this plant theory."

Reid walked Nathaniel back to his bedroom to tell him the latest tale about Jay Sykes.

"What the hell? If he can find us, so can Consuelos."

"He found us by going through files of the latest cops to leave the force. He figured you'd come to one of us for help."

"I don't give a damn how he did it. He's going to try to lure Consuelos here. That's his only motive, and he knows how to get the word out to the lowlifes in Atlanta. He could be in Hayden now!"

"Nathaniel, I don't believe that, but I can get you out of here. I'll call Nick Solomon."

"Hell no! I'm not going to run from that son-of-a-bitch for the rest of my life. We're staying right here. Maybe it's for the best if he's lured out. He has to be found eventually, or we'll never be free."

"Nathaniel, think about what you're saying. We're talking about Gracie's and Laverne's safety, and—"

"That's exactly right. We need to end this once and for all. I refuse to have my family constantly uprooted, running from state to state just to get away from some monster. What kind of life would that be? I want more for my daughter."

"She isn't legally *your* daughter, Nathaniel. I hate to say that, but it's the truth. The Marshals can and will come in and take her if they feel she's at risk." Reid was saved by the doorbell and any further conversation as he went to answer it. "Glad to see you, ladies," he said as he opened the front door.

"Happy to be here again," Vaughn said. "Smells like you have a good dinner waiting for us."

"Courtesy of Nathaniel," he answered.

"Good evening, ladies. Let's eat and get to work. Gracie needs her rest."

"And who is Gracie?" Vaughn asked, acting as though she didn't see her cuddled up on the sofa.

"I'm Gracie," she said, sitting up to see who the pretty lady was. "That's my Daddy. My Mommy died, so he doesn't have a wife anymore…till he finds a new one."

"Gracie!" Nathaniel said, attempting to scold her.

"What? You don't," she said teasingly.

"Let's eat," Reid suggested.

The meal was eaten and everyone was anxious to get to work. The sound of Gracie's movie played in the background at a low volume.

"I'm going with the plant theory too," Vaughn said without hesitation. "And like Anne, I'd put my bet on monkshood. I don't know why. Maybe I'm psychic. I've brought all the information I could find on it, and you can review it later. My concern now is who in this community might fit some of our profiles."

Reid started with the Sewell brothers, letting everyone know he'd found out they lived together in a small trailer behind their parents' home. "They seem like nice guys," he continued, "but for the first time the other day, I thought of them as suspects. Their mother is upset about their lack of a social life, and even asked us to set one of them up with Nathaniel's sister."

Vaughn didn't answer but waited for him to continue, as she soaked it all in.

"The real suspect is the funeral home owner's son. He

was shunned in high school by some of these very same girls and, quite frankly, he's as strange as they get—you know, one of those guys who hides in the shadows, kind of a lurker if that's even a word?"

"I think it is," she answered.

"I hate to say it, but one of my deputies is in question as well. He's young and knew all of the victims. He's somewhat of a...well, a nerd. I don't expect he was very popular in high school either. He lives by himself, in a small efficiency apartment. He's a good deputy, but the deaths have devastated him. I feel guilty even suspecting that Maloney could've done it."

"You have to look at everyone, Sheriff. It's your job to be objective. Don't let personal feelings come into play here."

"Isn't it also possible that it's someone from outside of Hayden?" Reid asked.

"Of course it's possible. We're just trying to start at the most logical place first. Any other single men who live alone?"

"A couple of middle-aged teachers, one of our paramedics, and a couple of stock boys from the local grocery store."

"Tell me about this paramedic. Is he a loner? Does he get involved in community activities?"

"Oh, Lord," Anne interjected. "I can't even imagine Joe Hill being a suspect. He's not exactly a social butterfly, but I think that's because of his weight. He's awfully shy until you get to know him. He's worked as an EMT for years. Everyone in Hayden knows him."

"Hmm..." Vaughn pondered. "Sometimes, it's those we least expect. About how old is he?"

"I don't know exactly. Mid to late thirties," she answered.

A silence fell over the room as everyone pondered the ridiculous possibility that Joe Hill, the faithful paramedic, could be a killer.

"You know," Reid said, his head down in shame for even thinking of saying what was to come next, "when you really think about it, Joe is kind of an oddball."

"Reid!" Anne said. "That's one of the ugliest things I've ever heard you say!"

"I know, and I feel like shit for sayin' it, but he's just always so nervous, so...well, so sweaty."

"He's overweight, and his work is physically demanding," Anne snapped protectively. "How many times have you loaded a body into an ambulance?"

"Look," Vaughn interrupted, "I don't know him myself, but sometimes discussing possibilities can be positive, even if it appears hurtful."

"I just see him as one of the good guys," Anne answered defiantly. "He works hard in this community to save lives, not to end them."

"That may very well be true," Vaughn answered, aware she may be treading on thin ice with the issue, "but as a medical professional, Anne, you know there are many nurses and doctors who've killed their patients. Some have even taken their patients very close to death, only to bring them back just for the atta-boy and a pat on the back."

"Point taken. Let's move on."

The phone rang and took everyone's mind away from sweaty, Joe Hill.

"Langley," Reid answered.

The group watched as the color drained from his face and his hand trembled beneath the weight of the phone.

"I'll be right there. Don't let anyone in to talk to him, not a damn soul. You hear me?" After he laid the phone down on its cradle, Reid pounded his fist down hard on the counter.

Gracie sat up from the couch and passed him a worried look. "Is everything all right, Uncle Reid?" the girl asked.

"Yes, Baby. Just watch your movie." He sat back

down at the table, attempting to hide his shock and sorrow. "It's Matthew Maloney. He's at Mountainside, fighting for his life. He...God, the kid slit his wrists."

A collective gasp from the crowd followed, and everyone began to gather up their coats and keys.

"Where are you all going?" Gracie asked, confusion crossing her little face.

"They're going to the hospital," Nathaniel answered. "Everything is okay, Honey."

"I'll stay here with Gracie," Vaughn suggested. "You go ahead, Nathaniel."

"No, I think your expertise is far greater than mine in this situation. Somebody, please call me and let me know what's going on. Don't just leave me hanging."

"We won't," Reid promised as the three rushed out the door, hoping to find an alive and coherent Deputy Maloney.

Once they were gone, Nathaniel smiled at Gracie. "So, little one, it's just the two of us now, I can watch the movie with you. I haven't seen it before, do you mind starting over from the beginning?"

"Of course, Daddy," Gracie said, "you can't watch *it* from the middle."

Chapter 83

Matthew was alive but groggy from the painkillers and sedatives he'd been given.

Deputy Ray was standing outside of his room, doing his duty to keep anyone out except for Maloney's parents.

"How is he?" Reid asked.

"Disoriented and tired. He's a good boy, Sheriff. I didn't see this coming, or I would've talked to him. He just needed a friend."

"There's no one to blame for this," Vaughn said, stepping up to introduce herself, deliberately leaving off her Doctor title. She'd never felt comfortable using it. It seemed to intimidate people, making her job more difficult. "When someone has their mind set on suicide, there's very little anyone can do."

Deputy Ray studied her face, giving her a questionable stare. Vaughn was a stranger who'd stepped into their family uninvited, and he wouldn't waste time asking why she was there.

Vaughn was accustomed to such a reaction and left well enough alone for the moment.

"I need to see him," Reid said. "I'm going in."

Matthew was lying in the bed, looking up at the ceiling with a blank stare. His parents were seated on either side of the bed, their eyes red from crying and the simple shock of it all.

"Hey, Sheriff," Mr. Maloney said, standing and holding out his hand. "I know Matthew is glad to see you."

"And I'm glad to see him. I know you both want to be by his side, but I was wondering if I might have a few minutes alone with him."

"That'd be a good idea. His mother and I could use a strong cup of coffee and some fresh air."

"Thank you very much. I can't imagine how difficult this must be. If I'd seen it coming, I surely would have…"

"Don't even say it, Sheriff," Mrs. Maloney interrupted as she walked over to him. "You've been very good to our son and a positive mentor. No one could've stopped this. We're just grateful that he's going to be okay. We plan to get him some professional help."

Reid waited until they left the room before he took a seat next to Matthew's bed. "What's the deal, buddy? You're late for work and I have a good mind to dock your ass."

The banter brought a slight smile from his young deputy, but his eyes remained fixated on the ceiling.

Reid tried desperately not to look at the thick gauze wound around his wrists as he said, "Matthew, so many people care about you, and if we failed you in any way, we're certainly sorry."

Maloney slowly turned his head to make eye contact with his boss. "No one has let me down. I love my job, I love the people I work with, and I love helping this community."

Reid considered how to continue, but Matthew beat him to it.

"I guess you're probably wondering why I'd do such a thing."

"Yes, but whatever the reason, I'm here for you. We can get you help."

"I just started taking the deaths of those girls too hard, Sheriff. I didn't realize how much it was affecting me until now. I'm just weak. Maybe I'm not cut out to be a police officer."

"You're not weak, Matthew. You handled those situations with compassion. That's what makes a good cop."

"It was an act."

"Maloney, cops have to put on an act far more than most people realize. We saw those young girls lying there, knowing there was nothing we could do, but we had to stay strong for the families because they needed us. You're a damn good cop. Don't you think the rest of the department went home and shed a few tears? Don't you think we're frustrated as hell because we can't solve this fucking case?"

"It's not that, Sheriff."

Reid held his breath until he felt he'd explode. *Please don't confess,* he prayed silently. *If you did it, I can't bear to hear it.*

"I feel guilty because of how I felt about those girls."

Oh, God. "What do you mean?"

"They were out of my league, always bunched up in their little cliques, treating me like I was invisible. Don't get me wrong. They weren't ever cruel to me. They just avoided me. I was one of those kids no one ever noticed. Do you know what it feels like to never be included in anything? I wasn't even invited to one birthday party the whole time I was in elementary school."

"What are you saying, Matthew?"

"I'm saying I feel guilty as hell. So many times, I

wished bad things would happen to them so they wouldn't be better than me. I even wished they'd all be in a car accident that'd disfigure them so they would be as invisible as I was. Now that this is happening, I feel like…well, I'm afraid my awful feelings made all of this happen."

"You can't really believe that, Matthew," Reid said, reaching across to pat him a couple of times on his scrawny shoulder. "Hell, we all wish things we shouldn't, like evil and harm on people who've hurt us. We don't really mean it. Believe me, son, you had nothing to do with this."

"I wish I could believe you, Sheriff."

"Well, you will when we catch the bastard who *is* responsible for all of this! You just get better and get your ass out of here. We need you on this case!"

That made Matthew laugh for the first time, and it was music to Reid's ears. At the very least, he could count his young deputy out of the equation. Matthew Maloney was no killer, and it was a huge relief.

Chapter 84

Mad Dog finished off his breakfast at the small diner, then headed back to his room. Studying the map again, he realized it could literally take him years to find the place where the two were hidden. Then, in some kind of epiphany, the answer came to him. It was so obvious that he could've kicked himself for not thinking of it earlier.

Laverne Lewis was a chubby, unattractive, single woman, and all she had in life was her brother and her job. He picked up the Yellow Pages and looked under hospitals. It would take awhile, but he would find her, and when he did, she'd lead him right to them.

He called the two hospitals in the area without any success. His story was certainly believable. He could sound professional when absolutely necessary, even dropping some of his Hispanic accent. "Hello. I have an old friend who just moved to this area, and she told me she has a new job at a hospital. I just happen to be here on business and would love to surprise her. Her name is Laverne Lewis, but I believe she's going by her maiden name now. For the life of me, I can't remember it. She's heavyset, friendly, a very good nurse..."After several transfers to different departments and at least that many rejections, he thought of giving up, but decided to visit the motel office and see if they could provide other local phonebooks. Even with growing doubts, he still had a good feeling about it. *Yeah, that's where I'll find them,* he convinced himself.

Chapter 85

The crowd arrived back at Reid's house to find Gracie and Nathaniel gone. A note on the coffee table requested that they call him, no matter how late.

"Evenin'," Reid said.

"Sorry, but I needed to put Gracie to sleep. I don't want her getting off schedule. What about the kid, your deputy? Is he going to be all right?"

"Looks that way. He seems to be carrying some guilt about the girls ignoring him in high school. Nell warned me, but I didn't listen. I guess I expect everyone to have thick skin."

"Does that make him an obvious suspect or clear him?"

"It clears him."

"Remember what Vaughn said. The ones you least expect may just be the ones who surprise you."

"Well, I was there and talked to him. If he was

fabricating a tale, he should be up for an Oscar. Believe me, Maloney isn't that smart."

"Okay, so what does tomorrow hold?"

"I say we make a few house calls. Joe Hill is first on my list."

"I'll meet you at your office as soon as I drop Gracie off."

"Ten-four."

Chapter 86

Reid went to his office first thing the next morning, only to find Nell sitting across from his desk, nursing a cup of warm coffee. Somehow, he'd known she'd be there, but selfishly hoped she wouldn't.

"Morning, Sheriff," she said warmly. "I'm not here to say I told you so. I know you're hurting just like the rest of us."

He sighed heavily and sat down behind his desk. He wasn't one to discuss his feelings, but at the moment, they were dangling from his sleeve. "I feel like shit, Nell. I should've listened to you. You saw this coming and came to me to fix it. But I brushed it off, just like I do so many things."

"If you're looking for pity, you won't get it here. You know this isn't your fault. Besides, you *did* talk to him."

"A lot of good that did."

"I spoke with Mrs. Maloney today, and she tells me

Matthew is up and walking around. The hospital plans to keep him for a few days to make sure he sees a psychiatrist. That's what he needs right now."

"That's good. I'm glad to hear it."

"Are you going to let him back on the force?"

"Why wouldn't I? Of course, he'll have to have a full release from his doctor, but Maloney's a good kid. I kind of like having him around."

A smile spread almost the width of Nell's face and, without further comment, she threw her empty coffee cup in the trash and went on about her business.

Nathaniel came in almost as soon as his office had cleared, carrying a bag from Kaleb's Diner.

"Two sausage biscuits and a couple of coffees."

"What is it with you and food? You never show up anywhere without it."

"I guess it's a side effect from all those stakeouts. You never knew when you might have to go hours without it."

"I can see your point."

"I seem to be making friends with Mrs. Sewell. I'm playing big brother, trying to find out more about her sons before I let them meet Laverne."

"Not a bad idea. What have you got so far?"

"They each split part of the day shift, and both work in the evening to clean and cook for any late-nighters. Looks like we might be able to do a little snooping around the trailer in the middle of the night."

"You're from the bounty-hunting business, so you're used to a little more leeway, Nathaniel. But I'm bound by laws and search and seizure warrants signed by a judge."

"I'm not saying we should break into the place. Maybe we can just walk around it a bit."

"I'll think about it, but I thought we decided to give Joe Hill a visit."

"Oh yeah." Nathaniel looked at his watch. "Do you think 8:30's too early to knock on his door?"

"Well, we're both up. If he isn't, he should be."

Winter had settled in but was going fairly easy on Hayden. The wind was the toughest thing to bear, but when mixed with snow, it was really tough to handle. The sun was shining brightly, and the wind was at its mildest during this time of year.

The ride was a quick one. Joe Hill's cabin was tucked neatly in a forest of various trees and plants. The outside needed some work, but it was still orderly.

Nathaniel held his breath as Reid rang the bell.

Heavy footsteps plodded to the door, then Joe peeked around the curtain before he opened it. "How ya doin', Sheriff?"

"Pretty good. This is a friend of mine from out of state, Nathaniel Smith."

"Nice to make your acquaintance. I've heard a lot about you already. People here seem to be taking well to you."

"That's certainly nice to hear," Nathaniel answered.

"Oh, where are my manners? Sorry, gentlemen," Joe said, shuffling his feet uncomfortably. "Come on in. I'm not used to visitors, but Jane did come by a few days ago."

"We should've called," Reid said. "I just wanted to check on you."

"Check on me? Is something wrong?"

"Oh no, nothing like that," Reid answered. "I guess after what happened to Matthew, I wanted to make sure you were okay."

"Me? I'm afraid I don't understand. I mean, I like the kid, but we aren't exactly buddies, so—"

"This is coming out all wrong," Reid said, stepping lightly into the conversation. "Do you mind if we sit down?"

A look of confusion and concern crossed Joe's face, but he led them into the small den, taking the recliner for himself.

"Thing is," Reid continued, "I feel a little responsible for Matthew's suicide attempt."

"And why would you say that?" Joe asked suspiciously.

"Nell came to me a couple of weeks ago to tell me how hard he's been taking all these deaths, and I didn't take the time to really talk to him. I've been in this business for a long time, and I guess I've learned to disassociate myself when things like this happen. Matthew hasn't had much experience."

"No need to blame yourself, Sheriff," Joe said, his body language appearing more comfortable as he leaned back in the chair.

"I'm used to big-city crime, but Hayden's no metropolis. I need to work harder on taking people's feelings into account. I know these murders have taken a toll on you and Jane. You two are almost always the first on the scene, and I'm here for you if you ever need to talk."

"I appreciate it, Sheriff," Joe said, taking in a deep, breath. "I've been in this business a while, too, and I know what I'm up against. I hate to say it, but these things happen."

Nathaniel pondered the strange comment. *These things happen? In a small town like this?* He found Joe not only arrogant but seriously lacking in compassion. Even if the people in Hayden liked the paramedic, something about the man didn't sit right with Nathaniel. When a mound of cold medicines caught his eye he said, "Looks like you've had a cold, Mr. Hill. Which one of those works best for you? I can't ever find any over the counter meds that work, especially when my sinuses are bothering me."

Joe looked at Nathaniel for several seconds as if he'd suddenly just noticed he was there. "Haven't found one yet that'll take away a prolonged cold, and I can safely say I've tried just about all of 'em."

"It's all a racket anyway. The advertising agencies

probably make a mint with all their bullshit promises."

"You got that right."

"Well, Joe," Reid said, standing and stretching his back, "just wanted you to know the community appreciates your efforts and dedication. If you ever need me, just let me know. I think we're going to go by and visit Jane for a few minutes."

"She'll enjoy that," he answered. "She doesn't get many visitors either."

"Oh yeah, I hate to bother you, but could I use your bathroom? Nathaniel's been filling me full of coffee. I'm not sure I can even make the ten-minute drive to Jane's."

"Sorry about that, Sheriff," Joe said, standing and trying inconspicuously to block the path to the hallway. "Funny thing is, I'm having trouble with my plumbing. Should have it fixed in a couple of days. You're welcome to that old outhouse out back. I've had to use it since yesterday. Damn plumbers make more than doctors."

"You called Andy Simms, I take it. He's about the only plumber left in town, isn't he?"

"Yeah, that leaves me, my clogged pipes, and my wallet at his mercy."

"Guess I'll use the outhouse then. Wouldn't want one of my deputies to catch me pissing on the side of the road."

After Joe saw them out, Reid walked down to the outhouse, trying to make the restroom request sound more believable. *Funny*, he thought to himself, as he opened the creaky door. *If he's been using this outhouse since yesterday, why are cobwebs covering the doorway?*

Chapter 87

The visit with Jane was a much more pleasant one, but the two men found it hard to get away from her. She enjoyed their company and loved talking about her job. It was obvious that she had compassion for the families of the deceased, but she also enjoyed the excitement of something happening, something she was right in the middle of. Reid had seen it many times with new recruits, that strange desire to see something others may never see: fatal car crashes, suicides, and murders.

Back at the station, things were going smoothly, and the two men prayed it'd stay that way. Another murder would be too much.

"I wish we could get into Jonathon Stephens's apartment," Nathaniel commented. "Maybe he and Joe Hill are in this together. They're both creepy."

"I've never thought of Joe as creepy," Reid answered, "but today, I have tell ya, he made the hair stand up on the back of my neck. There were cobwebs across the door of the outhouse, Nathaniel. That alleged plumbing problem was bullshit. For some reason, the man didn't want me in his bathroom."

"That doesn't surprise me. And what about all that cold medicine? Who buys every brand on the shelves? He must have spent a hundred bucks on that stuff. You think he's been whipping up a nasty little potion in his bathroom?"

"I'll talk to Anne and see what she thinks. In the meantime, do you need me to call Nell?"

"For what?"

"I figured you wouldn't want Gracie going on our little field trip to the Sewell brothers' trailer."

"Oh yeah. I forgot. That crazy guy from the Atlanta PD has me worried out of my damn mind. Suppose Consuelos has him on the payroll. I think we're taking it too lightly."

"I haven't heard back from him. He was probably all talk and ran back to Georgia with his tail tucked between his legs. If he meant any harm, you'd already be dead."

"That's comforting."

"See you tonight…say, ten o'clock?"

"If Nell is available, sure. Otherwise, I'm afraid I'll have to take a raincheck," Nathaniel said.

Chapter 88

Consuelos put on his most attractive Wal-Mart outfit and moseyed into the front office of the dingy motel. Just as he'd hoped, a young girl was sitting behind the counter. She had a bad case of acne, was smoking Kool cigarettes, and gnawing on her grubby nails. *Ah, how easily this one will be bought,* Mad Dog thought. *Minimum wage, probably has a couple of snotty-nosed kids at home, and can barely scratch up the money for her next pack of cheap-ass cigs.* "Hey, beautiful," he said, looking her up and down.

"Can I help you?"

"Well, first, the obvious question is, what's a good-looking girl like you doing working in a dump like this?"

She gave him a sideways glance, then took a long drag on her cigarette before stubbing it out into the overflowing ashtray. "It pays the bills—sort of. What's a guy like you doing *staying* in a dump like this?"

"Ah, and she's smart too."

He slid two hundred dollars across the counter. "I could use some help."

"I ain't no hooker if that's the kind of help yer lookin' for."

"Listen, Honey," he answered smoothly, "if I was looking for a hooker, I wouldn't insult a classy girl like you with a mere two hundred bucks."

She seemed pleased and lit another cigarette. "All right. What kinda help you need?" she asked as she pulled the two bills toward her, folded them, and put them in her jeans pocket. "I'm on probation, and I ain't 'bout to go back to jail."

"Oh, I wouldn't ask you to do anything illegal, Baby. I'm looking for somebody. I could use a female voice and a list of hospitals within a hundred miles of here."

"Got another one of them hundred dollar bills?"

"Greedy little thing, aren't ya? You better pay off for this kind of money."

"Just tell me what to do."

In less than forty-five minutes, the poor, distraught, little second cousin with nowhere to go, had located her aunt. "I have cab money to get there," she assured the older Pink Lady, "so don't tell her I'm comin'. I wouldn't want her to worry any longer than necessary."

"Oh, Honey," the old lady said kindly, "I wouldn't ever worry sweet Laverne."

"I don't want to interrupt her shift or anything," the desk clerk said, smiling at Consuelos. "When does she get off?"

"She works 3:00 pm to 11:00 pm, dear."

Consuelos laughed viciously, making the young girl uncomfortable.

The deal's sealed now, you stupid broad, he thought. *I'd put a bullet in your head if it wouldn't lead the cops right to me.*

Chapter 89

Nell showed up early with gummy bears, new satin ribbons, and a coloring book.

"Oh Lord." Nathaniel teased. "All she needs is someone else to spoil her."

"She *does*," Nell replied defiantly. "A good girl needs lots of spoiling, doesn't she, Gracie?"

"Yes, Ma'am," she answered. "I need lots of spoiling."

"I think we may need to change babysitters," Nathaniel joked.

Gracie answered him by giving Nell a bear hug. "No way, Daddy!"

"I'm just kidding, Sweetie. I'll be home later, but you'll probably be in bed. I'll wake you in the morning."

"Okay," she answered quickly, then turned back to Nell and the new coloring book.

Reid was waiting outside when Nathaniel drove up the driveway.

"Shit! I almost didn't see you in all that black. I thought we might drop by Kaleb's to get a burger before going to case the place, but you look like a ninja."

"Give me a break." Reid said. "Doesn't it make you feel just a little deceitful to eat at their restaurant and then go sneaking around their house?"

"It'll let us know for sure that they're tied up at the diner. Being a little proactive never hurt anybody."

"All right. I see your point."

The brothers were at the diner, Adam behind the grill and Aaron mopping. They only had three tables of customers, the average 8:00 p.m. crowd.

Nathaniel and Reid took a seat at the counter.

"How're you guys doing tonight?" Adam asked, stepping away from the grill to take their orders.

"Not too bad," Reid answered. "I'll have a cheeseburger plate, well done, with extra onions."

"I'll have the same," Nathaniel answered, "and a sweet tea."

Adam looked at him like he was an alien. "Huh?"

Reid gave a hearty laugh. "You aren't in the South anymore," he said as he continued to laugh. "If you want sweet tea, you'll have to add the sugar yourself."

Adam still wore a look of confusion as he walked toward the back. "What ya want to drink, Sheriff?" he asked over his shoulder.

"Strawberry soda."

He returned quickly with their drinks, then hurried back to his grill.

Aaron mopped his way over to them, then took a seat on one of the stools. "What's new, Sheriff?" he asked.

"Thank God I can say we've had a couple of uneventful days. How are your folks?"

"Doing well. Between you and me, I think they're getting a little old to be working so hard. Adam and I could run this place ourselves with a couple of waitresses. We wouldn't stay open all night though. It's never been profitable for us, but Dad has always insisted on it."

"Well, I suppose your parents are from a generation who doesn't know anything but hard work. Too bad some of our younger kids don't hold the same work ethic. This diner just may be what keeps your mom and dad going."

"I suppose so," he answered, then got up to continue his mopping detail. "Good to see both of you."

"You too, Aaron."

The burgers were delicious, and both men left feeling as full as they felt guilty.

"They seem like nice guys," Nathaniel said.

"So did John Wayne Gacy."

"Give me a break, Reid."

"I'm just sayin', you can never be sure. Dahmer worked in a chocolate factory, for God's sake, and his neighbor lady thought he was the nicest guy."

"Let's check out the trailer and get home. It's cold as hell out here, and I—"

"Yes, I know. You've got to get back to Gracie."

The two were surprised to find the trailer so large, surrounded by a well-manicured lawn, with wooden rocking chairs on the front porch.

"I'm sure that's Mrs. Sewell's doings," Reid said. "Either that or they're gay. What grown men would put rocking chairs on their front porch?"

"Don't you have some?"

"Screw you, Nathaniel. I happen to have a beautiful view I like to enjoy whenever I get a few minutes of free time."

"Wow. All these years we've known each other, and I had no idea you were checking me out."

"I'll ignore that because we have to get in and out of here. I refuse to sit here and argue with you like you're a woman."

"*I'm* a woman? I'm not the one with rocker on my

porch."

"Shut up, Nathaniel."

They circled the perimeter of the trailer, peeking in any windows that didn't have the blinds closed. Nothing unusual caught their eye, but they weren't inside the structure, so there were still infinite possibilities. As they were peering through the sliding glass door, they heard the distinct sound of a bullet being chambered.

"One move, and I'll blow your brains out!"

Chapter 90

A repeated hard knock at the door, along with the constant ringing of the doorbell, startled and frightened Nell. "Gracie, go up to the loft, honey," she said sternly.

As usual, the girl did as she was told.

Nell slowly made her way to the door but not before pulling a large butcher knife from the block on the counter. "Who the hell's out there?" she demanded.

"I'm US Marshal Nick Solomon," said an unfamiliar male voice. "If you pull back the curtains, I'll show you my credentials."

Nell pulled them back slowly and looked through the glass at the man's badge.

"Please open the door, Ma'am…quickly," an unfamiliar male voice directed. "We don't have time for dialogue. Lives could be at stake."

Nell inhaled deeply, in an effort to calm her nerves. Gripping the knife tightly, she unlocked the door with more than a little apprehension.

"Is Nathaniel here?"

"No. He's with the Sheriff. What do you want?"

"Where is Gracie?"

"Why are you asking? And what business do you have here?"

"That's strictly confidential, Ma'am. I need the girl. She's in grave danger!"

"I won't hand over a child who's in my care. Are you crazy?"

Gracie stood at the top of the loft and peered over the banister. "My real daddy has found me, hasn't he? He wants to kill me so I can't tell what he did to me and my mommy."

"Sweetheart," Nick answered, "we're here to make sure you're safe. We won't let your father anywhere near you."

"But I can't leave my new daddy. I'm happy here. Mr. Smith will be scared if I'm not here when he gets back."

Nell shook her head in sheer confusion. "What the hell's going on here?"

"Mr. Smith, as you know him, as well as Gracie and Laverne are enrolled in the Federal Witness Protection Program, Ma'am. I realize what a shock this must be, but I have to get the child out of here. Gracie, honey, come on down. I'll make sure you're back with Nathaniel real soon, I promise."

She reached for her new bear and, with tears streaming down her face, climbed down the ladder and hugged Nell. "It'll be all right, Miss Nell. He'll take care of me." With that, she took Nick's hand and walked into the night, to yet another black Suburban that'd carry her away.

Nell sat on the couch, wringing her hands, wondering how she'd ever be able to break the news to Nathaniel. "And Witness Protection? Whatever for?"

Chapter 91

Consuelos sped the entire way to Hayden, even at the risk of being pulled over in his stolen car. He was too close to let it all slip through his hands now. He hoped the motel girl had given him adequate directions or she, too, would pay. His heart raced as he savored the taste of adrenaline, one he'd missed for so long.

He pulled around the back of the hospital and saw that the back exits were merely loading docks. The only parking lot was in the front of the hospital, the perfect place to spot and follow his prey.

He was fifteen minutes early, which gave him plenty of time to prematurely relish the moments to come. Time passed quickly, and before he knew it, the chubby nurse he remembered so well was walking to her car.

He waited until Laverne pulled out of the parking lot before he turned on his lights and began his pursuit. She was a cautious driver, which made it more difficult to follow her without being noticed. The backwoods town had very little traffic for him to disappear into.

Twenty minutes later, she pulled into a dirt driveway. He could've pulled over down the road, but he refused to risk her getting in the house. He was sure the bounty hunter would have a gun, and that'd only complicate things.

The nurse didn't seem concerned when his lights followed her into the drive, and as she got out, she even walked back toward his car. It took her brain a minute to register that she didn't recognize the vehicle. When she realized it, she turned and hurriedly walked toward the house.

Consuelos was out of the car and on her like a lion on an injured gazelle before she had the opportunity to react.

A gasp was all she could get out before he covered her mouth. She felt nails digging into her face as she struggled against his strong grip.

"Where are they, you fat bitch? Get me the kid and that bounty hunter, or I'll snap your neck right now."

"I-I don't know," she said, struggling to breathe. "Can't...breathe. Please!"

He loosened his grip just enough to let her get a few words out.

"The Jeep is gone. They must not be home."

"Whose car is that?" he asked, pointing to Nell's vehicle.

"One of the local deputies."

"A deputy? Why's he here?"

"I-I don't know...really," she said, not giving away that Nell was, in fact, a she. "I've been at work and—"

"Tell me where they are now, or you die...and so will Jeremy, that brother of yours back in the big city. The one who likes to watch reruns," he spat, making sure she knew just how much of a threat he was to her and her only living kin.

Salty tears streamed down Laverne's face as she tried

desperately to come up with a plan. Her mind just wasn't cooperating. "Please Lord," she prayed, "give me an answer."

"I'm gonna count to three, and you're dead, simple as that. I know where they live now, and I can wait this one out."

She knew he was telling the truth, and she closed her eyes and prepared for her own death. *Poor Gracie. Poor Nathaniel.* She could never give them up.

Nell watched helplessly from the window, knowing there was nothing she could do. The headlights gave a vivid picture of what was happening. Before she could even get out the door, Laverne would be dead, and she'd be next. It'd all happened in such a whirlwind—the US Marshal showing up, followed by Laverne being accosted in the driveway—and she wondered if she were only dreaming.

"One…two…"

Laverne gasped, knowing she was doing what she had to do.

"You never could stop the killing, could you?" said an unfamiliar voice from somewhere close behind them. "Killing this lady, Nathaniel Collier, and your own daughter will still not be enough."

"Sykes? Officer Jay Sykes? Humph. I'm surprised you have the balls to be here. Are these people worth your life too?" Consuelos asked, letting Laverne go as he turned to face Sykes.

"What life? You saw to it that I don't have one left."

Laverne was shaking violently, fighting the feeling that she'd soon pass out. She slowly backed away, hoping no one noticed her attempt to escape.

Consuelos reached around to the back of his pants and felt the cool steel of his 9 mm. It was full with one in the chamber, and no one had ever beaten him to a draw. "You're right, Sykes. You don't have a life."

Sykes laughed as he unloaded his weapon, center-mass, into Mad Dog Consuelos.

It was almost like a movie. Mad Dog looked at Sykes in disbelief, dropping slowly to his knees, then falling flat on his face.

"Oh, my God!" Laverne said, running to the stranger who'd saved all of their lives. The evil was dead, gone for good, and she wanted to thank him. But before she could reach him, she heard another gunshot that pierced the night, a bullet that went straight into the temple of their savior.

Chapter 92

Nathaniel and Reid held their hands up in surrender and refused to turn around.

"What in God's name are you two doin' rambling around my boys' place?"

"Thank God," Reid said, ready for a believable story. "It's Sheriff Langley, Mr. Sewell. Can I turn around?"

"Sheriff Langley? What the hell are you doing here?"

"The station got an anonymous tip that somebody was prowling around out here. We were out anyway, so I told them we'd check it out. I didn't want to wake you and Mrs. Sewell unnecessarily."

"Good gracious, Son," he said, relief washing over him. "I might've shot you."

"My sincere apologies, Sir."

"Well, since we're all wired up, come on in for a warm cup of coffee. The wife is up, too, worried to death."

"We appreciate that," Nathaniel answered, "but I need

to get going. Nell is babysitting Gracie, and I'm sure she's ready to head home."

"I understand young fella. Sheriff, let me know if this happens again so I don't go shootin' one of the good guys."

"Will do, Mr. Sewell. My apologies again."

They were making their way to Nathaniel's car when Reid's cell phone went off.

"Langley here," he answered.

"Sheriff," Deputy Ray said, "you need to get over to your buddy Nathaniel's house right away. There are two dead people in the front yard!"

"What? I must've heard you wrong. Say that again."

"No, Sir, you heard me correctly. Two dead at Nathaniel Smith's house. I don't have any details, but I'm on my way."

Reid turned to his friend and wondered how he could possibly break the news to him. *God, don't let it be Laverne or Gracie,* he thought. "Nathaniel, that was Ray, calling about your house. Apparently, something is going on over there."

Panic rose in his voice. "What? Oh, my God! Why didn't Nell call? Is Gracie all right?"

"I'm sure she is. Let's just get there as quickly as we can."

The ride seemed to take hours, and Nathaniel prayed out loud the whole way, begging the Lord to spare Gracie.

The scene greeting them was frightening. The bright lights from the patrol cars and the ambulance lit up the night.

Nathaniel was out of the car almost before the vehicle stopped. He ran past everyone, pushing anyone who tried to stop him out of the way.

Laverne ran into his arms, her body wracked with sobs. "They're dead, Nathaniel! They're both dead."

"Who, Laverne? Tell me it's not Gracie."

"No, Gracie's fine…and Nathaniel, we're finally free!"

"I-I-don't-understand. Free?"

"Yes! One of them was Consuelos. He was going to kill me, but some man showed up and shot him, then shot himself."

Reid and Nell walked over to them. "It seems Jay Sykes was legit," Reid said. "He came to get Consuelos, and he did. It's over now."

Nathaniel felt his knees go weak. "Where's my daughter? Did she see this?"

"Let's go inside Nathaniel," Nell said, taking him by the hand. "She's okay, but we need to talk."

Chapter 93

It didn't take long for word to get around town about Reid's friend and the Witness Protection Program. The townspeople seemed to accept it, and although it'd led a killer to their town, they were forgiving.

While Reid was spending all of his time looking for the serial killer, Nathaniel was spending all of his trying to get Gracie back. Things looked pretty good, but it'd be at least two weeks before the red tape could be taken care of and she could come back home. He was allowed to talk to her every day, which made the situation somewhat bearable. The best news was that he'd be picking her up in Atlanta, where he'd go to court to legally adopt her. He decided they'd make Hayden their permanent home, but since he was no longer on the witness protection payroll, he'd have to find a job quickly.

Laverne had already flown back to Atlanta to visit her brother and to watch *Cheers* reruns, but she'd purchased a round-trip ticket back home to Wyoming. At least now, she and her brother could visit regularly, and she could keep her job at Mountainside Memorial.

Chapter 94

Reid was sitting at his desk, reading the latest internet information on the monkshood plant. The toxicology reports had found aconitine in all of the murdered girls, the chemical found in the roots and leaves of the deadly plant. Vaughn, Anne, and Reid had done enough reading about it to grow the plants themselves, but all that knowledge didn't seem to get them any closer to their killer.

"Let's see," Reid read aloud, "it says here that western monkshood is found at higher altitudes in the Pacific Coast states, yellow monkshood from Idaho to New Mexico, and wild monkshood from Pennsylvania to Georgia. Wow. That really narrows it down," he said sarcastically to himself.

He shut down his computer and rubbed his eyes. He reached for an aspirin, but thought a meal might do him better. He walked across the street to Kaleb's and ordered a grilled ham and cheese sandwich from Mrs. Sewell.

She brought it to him, hot off the grill, with his usual

strawberry soda.

"Thanks," he said as he took a napkin from the dispenser. "I need this. I've been fighting a headache all day."

"Maybe you're working too hard," she said. "Being Sheriff is a tough responsibility."

Two bites into his sandwich, a light went off in Reid's head, and he slammed his fist on the counter. "Damn! I should've known it all along!"

The large lunch crowd all turned to see what the commotion was about.

"Are you all right, Sheriff?" Mrs. Sewell hurried over to ask.

He dropped ten dollars on the counter and answered excitedly, "Yes, I'm fine. I hate to eat and run, but I've got a killer to arrest!"

Chapter 95

"Doctor Anne Novus," she answered into her office phone.

"Meet me in front of the hospital," Reid said. "I'm picking you up in five minutes, and we're going to arrest our killer."

"What?"

"Just be there," he demanded, then hung up and hurriedly dialed Nathaniel. "Meet me at the end of your driveway. I'm on my way,"

"What's up?"

"I need you to help arrest our killer."

Reid picked Nathaniel up first, then Anne. Both sat in the patrol car in total confusion.

"What's going on, Man?" Nathaniel asked. "Have you been working too hard?"

"No. It all makes sense, and we should've seen it before now, especially you, Anne."

"Gee, thanks for the vote of confidence. Don't keep us

in suspense. Who's our guy?"

"Henry! It's Henry Hartwell, the damn coroner." He didn't give them time to react before he continued. "He's had it out for both of us for a long time, especially you, Anne. He doesn't like how things are changing or that his job as coroner is quickly being outdated. A person just has to watch a little cable, some *CSI* or *Forensic Files,* to see that medicine has come a long way. Putting his John Hancock on those death certificates was the only thing that gave him any clout in this town. He certainly isn't getting that from his trash removal service. He had the perfect plan. He knew we wouldn't figure out the poisonous plants, at least not for a while, and they wouldn't show up in an autopsy. He was trying to make us look like fools while he played the role of the compassionate coroner, the guy people here have always believed him to be. Remember the night he came to my house drunk? He said he'd been visiting a sister in Idaho and a brother in Pennsylvania. It just so happens that different species of monkshood are found in both areas."

"But the murders occurred during his vacation, Reid. He wasn't even here to commit them."

"Ah, but he could've gone and gotten the plants and come back. We aren't sure how long he was really gone.

"What if he made up where he went on vacation?" Nathanial asked.

"We can ask Elijah at the post office if he receives any family mail from those states. Our good ol' postmaster is nosey enough. He'll remember, but I don't think it'll come to that. Henry is weak and hotheaded. I'm sure we can bluff our way through this one."

Chapter 96

Anne took great pleasure in ringing the doorbell of Henry Hartwell's home. His dump truck was outside, so they knew he was there.

A couple of seconds later, he answered the door in the mood they'd expected, a foul one. "What the hell do you people want?"

"I think I've found our killer, Henry," Reid said, "and since you're the Coroner, I wanted you to be the first to know."

"Is that so?"

"Can we come in?"

"Nah, lemme just step out on the porch. I don't have long. So…who'd you end up arrestin' for killing those pretty little things, God rest their souls."

"Nobody yet."

"If you know who the killer is, why the hell aren't you out there slapping the cuffs on him instead of over here bothering me?"

"They're one in the same, Henry," Reid said.

"What the hell are you talking about?"

"We know it's you, Henry," Anne said. "We should've known it all along. You got the monkshood from Idaho and Pennsylvania where your family lives. You brought it back here to fool us so we'd looked like idiots and everyone would still vote for you on the next ballot."

Sweat beaded on the old man's forehead, but he brushed it away quickly, hoping they hadn't noticed. "What are you talking about? That's about the craziest thing I've ever heard."

"Actually, Henry, it's quite brilliant—much more clever than I'd ever given you credit for. You thought you were going to lose your job as Coroner, and you had to do something to make yourself look important while making us look like fools. Reputation is everything in these small communities, especially for elected officials. These were the perfect murders until we found the aconitine in toxicology reports and placed you in the only two states that carry that particular plant," Reid said.

Nathaniel was impressed with his bluff.

"This is preposterous, and I don't have to listen to it!"

"Henry, if it's so preposterous, why don't you let us take a look inside?"

"I don't have anything to hide."

"Does that mean we have your consent to search the premises?"

"Hell, yeah."

"Okay. In that case, step aside," Reid said.

"You know, Sheriff, on second thought, I think I'll wait for a warrant from Judge Jones. That should take you at least a couple of days."

"I'm sorry, Henry, but I have two witnesses who heard you give verbal consent to a search. That gives me the right to tell you to step aside."

"Wait! Hold on a damn minute!" he screamed. "You can't do this! You can't just barge into a man's home and—"

"We can and we will. Nathaniel, will you stay out here with Mr. Hartwell?"

"Sure."

Anne and Reid were back outside in less than five minutes.

"Quite a little setup you have in there, Henry," Reid said. "Looks like I'll have to call the State police in on this one. You should start talking if you don't want that lethal needle going into your arm."

Nathaniel sat in back beside a sobbing Henry Hartwell as they drove to the police station.

Inside, the Sheriff motioned to a video camera and a tape recorder. "Do you consent to this interview, Mr. Hartwell?"

Defeated, the old man nodded his head.

"I'm sorry, but we need a verbal response."

"Fine! Yes, I consent!" Henry spat. His nose was running into his mouth, but none of them offered the scum a tissue. He wasn't even deserving of that small luxury.

"Have you been read your Miranda rights?"

"Yes."

"Do you understand them?"

"Of course. I'm not an idiot."

"Henry Hartwell, do you admit to causing the deaths of Joanna Sibley, Lauren Lowe, Haley Monroe, and Madison Aldridge?"

"Yes."

In a tearful confession, the old Coroner provided the gory details of each murder. He spoke of his resentment of Doctor Novus and Sheriff Langley, both of whom he felt were out to get him and his position. In his mind, they were incompetent and couldn't even figure out a simple death. "I was sure I'd see you fired and replaced by more competent folks, and the people of Hayden would've supported me. If you'da been smart enough to figure it out in the first place, them other three girls wouldn't have had to die."

They placed Henry in a cell and retreated to Reid's office so they could call the State police. The three just shook their heads. None of them could believe how sick he really was.

"It's amazing that these psychotic tendencies never came out before," Anne said.

"Yep," Reid answered, "and it's a damn shame four girls had to die to bring them to light."

Epilogue

Gracie and Nathaniel held hands at the Fulton County Courthouse. They were surrounded by Reid, Laverne, Anne, Vaughn, and US Marshals TJ Davis, Nick Solomon, and Julie Harmon. State Attorney General Pete Lancaster had even taken the time to attend. When the judge slammed down his gavel, making Gracie legally Nathaniel's daughter, cheers erupted in the courtroom.

Nathaniel treated everyone to the delicious greasy food at The Varsity and thanked them all for the important role they'd played in bringing them together and keeping them safe.

"We've come a long way since I called you from the hospital in Atlanta, huh, Reid?" Nathaniel asked.

"You got that right. If I'd only *known* what I was getting myself into."

"Would you do it again?" Laverne asked.

"In a heartbeat."

The crowd laughed and stood to go.

On the way out, Gracie tugged on Vaughn's sleeve. "My Daddy's still not married," she whispered up with a grin.

"Gracie!" Nathaniel said.

"Well, maybe you can convince your Daddy to ask me out to dinner sometime, and we can talk about that."

"And maybe her Daddy will do just that," Nathaniel said, smiling and feeling warmer than he had in a long, long time, in spite of the cold climate they were headed back to.

The End

Sneak Peek

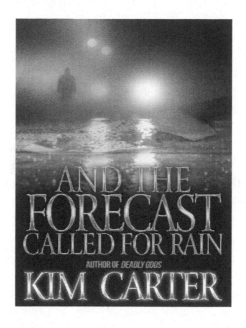

Sneak Peek of And The Forecast Called For Rain

Detective Jose Ramirez and the Sierra Hills Police Department are scrambling for leads on a killer who has already struck five times, each time leaving his signature trademark: large butcher knives piercing the abdomens of his young female victims.

Profiling the killer is proving to be difficult, and Detective Ramirez knows that it's only a matter of time before their perpetrator strikes again.

As if Ramirez isn't frustrated enough, to his dismay, he is assigned a partner. Officer Daniel Chatham, a handsome, young man, fresh out of grad school, has pulled some strings to join the division and becomes Ramirez's right-hand man. The lead detective's anger slowly begins to dissipate as he discovers the book smart kid can be quite the asset.

With Ramirez's experience, Chatham's sharp mind and quick thinking, and the insight of Erin Sommers, a beautiful, young journalist, the three make a powerful team gaining on their criminal.

It's raining… it's pouring, and a killer is on the loose in the rainy Sierra Hills of Washington State. No one is who they seem, and the plot thickens with every turn. You'll never guess the ending of this enigmatic tale.

Sneak Peek at Sweet Dreams, Baby Belle

Waitress Lizzie Headrick thought she had finally met her prince charming in Doctor Grant Chatsworth. She was young and in love, and their quick courtship ended with the four carat diamond engagement ring of her dreams.

Now residing in one of Buckhead's finest estates, Lizzie soon learns all that glitters is not gold. Her handsome husband, a renowned cardiac surgeon and developer of a new congestive heart failure drug, was becoming cruel and controlling. She finds herself captive in the vast expanse of his estate without a phone or car, and under the watchful eye of Flossie who runs the household.

When Lizzie discovers that Cardiac Care Research, his drug development company, is a Ponzi scheme, she realizes her life could be in danger if she doesn't somehow escape the gated mansion on the hill.

Her only hope is to get to Biloxi, Mississippi and seek refuge with her sister, Maggie. Maggie and her husband, Leland, quickly find a safe harbor for Lizzie in a house on the bayou. However, the house at the end of the street might not be the quiet retreat Lizzie was hoping for.

As the confines of her hideaway close in on her, she retreats to the small historical cemetery next door where the small, damaged tombstone of a child soon catches her eye and captures her heart. Just when Lizzie Chatsworth thinks her world can't get any more complicated, she finds herself in the middle of a mystery from the 1800's that is pulling her in and demanding she seek justice.

As her husband's empire begins to crumble, he's more determined than ever to find Lizzie and eliminate her. But, will the mystery of the small tombstone end Lizzie's life first?

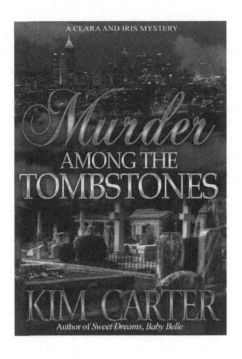

Sneak Peek at Murder Among The Tombstones

A Clara and Iris Mystery

When Atlanta homicide detectives are called in to investigate the murder of a nineteen-year-old girl found dumped in historic Oakland Cemetery, they immediately begin working the case. But with no leads to follow, and their case log growing larger by the day, the murder quickly grows cold.

Desperate to keep the investigation of her deceased sister going, Ginger Baines hires two novice sleuths to solve the case. Widowed, well into their seventies, and new to the world of private investigating, Clara Samples and Iris Hadley aren't your average private eyes.

When a second body is found in a neighboring cemetery, the plot thickens. With two bodies wrapped, almost lovingly, in a soft blanket before being discarded in a cemetery, could a serial killer be on the loose?

Joined by their young apprentice Quita, Clara and Iris are determined to stop at nothing to find the killer before they can strike again. But, will their bodies be the next ones discovered among the tombstones?

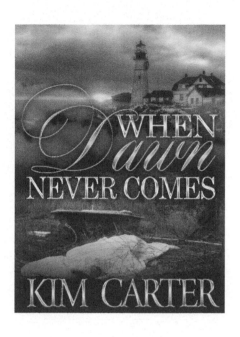

Sneak Peek at When Dawn Never Comes

Jordan Maxwell, a twenty-seven-year-old freelance journalist, ventures to New York City to make a name for herself. With both of her parents dead, she struggles to get by living in one of the worst neighborhoods in the city. In a twist of fate, Jordan finds herself the sole heir to her great-uncle's estate in Solomon Cove, Maine.

Packing her bags, she heads to Maine where she soon realizes that her rags to riches journey entails much more than she bargained for.

Crime was unheard of in the small fishing village of Solomon Cove, a town where everyone knows everyone. It was the last place anyone expected crime, especially murder. However, the tides turn for this quaint town when the body of a young girl comes crashing in with the waves.

As the victims continue to mount, Jordan starts to believe the murders are connected to her and the family she never knew. Digging deeper into the past, Jordan must protect herself before she becomes the serial killer's next target.

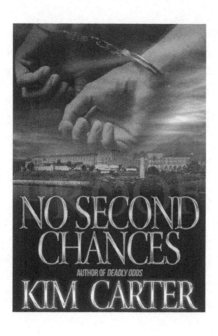

Sneak Peek at No Second Chances

Falling from a life of wealth and substance, to inside one of America's most notorious prisons, prominent orthopedic surgeon Phil Sawyer is incarcerated for the voluntary manslaughter of his wife. While confined, he finds himself on the trail of a serial killer that infiltrates the walls of San Quentin. After finding himself in the infirmary for getting involved in an incident that didn't concern him, Phil struggles with the decision to stick his neck out. But he can't ignore the rise in suspicious deaths among the African American inmates. With the aid of an empathetic nurse and help from the outside, he tries to identify the unexplained cause of their cardiac arrests. He finds himself out on early release and heads to Solomon Cove, a peaceful town in Maine. But, could the tranquil town all be a façade, or has the serial killer made their way across the country to seek revenge?

From wealthy Los Angeles, to the justice in San Quentin, and the serene landscapes of Maine, you will applaud the friendships and hear the cry as you ride the roller coaster of emotions this story will bring.

About the Author

Kim Carter is an author of contemporary mystery, suspense, and thrillers. She has won the 2017 Readers' Choice Award for Murder Among The Tombstones. This is the first book in her Clara and Iris Mystery series. Her other titles include: When Dawn Never Comes, Deadly Odds, No Second Chances, And The Forecast Called For Rain, and Sweet Dreams, Baby Belle.

Kim has been writing mysteries for some time and has a large reader fan base that she enjoys interacting and engaging with. One of her favorite things about writing mysteries is the research and traveling she does to bring her novels to life. Her research has taken her to places such as morgues, death row, and midnight cemetery visits.

Kim and her husband have raised three successful grown children. They now spend their time in Atlanta with their three retired greyhounds.

She is a college graduate of Saint Leo University, has a Bachelor Degree of Arts in Sociology, and now has become a career writer and author. Between reading and traveling, she will continue to write mysteries.

Get In Touch With Kim Carter:

Website: https://www.kimcarterauthor.com/

Email: kimcarterauthor@gmail.com

Facebook: https://www.facebook.com/kimcarterauthor/

Instagram:
https://www.instagram.com/kimcarterauthor/?hl=en

About.Me: https://about.me/kimcarter.mysteryauthor

Amazon Author Page:
https://www.amazon.com/Kim-Carter/e/B019QSNFI0/

GoodReads:https://www.goodreads.com/author/show/4075
351.Kim_Carter

Twitter: https://twitter.com/KimCarterAuthor

Google+ https://plus.google.com/105425029849895301377

For speaking engagements, interviews, and book copies, please get in touch with Raven South Publishing info@ravensouthpublishing.com.

I hope you enjoyed reading Deadly Odds. I'd appreciate it if you would post a review on the site you purchased it from, as well as on Amazon and Goodreads. I'm grateful for every one I receive. Feel free to contact me on Facebook and my website if you have any questions or thoughts about the stories. I love hearing from readers.

Very best regards,

Kim Carter

Facebook: kimcarterauthor
www.kimcarterauthour.com
kimcarterauthor@gmail.com

Made in United States
Orlando, FL
30 December 2021

12689560R00243